Sentinel

K. A. Moore

Published by K. A. Moore, 2022.

This is a work of fiction. Names, characters, businesses, places, events, locales, and incidents are either the products of the author's imagination or used in a fictitious manner. Any resemblance to actual persons, living or dead, or actual events is purely coincidental.

Book cover design by Betibup

Editing by Ginny at Bookhelpline

ISBN 9781957223001 (ebook)

ISBN 9781957223117 (paperback)

Also by K. A. Moore

Relics Series

Relics

The Key

The Chosen

Standalone

Watching Her Sleep

Sentinel

Weeping Widow's Heirloom

One

You could set your clock by the mystery woman's daily runs. She'd been jogging past their building regularly for the last couple of weeks. Due to come by at any moment, employees scrambled to the monitors to catch a glimpse of her. Riley Strong, a retired police sergeant who owned the business, didn't like that she was so predictable. It wasn't safe for a woman in this day and age to keep such an obvious schedule. Variation was key in not getting complacent and making yourself an easy target for the viciousness of the world most people were too naive to admit existed. He started the company a few years before, after retiring with over twenty years on the force. His employees he trusted with his life. They were all either former officers or military. Several had been his friends for years.

The corner of his mouth twitched as his men stood glued to the screens in the control room of the building that he'd bought last year. The highest resolution digital cameras money could buy, mounted on the outside, covered every possible angle, and the images were piped into the observation room, where they were monitored all hours of the day and night. How could they sell their security and investigative services if they couldn't show their clients how secure they could make an office or house for that matter?

She was petite. He'd guess she wasn't much taller than five foot three and maybe one hundred fifteen pounds soaking wet. Her sun-kissed blonde hair, pulled high on her head into a ponytail, swept from side to side with her short strides. Her calf and thigh muscles were well-developed from years of running.

The distinct rumble of an engine sounded in the distance through the audio feed as she approached the building at a steady pace. Her feet in brightly-colored running shoes slapped the pavement with each footfall. The road ended with your only option to take a ninety-degree angle before heading to the north and the seedier part of the city with graffitied buildings overrun by gangs who did nothing all day except hang out on the front stoops flashing their gang colors. Windows became empty shells with plywood sealing them in instead of glass to showcase the wares of the businesses that had lost the battle to stay open decades before. It was early; the sun just rising on the horizon.

The men raced for the door as the gunned engine interrupted nature's morning song including everything from the birds to the crickets before they slept for the day, no doubt, pedal pressed to the floor. Riley got there first and flung the door open, gun drawn. She swung around, her ponytail whipping through the air around her face as the car changed its deadly course heading straight for her. Eyes widened with alarm, she tried to jump out of the way, her expression giving away that she wouldn't be able to move fast enough. The passenger mirror clipped her in the side, tossing her across and over the tufts of grass that encroached at the edge of the road into the asphalt's space before she rolled down the modest slope of the pavement. The car skidded to a stop with two men exiting, guns drawn as she ended up only a few feet away.

Riley and his men raised their weapons as he said a silent prayer to keep his men and this woman safe. They outnumbered the men in the vehicle four to one. Recognition crossed over her features, awareness of the identity of the two who emerged from the beat-up sedan that had seen better days, as Riley stared down, her green eyes locked on his.

A sharp, ear-piercing report sounded milliseconds after a bullet ripped past him, as the passenger scrambled around to the driver's side, taking cover behind the back fender. Riley dropped to a knee, returning fire. His men followed suit. The female screamed and curled into the fetal position, flinching with every pull of the trigger from either side. The two men dove into the car and bolted, racing down the road. He reached her in three long steps. He plucked her off the ground, her cry of pain sounding in the open courtyard of the building, bouncing off the front of the structure behind them that appeared to be more windows than concrete and steel.

"Hold on." His gruff voice penetrated the morning air that still had a crisp bite to it, sending his breath out partially steamed since spring wasn't due for another month.

She wrapped her left arm around his neck, her modestly short nails digging into his skin in a death grip. He cringed but didn't say anything.

"Monroe!" Riley barked.

His team secured the bullet-resistant doors once Riley was inside with the woman. She cried out and her grip tightened on his shoulder when he lowered her legs. Her head landed on the side of his neck; her steamy breath blew against his skin as she exhaled.

"Call the police and also the fire department to send an ambulance," he commanded.

"No!" Panic flooded her face, which was now only inches from his. Their eyes locked as she tried to push away from him, her hand fiercely shoving against his chest before dropping to press against her side.

He held her to him and she turned her hand over, palm up. Blood covered the delicate creamy skin. The color leached from her face. Monroe, a former combat medic and an imposing man at just over six foot—his build almost rivaled Riley's—ran up with a medic bag and applied pressure with a wad of bandages. She winced and clung to Riley.

"You need a hospital." Riley studied her green eyes. She barely came up to his chin. No doubt her running shoes gave her an extra inch or two in height, he guessed as he took in the thick, iridescent rubber soles. Even her long blonde hair perched on top of her head in a ponytail added to it, but still made her short compared to his six-foot frame.

"No!" Her head drooped, landing on his shoulder again, her hot breath scorching through his shirt to his skin as she pulled in a deep breath before shuddering its release. "He'll find me."

Sweat beaded across her forehead. Riley's muscles flexed as she squirmed under the pressure Monroe applied to her side. She grabbed Monroe's wrist that held the bandage and pushed it away. Riley grabbed her hand and wrapped it around her back, passing her wrist off to his other hand behind her arm that was thrown over his shoulder. He nodded to Monroe, who pressed the dressing back to her wound as she sucked in air between gritted teeth.

"No, no hospital or police!" Her knees buckled and the fingers on her left hand dug in further on his shoulder. She took a deep breath and tried to pull away again. His muscles strained against his shirt as he tightened his grip on her right wrist, which she tried to pull up and away from his grasp.

"Stop fighting us. We aren't the bad guys." She was no match for his size. "Let us help you. We can keep you safe."

Monroe continued pressing on her side, adding another wad of bandages, and mouthed "Hospital" to Riley.

Sirens from an ambulance cut through the tension, interrupting them. Her head snapped up and her eyes widened. "No!" She peered over his shoulder to the doors as the ambulance drove down the circle drive. When she turned to face him, he stared into her fearful eyes, a single tear trekked down her cheek as she shook her head the tiniest fraction.

The paramedics unloaded the gurney and jogged to the doors. Riley nodded for his team to unlock them.

Paramedics grabbed several bandages with their blue nitrile-gloved hands. Riley held up his unoccupied hand. "Let them help you. You need to go with them."

"No! I refuse treatment!"

A paramedic peered at her side and held his hands up as if in surrender. "Ma'am, let us take a look. There is a lot of blood."

Sweat dripped from her forehead, her skin ashen. She sunk into his arms as he supported her, grasping her under her right arm as she lost consciousness.

"I think she's in shock. She bounced off the side of a car," Riley informed them.

One paramedic inspected the wound; no doubt the pain was intense as the woman reflexively tried to pull away in her unconscious state. Palpitating her ribs led to another involuntary response, her body's way of trying to defend against the discomfort. "My guess a few are either severely bruised if not cracked."

The second paramedic nodded in agreement with the assessment. "We can't close this wound here; she will need stitches along with x-rays to check for any internal bleeding that could lead to an even worse outcome."

"I agree, maybe you can get her loaded up before she comes back around." Riley shifted his hand, gripping her wrist.

Two police cruisers pulled up outside. Riley gave a quick sharp nod to Duffy, who he talked into working for him after a referral from one of Riley's employees—he'd jumped at the chance. Only coming to five foot ten inches, he was stocky yet nimble. His hair was streaked with more gray than brown; he was the oldest one in the group. Duffy met the officers at the doors. They talked in hushed tones. He pointed to the street and then turned and showed them the building, pointing to the damage from the bullets.

Meanwhile, the paramedic applied pressure to her side. She responded to the pain with a grunt, rousing her to consciousness, but she kept her eyes closed, sucking in air through gritted teeth. She then opened her eyes wide. "I want to go home."

The paramedic shook his head. "You can't. We have to transport you to the hospital."

"No, you can't. I refuse treatment," she rasped out.

The paramedic held her wrist. His two fingers pressed into her skin at her pulse point.

Her pale face pinched in pain.

"I'm sorry. With the injuries and our assessment of you, we aren't convinced you're able to make that decision for yourself." The paramedic gave a slight nod to Riley.

The officers strolled into the office. One tipped his chin in acknowledgment and then glanced at the woman in his arms while the paramedics prepared the gurney for her.

"Now he'll find me." Her brow furrowed, her eyes pleading.

Riley's eyes met hers; she wasn't lying. He slid his hand down to her waist. She flinched when he fished her identification out of the side pocket in the waistband of her running pants, palming it before he slipped it into his pocket as the paramedics took her from him. One buckled her trembling body, coming down from an adrenaline dump, to the gurney as the other put a neck brace on to strap her head to the dreaded foam pads on either side.

Claustrophobia took hold and panic kicked in as she gasped for air, her hands instinctively clawed at the neck brace. Riley had seen it numerous times when he worked for the local police department. For some reason, a lot of people couldn't handle having their heads bracketed for transport and strapped down not allowing movement. He wanted to go to her but held back. She cried out as they applied pressure to the wound on her side. Blood seeped through the bandage as her arms fell, lifeless on either side of the gurney. The paramedics tucked her arms under the straps as officers talked in hushed whispers. One moved outside and put his cruiser in position to follow the ambulance. Riley said a quiet prayer to keep her safe on the transport to the hospital.

"We gotta move. Do you know her name?" The paramedic captured the handles of his bag off the floor with one of his meaty hands.

Riley didn't blink. "No. What hospital are you taking her to?"

"Sorry, we can't release that information if you're not family." They pushed the gurney through the doors toward the waiting ambulance.

"Bear, follow them. Keep me updated on where they take her," Riley muttered to his employee and best friend since childhood.

Bear, with his black hair still cut according to military regulation, was massive at six foot five inches and a muscled two hundred thirty pounds. He jogged to the back lot. Most people thought his name was due to his size, but it actually started in elementary school when he shot up past all the other kids their age. His last name being Bearden, it was shortened to Bear and it stuck. He knew God had a sense of humor to have a nickname fit him so perfectly off his given name. Half of their friends would probably spit if they knew his first name was Shamus. Riley wouldn't be surprised if he could lift a car, though; his arms and chest were massive. He worked out nonstop when he wasn't on assignment for Riley. He was also Riley's best friend; they'd known each other since they were kids. They grew up in a bad neighborhood, full of violence and gangs. Riley chose to be a police officer; Bear chose the military. They stayed in touch through Bear's deployments, and when Riley started his company, he knew Bear would want to jump on board. They both chose a life protecting people. This was a no-brainer that they'd work together to continue that service.

Bear raced after the ambulance in one of the company's silver Audi sedans, keeping several car lengths between himself and the police cruiser before Riley lost sight of him as they made the ninety-degree turn and disappeared.

Riley tilted his head toward his office. The first floor held the lobby along with several workstations. The kitchen ran off to the right down a hallway that also led to the back door and several doors along the way. One included access to the workout room in the basement, their weapons lockers, and storage. The second floor held a conference room as well as their control room, which monitored all activity on their twenty-four-hour surveillance accounts. The next two floors were comprised of apartments that his staff stayed in, one of the perks of working for him, along with a couple of apartments they kept available for security reasons. The top floor held his own apartment and stretched the length of the north side of the building. It had roof access if they needed it.

"Officer Ayers, good to see you again." He hadn't seen a lot of Ayers since he'd worked numerous shifts with him over the years before now.

The officer pulled his spiral notebook from the front pocket of his shirt and flipped the pages until he found an unused sheet, pen poised over the pad. "Strong, you retired, what, two years ago, and still manage to get caught up in crazy cases? Can you tell me what happened?"

"The female has been running past the building for a few weeks. Today was different. A tan old junk Crown Vic late nineties model intentionally swerved to hit her. We left the building to help and two men jumped out of the vehicle. They fired the first shot. We returned fire, hitting their vehicle numerous times."

Ayers's eyebrows almost hit his hairline. "You didn't take them down? You're a better shot than that."

"They were amateurs. Their shots went wide before they ducked behind the vehicle, giving them cover to avoid ours. Hoped they would be in custody so you could haul them in."

Ayers furiously scribbled. "Do you have their description?"

"Even better, we have them on video. Erickson is making a copy as we speak." Riley motioned to his computer and pulled up the footage to show him.

Ayers sauntered around the desk and joined Riley to view the material queued up on the monitor. He whistled when they observed how far it knocked her into the grass. He stopped the recording as the car left.

"So, do you know her?" Ayers strolled to the other side of the desk and planted his feet shoulder-width apart, hooking his thumbs through the armholes of his ballistics vest.

"No, never spoke to her. She was consistent in the time she ran." Riley glanced around Ayers when there was a knock on his office door frame. He motioned for Erickson to come in.

"Officer, here are the video and stills of the two men." Connor Erickson was the latest hire that Riley had added to his team. Ex-military, he was exceptional and devoted to his job. His shaggy surfer-style brown hair and penetrating brown eyes made him popular with the women, especially with his runner build with sinewy muscles. His physique was misleading and gave a false sense of a non-threatening appearance, distracting from his actual strength. He easily fit into scenarios where Riley needed him to blend in while he tailed someone.

"Thanks," Officer Ayers took the photos. They were sharp, clear images. He checked his phone as it buzzed in his pocket. "I'm going to head to the hospital to check on my partner. He wasn't able to gain anything from the woman. She claims to not know anything." Ayers scrolled through his texts, his jaw clamped together.

"Hopefully those will be able to help identify and locate the two responsible." Riley motioned with his right hand to the evidence they handed over.

"Not real smart to be so predictable running past here daily for the past couple of weeks," Ayers mumbled.

"Not everyone thinks of things like that. That's why it's called job security for both of us." Riley shook his head. He could remember dealing with that when he still worked with Ayers.

As soon as Ayers left his office, Riley pulled up a search engine and ran a background check on one Annie Divers from the identification he lifted. Since she was apparently running from someone, perhaps he could get lucky enough that the computer check would tell him who, so he could help her. Was it the men who ran her down, or were they working for someone else who hunted her? And what was she doing out in the open like this if someone was after her? Those were questions he couldn't wait to get the answers to.

Two

Riley snatched his phone off his belt when it rang. "Talk to me."

"We're at St Mary's. They have her in for a scan now. She didn't tell the officer anything, but she's definitely hiding something or running from someone," Bear's voice informed him.

"Stay with her. Don't let anyone get to her."

"Yes, sir."

Her name didn't show anything before nine months ago. He skimmed the documents a third time. She didn't exist before then. He tipped back in his chair and studied the picture on her license. Her lack of history and digital footprint piqued his interest. He pulled up the address on her identification. An aerial view showed a field.

He scanned her photo and ran a search. Nothing. No social networking; this mystery woman was a ghost. He was impressed. It was hard to make yourself disappear like this. She was either very good or someone helped her. She was definitely hiding from someone, and with the interaction that she had this morning, they would find her soon enough if she stayed at the hospital. He nabbed his phone from where he placed it on his desk when it rang again.

"They just brought her back from a scan. She has a concussion and it took seventeen stitches to close the wound on her side. She also has a couple of cracked ribs. Some fellow just showed up asking about his wife. He gives me a bad vibe. There's something off; he's demanding and trying to push the staff around as if he has clout and shouldn't be denied any request, throwing legal jargon left and right as if he's either been to law school or knows someone who has, coaching him on what to say."

"Did you get his name?" Riley rubbed his forehead. "Take a picture or video of him?"

"No, I couldn't get close enough without him noticing. It's not like I can blend in like Connor. Now he's trying to push past the nurses who are physically standing in his way as they wait for the security they requested moments ago. He's going to find her." Bear's voice dropped to a whisper.

"Move her. I'm on my way." Riley snagged the keys for his Audi from the top of his desk. They jingled as he palmed them.

"Sir." Bear disconnected.

He lifted her identification and left his office, praying he had time to get there before the men from this morning's incident did, no doubt joining the aggressive man trying to get to her. "Keep the building on lockdown. I'm going to pick her up."

"Yes, sir." Monroe swiveled around in his chair.

"Have Sasha go up and get the empty unit ready," he yelled back over his shoulder, knowing she was likely cleaning the workout room in the basement he had fully kitted out with every possible workout equipment you could imagine. He knew their cleaning schedule since he and Sasha sat down and created it to maximize her ability to keep up with the size of the building to include empty apartment units, the offices, control room, and basement workout area.

"It'll be done." Monroe had the receiver in his hand before Riley made it to the door.

Riley pulled out of the back lot and pointed his car toward St Mary's. He punched the gas and rocketed down the street. He was ten minutes from the hospital. He knew that wasn't fast enough. He called the control room from the phone system in the car. "I need green lights." It wasn't exactly legal to go in the back door of the city lights grid computer system and manipulate them, but he'd only done it one other time before and only issued the order in case of emergencies.

The emerald-colored orbs lit the way as the sun rose in the east. Pollution hung heavy in the air, marring the skyline as he drove, yet creating a beautiful sunrise as the rays hit the smog, making it almost shimmer in hues of pinks and oranges.

Three minutes later, he pulled into the parking garage, bypassing the two unoccupied police cruisers angled outside the emergency room entrance. His tires squealed on his Audi as they gripped the pavement while he raced up two levels.

Bear held the mystery woman in his arms when Riley pulled up. Riley pushed the passenger door open for him, and Bear gingerly placed her in the seat.

"She's still out. They had to sedate her for the scan. She freaked when they tried to put her in the machine. The staff never let the guy near her. The man asking about her said she was involved in a bad accident and he was worried that she would need emergency surgery for internal injuries. The officers didn't see me take her. They were too busy with him to notice me turn off her machines so the alarm at the nurse's station wouldn't go off when I unplugged the leads monitoring her heart and lungs." Bear pulled the safety belt away from the door.

"How would he know about her injuries if he wasn't involved. He could have only gotten that information from the two embroiled in this?" Riley grabbed the seatbelt from Bear to buckle it over her small fragile frame.

"My thoughts exactly. He wasn't one of the two that were in the car this morning but seemed to know the extent of the injuries. I missed him giving her name so we still don't have that." Bear nodded and started to close the car door.

Riley held up his hand stopping him. "I lifted her ID before they transported her. We can go over her file back at the office."

As soon as the door latched, he punched the gas and took off. He knew Bear would meet him at the office.

Bear pulled into the back lot as Riley lifted her from the car. She moaned. "It's okay, you're safe. I won't let him get to you."

Monroe opened the door for them, raking his fingers through his blonde hair. "The room's ready."

Bear went to his station while Riley and Monroe took the elevator to the third floor. Monroe reached the apartment first and held the door open for Riley.

He placed her on the freshly made bed and then lifted her feet to pull the blanket out from under her, covering her with it.

Monroe took her pulse and checked her incision; bruising ran down her side just above the gash the hospital expertly sutured closed. He scanned through the chart on the tablet Bear retrieved from the hospital and had handed him before they got into the elevator. They would need to slip it back, or they'd get in trouble for lifting it. He always tried to keep in good with the local hospitals and police departments in case he needed them.

"Well, will she be okay here?" Riley frowned at her unconscious form. He didn't like that he snuck her out of the hospital behind the officers' backs like that, but what else could he do? His gut ached, a sensation he hadn't felt in a long time, not since he lost the one person who was his whole world.

He'd make sure her bills were covered until they could figure out what was going on with this woman, who appeared so fragile in front of him. He hoped he could convince her he wouldn't hurt her and that she could trust him. The amount of effort she went to, to hide and erase all traces of herself online, told him that could be harder than anything he faced when he was on the force.

"Yeah, no major internal injuries, which is a miracle in itself. Let's see," his finger ran over the screen as he skimmed the chart. "Three cracked ribs, a grade one concussion, and stitches. Looks like she almost got out of the way, or this could have been much, much worse. The bruising makes it look harsher than her injuries actually are. I'll get her set up on antibiotics." Monroe tossed the device onto the dresser as he left.

"Who are you?" Riley leaned against the door frame. He took a small camera out of his pocket and hooked it to the top of the doorway, facing the bed and door to the bathroom and walk-in closet. He queued up the image on his phone and adjusted the angle twice before he was happy with the view. This way they could keep an eye out to make sure no one slipped past them to get to her. Monroe could also keep an eye on her in case she needed anything. He would talk to her as soon as she woke to let her know he could protect her and keep her safe. His stomach knotted at the thought she wouldn't trust him. He rubbed at the spot on his chest just over his heart.

His phone vibrated. "Yeah?"

"You're needed downstairs. We have visitors," Bear grumbled.

He stuffed his phone in his pocket and left. He locked the door from the outside, punching in a special code so it couldn't be opened from the inside either. He bounded down the stairs, deciding not to use the elevator so the numbers on the first floor wouldn't light up with the floor he came from. When he turned the corner toward the front doors, the two goons from this morning were joined by an impeccably well-dressed man waiting on the outside. At approximately six feet tall, he was solid muscle. On reflex, Riley's hand settled on the gun on his hip. Riley wasn't intimidated by his physique due to his training while working at the police department. Even though they were approximately the same size, he had no doubt he'd be able to take the stranger down and restrain him easily enough. "Can I help you?"

"Yes, I'm looking for someone very dear to me. My wife went missing several months ago. My associates said they saw her in the area this morning. She may have been in an accident and injured. If she is here, I need to get her medical help and then take her home where I can care for her myself."

"And you are here because..." Riley tilted his head to the left.

"Like I said my associates saw her here this morning."

"Do you have a picture of her?" Riley didn't move.

"Oh, sure. Here." He pressed his thumb against the scanner on his phone and opened the gallery before scrolling to a picture, and then turned it toward Riley. It set off red flags. The picture was of the mysterious unconscious female upstairs. She leaned away from him and fear clouded her eyes. His knuckles were white from the grasp he had on her own petite hands. He had no doubt from the image he studied that she hid the pain from his grip.

"What's her name?"

"Megan. Megan Montgomery."

That didn't match what was on her license. "Sorry, don't know anyone by that name. This morning, an ambulance transported someone who was hit by a car your two associates were driving."

"Are you sure?" He narrowed his eyes at Riley as he flexed his chest muscles, an intimidation tactic that didn't affect him in the least. Riley wasn't impressed or threatened by this man. "And that is a dangerous accusation that you're making."

"Am I sure about what?" Riley met his stare. He wouldn't back down.

"My associates advised me you carried her into this building. Maybe she's still here?"

"An ambulance transported her after your associates ran her down and shot at us."

"It wouldn't hurt to look around, would it?" He stepped toward Riley, dismissing his comment.

Three of Riley's men stood. Their hands migrated to the holsters on their hips.

Riley didn't flinch. His eyes never strayed from the tyrant that stood before him. "That's not happening."

"It wouldn't be smart to keep me from my wife. I know how pretty she is, but she belongs to me." He narrowed his eyes at Riley. "Don't get any inappropriate ideas about her. It wouldn't end well for you if you did."

Riley released the lock on his holster. "First, she isn't here. Second, I think we are done and you need to leave the premises since the police have video of your *associates* shooting at her this morning. See, that's the great thing about owning a security company. I get to test all different types and styles of cameras to see which ones are the best. And I have the best."

The man's eyes darted to several corners in the front lobby area, his hands clenched into fists and his chest heaving as if he struggled to stop himself from lashing out. "Alright. Here's my card. If you come *across* her, I suggest you call me. She isn't well and this wouldn't be the first time she jumped in front of a car. I'm concerned she may hurt herself again. I need to get her back to a facility that can help her and administer the right dosage of meds to keep this from happening again."

Riley took the card, it read Dr. Alan Michael Montgomery. Surgeon. It also mentioned the hospital he currently worked for on the other side of the state. He gave a curt nod in his direction.

The doctor backed out of the office, and his goons followed him like good Labrador Retrievers.

"Keep this door locked. Make sure the outside cameras are monitored as a priority. Bear, run a background on our good doctor if you would. It's time I had a talk with Megan." Riley handed the business card to Bear before spinning on his heels, the elevator his next stop. He'd seen too many domestic situations go from bad to worse with results that you couldn't change because they didn't have all the facts about the case.

He got off on the third floor. Monroe waited for him at the door. Riley used his code on the security panel, disengaging the setting for the locks to only open to him since the building was secure again. The door swung open and Monroe followed him in.

Megan's unconscious form hadn't moved since they were downstairs. Monroe took her pulse and then pulled a syringe out of his bag, injecting her with her first dose of antibiotics. "I'll need to give her one every six hours. This is a high dose and will take care of any infection that will try to take hold with her injuries."

Riley didn't question where Monroe got the medications; he procured but knew he would never jeopardize his business. "Thanks, bring me a laptop. I need to run a search on her now that we have her real name. And tell Sasha to take this apartment off her cleaning rotation until further notice."

"Got it. Her license is a fake?" Monroe stopped mid-stride on his way out of the room.

Riley shrugged his shoulders. "It came back in the background check as legit, unless she had someone who was able to hack into the DMV and her file. That makes me think it's real. She changed her name and the good doctor doesn't have a clue what it is now."

Monroe left. Riley heard the elevator doors ding moments later when it reached their floor again. Megan moaned and her fingers on her left hand twitched under the blanket. Riley stood over her, his eyebrows drawn together as he waited to see if she would open her eyes. He didn't like the pompous man who tried to search his building. People didn't normally bother him; he knew people and most weren't inherently bad. But not this guy; this guy made his skin crawl. It wasn't good that he stated she *belonged* to him. She wasn't property to be claimed.

Monroe came back with Riley's laptop and left again without a word. Riley pulled a chair to the end of the bed. He pushed the lid up, angling it so the overhead lights didn't glare off the screen, then pulled up his search engines. He ran Megan's name through his background check software. It was top of the line. He needed it to be. He ran investigative background checks for employers and citizens who hired people to do work in their homes. He also ran a security company and offered protective services when celebrities or politicians were in town.

The computer notified him it was done with the search. He printed the reports to his wireless printer in his office. He dialed his phone. Bear answered. "Bring me the printouts in my office. Let's see what she's hiding."

"We also have the good doctor's ready. Did you want me to bring his up to you?"

"Yes, thanks."

Several minutes passed before the ding of the elevator and then the sound of doors sliding open seeped in through the cracked door from out in the hall. Bear sauntered in with two folders. "How is she?" He watched her, hesitant to enter the room.

Riley held out his hand for the folders. "Still unconscious. Check with Monroe and ask him about pain meds. She keeps shifting around and then groans."

"Yes sir. And you know we could easily send you the files on your computer." Bear leaned his shoulder against the door. His shirt stretched even further against his taught muscles.

"I don't like files only being digital, they can be hacked and changed or deleted altogether. Hard copies are easier to control, and having the actual pages in front of me helps me review the files easier than a digital one can. And Bear, how many times do I have to remind you I am not a superior from your military days. Stop calling me sir." Riley didn't look up from the pages he was thumbing through.

"Yes sir." Bear's chuckle faded as he left.

Riley leafed through her file. Definitely more than he could find from the name on her license. She used the same birthday. Her maiden name was Megan Ann Becker. She married Alan when she was twenty-five. They didn't have any kids. Her parents were killed in a car crash three years after her marriage. She didn't work; it looked like she was a stay-at-home wife. The next page caused him to hold his breath. He didn't look at the records on his computer, but there were pictures of her. Black eyes, cuts, burns. He stood and dropped the folder on the end of the blankets. Riley hurried to the side of the bed as Monroe came into the apartment.

Monroe stopped halfway through the doorway. "I know that face. What's wrong?"

"Help me roll her." Riley pulled the blanket back.

"We need to be careful of the incision." Monroe dropped his bag on the floor and gently rolled her to her stomach. She moaned and tried to roll back over.

Riley opened the back of her hospital shirt. Monroe gawked. "What happened?"

They stared at her back, which showed faint scars from cuts and burns. They were in varying degrees of healing. Some were so faint they were barely visible while others were newer, showing the angry puckered skin around the injury and probably not even a year old. That was the same time he said she went missing. She was running from a monster.

Riley didn't say a word but closed the back of her gown before rolling her onto her back. He covered her once again. When he was back at the foot of the bed, he handed the file to Monroe before grabbing Alan's file to thumb through it. He shook his head. This was bad. None of the abuse allegations were followed up on. No charges were ever filed; police records showed all the cases closed unfounded. How in the heck did they come to the conclusion scars were unfounded? This was a blatant disregard for finding justice for the victim.

His previous two wives suffered at his hand before they disappeared and then were discovered dead in very similar car crashes. Both ejected over the same stretch of road. Alan was part of a fraternity in college, and the college photo showed his two goons by his side.

Monroe whistled when he finished Megan's file. "This shows she divorced him nine months ago through court on a contested case. They aren't married. He wants to get revenge."

"No, he thinks of her as his property. She looks like the first one to make it out of a marriage with him alive. His two previous wives weren't so lucky. They were also abused before they disappeared when they filed for divorce. He received large insurance settlements after they were declared deceased from car crashes while he was out of town at medical conferences." Riley studied Megan; her eyes fluttered open. She stared at him. Her hands clenched the blanket and pulled it up higher.

Three

"Who are you?" Annie tried to move up the bed toward the headboard. She cringed when she twisted her torso to pull her legs up to herself. Two men, very large men, towered over the side of the mattress. She was still in the scrub pants and hospital gown they changed her into when the hospital assessed her injuries.

"My name is Riley Strong. I own the building you were in front of when you were run down while on your run this morning. This is Monroe. He helped you and works for me."

"How did I get here? I was taken to the hospital." She blew out a breath as she scrunched her eyes closed. Did they work for Alan?

"Here, I can help with the pain." Monroe grabbed a syringe.

Annie's eyes grew wide and she scampered away from him to the other side of the bed. She cried out and her right hand clutched her stomach as a wave of dizziness made her head swim. Wow that hurt; she needed to get home and pack. Sam and Mark found her, which meant Alan wouldn't be far behind. Did she need to look at moving out of state? There were so many things she didn't have answers to.

"It's okay, we aren't going to hurt you." Monroe held out his hands. "I was a medic in the military. I wouldn't hurt you. We brought you here from the hospital to keep you safe."

Riley worked his way around to her while Monroe kept her focus on him. She dropped her legs to the floor and attempted to stand. She cried out and crumpled into Riley's waiting arms. Her fingers dug into his thickly muscled biceps as she clung to him. The prominent veins—a roadmap up and down his forearms—were impressive and hinted at his strength.

"Shh, it's okay. We aren't going to hurt you, Megan."

She shoved him in the chest and twisted around away from him. How did he know that name? She stumbled to the nightstand. Backed into the corner of the room, she clutched the lamp from its place next to the bed, holding it over her head awkwardly, her other arm wrapped around her waist. Riley put his hands up, palms toward her. With his size, he could easily restrain her.

"How do you know my name?" Her eyes darted from Monroe to Riley.

"Someone came looking for you with the two men who ran you down this morning."

Her chin trembled. "Alan?"

"Yes, he said you were his wife and he was worried about you. I didn't believe him."

She jerked her head toward Riley. "He doesn't know I'm here?"

"No, I told him the ambulance took you to the hospital. Which is true, but what I didn't tell him was that we brought you back here without anyone's knowledge."

She darted her eyes from one to the other as she tried to work out what he was telling her. "Why would you do that?"

"Gut feeling."

She stared at Riley and then at Monroe. She still held the lamp over her head, but her eyes started to droop as darkness crept into her vision. She couldn't allow herself to go unconscious in front of these two men. But wasn't she that way when they brought her here? Wherever here was.

"Megan, we aren't going to hurt you." Riley offered her his hand.

"My name isn't Megan anymore. I had it changed."

"Annie Divers?"

Her eyes grew wide. "Are you following me? Did Alan send you to mess with me? He likes to play games, mess with people's heads. It's sick entertainment for him." Her breathing picked up with quick inhales. Yet she felt like she couldn't pull in a full breath, as if there was a weight on her chest.

"No, it's on your license." Riley pointed to the dresser where the laminated photo ID lay.

"I need to get home and pack. He knows what city I'm in. It's only a matter of time before he finds my house and my new name. Am I free to leave?" She gulped in air, concerned about how far from her house she was. Not able to order an uber, she would have to walk. No one knew where she lived and she was perfectly happy with that.

"I don't think that's a good idea. He didn't leave that long ago. My guess is he's out there with his friends. I don't think he believed me when I told him you weren't here."

"Why can't he leave me alone?" Annie dropped the lamp onto the nightstand as she sunk to the floor.

Riley knelt next to her and pulled her to him. Her muscles tensed as his hands grasped her arms. "Come on, you need to rest or you'll injure yourself worse than you already are. Your body needs time to recuperate."

He helped her to the bed. She glanced at the end with the scrunched covers and her name on the file folder. "It's my job. I do security and background checks on people for a living. I used to be an officer, and as Monroe stated, he was a medic in the military. I was just trying to figure out what was going on with you and how much danger you're in."

She took a quick glance at him. "And did you figure out how much danger I'm in?"

"A lot." He didn't hold any punches.

She held tight to his arm, her fingers turning white. He helped her lay back as she buckled from the pain. Monroe grabbed the syringe. "This is for the pain."

"No, I don't want it." Her vision was already blurry.

"This is only temporary until your body starts healing. If I don't give you this, you'll be in excruciating pain in a couple of hours after what the hospital gave you wears off. Trust me, broken ribs hurt. I've had my fair share."

"Take it, you'll need it." Riley pried her fingers off his arm but didn't let go of her hand, intertwining their fingers.

She shook her head and turned away. Riley smoothed her hair away from her sweat-dotted forehead when she closed her eyes. She grimaced and her face pinched in pain as she curled into a ball.

• • • •

"I'LL BE BACK IN A FEW hours for the next antibiotic dose." Monroe recapped the unused syringe. He grabbed his bag and strolled from the room.

Riley picked up Alan's file and continued reading. The fraternity looked to be a haven for misfits whose rich parents bought their way out of jail. Between the property damages, rapes, assaults, and a whole list of other crimes, Riley knew this guy would stop at nothing to get what he wanted. And what he wanted was Annie.

Riley stood and grasped his hands together behind his back, raising his arms and stretching his muscles. Annie moaned, causing him to hesitate. She settled down and was quiet again. He removed the folders from the bed before he knelt and whispered to her, "I'll be back. You're safe here."

As he went out of the room, he punched in his priority code locking her in and everyone else out, except for him. He didn't want to take the chance that she would get out and Alan saw her, it would be an all-out fight to keep her from him. He closed his eyes and shook his head; this was a bad case. He'd never worked one this bad when he was an officer. The fact that he still called her his wife even though the divorce had been finalized nine months ago told him this guy wasn't going to give up easily. To keep her alive and away from her abuser, whom she had the strength and courage to separate herself from to escape unimaginable terror and pain, he would need a lot more resources than he normally used in the day-to-day operations of his business.

He grabbed a sandwich off the lunch table when he went back down to his men. He dropped the folders in Bear's box on his desk. "Check this guy out. This could get ugly."

"Yeah, I passed around a copy for us down here. Everyone's caught up on what he's capable of. Looks like he has friends everywhere to help him cover up his crimes." Bear's chair groaned when he leaned back.

"That's not good. Any sign of him outside? Him or his goons?" Riley took a bite of the sandwich as he peered out of the front windows. The bullet-resistant glass held up nicely during this morning's fiasco. He would call the window company anyway and get an order in for replacement panes. They would more than likely be fine, but he would rather replace them and not advertise the damage and nicks from the shooting this morning to his customers.

"No, Tracker thought he saw the car approximately thirty minutes ago but nothing since." He'd first met Tracker when Bear introduced them six years ago. Bear had been in the military with him, and Tracker picked up the name when he was asked to track down a group who had taken out part of their unit. Tracker was mean-looking. If anyone didn't know better, he always looked to be in a bad mood. It wasn't his fault; he didn't scowl, but the harsh lines of his face hid his easy-going nature. At six foot two, he was the second tallest of Riley's staff. His blonde hair and blue eyes were a deep contrast to his always sun-kissed skin. He never stopped when he caught a trail, and people swore he was part bloodhound. The smallest thing led him to where someone had gone. He said he'd always been able to track anything and practiced when he was a boy to see if he could find someone.

"Okay, let everyone know to be on high alert until we figure this out. If he has high enough friends, and it looks like he does, we could be in trouble." Riley sauntered back into the kitchen, putting together a tray with different sandwich choices and a couple of bottles of water. He would leave them on the dresser in Annie's room if she wanted to eat something the next time she woke. Back in his office a few minutes later, he needed to run a few more searches and get more background on the colleagues and who they were associated with.

He closed the solid steel door to his office. This could take a while. He pulled up several search databases and typed in what information he had. He sent the image from his phone to the tv on the wall. He had Annie full screen. She tossed from one side to the other. The pain showed on her face. He stood when she swung her legs out from under the blankets. She faltered and stumbled to the wall. A couple of steps took her to the bathroom where she closed the door and was out of his sight.

He selected the print option for goon number one, Sam Berger, and then pulled a search for goon number two, Mark Murphy. The picture of the fraternity group lay on his desk; might as well run all of them. The printer beeped and he loaded more paper, pulling off what was already printed. An hour later he had eight folders on his desk. The two goons seemed to be the ones who did the rest of the fraternity's bidding. Troy Blair became a lawyer and worked at a prestigious law firm. Brett Gephardt was in banking, while Kurt Sherman was in construction and Heath Mosbacher in politics. Alan, a doctor with more money than he could ever spend, had endless options to keep his name clean and away from any bad press.

There was no trail on social media for any of the members. They apparently liked to keep a low profile. He glanced at the TV and noticed Annie hadn't gotten into bed. Riley jumped from his chair, causing it to roll back, slamming into the credenza behind it, and raced out of his office. "Monroe!"

Monroe leaped out of his chair to follow him with his bag in his hand.

They slowly opened the door to the apartment. "Annie?"

A couple of steps into the bedroom, still no Annie. Riley knocked on the bathroom door. "Annie."

Riley edged the door open. Annie lay on the floor, curled into a ball. He raced to her side; sweat gleamed on her forehead and dotted her upper lip. Monroe grabbed the syringe she declined earlier; Riley held her arm out. The needle pierced her delicate skin. The fluid disappeared through the needle into her arm. Riley watched the pain ease from her furrowed brow as she relaxed. He slid one arm under her knees and the other under her shoulders. She cried out as he lifted her off the floor.

Monroe took her vitals after Riley laid her on the bed. She gasped as she held her side. "Let me take a look."

Blood seeped through her bandage. Monroe looked at Riley. "She tore a couple of stitches."

"Does she need to go back to the hospital?" Riley didn't like the idea of leaving the building with her. He knew they were out there somewhere watching them.

"I can take care of it here, but it's gonna hurt."

"No hospital!" Annie sucked in air through clenched teeth.

"Riley, hold her. Annie, I'll try and numb it first, but I don't have anything close to what you'll need. You'll still feel all of this, and for that I'm sorry." Monroe grabbed sutures from his kit. Riley scooted next to her and grabbed both her hands in his. She tightened her grip and turned her head away from Monroe.

A cool liquid hit her stomach; she tried to sit up and see what it was. It stung; she cringed and sucked air through her clamped jaw. She turned her head to Riley, who waited while watching Monroe work. The needle pierced the skin and she scrunched her stomach muscles and dug her fingers into his hands. He tightened his grip; his muscles tensed as she strained against him. She tried to pull her legs up to her stomach on instinct. Monroe was quick; he threw a leg on each side and sat on her upper legs, pinning them to the bed.

"Just a couple more. Sorry, Annie." Monroe started the next stitch when she tried to sit up.

"I'm sorry," Annie muttered and squeezed Riley's hands tighter, the tips of her fingers turning white.

She was apologizing to them? She never screamed out, never cried, just held onto him as if he were a lifeline she could anchor to. "Hold on, just a couple more," Riley whispered in her ear. She was so strong and he wasn't sure she even knew it. He vowed right then and there to make sure he did everything humanly possible to get her free and clear of her ex and show her how strong a fighter she was. Everything else he would leave up to God to handle.

Her breathing picked up as she strained against Riley's massive arms. She released a pent-up breath in her lungs through her nose and pushed her head back into the pillow. Monroe pulled the tape taut against her skin over new bandages on her newly stitched stomach. She relaxed against the pillows; sweat beaded across her forehead.

"Thank you." She closed her eyes and released his hands from the death grip as her arms fell slack at her sides.

Riley angled himself off the bed, trying not to disturb her. He took a washcloth from the bathroom, ran cool water over it, and then wrung it out. He wiped the sweat away when she closed her eyes again. Heavy breaths filled the room. Monroe got off her legs and finished cleaning up. He removed his gloves, tossing them into a bag along with her old bandage. He nodded to Riley before he strolled out of the room.

The gown slipped over her left shoulder a couple of inches, exposing her delicate pale skin. He cringed when he saw the initials AM branded on her shoulder. He didn't see this when they looked at her back earlier. The raised flesh looked pink and angry, not completely healed. He couldn't take his eyes off Annie. Motionless, the pain meds had taken full effect as her body sagged with exhaustion. The blanket had slipped off the bed and lay in a crumpled pile on the floor. He covered her shoulder with the corner of the gown before covering her with the blanket he pilfered from the floor. He took the Bible he put on the dresser when he came in and placed it next to her on the table by the bed. The note he wrote poked out of the cover at the top explaining how much the Bible helped him during the lowest time in his life. He could only pray she would be curious and pick it up, like he had all those years ago when he was hurting and had nowhere else to turn.

Backing out of the room, he marched through the door and punched in his code. Monroe lingered in the hall. "She okay?"

"She's out right now but we need to keep an eye on her. She won't ask for help." Riley punched the button to bring the elevator to them hard enough to make the elevator panel rattle. "He branded her."

"He did what?"

"On her left shoulder the initials AM, I say about the size of a cufflink." Riley tilted his head back, staring at the ceiling and trying to get his anger under control.

"You saw the cigar burns on her arm, didn't you?"

"No, I didn't." Riley ground his teeth together.

"On the inside upper arm. I saw it when I gave her the injection." Monroe's hands tightened around the worn faded canvas handles of his bag.

"He's someone who thinks he's above the law and will do anything to get her back. I fought against monsters like this when I worked for the local department. They think their wives are their property and they can treat them any way they want to. They definitely don't like to lose."

"That's not a good combination." Monroe stepped into the elevator.

"No, it's not. All we can do is keep her here."

The doors slid closed as Monroe asked, "What about when she wants to leave?"

"I don't want to think about that. We can't keep her here against her will. We can't break the law to that degree. It would only hurt the relationship we have with the local precinct here. Let's just pray she doesn't want to leave. I don't want to jeopardize her trust in us that she thinks we act no better than the Neanderthal that was married to her and keep her here where she will feel like a prisoner. Maybe she'll realize how secure this place is, and we can keep her safe with us."

"The bandage should hold. I wrapped it more than I normally would. I would give her at least two days before we even think about letting her leave. It's a nasty gash from the impact with the side mirror, coupled with the fractured ribs. If he gets a hold of her in this condition, it wouldn't take much to kill her."

"Copy that. We'll have a talk with her the next time she wakes." Riley pulled up the video on his phone. She lay curled under the blanket he had draped over her unconscious form.

Monroe sauntered back to his desk and dropped the bag on the floor for easy access when he was needed again.

Riley slid the files across the top of his desk and opened the first drawer on the left. Several small metal strips with minuscule circuits embedded in the thin foil film lay in the tray below his pens, paperclips, and sticky notes. He slipped one out and pulled Annie's license from his pocket. He carefully used a razor to open a small slit in the side to wedge the metal strip into her license. He would know it was there but no one else would. The smallest drop of super glue sealed the opening. They were top of the line, and he paid a hefty price for them.

Four

It was early morning; he had worked through the night, and his employees were just coming in for their shift. Bear nodded at him before he sat behind his bank of monitors, watching the high-end accounts assigned to him. Bear got the privilege of monitoring their high-target security accounts during the day.

Riley jumped out of his chair when he glanced at his phone and saw Annie wasn't in the bedroom. He strolled to the elevator and took it to the third floor. Punching in his code, he let himself into the secured apartment. The rumpled sheets and blanket piled on the floor made his chest tighten. The food tray was empty from the meal he brought her last night. They had convinced her to stay at least two days to give herself a couple of days of healing. She apparently took him literally. This was the third day, and he was still no closer to figuring out what their next step would be. He wasn't sure what he would be able to say to convince her to give them more time. She refused to talk to them, and he knew he would have to do a lot to earn any sort of trust from her.

"Give me the location for Annie's GPS chip." Riley had Bear on the other line while he searched the empty apartment, already knowing she was gone. He had dropped her license back on the table in the apartment the first night while she slept when he checked on her. He wasn't sure how she got out of the building, but her license was gone, so he knew she had somehow. His code was the only one that would open the door when he enabled it. The solid steel door was locked when he came up to the apartment. He yanked open closet doors only to expose the empty space where no one hid. He was ready to take her home today if she was still adamant she wanted to leave, but he didn't want her to leave like this. She was vulnerable in her condition and he preferred to at least have a general knowledge of the area she lived in so he could suggest security or even a system to keep her house safeguarded from Alan. He prayed he could find her before Alan had a chance to.

"Shows she's on the street outside our building. It's not moving fast; she must be walking. She's exposed if she's on foot."

"Send Tracker and Monroe out to get her. If she wants to go home, have them tell her that I'll take her home."

"Sir."

He turned with a grimace as his jaw muscles tensed. He inspected the door, there were no marks. How did she get out? He pulled up the camera and rewound the footage for the past thirty minutes. All it showed him was an empty bed. He queued it up for another fifteen minutes before that. She lay there but rolled from side to side every couple of minutes. By the scrunched brow and pale skin, he knew the pain meds had worn off. She was in too fragile of a state to leave. He should have put someone outside the door.

She left the bedroom for the front door and was out of camera range. There was no camera in the living room or by the front door to show him how she got out.

His phone rang. "Go."

"We found her ID. There's blood on it. Tracker's following footsteps in the grass. We'll let you know when we catch up to her."

"Copy." He knew if Alan hadn't gotten to her yet then no one else would be able to find her as fast as Tracker.

Riley blew out his breath and closed the door behind him. "Sasha," he spoke into his phone.

"Yes."

"Can you make sure the apartment is cleaned?" He had her grab some clothes for Annie while she was here and knew she would be wearing a black shirt and gray sweatpants.

"Yes sir, I'll be right up."

He dropped his phone into his tan cargo pants pocket and strolled to the elevator. He blew out another sigh and punched the button to take him back to the ground level. The sound of jingling keys filled the air in the elevator as he fished them out of his pocket. He would drive around and see if he could find her.

Riley pulled out of the lot and pointed his car north. The silver Audi's engine was almost completely silent as he pulled alongside Monroe and Tracker. He rolled down the passenger window, and Monroe handed him her license.

"She definitely went this direction. She's not raising her right leg completely when she takes a step. You can see the gravel on the side of the road disturbed from the foot she's not lifting as high as the other. It's on the side with her injured ribs. Probably trying to move that side as little as possible to keep the pain at a minimum. Then you see the dew is interrupted where her other foot lands." Tracker pointed to the disturbed gravel and dew-laden grass where it was darker from knocking the dew from the thin knife-like leaves.

Up ahead they saw another drag mark he pointed to; they were headed in the right direction. "I'm going to drive ahead and see if I can spot her. Keep going in case she went off-road, and I'll circle back around if I don't see her and catch back up to you."

They gave a small nod and salute with a couple of fingers. Riley rolled up the window and punched the accelerator leaving them to continue on foot. "Annie. What are you doing?"

He knew what she was doing; she was running. She didn't trust anyone, and he couldn't blame her for that. He hated that someone took that away from her. He'd seen a lot when he was an officer, and he always fought for victims of domestic violence. That was one crime he couldn't wrap his head around. You were supposed to love and protect the one you promised to love forever. How could someone brutalize their loved ones?

He still struggled with the death of his wife eight years ago. The cancer that stole away their happily ever after still made him mad. He knew many who had turned to alcohol after the death of a spouse. He wouldn't tarnish what he had with his wife. She wouldn't want him to do that. So he threw himself into building his business. He smiled as he pictured her beautiful face. They had a good life together. She'd been a nurse while he was an officer. She was in a better place, and he knew one day he would be there with her for eternity.

Until then, he would help people like Annie fight for their right to live a life where they could feel safe.

Chance brought him and his wife together one night when he was assaulted by a drunk at a tavern disturbance he was dispatched to. He needed staples to close the gash on the side of his head. She had cleaned up the wound for the doctor. She apologized when he winced and placed her hand on his shoulder. It was at that point he knew she was the one. Her soft brown eyes with just a hint of copper in them paired with her long thick black lashes drove him crazy.

They dated for a few months before they both knew it was forever for them. The guys at the station had given him a hard time, but he didn't care. They were married six months later and had several years together. One morning he couldn't wake her up. He called an ambulance and three months later she was gone. It had been a fast-growing tumor that started in her brain. He watched in agony as she struggled to form even the smallest words in the end. He hated cancer.

It was after her death that he launched the plans they had discussed before she got sick. He would retire and start his own security company. She had talked to him about going into business for himself for months after he told her his ambitions. She said he could do anything he wanted, that he was the most brilliant man she'd ever met. He had laughed at her and brushed off the compliment. She was his biggest supporter and champion in the short time they had been together.

Two years ago, he retired and within a year he had people who jumped at the chance to help his business succeed. He assisted the local police department and the county sheriff's office with high-end domestic cases. He was given a little more leniency than the law allowed officers.

He crested the next hill and turned to enter a residential area. It was the last subdivision before the main road took someone to the interstate and the inner city. This was the only possible location of her house since she had to live in the area for her scheduled jog to take her past his office. Still no Annie. He was ready to turn around when his headlights picked up a moving dark form in the distance. It looked like a lone figure. The white skin of their feet told him they were shoeless. He accelerated as the figure walked down a driveway. The large wrought-iron gates closed behind her. She struggled with each step to the house. No, not a house. This qualified as more of an estate. He sat there and watched her wrestle with the front door. The yard was immense. Where did she get the money to stay at this place? Was it a friend's so she wouldn't face Alan alone if he found her? A boyfriend's? Why did the thought of her seeing someone twist his stomach in knots?

He knew from reading her file she didn't get anything in the divorce. She requested to be able to leave with the clothes on her back. She wanted to disappear. He wasn't sure Alan would even think to look for her here. He dialed the office.

"Yo, Bear here."

"Pull up what you can about 1134 Lone Hill Drive. I think this is where she lives."

"Sir." A dial tone sounded in his ear. He hung up; Bear was not a man of many words.

Tracker and Monroe were small dots in the rearview mirror. He waited while they approached the car before he got out. He kept his eyes peeled, looking for Alan and his two cronies. He noticed things normal people didn't. He was trained to look for the unusual. The lady walking her miniature schnauzer was someone who knew the area; she was confident and comfortable with where she was and didn't look around.

The elderly male who took his trash to the curb was wary of people. He glared at the lady with the dog as if she encroached on his space. Then he scowled at Riley as he noticed him sitting in the car. When Tracker and Monroe caught up to him, he scurried back into the house, no doubt watching from behind the curtained windows at the front of the residence. No cars were in the area. It was still early enough that people wouldn't be leaving for work just yet.

"She went in there," Riley slid out of his Audi.

"Wow, nice digs." Tracker whistled. "Her trail ended at the driveway."

"Did you see anyone in the area on the way here?" Riley leaned back against the car and crossed his arms.

"No, still early, no traffic out on the roads yet."

Riley's phone rang. "Go."

"House is in Annie Divers's name. She paid cash for it a month ago through a holding company and then an LLC. Looks like she's trying to hide her tracks."

"Where did she get enough cash to buy this house outright?" Riley wondered if Alan wasn't just interested in her, but did she take money also?

"Not sure, but according to property records she paid for it in hard cash and moved in the day she finalized the paperwork. Bank owned it and was happy to take the payment. She got a great deal on it. Previous owner lost it when the market tanked a year ago. It was almost paid off before the owner bailed and left everything."

"What did she pay for it?" Riley was curious how good of a deal she got.

"Less than a quarter of a mil."

Riley whistled. "Wow."

"Yeah, had I known about it, I'd be living there." Bear disconnected.

He slid his phone into his pocket and stared at the house that could easily sell for three times that. It reminded him of his house, the house that he hadn't stepped foot in in years, only this was easily three times its size. He couldn't think of Helen. Right now, he needed to concentrate on the woman who needed his help more than his deceased wife who was in heaven; no place safer. Even though she got it for a great price, that still didn't explain where she got her hands on that much green.

"What's the plan." Monroe shifted his medic bag to his other shoulder.

"We go in and talk to her." Riley walked up to the intercom button and pressed it.

If she didn't answer, he wouldn't hesitate to let himself in. She could need help and may not be able to answer, although that wouldn't help her trust issues. He pushed the button again.

The speaker squawked static. "Who's there?"

"Annie, it's Riley. Are you okay?"

"How did you find me?" Her whisper filtered through the electrical hum.

"Can we come in?" The antiquated box squawked with his every transmission.

Static almost overrode her voice. "Who's with you?"

"You know who's here." He waved at the camera mounted on the gate.

"Annie, you need another dose of your antibiotic. It's only been three days, and you need them for at least ten. Trust me, an infection from something like this would be fatal." Monroe volunteered.

There was silence. Static squelched through the speaker, and then it went silent. Static again. Nothing.

The gate started to open. "Pull in and hide your car around back."

Riley unlocked the Audi and they all piled in. The driveway curved around the front of the house, but he could also see an unkept disintegrating concrete drive past the garages that went behind the residence. The gate closed behind them.

Once out of the car, they approached the back door and found it open. He pulled his gun from the holster on his hip; the others followed suit. "Annie?"

His flashlight beam lit the expansive interior. There wasn't much in the way of furniture, but the pieces she did have looked to be antiques. He panned his flashlight around when he saw movement from the kitchen. The overhead light blinded them as she flipped the switch. She held a gun aimed at his chest.

Five

"Annie, I'm not going to hurt you." Riley's rich baritone voice filled the air, sending goosebumps down her arms. Slowly, he put his flashlight back on his belt and holstered his weapon, keeping his movements slow and even.

Tracker and Monroe did the same. Annie's ashen face contorted into a grimace. She was well past any sort of lingering effects of the pain meds Monroe administered the previous night. Sweat glistened on her forehead as pain pinched her delicate features. She didn't want them to know the extent of her discomfort.

"Why are you here?" She refused to lower her gun.

Riley held up his hand to her. "Please put the gun down."

She held her breath and tried to hide the wince as the muscles twitched in her face. "No, I think I need it."

He tilted his head. "Why do you think you need it?"

"I saw the files you carried out of my room. It had Alan's name on it. Are you working for him?" Annoyed her voice faltered.

"No. I felt he was a threat so I did some research on him." Riley's mouth slightly spasmed at the corner when her finger came to rest on the trigger; the pulse in his neck jumped.

Annie's shoulders convulsed slightly as she tried to hide her grunt of pain. "And what did you find?"

"That he's gotten away with this long enough. That he makes his wives disappear when they try to escape from him. He discards them as if they are nothing to him. He has a group of friends who help him cover his tracks and they are powerful enough; no one has challenged them yet. And that he branded you as if you were his property." He watched her when he said the last. Monroe spared a glance at Riley and then back at her.

Annie flinched; her finger moved away from the trigger. She didn't need a twinge of pain to cause her to shoot them unintentionally. "How do you know that?" A tear glinted in the corner of her eye.

"The hospital gown fell off your shoulder when we were helping you."

"It was his cufflink. He got it hot with his cigar lighter. Mark and Sam held me down while he pressed it to my skin, laughing while I screamed. He whispered in my ear that no one would want me now that I was marked as his possession." The words tumbled out. She ought to stop talking, but there was something about this man that affected her like no one else had. She wanted to trust him. His copper hazel eyes pulled to her.

Riley held out his hand. "Let us help you."

"No!" Her eyes widened. She blinked away the tears that had yet to fall and moved her finger back to the trigger.

"I don't think you want to shoot us. You aren't the type to murder someone."

Annie blinked several times to clear her vision. "You're in my house. Castle law."

"Do you know how to use that?"

"Safety off." She flipped it off with her thumb. "Point at what you want to shoot." The barrel lifted to chest level. "Pull the trigger. Yes, I know how to use this," she stated matter-of-factly, no emotion in her monotone voice but fierce determination burned in her eyes. Did he really think she didn't know what she was doing if he knew as much about her as he apparently did? He read the files, so he knew what she was up against. One of the first things she learned when she left him was how to shoot. And she was pretty good with a killer aim.

"Think about this, we haven't done anything to hurt you. We hid you from your ex. We helped stitch you back up so you didn't have to go back to the hospital and could stay unseen. Nothing we have done was to hurt you." Riley took a tentative step forward.

"You can't help me." She slightly bent at her side. Why on earth did cracked ribs hurt so much?

Riley inched forward again. "How do you know?"

Barely a whisper escaped her lips. "No one has been able to help me. Do you know how many people he has in his back pocket? Forget police departments, lawyers, judges, you name it. It goes higher than that. For years, I asked for help and everyone turned me back over to that man. I should have left the state."

"Annie, we're good at what we do. We protect people for a living. I can help make your home more secure. I own the company where we had you. It's a security company. We're the best out there. You don't have to leave. He'll never think you'd be in a house like this. I believe we can keep it that way." Riley's eyes left hers for just a moment to glimpse at the gun and then back to her.

Several minutes turned into fifteen. She still held the gun but eased her finger off the trigger back to the slide of the gun, trying to hide the slight tremble in her hand. "What do you mean, make this more secure?" That was all she ever wanted, to feel safe again. To not be scared every second that he might find her. She thought once the divorce was final, she would have a second chance. At what, she wasn't sure, but it was better than what she had been living through. She fought for a divorce, meeting behind Alan's back, being the dutiful wife in front of him if only to get the code to the safe. And she memorized who he associated with so she could avoid those people. Convincing him she was going to lunch with the Sheriff's wife, he let his guard down. He was furious later when he learned it was her attorney picking her up when she climbed into the back of the Lincoln, and not the wife of his best friend.

"Better cameras, motion sensors, more secure locks on the doors. You would have a bank of monitors to see every part of the outside of the house behind the safety of your locked doors. Alerts to your phone if a motion sensor is triggered. We'd also monitor the house. We offer to respond to any alarm set off here. You are close enough that we could be here in a matter of minutes." Riley's voice pulled her back from her musings

She nodded but didn't say anything. Her mouth was set in a scowl. Could he really give her everything he promised? "Annie, we can also help with the pain. You wouldn't have to go to the hospital."

She furrowed her brow. "Why are you doing this? What do you want?" What was he getting out of this?

"It's who we are. I worked domestic violence crimes for a police department my entire career. I'll be honest, yours is the worst I've seen. And sometimes people want to help just to help. They don't want anything in return."

Annie shook her head. "I must insist on paying for the security system and monitoring. Treat me as a client." Wait, was she really agreeing with this?

"Of course. Did you want Monroe to look at you?" Riley still hadn't moved. He didn't try to sidle up to her and convince her he was a good guy she could trust but stayed where he was, letting her set the pace and make the decisions herself. Alan had never done that. She hadn't realized the day she met him that all choice and free will went out the window with his commanding, narcissistic ways, his need to overpower and dominate whoever was in his life.

She nodded, flipped the safety on, and placed the gun on the kitchen island. Her hands clutched the edges of the counter as she controlled her breaths; her arms shook.

Monroe yanked his bag off his shoulder and opened it on the island in front of Annie. "Let me see."

She had managed to take a quick five minute shower in the time it took them to figure out where she was. She wore yoga pants with a loose-fitting t-shirt that Monroe lifted, the band to her pants riding just below a new bandage. He gently peeled back the tape. The skin around the stitches was red and swollen. Her skin was hot to the touch. "This is infected. We need to keep up with your antibiotics. I can give you some to take with water, or I can come to see you every six hours and administer an injection, but the two days you were with us weren't long enough to be done with the meds."

"What will work best and the quickest?" Sweat dotted above her upper lip as she swayed on her feet.

"Injections."

She nodded.

"Annie, I have to ask something."

She jerked her head to Riley, who was no doubt able to see the pain etched on her face as she tried to steady herself. "What?"

"How did you pay for this house with cash? If you accessed one of his accounts, that could be a reason he's so fixated on you. I'm only asking to know what we're dealing with here."

She smiled. It was the first time she was able to smile since meeting him. For the first time in almost a year, she was proud of herself and her accomplishments. "Look at the books. Second shelf in from the left, the book with a blue dust jacket."

Riley strolled to the bookcase and ran his finger across the books until he came to the blue dust jacket. "*Married to the Devil.*" He pulled it toward him, sliding it off the shelf, the dust jacket scraping against the ledge as he read the title. Annie Divers Becker was the listed author on the cover. He turned to her. "You wrote this?"

"Yes, I wrote about my life. Once I started, the words just flowed. It was also cathartic and felt like I was finally putting the worst chapter of my life behind me. No publishing agency would touch me being an unknown. It was nerve-racking waiting for a response when I started looking at self-publishing. A couple of book edits and voila, I have an e-book and the royalties are beyond anything I could imagine. My book went viral, which is unheard of, and within the first sixty days I saw money start filtering in."

"It says it's fiction, but it's based on a true story. Your story." He raised an eyebrow at her.

"No one knows it really happened. And no one will. It's poetic, I think. He said I would be nothing without him, yet I've made something out of myself and am so much more than I would have been if I stayed with him."

He thumbed through the book and looked the dust jacket over. "Your picture isn't on here."

"That was the one part I was adamant about. No pictures of me will ever be on my book covers. I have another manuscript at the editors now." She flinched as Monroe replaced the bandage.

"Sorry, let me get antibiotics on board. Hold on." Monroe fiddled with a syringe, filling it with a clear liquid.

"Can I sit? I'm dizzy." She didn't feel the least bit of nervous energy she thought she would, having three monstrous alpha males in her house. Did she dare to believe her life was finally her own without Alan lurking in the dark shadows of her fears? Oh, she had no delusions that she didn't have more to work through before she felt whole again. She still couldn't stand when someone yelled. It triggered her flashbacks where her ex used to belittle her, degrade her, and make her feel worthless. But there was hope looking at these three men that she would get there again.

Monroe grabbed her arm, guiding her onto a stool.

"With how easy it is to find out information online, aren't you worried about the media or some individual being able to dig up your real identity?" Riley placed the book on the counter.

"My lawyer is good and knows people who keep my identity hidden," she offered as an explanation.

Riley pulled his phone off his belt. "Bear, give me a workup on an outside security system for the gate and the house."

"Sir." A voice cut through the speaker on the phone.

He slipped his phone into his pocket and took a couple of steps to where Monroe was just finishing up. "So, you wrote after you got away from him and made all the profits after the divorce?"

"Yes and no. I started writing it before I left him. It was more of journaling and tracking what he did in case I came up missing. I hoped someone would find it and he would be charged with my death. But I didn't put it into a manuscript and publish it until after I left him."

"Good, I was afraid you'd helped yourself to some of his money, and that was his true motivation for wanting you back." His shoulders sagged. "Not that you don't deserve every dime he has, with what he put you through."

"No, I left him the same way I went into the marriage, penniless. He refused to let me work. At first, I thought it was romantic and he was a knight in shining armor. That he wanted to take care of me and...oh, I don't know, spoil me. The second week into the marriage, I met the monster that he was. It took seven years to get away from him. My parents never knew. I'm glad they weren't there to see what he did to me." Her voice caught in her throat as she twisted her hands in her lap.

"This will help with the pain." Monroe has another syringe ready.

"No, I don't want to be out of it and not be able to get away from him. I'll be an easy target if he finds me with that coursing through my veins." She pointed a shaky finger at the hypodermic needle.

"You won't be alone. One of my guys will stay with you until the security system is up and running."

She jerked her head around and met his eyes. "Oh no. I couldn't ask you to do that."

"That's my recommendation until we can fully monitor your house to keep you safe." Riley implored her to agree, standing in the least imposing stance she knew he struggled with. This man was far from unimpressive.

Did he understand her trepidation with essentially being at someone's mercy? She had to make the decision to trust him. They'd done nothing but take care of her for the two days she stayed in that apartment. Bringing her meals, checking on her injuries, nothing besides being open about who and what they were. Sentinels, guarding the weak. But was she weak? Not anymore, she wasn't. Annie squirmed and her hand went instinctively to her side. She blew out a breath, her eyes closed. She nodded.

Monroe took her arm and plunged the needle, piercing the delicate skin in the crook of her elbow before she could change her mind. Seconds later, her face smoothed out. She no longer felt the pain. "We need to lay you down somewhere. Where's your room?"

She pointed to the top of a tall half-moon staircase. She huffed out a breath. Why did it seem like such a long walk up that flight of stairs to handle by herself?

• • • •

"DO YOU MIND?" RILEY set the book on the counter and held out his hands.

She shook her head before placing her hand in his. He felt the tremble through her palm. She was scared and it was of him. He wasn't sure if it was the fear of trusting someone or if she was afraid of all men at this point in her life. It bothered him more than he wanted to admit that she had put him in the same category as her psychotic ex.

He wrapped an arm around her waist, keeping her incision on the side closest to him so he wouldn't put pressure on the wound with his hand. He guided her to the stairs. On her first tentative step up, she grunted.

"Sorry if this bothers you. You can trust me." Riley swung her up into his arms. His shirt strained against his flexed muscles.

Annie closed her eyes; her body trembled all over. "Please...don't...h-hurt me." Her head drooped forward, coming to rest on his shoulder, her words slurring, her eyes closed.

He spun and raised his eyebrows to Monroe, who only motioned for him to take her up the stairs. Several doors stood open. He glanced in a couple before he found the master bedroom behind a set of ornately designed double doors. Monroe followed him and pulled the comforter back for Riley to lay her on the bed. He placed her on her side, wound up so she wouldn't put pressure on it.

"I gave her a little more than I normally would. She needs to rest and stop moving around. I don't like the look of her wound. It's too red and swollen. I can only hope the continued injections will tackle the infection and clear it out."

"You have first watch. I'll send someone to relieve you at noon after you give her the next dose." Riley pulled up his schedule and started a rotating shift of watches for Annie.

"I'll keep her in bed. She needs to give her body time to recuperate more than the two days she had at the office. But I'm sure with what we've seen of the scars and demons she's had to deal with, she won't be used to giving herself time to heal." Monroe leaned his back against the door frame and crossed his arms.

"I'm heading back to the office to work on a security system for her. I have a few ideas but will come back to start on the actual installation. I'll do that myself." Riley pulled her license from her pocket and placed it on her nightstand. He stared down at her and remembered her smile. He wanted to help her have a reason to smile more. He prayed that he'd be able to stop this callous man that was after her and with God's help, put him away for good.

He strolled out of the room. The stairs would be a problem for her if she got hungry. She probably hadn't eaten since last night when he took dinner to her room at the office. He slid her book off the island and took it with him as he passed through the kitchen. "Let's go. We need to get the security up and running on this house as soon as possible."

"Yes, sir." Tracker followed him through the back door.

"Stop with the sir crap," Riley growled.

"Yes, sir." Tracker hid his smirk behind his hand with a fake cough.

Riley laughed. "Jerk."

Six

Riley pulled into the secured lot around the back of the building. The sun's hues of pinks and oranges dotted the sky on the few wispy clouds that lingered in the polluted air above the downtown skyline.

"Someone's here to see you." Bear motioned with his head toward the front door.

"It's been three days. Why is he in such a huff when she divorced him nine months ago?"

Bear squinted. "Are you seriously trying to understand his actions?"

Alan, flanked by two police officers, a grin of conceit and arrogance plastered on his face, placed his hands on his hips. He felt he was better than Riley, and all Riley wanted to do was wipe the smug look off his face permanently. Relief flooded him that Annie wasn't in the same building as this ruthless man.

Riley unlocked the doors, barely pushing them open enough for his massive shoulders to fill the opening. "We aren't open yet. Can I help you?"

"Strong." Officer Ayers stood there with a scowl. His eyes darted to Alan then he rolled his eyes.

"Ayers." Riley's mouth twitched, hiding the smirk he almost let show.

"Mr. Montgomery reported that you may have his wife in your building against her will."

"No one is in this building against their will."

Ayers looked at Alan.

"First, it's Dr. Montgomery. I earned that title and you will use it. Second, I know for a fact he has her here."

"Mr. Montgomery, you aren't even married. So how can I have your wife here if you don't have one? And where are your two friends you never seem to go anywhere without?" Riley waited for steam to roll out of his ears. He knew his friends weren't able to be with them since the police were looking for them in questioning about the shooting that occurred at this very building.

"It's *Dr.* Montgomery. My friends have other things to attend to this morning. And I am married. The courts let the wrong documents through, and I'm in the middle of appealing the divorce. She went behind my back and refused to see the judge that was recommended." Alan's hands twisted and balled into fists.

"You mean the judge you were in a fraternity with? The one who probably has covered up more than one of your crimes. That judge? Or are your friends not with you since they are the ones who shot at my building, and that video was turned over to the police?" Riley shook his head. "Wait, can you even appeal a divorce proceeding?"

Alan tried to step around Officer Ayers, who didn't budge but held up his hand. "How dare you! I could sue you for slander! And as a matter of fact, you can appeal a divorce if your attorney can find proof the judge didn't follow the law."

"You can try." Riley stood his ground.

Sasha came through the back door and stopped dead in her tracks.

"Sasha, go ahead and clean the upstairs rooms that are on your cleaning schedule." Riley didn't want to scare her with what may transpire with Mr. Montgomery. He waited until the elevator doors closed before turning back to Alan.

"I demand you give me my wife!" Saliva gathered in disgusting foamy bubbles in the corners of Alan's mouth. He yanked a handkerchief from his pocket and dabbed at the noxious slobber.

The corner of Riley's mouth ticked up. "You aren't married, even you admitted that."

"Sir, we can't search a building for a wife you don't have." Ayers stood with his thumbs hooked into the armholes of his vest. His left eye twitched.

"Yes, she *is* my wife!"

Riley never took his eyes from Alan. "You mean the one you just admitted you aren't married to anymore?"

Alan practically spit. "That issue will be rectified as soon as I can get it taken care of! I had the police respond due to this man having someone here against their will. How about we address that concern first and then worry about the other."

"Riley, do you have anyone here that you are refusing to let leave?" Officer Ayers rested his hands on his duty belt.

"Nope."

"He doesn't have anyone against their will." The officer raised an eyebrow at Alan.

"You can't just take his word for it. Search this whole building. I know he has apartments on the third and fourth floor. I demand you search them all," Alan sneered. He'd done his homework but not well enough to include Riley's expansive apartment on the fifth.

"Sir, we would need a search warrant. Those take time. Unless the owner of the building gives us permission, we can't just barge in here on one person's word."

"Oh, you can search any room you feel you need to, Officer."

"Thanks, Strong." Ayers took two steps into the building, stepping around Riley. Alan was hot on his heels with a smug grin plastered on his chiseled face.

"Oh, I'm sorry. The officer has permission to look inside my building. You don't." Riley stepped in front of Alan.

"Oh no, I'm going with the officer!" Alan pointed over Riley's shoulder to Ayers, who stood behind him.

"I'm sorry, sir. He's correct. By law, he can refuse to allow anyone on his private property. I'll look around and let you know if we find the wife you don't have." Ayers pinched his lips together, turned his back on them, and strolled to the elevator.

Alan stepped forward so that he was nose to nose with Riley. "No, I demand to go with him!"

The second officer put his hand on Alan's shoulder to guide him back away from Riley. "I'm sorry, sir. You heard my partner. You aren't allowed on the premises unless the owner gives you permission."

"Are you kidding? What kind of podunk police department is this?" Alan gritted his teeth.

Riley nodded to the officer. "What's the matter, *Mr.* Montgomery. I guess you aren't used to not getting your way?"

Alan spun to Riley and balled his hands even tighter. His knuckles turned white. His face flushed; red crept up from the collar of his pristinely pressed button-down shirt that no doubt cost more than most of Riley's clothes did all together. "You have no idea who you are dealing with. I'd be very careful if I were you."

"Sir, did you just threaten this gentleman?" The officer put his hand on his gun.

Alan glanced to his left at the officer's hand. "No, just concerned for his safety. You never know with the dangers in the world out there. Someone could be mugged on the walk to their car and killed. Can't trust anyone this day and age."

Several minutes later Riley heard the ding of the elevator announcing the arrival of Officer Ayers. He never took his eyes off Alan.

"No one's here." He nodded to Riley on his way back through the front door.

"Told you, *Mr.* Montgomery." Riley crossed his arms; a smirk touched the corner of his mouth.

"We'll see. We'll just see about that." Alan stormed away from the building, snatching his phone from his back pocket.

"What was that about?" Officer Ayers shook his head, hooking his hands into the sides of his vest.

"He's bad news. Watch your backs out there. It's not good when he's upset with someone. He probably thought he could bully you into letting him search the building." Riley kept his eyes on Alan, not turning his back to him.

"Well, he picked the wrong officer for that." Ayers shook Riley's hand. He half-turned back to Riley when the other officer was out of earshot. "Keep her safe."

"Already done. Have a good one." Riley locked the doors after they left. Ayers was a rock-solid officer; he knew he wouldn't have a problem with him. He planned to add him to his team when he retired in a few years.

Ayers approached Alan and motioned to the building. With a finger practically jammed into his chest, Alan ranted at Ayers a moment longer. Attempting to calm the agitated doctor, Ayers continued to talk to him and motioned to the building. After another rant, Alan jumped in his car and peeled out, spraying gravel from the side of the road across the sloped grass of their courtyard.

"Okay, let's do the work to set up our top-of-the-line security system for her house. I want *everything* on that house." Riley marched to his office.

A short time later, Bear brought in the aerial photos with marked locations for security cameras. Riley thumbed through the pages. He liked what he saw but added an additional three cameras. "Have Tracker get started. I'll meet him out there in a few."

Riley tapped out a text to Monroe, asking how she was and prayed it was good news. She was sleeping after he got her to eat a little soup. He thanked God for letting her find the rest for what she may face next. He informed Monroe to check the garage; he wanted his cars out of sight and not just hidden behind the house. He didn't want to advertise that they were installing a security system on a house this close to the building, especially since she was targeted while running in the area. Monroe said he would check and let him know.

Monroe messaged back that there were a couple of garage stalls empty. Riley sent him to open one for Tracker; he was on the way to start installation.

Seven

Riley initialized a search on the computer and typed in the first wife's name. Several images loaded on the screen. She was pretty with long blonde hair and dark brown, expressive doe eyes. The insurance payout was a little over a million. They found the car off a ravine but didn't find her body for several days. She was young at only twenty-one at her time of death. The coroner's report stated death from internal injuries from being ejected from the car as it flipped end-over-end down the ravine. They found several vodka bottles in the car. He flipped to the next page on the screen. No one would be able to tell it was her by the decomp and the damage to her head. Dental records were the only option they could resort to for identification.

He typed in the second wife's name and waited for the search to finish. He picked up Annie's book. *Married to the Devil.* How fitting. He read several pages before the search finished. This report was more detailed with hospital records attached. Numerous accounts of broken bones, skull fractures, and burns; not a single police report had been filed on any of those cases. The sheriff's name was familiar. He grabbed the fraternity list. Yep, number six from the left stood the haughty sheriff where Alan lived. Convenient.

"Bear," Riley called out.

He appeared in the doorway seconds later. "Yo."

"Do you still have that friend at the county coroner's office?" Riley peered over the pages he held in his hands.

Bear raised his eyebrow.

Riley chuckled. "I need you to make a call." He flipped through certain pages from the hospital records for the second wife. The wounds were almost an exact match to Annie's. This man got a rush exacting pain. He handed Bear the pages he separated from the others; he didn't need to clarify what he wanted. Bear would know. Riley grabbed the book off his desk, thumbing to the page he left off on.

Hours later he dropped the book on his desk. He couldn't read anymore. What the world knew as a great fiction book happened to be a harsh reality to three women, two of which didn't survive this madman. Anger burned just under the surface. This man was evil, plain and simple. No wonder it was a bestseller in such a short time. It made him cringe and his skin crawl. It was too horrendous to even think evil like that existed in the real world.

Bear was at the door, files in his hand. "This isn't right."

"Let me see." Riley held out his hand.

He leafed through the printed screenshots of files. There were two autopsy reports per victim. He raised an eyebrow to Bear who only said, "Trust me, you want to read both."

The first wife showed blunt force trauma, scars, and stab wounds. None of that was in the official report. He literally beat the life out of his first wife. The official report stated wounds consistent with ejection over a ravine and that branches and rocks were the cause of the wounds. Any moron would know the difference, and you wouldn't have scars. The body stops healing when you die. Those scars were from months of torment. He slid the reports out of the second wife's folder. They were the same, crash over a ravine, tragic death by ejection. The wounds were much more severe than the previous wife. Burns on hands from an electric stove coil. He held her hands on the coil as it melted and burned her skin until there was nothing left. How did he even have access to those—with the money he made, he no doubt had all newer appliances that don't use coil burners anymore. Blunt force trauma...so vicious an attack that they couldn't find all the pieces of her skull. The blunt force was the cause of death, but the torture she suffered before he took her life was unspeakable.

He prayed God would give him the strength to keep Annie safe and to be her sentinel charged with her safety and life. To be a beacon in the dark for the woman who was starting to awaken his closed-off heart.

The terror that these women went through, he thought. He tossed the folder on his desk and then shoved his chair back. He stalked to the window. Across the street, Alan sat parked in his expensive ostentatious sports car, watching the building. His two goons accompanied him, taking up residence in the front and back seats. Riley marched out of his office.

"Wait." Bear jogged to catch up to him.

"No, I want to have a talk with him." Riley barged through the front door and didn't stop until he was at the driver's side of Alan's swanky top-of-the-line Porsche.

The window silently slid down, exposing Alan behind the wheel. "Yes, Mr. Strong. How can I help you?"

"You are done."

"Done?" Alan acted defiantly of any wrongdoing.

"I have the autopsy files from your first two wives. The original files, not the ones that you had your sheriff buddy lean on the coroner to change. Someone didn't follow your instructions to destroy the original set, and now I have them. Guess your word isn't law to everyone in your little group." Riley fisted his hands on his hips.

Bear turned his back and furiously dialed.

Alan's hand gripped the steering wheel tightly enough that they squeaked as he twisted his grip over the leather-wrapped carbon fiber. "Sorry, I don't know what you're talking about. I only know of the files that are on the official report. Other files don't exist."

Riley was about to poke the bear. "Oh, you mean the files where you held Sheila's hand to a stovetop coil until her skin melted off before you bludgeoned her to death?"

The color drained from Alan's face. His leathered tan skin turned ashen a split second before red flashed across his cheeks, down his neck, disappearing under the collar of his shirt that was too tight so that it showed his muscles that he no doubt spent hours developing. "You have no clue who you're messing with. You're in over your head. Just cut your losses and hand her over."

Riley placed his hand on the top of the car and leaned in so he was in Alan's space before uttering in a hard, deep tone, "You will never get her, *Mr.* Montgomery." He spun on his heels and marched across the road toward the building.

The sound of a slide being pulled back on a Glock reached Riley's ears. He spun, gun drawn and aimed at Alan's head. Bear stood next to Riley, weapon out, eyes on the same target.

Alan raised his eyebrows and smirked. He put the car in gear and roared down the road.

"Did your friend get them?" Riley trusted the men he worked with, with his life. They never let him down.

"Yes, they'll be here tomorrow, in the overnight express." Bear holstered his sidearm.

Riley clapped him on the shoulder. "Good, thanks."

"Can we keep her safe from him? He gives me the creeps." Bear reached the door first.

A smile crept across Riley's face. "Didn't know anyone scared you."

Bear grunted. "Not many, but count him in the select few."

Riley knew what he meant. Until they could build a case against Alan with more than just autopsy reports that didn't match the official ones, they would have their hands full trying to stay one step ahead of him. How far up the chain did this corruption go? If they gave the files to someone now, would they disappear like everything else against Alan? It gave him comfort to know he was watching this building, which meant he didn't know where Annie was.

"Bear, pull up our tracer units."

Bear grinned ear to ear. "You didn't!"

"Oh yeah." Riley had rested his hand on the top of the Porsche when he spoke with Alan. He knew he took a risk being that close, knowing they were armed. Just inside the rubber trim at the top edge of the driver's side door was one of their state-of-the-art GPS tags. Now they would know where he was, or at least his car.

Bear punched up their tracking software. There were several blips on the screen. Some of their clients requested constant surveillance while others just wanted to know that if their cars were stolen, they could track them. It was amazing what things people paid for nowadays. A red dot appeared over Annie's house, for the one he slipped inside her license. Another red dot flew down the interstate. Alan was on the way to his high-rise hotel room he acquired when he showed up in town. Riley had Duffy follow him when he left earlier. Now they could get to Annie's and not be seen. They would bundle everything into one SUV and only take two vehicles so they could hide them in the empty garages.

"Let's load up." Riley stepped away from Bear's desk.

Bear nodded to Duffy, who was on his feet before Bear finished the slight tilt to his head. They strolled to the storage room; Riley gave them a list of what they would need. Tracker would already be there, installing the cameras on the backside of the house.

In less than fifteen minutes they had everything loaded up and were on the move. Riley had Bear with him, the tablet queued up to Alan's location. They weren't sure how much time they would need. Riley pulled up to Annie's gate and rang the buzzer.

"Come on in. I have that camera already changed out. We'll need to work on the gate access." Trackers' staticky voice filtered through the ancient intercom.

Riley nodded to Bear, who hopped out of the Audi. They opened the back of the SUV and pulled out a new security access panel for the gate. Duffy left Bear with what he would need before he joined Riley in the garage.

Riley helped Duffy and Tracker unload the rest of the gear for the outside installation before he grabbed a bag for the inside. Monroe came around the wall with his hand on the gun strapped to his leg when he let himself in through the unlocked back door.

Riley gave him a chin lift. "How is she?"

Monroe dropped his hand from the butt of his gun. "Better. She didn't fight me on the next dose of pain meds. I think she feels safe enough here to let her guard down. I was also able to get her to eat some more. That will go a long way toward turning the infection around."

"Good. I have a couple of folders I want you to read so you can know what we're dealing with." Riley fished around in his soft-sided briefcase.

Monroe took the files. "Did you want me to read these now or help with interior installation?"

"Help with the interior. I made him mad this afternoon. I'm hoping it makes me his next target and he focuses on taking me out before he goes after Annie."

"Is that wise?"

"No, but I can't think of anything else, after reading the autopsy reports on his first two wives, to get his mind off of Annie." Riley unboxed several cameras lining them up on the table.

"Bear, call his guy again?" Monroe took one of the cameras and worked on the mount.

"Yup, came through for us on this one. I told Alan I had the original files. Not sure how they still exist?"

Monroe gawked at Riley. "Oh, that ain't gonna sit well with him. Maybe the coroner hid the first reports as insurance in case something happened to him?"

"Nope, already pulled a gun on me. Wish he would have fired, then he would be dead and Annie would be safe. That is something we need to figure out: why both files exist if Alan's friends covered this up."

Monroe dropped the screw to the back of the mount; his hand fumbled trying to chase it around the marble countertop before finally catching it between two fingers. "And if he shot you? Where would Annie be?"

"Safe. Alan would be dead. I had Bear with me." Riley didn't look up as he laid out the cameras according to where he wanted them.

Monroe only nodded and grabbed the next camera.

• • • •

SEVERAL HOURS LATER, the sun hovered on the horizon. The outside cameras were up and they had the monitors in Annie's office per her request. There were eight monitors displaying the views of the exterior. She could also use two of the monitors for inside cameras. One they programmed to scan so it would cycle through the exterior ones while another allowed her to select which camera she wanted. She felt like she was part of some secret undercover agency with the monitors taking up much of one side of her office on all the brackets they added to showcase her system.

Monroe had helped her down the stairs to the office so Riley could show her everything they did. The small monitor for the gate had been replaced with one that had better resolution to match the camera.

"The image looks like I'm standing out there." She almost smiled.

"I need to talk to you." Riley motioned with his head to the living room. His team left the office and retreated out of earshot. "Some of this will be hard to hear. Do you think you are up for it?"

"Yes, I need to know." Annie pulled her lips in between her teeth for a second then released them again. She didn't have a good feeling about this; her stomach in knots, she barely kept from rubbing the outside of her abdomen to negate the urge to retch.

He started with the original search he ran on Alan and all the crimes that were covered up. He explained everything in detail so she would know exactly what he did, which she appreciated more than he could ever know. Next were his wives. She didn't know there was a first wife. Alan only told her the horrible grief he went through when his wife—who Annie now learned was his second wife—died. She believed him and that was the starting point where she fell for him. Riley continued with the autopsy reports. The color leeched from her already pale complexion. Her breathing sped up; she recognized the signs of the impending panic attack. She had had several over the years. Alan chalked it up to her wanting attention, which he would deliver with the back of his hand.

Riley rushed over to her. "Slow your breathing." He put his hand on the back of her head and guided her head down as much as he could without causing her pain.

"He killed them?" Annie gasped. "I thought I could hear this but..."

"Yes, he did. I'm sorry, maybe I shouldn't have told you. Come on, slow your breathing. Shh." The heat of his hand seared her skin through her shirt. He crouched in front of her.

She grasped his hand on her leg in an iron grip. Her knuckles turned white.

"I'm here. He isn't going to get to you. I promise." He squeezed her hand back.

"How can you make that promise?" She trembled.

Her breathing began to slow as she fought the panic that tried to take hold, as his voice lowered. "Because I'm going to get enough on him to have him tried for the murder of his first two wives, but I need you to trust me to do what I think is in your best interest to keep you safe."

"The sheriff's his friend. The judge also." She felt a blush rise on her cheeks as she let go of his hand. She missed the heat. Why couldn't she get the little niggle in the back of her mind to quit? There was something different about this man. He wasn't like Alan at all. She shook her head; she wasn't in a place mentally or emotionally to even think about a relationship. Could she let someone in again after what she went through? Would it be fair to the man if she tried and wasn't able to work through her fears, insecurities along with trust?

"I have better friends, who will take this to the state level to get it out of the local government's hands. Come on, let's get you back upstairs. I'd rather you have a couple more days' rest while I get some evidence together. I made him mad today. I'm hoping he comes after me and forgets about you until we can put him away for good. Have you eaten?"

She used the side of the end table to push herself to her feet. Short, shuffled steps took her out of the office. "Not yet." The men in her kitchen fidgeted as she passed them on her way to the stairs.

"I'll bring you up something in a bit if that's okay with you." Riley took her hand and helped her maneuver the stairs.

She nodded. Once in her room, she stared at the gun on her nightstand.

"Just in case." Riley had Monroe move it while he watched over her. He wanted her to be armed in case Alan made it past his men. He also placed a Bible next to it. She missed him carrying it upstairs with him. "This can also help."

"No offense, but that really isn't my thing." She blinked to clear her tears. She wasn't sure why that book stirred so many emotions. She was dealing with enough without bringing more to the surface.

"Keep it, just in case. That book got me through one of the hardest times in my life. It saved my life." He ran his fingers over the burgundy cracked leather that told of its years of use.

She could only nod, not trusting herself to say anything.

"Annie, I need your permission to watch the cameras inside. I have a contract ready to go for surveillance of your home. I will be the only one to watch the interior ones, mainly on the lower level. Bathrooms and bedrooms are off-limits so there will be no installations in those rooms." Riley pulled a rolled-up piece of paper out of his back pocket and held out a pen for her.

"Only you?" Annie didn't reach for the pen. This felt like Alan all over again; her breath hitched.

"Yes, just until this is over. Then you'll be safe and the interior cameras will be switched off and even removed if you wish. There will be key personnel who will have the codes and keys to get into your house as part of the contract, including Monroe, Bear, and myself." He still held the pen out, giving her the choice to take this step.

Her respect for him grew in that small, measured level of trust he apparently knew she had to take on her own. With her background and what she'd been through this would be a tough decision to let someone get that close to her again. She studied him, his eyes never leaving hers, locked in submission to her decision. She had the power here; she knew what he was doing. But did she have the faith to take the leap and find it in her to proceed?

She slowly nodded and took the pen; her fingers brushed his. She signed her name and handed the pen back.

"Thanks, Annie. I promise I'll do everything I can to keep him away from you. I want you to know this could get ugly if he is as evil as I think he is." Riley turned for the door.

"Thank you, Mr. Strong. Please don't make me regret this. I don't know why but I trust you, and I haven't trusted anyone in a long, long time." Annie smiled and the pulse in his neck galloped at an increased pace. Did he feel something? Was this affecting him the same way it was her?

"Please call me Riley." His fingers gripped the edge of the door.

"Okay, Riley it is." She laid back and closed her eyes and blew out the air in her lungs as he pulled the door closed.

Eight

Riley joined his men in the living room. He knew he would need God on this one. He couldn't explain it but his gut told him this would be one of the hardest cases he'd ever worked on if it went the way he knew it could go. He also prayed he wouldn't let his attraction to her get in his way and mar his ability to think clearly and act quickly if he needed to. He would get her something to eat first and then finish the installation.

"Okay, I made us enemies in Alan's eyes today. Stay on guard. Report anything, no matter how small. We do this by the book. He'll be looking for anything to use against us to get to me. He thinks I'm competition and will keep Annie from him. And he's partly right. While I'm alive, he won't get to her without going through me. This house will be a twenty-four-seven watch detail. She's now officially a client since we have a signed contract. With what we set up today, we can keep vigilant and watch on any and all activity. I'll keep eyes on the inside security of the house."

"I need to get the next dose for her. I'll be back." Monroe took the stairs two at a time.

"I need you guys to pull in markers. We need to get a lot done in a short amount of time. I'll owe you guys for this." Riley met their eyes.

"You don't owe us anything." Duffy crossed his massive arms. "What do you need?"

"We need hospital reports on the first two wives. We need dirt on the Sheriff. The lawyer who helped with the life insurance claims has to be in on this. There's proof somewhere on these people. They have to be hiding something since they are willing to help him hide murders and commit insurance fraud. If there's a money trail from him to them then maybe we can flip them when we show them the evidence."

Tracker nodded. "I've got someone who can take care of the lawyer."

Monroe came down the stairs. "I have the hospital reports covered."

No one stepped forward for the Sheriff. "Thanks, you two. I may have someone I can go to for the Sheriff."

"We need better locks on the doors. I made a call to check our supplies. I'll pick them up after we leave here. I can have them installed before she needs her next dose from Monroe." Bear grunted. "What about your house? What if we set her up there? It's smaller and it wouldn't take as much to secure as opposed to this monstrosity."

"Yeah, except with it being in my name, it wouldn't take but seconds to find it, and I don't want to bring Roger and Rebecca into this. They have already gone above and beyond taking care of the place after I moved out in the months after Helen's death."

Bear hung his head. "You have a point. I'll check supplies."

"Thanks." Riley stacked the boxes for the equipment on the counter to take them back to the cars to dispose of at their office. "I'll stay until you're back with the locks. Where's Alan's car?"

Bear snatched the tablet off the counter, punched up a few screens, and the red blip moved on the display. "He's outside our office building."

"Bring up our cameras." Riley peered over his shoulder as the others joined him.

Alan's Porsche sat on the street, the driver's seat empty. A shadow moved across the side of the building, just as their phones all vibrated with an alert there was motion activation on the east side sensors.

"Punch up the other cameras."

The screen was split, showing four different angles. Three shadows were on the move. Alan came into view under the front door camera frame. He tugged on the doors. With his hands cupped around his eyes, he peered through the glass.

"We're safe to leave here without exposing Annie." Riley started for the door to the garage.

Everyone jumped into the SUV except Riley and Monroe. They jumped in the sports coupé. Both Audis pulled out from the garage and left Annie alone under a multitude of surveillance cameras. It wasn't the ideal situation since Alan was still hunting her, but maybe Riley could dissuade him from that pursuit. His knuckles turned white as he seized the steering wheel in a death grip.

Riley led the team back to the office. He didn't know what lay ahead of him and if Alan would be bold enough to try something. Riley almost hoped he would. He didn't want to take himself out of the equation, but if it kept Annie safe and took Alan down, he would. If she was strong enough to get away from him and find a court to see her divorce case going around his conspirator friends, she more than earned the life she dreamed of living.

The Porsche was still on the road in front of his building. He didn't receive any alerts on his phone that they'd made entry into the office. Riley parked and pulled his gun. Monroe joined him seconds later.

All five stalked to the building, keeping in the shadows, guns drawn. They were at the back of the building. Riley signaled that he and Bear would go around the south side and make their way to the front while the other three took the north side.

Riley and Bear tracked to the front of the building from the south side. Quick, hushed whispers drifted around the corner to their position.

"No, he won't get away with this. She's mine! I put too much work into training her and getting her where I want her. It won't take much to get her back where she belongs: subservient to me!" Alan seethed.

"I'm not saying that, but I don't like that guy. I say we go after Megan and leave this guy behind." One of Alan's goons whispered loud enough he wasn't sure it qualified as a whisper.

"Did you not hear how he talked to me? No one talks to me like that. He thinks he has a chance with my wife. He's wrong. I own her! He goes down first and then it's her turn. I have special plans for her. Sheila didn't see the last moments of her life coming, but Megan will. She'll have a front-row seat to what I have designed for her." Raucous laughter filtered through the air.

Riley ground his back teeth together, raised his gun, and prowled around the corner. Maybe he could draw him into a firefight and end this here and now.

"Come on. No one's here. We can't get through these doors; they have a special hydraulic locking system on them that will jam the doors closed. Trust me, I know. We would have to cut the power before we could get these to open."

"So, cut the power!"

"Well, he was smart on that. He put the main power cut off inside instead of at the power junction box like everyone else. Without knowing where the cables are buried, we can't do that."

"So, blow up the power junction box," Alan hissed, his gravelly voice dripping with anger.

"I can't. Taking out the junction box would only put the building on lockdown. The computers would sense an attack, so to speak, and lock the entire building. This guy knows what he's doing," the second goon tried to rationalize.

Alan waved his gun in the air, pointing it toward the building. "Fine, then shoot out the windows."

A large hissing sigh escaped the first goon's lips before he explained as if speaking with a child, "Sir, we can't do that either. The resistant glass he used would need to have high-caliber rounds to pierce it. Even then, it would take several rounds concentrated in one area before the glass gives way. The police would be here before we could even breach the polycarbonate-clad glass, which I noticed is several panes thick. This is complete overkill for this building's ability to withstand a bullet."

Alan stormed over to one of the goons and peered down at him. "You act like we are standing outside Fort Knox!"

Number one glanced at number two. "In a way we are. I've never seen this much security on an office building. Maybe he has something to hide. Something we can use to buy this guy off."

"This sorry excuse for a man is not easily bought off. He has a hero complex. He wants to be the good guy so bad it's sickening. So, we have a plan, we come back with high caliber rounds and take this building down. Riley Strong has no clue who he's messing with."

"Sir, we aren't in a jurisdiction where it would be in your benefit to pull off something like that. We need to be smart about this." Goon number two fidgeted, transferring his weight from one leg to the other.

"Oh, don't start with me. Everyone can be bought. I'm having fun." He turned to the side.

Goon number one growled, "You just said he can't be bought!"

"I can't." Riley had Alan in his sights, and he itched to pull the trigger.

Alan spun around at Riley's voice; his hand gripped a gun, tapping it against his leg. "Give me my wife."

Riley aimed for center mass. "I believe we've already established she isn't your wife."

"What? Are you sleeping with her? Is that it? Figures, anyone else would have handed over my property by now." His hand jerked on the gun still at his side.

"You can believe what you want, but she isn't property. She made the choice to leave you, and you can't stand it."

Alan started to raise his gun but flinched as shadows in the glass reflected three men approaching from behind. Bear stepped next to Riley. The front doors unlocked, and three more employees joined Riley's team, guns drawn. "By the way, smile for the cameras recording both audio and video of this little exchange. I'm sure the police would like to see and hear everything you just said and did."

Sweat dotted Alan's forehead. Riley was sure he wasn't used to having the roles reversed and finding himself on the losing side. His thugs fidgeted and inched their way toward the car. Alan lowered his arm, smiled, and nodded his head.

"Guess you won this round. See you for the next one." Alan smirked and holstered his weapon before pulling his sports coat around and buttoning the top button. His cufflinks glinted against the outside lights.

He left without further incident. At least he was focused on this building, so Annie was still safe. Riley joined his men. "Hope everyone has plenty of caffeine because I don't think we'll be sleeping any sort of normal hours for the foreseeable future. Connor, make a copy of the camera captured and get it over to Ayers," Riley called out over his shoulder.

Bear secured the doors behind them when they entered the building. Riley joined him in the storage room to select state-of-the-art locks for Annie's house. He tossed several into a duffel bag. Jogging out to his car, he left Bear in the building tracking Alan while he installed the new deadbolts. He was to inform him of any movement around Annie's.

He remoted himself through the gate. He needed to talk to Annie and let her know his concerns. With the car hidden behind the garage, he kept to the shadows and crept around to the back door to let himself in. He punched in the code to the alarm and called out Annie's name.

No answer. The downstairs of her home was dark except for the faint glow from the monitors around the back of the kitchen that filtered through the door that was cracked open. He clicked on his flashlight and illuminated the dining room and kitchen areas.

"Hello?" Annie's voice drifted down the stairs.

"Annie, it's Riley."

"Is everything okay?" Her voice faltered.

"Yes, stay where you are. I'll come to you. I don't want you taking the stairs more than you should."

The light at the top of the stairs cast shadows across the marble entryway. A dark form passed by the sidelights on either side of the front door. Riley clicked off his flashlight and froze. "Annie, get in your room now!" he hissed.

Riley dropped the duffel bag on the floor and pulled his gun. His left hand hit the speed dial for Bear. "Where is he?"

"Car shows to be at his hotel. What's up?"

"Shadow crossed in front of the door."

"Hold on. Pulling up the front door camera as we speak. Nothing there. Let me go to Duffy's station. He has night watch on the house."

Riley backed up to the stairs, taking one at a time, his feet finding the next step by feeling for it with the heel of his boot. His eyes never left the front door.

"No one is on the cameras. Monroe's headed to your location just in case." Bear disconnected.

Riley slipped his phone into his pocket and backed up the last three stairs. He glanced into Annie's room. She huddled near the top of her bed next to her headboard. He raised a finger to his lips. The shadow came back to the front door. Someone tried to turn the handle. It was locked. He pointed a finger at Annie. "Stay there!" Riley jogged down the stairs, gun trained on the front door.

A text came in, Monroe was approaching the front gate. Riley texted back about the subject at the front entrance. Monroe would approach on foot through the side pedestrian gate.

Mere seconds later, there was a scuffle at the front door. Riley yanked the door open. A shot interrupted the quiet serene night.

Nine

Sirens cut through the night as red and blue strobe lights displayed across the trees interrupted the tranquil neighborhood. Annie clenched her jaw at the attention brought to the house. Riley rushed upstairs before officers arrived and told her not to come out until he cleared the scene. She put her back to the wall next to the door and listened to the exchange downstairs, peeking every so often so she would know who was talking.

Two officers stood in front of Riley. The cranky, wary neighbor was red-faced and sweating. "Sir, what were you doing at this house?"

"I saw someone drive in and park behind the garage. Who does that?"

"Sir, you were carrying a gun and trying to get into the house instead of calling the police." Anger rolled off the older officer in waves.

Riley told her the gun had discharged and nicked the stone steps in front of the door. Monroe had startled him but luckily, the old man's eyesight wasn't what it used to be. Riley stood, feet shoulder-width apart, his arms crossed over his chest, and his shirt pulled tight across his biceps. She couldn't take her eyes off him.

"I'd like him trespassed. I have it authorized by the homeowner. They don't want him on their property." Riley's gruff voice was no-nonsense as he glanced up toward her door.

The old man's veins stood out on his neck. "You can't do that. You don't own this house!"

"Sir, is that right? The homeowner would like him trespassed?" The officer gave a slight nod to Riley.

"Yes, I run security for this house, and they expressed sincere concerns about people coming on the estate without permission. Sir, can I ask how you got past the gate?" Riley shook his head at the officer before turning his attention back to the elderly man.

He took a step forward but was restrained by the younger officer's hand on his chest. "That's none of your business! I have a right to make my neighborhood safe!"

"Sir, that's *our* job. In the future, call the police if you see something. And per the owner's request, you are not to come on their property again. If you do, you *will* be arrested and charged with trespassing." The older officer rocked back on his heels as he informed the nefariously nosey neighbor of the consequences.

The younger officer escorted the neighbor to his house. The officer who stayed turned to Riley as he keyed up his mic to tell dispatch to clear all units from the scene. Police cars left the neighborhood, letting the night take back over after their pulsing lights interrupted family dinners. Neighbors made their way back inside when they saw the police leave the area, their shadows and lights from the open doorways visible through the arched window over the front door that let her view the entire street from her second level.

"Can I talk to her?" The older officer took a step up onto the porch.

Her breath hitched as she spun back into her room. What if he happened to work with Alan?

"I don't know if she would want that." Riley glanced back toward the stairs as she peered around the bedroom entry.

"I understand, but me issuing a trespass warning to someone without speaking with the owner isn't how it's done. You know that, Strong."

"Yeah, but the neighbor doesn't know that. It's just to keep people away for a while."

"I'd still like to check on her and make sure," the officer demanded of Riley.

"Okay. Hold on." Riley took the steps two at a time. "Annie?" he called, out motioning her back to bed as he towered over her.

When she was huddled back under the blankets clutched in her hands and pulled up to her chin did she speak. "Is everything okay?"

"Officer Ayers needs to talk to you. I had him give the neighbor a trespass warning, but he needs to talk to you to confirm this."

"No, Alan will find me if you involve the police." Annie's eyes widened.

Riley drooped his head forward, rested his hands on his hips, and took a deep breath before he spoke again. "I trust him with my life. He's one of the good ones."

"I can't...you don't know what it was like...asking for help from the people who were sworn to help you only to take you back to your abuser." Anger seeped through Annie's words, her eyes alight with fire.

Riley sat at the end of the bed. "He would die trying to keep Alan from you. I promise you that."

She hesitated; eyes locked on him. He wanted to bring Ayers up here and let her judge for herself that he was one of the good ones, but he didn't know the full extent of who Alan had in his back pocket. "Okay." She nodded; something in the way he implored her to trust him got past one of her walls. Tension rolled through her shoulders. She needed to start trusting people again, and Riley was the first in a long line she needed to test the waters out on.

Riley sauntered to the doorway and motioned Ayers to join him.

"Ma'am?" Officer Ayers was the older of the two who responded and stood with one foot outside the room.

"Yes?"

"I just wanted to make sure you would like your neighbor trespassed and warned not to come back on your property. Is that correct?" Ayers nodded.

"Yes, sir." Annie never let go of the blankets but only clutched them tighter.

"Okay, I'll make sure that he understands that. Thank you for your time. If you need to file a report or talk to the police, have Mr. Strong call me and I'll handle it myself. That way no one else has to be aware that you're here. Okay?" Ayers smiled at her, but it didn't reach his eyes.

"Thank you." Annie loosened her grip on the blankets.

"I'll be back," Riley announced

Annie scooted to the end of the bed and stumbled to the wall by the door. Riley followed Ayers down the stairs to the front porch where they were no longer seen but she could hear them.

"Bad one?" Ayers's low voice was barely audible.

Riley's rich baritone carried through the night. "Yeah, worst one I've ever seen. You can't even fathom. I may need to call you for help on this one from the police side of things."

Ayers words broke through after an exhaustive silence. "I hope you know what you're doing. Just don't step over the line. I can only do so much. Hopefully, if she has one point of contact she trusts at the police department, it will help her trust you."

"I never do, and thanks for that. I think it'll help." Riley's hand was still stretched out as if he shook his hand when he backed back into the foyer.

Monroe joined her, interrupting her spying on everyone in her home. "Come on, off to bed."

• • • •

RILEY REMOTED THE GATE closed when the officers pulled out of the driveway. With everyone gone, he ripped his bag off the ground and quickly changed the locks on the front door. Monroe came down from Annie's room as he finished tightening the last screw.

"How is she?" Riley didn't lift his head.

"Better. Some of the redness is gone, and her skin isn't hot to the touch anymore."

"Good." His shoulders slumped as he picked up the next lock for the back door.

"What's wrong?"

"I can't keep her safe like this." Riley stalked to the back door.

Monroe kept pace with him. "How else can we keep her safe? You even said he'll never guess her buying and living in this house. There is the office which he knows about and your home. Again, easy to find her at either place."

"Just a gut feeling. I'm missing something and I can't put my finger on it." Riley looked down and studied his shoes.

The power screwdriver whirred as he removed the screws from the old lock. With the last lock in place, he dropped the old ones in the bag along with the remaining ones they didn't need. He pulled keys from his pocket and a remote to use on all the doors. One remote would secure all the doors in panic mode or unlock them one at a time. If the power was cut, the locks stayed secure unless you used the key to unlock them.

"Did you need anything else?" Monroe slung his bag over his shoulder.

"No, we're good here. Let Bear know I'll stay here for the night."

"Yup."

"Hey, check the road for Alan when you leave. I need to find a better way to track him than just his car."

"Will do." Monroe was gone.

Riley approached the stairs and hesitated before he climbed them with heavy legs. Annie's door was open. "Annie?"

Her mumble was unintelligible. He stood in the doorway, his silhouette casting a long shadow over the end of her bed. "Annie?"

"Is something wrong?"

"No, I'm sorry. I didn't mean to bother you. I just wanted you to know the locks have been changed and all the cameras are streaming to our control room and your office. You have a nosey neighbor who thinks it's his job to be the watch committee of the area. Officer Ayers gave him a trespass warning and told him not to come on your property again."

"Was it Mr. Havishaw? He's very cranky." She smiled. His heart raced.

"Is he the neighbor just to the north of you?" He returned her smile.

"Yes." She averted her eyes. "You trust Officer Ayers?"

"Yes, with my life. We worked together for years, and he has a spot on my team when he retires."

She only smiled and slid down between the blankets.

"Well, I didn't want to keep you from getting some sleep. I'll be downstairs if you need me. Just call out."

She sat up. Her body twitched from the quick movement. "Oh no, you don't have to stay. You've done so much already."

"It's no big deal. We run a twenty-four-seven business, so I'm used to late nights."

"Mr. Strong, please. I'd feel bad."

"Again, call me Riley, and nothing you say will make me go away. Get some sleep." He smiled and closed the door behind him after she nodded.

The lights were still off when he reached the bottom of the stairs. He used his flashlight to find his way to the office and the bank of monitors. The cameras displayed the outside of the house. Nothing moved. Many of the views had dark corners. Riley typed a few lines into the system and activated the option to access the infrared features. He glanced at the ceiling. He hoped his presence in her house wouldn't keep her from getting some sleep, but he was hesitant to leave and just monitor the system from the office.

He sat back and folded his arms over his chest. He studied the screens. Headlights from vehicles on the main road next to the subdivision dotted the background when they passed by in a blur. Riley called Bear.

"Sir."

"Everything's secure here. I'm going to get some sleep. Wake me if you see anything."

"How is she?" Bear's voice took on a protective tone.

"Seems to be doing better. She's asleep upstairs."

"I'll keep watch tonight." Bear hung up.

Riley disconnected and sauntered out of the office. A single sofa in the vast space between the windows on the back of the house and the kitchen was his only option for any sort of rest. He dropped down on the overstuffed velvety ruby-red cushions of the brass-plated embellished vintage sofa. The darkness and quiet of the house made it easy for him to drift off.

Ten

Annie stood at the bottom of the couch as Riley slept. His arms were crossed over his massive chest as if he was chilled. She shuffled to the hall closet and took out a blanket her mother had made years before. Her breath hitched as she remembered the birthday she presented it to her. The last one before they died.

She draped it over his feet, slowly sliding it up his body trying not to disturb him. She was laying the top over his muscled arms when he bolted up and grabbed her arms. He yanked her to his chest and secured her wrist between her back by nestling it in one of his calloused hands. She cried out in fear.

"Annie?" Riley had her pulled close to him with her hands restrained behind her back.

"I'm sorry...I didn't mean to startle you...I was just covering you with a blanket." She trembled, not meeting his eyes.

"Are you okay?" he placed his hands on her shoulders and took a step back but didn't break his hold.

"I'm sorry." She shook.

He ran his hand through his hair. She flinched; reflex caused her to put her hand up to shield herself from him. She was mad at herself she still reacted that way when anyone, even women, raised their hands. Annie knew it was a learned response due to what she'd been through the last several years. It didn't do anything to build confidence that she would ever not react like that.

"Hey, you have nothing to be sorry about. I should apologize to you." He pulled her hand down away from her face and held it.

"I just wanted to get you a blanket. You looked cold. I was thirsty and came down for something to drink. I think the antibiotics are making me dehydrated. I wanted to make sure you weren't cold. I'm sorry, I didn't mean to startle you," Annie rambled.

"Hey, hey, shh. It's okay. You don't have to explain anything to me. I'm not upset. I'm not Alan. Come here. Sit down." Riley motioned to the couch.

She glanced at the stairs; she wanted to distance herself from him. Yet she was drawn to him, and at the same time, her gut twisted when she thought of who she'd been drawn to before. Look how that turned out. He killed people. She wasn't sure if she had it in her to trust that much again.

"I won't hurt you. I know you have no reason to trust me. Just give me a chance." Riley motioned for her to sit.

She glanced at the stairs before she sighed and moved to the edge of the couch. She grimaced as she started to sit. Riley helped steady her with his hand under her elbow, easing her onto the cushion. He slid over, putting distance between them in the form of the middle sofa cushion. It was as if he could see inside her and what she needed to feel comfortable and to relax.

"How are you doing?"

"I'm fine. I'd still like to leave and put some distance between me and Alan." She squirmed and stared at her feet.

Headlights splashed across the windows on the front of the house. She gasped and leaped to her feet. Riley stepped in front of her, gun in hand. She clutched at the back of his shirt; even his back was muscles on muscles. He wrapped his left hand around his back to her. The headlights blinked off as the car approached the house. He backed up with his arm, guiding her to stay with him as he inched toward the office. A few quick keystrokes on the monitor system pulled up the driveway and side of the house where the vehicle headed.

Riley's phone buzzed. He slipped it out of his pocket. "It's Monroe. Here for your meds." He blew out his breath and holstered his weapon.

He turned to her. Relief washed over her. She leaned her head forward, resting it on his chest. Her heart raced when he wrapped his arms around her. She stiffened for a split second before relaxing, melting into his warm embrace. He pointed to the monitor and saw Monroe's form appear from the side of the garage headed for the back door. She nodded but didn't say anything. For the first time in years, she felt safe in a man's arms and didn't want him to let her go.

Seconds later, the back door opened with Monroe slipping in quietly. He glanced around before flicking on his flashlight.

"Monroe." Riley did a quick nod of his head. Annie peeked around him.

"Annie, what are you doing down here?" Monroe was upset.

"I was thirsty?" She raised her hands.

"Sorry. I should have taken water up to you to have when you needed it." Monroe pulled a syringe from his bag.

Her hand tightened on Riley's arm "Do we have to do pain meds?"

"No, if you aren't hurting like you were, I can just give you antibiotics, and if over-the-counter pain killers help, we can go that route." Monroe pulled a bottle from his bag.

"I don't like how they make me feel like I'm not in control." She turned her head as Monroe gave her the next dose of antibiotics.

"All done. Did you want me to relieve you or come back on her next dose?"

"Next dose is fine." Riley followed Monroe to the back door and locked it after he left.

Annie shifted from one foot to the next when Riley turned around to face her. Nervous energy twisted her gut. Her distrust of men but also people in general was taking a toll. She had a long road ahead of her, and she had yet to take those first crucial steps to start the healing besides getting away from Alan and divorcing him. When you dealt with individuals associated with the monster in your life, you learn real fast it is in your best interest to not trust them no matter what.

"Did you want to go upstairs? I can help you." He stooped trying to meet her eyes.

"No, I'm going to stay down here for a little bit. I think I overdid it when I came down for water." There was longing in her eyes when she looked at the stairs. She wanted to go back to bed.

"Come on, I'll help you." Riley held out his hand.

How did he read her so easily? "Why are you being so nice?"

"I'd be this way with anyone in your situation. I dealt with domestic cases when I worked for a police department before I retired two years ago."

She made eye contact and held his stare. His hand was warm as it engulfed hers. Riley went at her pace to the stairs. Three stairs up, she had to rest. Four more and she rested again. That was the pace they took while he escorted her to the top.

She eased under the covers. "Thanks for helping me."

"Sure, I can stay if you want."

Her eyes widened. "No."

• • • •

"OKAY, I'LL BE DOWNSTAIRS if you need me." Riley backed out of the room, closing the door behind him. His phone rang as he trudged down the stairs. "Riley."

"His car is moving," Bear alerted him.

He stopped midway down. "Where is he headed?"

"North. Away from both buildings."

"Keep me updated." Riley frowned. He was confused about where Alan could be going at this time of night.

"Sir." Bear disconnected.

Riley stretched as he stood in front of the bank of monitors. He sunk into the chair; he wouldn't sleep anymore tonight. Nothing moved outside. The cameras were operational. He pulled out his laptop and pulled up some of his other accounts. He knew the control room at work monitored everything, but he still checked in on them from time to time. His laptop let him access it while he was away from the office.

His phone rang and he snatched it out of his pocket. "Yeah."

"I found something you need to know about." Bear informed him.

"In-person or can you let me know over the phone?" Riley knew it wouldn't be good.

"Phone is fine. I researched Annie's parents' death..." Bear hesitated.

"Okay. And?"

"I think he had them killed also." Bear sighed.

"No!" Riley hung his head. Annie would struggle with their deaths if they could prove Alan was responsible.

"I know you didn't ask me to look into them, but when I read Annie's file again and I saw the car crash, I just had to look."

"No, you did the right thing. Can we get ahold of the autopsy reports on them also?" Riley watched headlights pass by Annie's house.

"Already done. They said their brakes went out. According to their vehicle records, they both had brand-new cars not even four months old. There's no way the brake lines were worn out like they put in the report..." Bear hesitated again.

"Out with it. What else?" Riley relaxed when they pulled into the neighbor's driveway.

"I think someone forced them off the road. Damage to the back bumper that can't be explained unless someone was bought off to fix the report. If they died from front-end impact after the brakes failed, there shouldn't be damage to the rear of the vehicle. And I got ahold of the evidence photos of the brake lines. They were cut. Any imbecile can see that." Bear's anger seeped through the phone.

"Thanks, I owe you. Did this happen in the same jurisdiction that Alan lives in?" Riley closed his eyes. He had no clue how he would tell Annie.

"Not the same city, but the same county. Either he paid someone off or had his little friends in the sheriff's department go over and talk to them and apply a little pressure."

"Do we have any concrete proof of the foul play?" Riley rubbed his eyes with the fingers and thumb of his left hand.

Bear sighed. "Yes and no. I have copies of the original reports showing the lines were tampered with, but nothing tying Alan to it. The county prosecutor denied charges in the city's case for lack of verifiable evidence. Anything in the small town where it happened has to go to county-level because they don't have the courts to handle a case for possible murder. Since it didn't go past county, no one at the state level knew to look into the case."

"How did you get those?" Riley watched the neighbors load up kids into a minivan and leave for the day. The sun peeked on the horizon. The cameras were flipping back over to day mode one by one as the sun edged up in the sky a couple of hours after he escorted Annie back to her room.

"I have a cousin, and that's all I can say at this point." Bear laughed.

Riley shook his head. Anytime Bear didn't want to explain something, he said he had a cousin. Riley knew not to ask further. He had a lot of cousins and some were of questionable character. "Got it. Thanks."

He tucked his cell phone back into his pocket and stretched his neck from side to side and yawned. He sauntered to the refrigerator and snagged a bottle of water. Lots of fruit and vegetables filled the chilled clear glass shelves. She definitely ate healthily.

His phone vibrated in his pocket as he was finishing the last of the water. "Yeah."

"You need to get here. Monroe's on his way to relieve you." Bear informed him.

"What's wrong?" Riley grabbed his keys off the counter in the kitchen and snagged his tablet, queuing up the monitors at the office. Alan's Porsche was outside along with a couple of state vehicles. He could only assume it wasn't good news.

"We are operating an illegal business, and they are here to shut us down," Bear grunted.

"Oh, two can play at this game." Riley saw Monroe pull through the gate around to the back of the house and met him at the back door.

"Boss?" Monroe held the door for him.

"I'll take care of it," Riley huffed.

"I have connections if you need it." Monroe offered.

"I know, but I don't want to play that card yet unless it's a last resort. I'll see what kind of stupid he is up to and will let you know." Riley started toward his car and then turned back around. "Monroe, thanks though."

"Yes sir." Monroe locked the door behind him and disappeared into the kitchen.

Riley yanked his car door open and blew a breath out before getting into his Audi. He kept calm on the way to the office and punched up contacts in his phone. He had all the proper forms and applications filled out when he started up his business. He never cut corners and did everything by the book. He knew he would probably make people mad, so he made sure everything was done to the letter of the law so they couldn't come back at him and try to close him down. Alan would have a hard time proving he didn't file the correct paperwork to stay in business.

Riley pulled into the back parking lot and took his time getting out of his car so he could finish his conversation before approaching the building. As he walked in, he could see Alan's red flushed face through the front doors. He was surprised the man hadn't had a heart attack since meeting him. He nodded to Bear, who joined him at the front door.

"Yes, can I help you, gentlemen?" Two suits flipped open credentials in a leather flip wallet when he opened the door for them.

"We have it under good authority that you are running an illegal business here and haven't sent in the correct paperwork to conduct the type of business you are. You may have filled out the state business license, but you never had it notarized and filed before the deadline. That doesn't even include the background checks and fingerprint cards needed for your employees to operate as security officers." The one on the left seemed to be the one in charge. He looked down his nose at Riley. He was tall and lanky, and the suit would never fit him right, even if he added forty pounds of pure muscle. "We will also have to check your supposed gun permits for all the different types of weapons on these premises and will have to confiscate anything not within the business scope of your license to operate."

"Oh, really? Well, since I came to the state's office in person and filed all the necessary papers two years ago to receive my operating license and security licenses for each and every employee on my payroll issued by your office, my guess is that you took a payoff from the man standing behind you to give me a hard time. And since that is illegal, I suggest you check with your supervisor Agent Hargis for those official documents that I have notarized copies of filed with not only the county but with the state office. Or did you want me to call him directly and wake him up on his day off because of his daughter's birthday?" Riley knew Tom was out of the office today. That was who he had a conversation with on the way to the building. What Alan didn't know was that he was personal friends with Tom and had gone to him when he wanted to start his company to check and see what all he would need to do it legally. He typed out a quick text with the two agents' names.

"Oh um, well, maybe we should go back to the office and check on that. I don't think interrupting him on his day off is necessary," the second male stuttered, backpedaling and stepping off the sidewalk leading to the building, almost falling.

"What do you mean? I told you he didn't have the correct paperwork and that I guarantee if you looked for it, it wouldn't be filed!" Alan spit out.

"Well sir, we'll need to check on that first before we do anything here." Mr. tall and lanky backed up, yanked his phone out and read the text message, and nudged his partner in crime showing him the screen. They scurried back to their state-issued four-door sedan painted the pale puke gray that was standard on all cars issued to the state's office.

Alan spun around and Riley hit record on his phone holding it up behind his back, recording the entire event. He also knew the men in the building were also zooming in with the exterior cameras to make sure it was recorded.

"I paid you good money!" Alan hissed under his breath.

"Yeah, about that. We're sorry we can't accept your donation at this time." The second male tossed an envelope at Alan, eyeing Riley who was recording the interaction.

"Yeah, sorry about wasting your time!" The lanky one also tossed an envelope at Alan. They jumped in their state-issued vehicle and spun the tires as they accelerated away from the building.

Riley smiled when Alan turned back around and saw the phone in his hand. "How'd that work out for you, *Mr.* Montgomery?"

Alan took two giant steps toward Riley, who didn't flinch. "It's *Doctor*!"

Riley locked eyes with him and didn't back down. They were eye to eye for several seconds before Riley saw Alan's hand flinch and pull a gun from his waistband. Riley reacted and had his own pointed at the other man's chest before Alan could raise his. His eyes glanced down at the barrel of Riley's, aimed at his heart.

"Well, look at you. I believe you just committed a crime by pointing a weapon at me." Alan narrowed his eyes.

"Not according to the cameras recording this interaction and you bribing city officials." Riley motioned toward the building with his head. His finger never moved to the trigger, and he knew that was captured in the video. "And now I have enough to get an injunction on you to keep you from being on my property. This video will be submitted into evidence to join the previous one the local police department already has, that you can't buy into making disappear. Both videos together should be enough to grab a judge's attention."

Alan glanced at the cameras on the building. "Are you sure they are at the right angle to catch the sight of the gun in my hand? I do believe you may be lacking in that department on the recording." His eyes locked on Riley's a split second before he hid the gun back in his pocket, not making any large movements. Riley's body blocked most of the view of the building behind him. "You have no idea who you're messing with."

"Someone who thinks they own everything and everyone around them. I'm here to tell you that isn't true and you will never own me, Megan, or anyone in this town." Riley narrowed his eyes at Alan. He knew the kind of man he was and that if he were to show any weakness, it would be over.

Alan glanced at the barrel of Riley's gun, still chest-high, and smirked. With his gun already tucked away, Alan backed up and nodded toward the building. "You won this round but you won't be so lucky the next time we meet."

"You keep saying that, but I have yet to see any action on your part." Riley lowered his gun when Alan strolled to his car as if he owned the street it was parked on, with arrogance in his determined steps. His tires left burn marks on the street as he punched the accelerator and tore down the asphalt.

With his gun holstered, Riley entered his building. "Duffy?"

Duffy's head popped up from behind his monitor. "Sir?"

"Scan copies of our legal business documents for operating in this state. Also make copies and put them in files on everyone's desk. I have a feeling my originals may disappear at the state building." Riley took the file Bear held out for him. He knew it was the dossier he found earlier on Annie's parents. He hadn't talked to her before he left for the office.

"I have copies of the altercation outside." Bear leaned his hulking body against the door frame.

"Perfect. I'll need a copy to take to Ayers after I finish a couple of things on some accounts I've been putting on the back burner. How is Monroe?" Riley leaned back in his swivel office chair his feet coming up off the floor.

"Good, nothing going on. He helped Annie downstairs and is going over the system again with her. He said she looks better today." Bear held out a thumb drive. "I also made a few more copies to keep here in the office for backups."

"We need to get ahead of this guy. Can you also make copies of the other night when they tried to get into the building? More than one set of backups needs to be stashed in case something happens to the ones at the police department."

"Already done." Bear tossed another drive at Riley, who caught it out of the air.

He only nodded as he stared at the drive. Bear disappeared from the doorway, leaving Riley to figure a few things out. He logged into his computer and pulled up the accounts that he needed to send monthly service bills to. His printer whirred as it warmed up and made a knocking noise. Riley grimaced. He would need to get a tech out to look at it and see what was wrong. It was still under warranty so it shouldn't be a problem getting it repaired. He leaned back and finally opened the folder on Annie's parents. He'd been putting it off, doing any other account activity he could so he wouldn't have to look at more of Alan's victims.

The car was demolished, but Bear had been right. The rear bumper had definite damage consistent with someone ramming the vehicle from behind. It was a classic cover-up job. He worked too many crashes when he worked the road as an officer to not notice the blatant misinformation on the police report that sat in front of him. He flipped the page to see the pictures of the brake lines that had been tampered with. How could someone who promised to uphold the law turn a blind eye to the murder of two innocent people?

He slammed the folder closed. Annie would be heartbroken at the thought that her parents had been murdered and not just died in a tragic crash. How was he going to break the news to her?

Eleven

Riley glanced at the clock and decided to go to his apartment upstairs and take a shower before the next watch over Annie's house started.

As he stood in the scalding hot shower, he thought about what she had gone through. He could hear his wife telling him to take care of her. He admitted to himself that he hadn't even thought about anyone else ever being in his life. The love he had for his wife even now was so strong, it made his heart ache when he thought about her. But when Annie smiled, he saw her as a woman who had never been abused. The appalling violence never happened, and she was happy. He prayed that God would use him to help her heal and get back her ability to trust people again. There were too many instances in which domestic violence took the victim from this world permanently, and he swore that wouldn't happen to Annie. How evil were Alan's friends that they helped this monster cover up his crimes? Were there more victims out there they hadn't found yet? He would have Bear do a more extensive background check on Alan.

As he got dressed, he knew he'd need to get a payment for the signed contract from Annie to show his reasons that he ran backgrounds on everyone that they had. He knew he had up to thirty days to show cause for the checks he ran, but he would get it taken care of as soon as possible. The fact that Alan went to the state and tried to bribe his way to ruin Riley's business worried him. It seemed that he could easily get people to do what he wanted.

After he checked his phone, he shoved it into his pocket and started for the door when someone knocked. He opened the door to Duffy. "Yes?"

"You need to see this." Duffy had never come up to his apartment before.

"Show me." He followed him down to his desk. He had a video queued up from a week before Annie was hit.

The tan, beat-up Crown Vic followed Annie on her morning run. They had known she was in town before she was aware of them.

"They had to have followed her home and know where she lives. Tell Monroe!" Riley ran for the back door.

"Already did," Duffy called after him.

Riley floored the Audi and punched up the phone system in the car and dialed Monroe. Several rings later, his voicemail picked up. Riley's heart hammered in his chest and he pushed the Audi's engine. As he turned onto Annie's street, he could see smoke from the Crown Vic's engine as it sat half-crashed into the gate. Luckily, the gate held up to the assault, and the only way in would be through the bent-up part or over the wall.

He pulled his phone from his pocket and called the office. Bear answered, "Yeah."

"Get everyone over here, including the police. They know where she lives and rammed the gate. Monroe isn't answering. I'm going in." Riley snapped his phone shut and jammed it into his pocket before Bear could acknowledge him. He stayed near the bushes and ran to the back of the house, gun drawn. His heart raced. She would be no match against all three of them in her condition, and the fact that

Monroe wasn't answering did nothing to calm his racing heart.

Gun up, he approached the back door and listened. No sound came from the house. He used the remote to enter silently, pushing the door open from above his head and leaving it open for his men to enter through. The living room was empty. The office sat at the back of the kitchen. He poked his head around the corner. Nothing. Something thudded upstairs. Back in the kitchen, he peered around the wall to the stairs that led to the second level of the house. He still didn't see anyone, but Monroe's phone on the counter didn't help his anxiety about what he would find.

The back door opened and he spun pointing his Glock at four of his men, who stood there. He motioned upstairs and all four backed him, guns drawn. A step past the wall and another thud sounded from above. Bear was first in line behind Riley, and he tapped his shoulder to indicate that they were ready.

Riley was on the first step when he heard muffled voices. He heard two distinctive tones and neither one sounded like the pompous Alan. He more than likely sent his goons so if they were arrested, he wouldn't have his name tarnished outside his little frat-run county.

At the top of the stairs, Bear went right while Riley went left. Left would take Riley to Annie's room. Duffy and Gavin, who normally worked only overnight hours due to his work as a night stalker when he was deployed and had trouble sleeping anytime the sun wasn't high in the sky, backed him while Erickson backed Bear. He carefully peeked around the doorway but didn't see anything to alarm him.

Voices filtered out of the second bedroom from their location. A quick sidestep into Annie's room and he noticed a lamp knocked over, a chair tipped on the side. It was hard to tell if Annie was involved. There was no blood and he took that as a good sign. The gun was missing from her nightstand, but the Bible was open, facedown as if marking the spot where she had been reading. Was she reading it or had it landed there when they tossed the room? He briefly closed his eyes, praying God would lead her to the perfect scripture to open her heart to Him. After clearing the master bath, he re-entered the hall and was met by Bear, who shook his head to indicate that the room he cleared didn't lead to anything.

They started for the bedroom that sat between the two rooms. Riley held up his fingers and counted to three and burst through the French doors to the room. Monroe stood there with goon one and two on the floor, tied with rope. A gash on Monroe's head didn't look good, but at least he was standing.

"Hey, boss." Annie's gun in his hand was pointed at the two assailants.

"Monroe?" Riley holstered his weapon as his employees did the same.

"These two came in uninvited and started a fight. They weren't too happy that I won." Monroe smirked.

"And our client?" Riley refused to say the name she was using in case it hadn't been found out yet, even though they were standing in her house and tax records were easy enough to get your hands on.

Monroe took Riley's lead. "Good. These two never got to them."

"Bear, meet the police at the gate regarding these two breaking and entering." Riley motioned for Duffy and Erickson to watch the goons and nodded outside to Monroe.

Out in the hallway, they closed the door and walked to Annie's room. "Where is she?"

"There's a panic room. We found it by mistake when the goon squad showed up and rammed the gate," he whispered and motioned Riley to follow him.

At the back of the walk-in closet, there was a small keypad that had previously been covered with clothes. Monroe walked up and punched in a few numbers and the door seal whooshed as it released before the door slid to the side. Annie sat on a couch with her feet curled under her and Monroe's gun pointed at them. She closed her eyes and blew out her breath, lowering the weapon.

Riley raised an eyebrow at Monroe, who explained, "Mine holds more rounds than hers. I figured if they got past me she would have a better chance with mine than hers."

Riley smiled and nodded at Annie. "Are you okay?"

"How did they find me? I thought you said I'd be safe here." Annie got up slowly with the support of the arm of the couch.

"We found out when I went to the office that they had been following you for a week before they ran you down. They probably knew all along. Alan will definitely know where you are." Riley peered down at her as she handed Monroe his sidearm.

"Do I run again? I thought it had been long enough and he quit looking for me. With the name change and moving to the other side of the state, I just didn't think he would find me like this. I should have left the state." Annie looked around her room, muttering the last sentence, her voice barely audible as she headed toward her bed.

Riley figured she would dread moving and starting over in an unfamiliar place. "We have a couple of options we can do if you want to stay."

"Okay." She sat on the edge of her bed with her arm tucked in close, protecting her side.

"You can stay in the apartment we first had you in. The building is impenetrable. Or we can step up security here and have armed guards outside and one in the house." Riley would prefer she move into his building for the time being. It was easier to defend with the security system he had in place.

She shook her head and blew out a breath as her shoulders heaved with the sigh. "I don't know."

Riley knelt in front of her and placed one hand on each side of her legs on the edge of the mattress. "Annie, if you run, he'll only find you again. And if he knows you live here, then he more than likely knows your new name. If you stay, we'll make sure we do everything in our power to keep you safe." He couldn't express how much he wanted to fix this for her. He wanted to go into the room with Alan's flunkies and show them how serious he was about them leaving this woman, who shook in front of him, alone.

"Okay, I'll stay and fight. I escaped from his clutches once. Maybe with help, I'll escape again...for good." She smiled and his heart raced.

He patted her on the knee, causing her to flinch. She wasn't quite there yet, but her wanting to stay was a start.

Twelve

The doorbell rang and Annie jumped. Riley spun around, his hand on his gun. Voices in the foyer told him the police had arrived. He turned to Annie, whose eyes were wide, her lips pressed into a thin line. He knew she could do this, and he nodded to her that he was here with her. She rose from the bed and walked to the doorway of her room, peering down the railing at the police in her home.

"Officers." Riley addressed the two who occupied the downstairs foyer. Officer Ayers was one of the two, and his partner from the other day accompanied him. At least they wouldn't have to explain a lot about the goons who were in custody upstairs. Riley motioned for his men to bring them out and take them downstairs.

Officer Ayers raised his eyebrows at the men who were brought down to him tied with rope. "Riley?"

"These two men broke into this house after ramming the car that is stuck in the gate at the end of the driveway and attempted to assault our client after assaulting one of my men." He motioned to Monroe.

"Did you need an ambulance?" Officer Ayers narrowed his eyes at the two goons.

"Yes, please. Since he was on the clock, I'll need that for the insurance on my staff." Riley nodded to Monroe, who only cringed. Riley knew he hated being checked on since he was once a medic in the military and could probably do just as good if not better at cleaning his own wounds.

Officer Ayers keyed up and requested a police tow for the car wedged into the gate and an ambulance, with instructions on how to get onto the property. Another officer knocked on the door frame and joined them in the foyer when Ayers motioned him in. "Please transport these two to detention for assault, property damage, and breaking into this house. Separate them for transport and put both on a twenty-four-hour hold for detectives."

"Yes sir." The other officer and Ayers's partner escorted them outside and put one in the back of each car parked at the edge of the gate on either side of the Crown Vic.

"Now tell me exactly what happened and who was here when they broke in." Ayers took out his trusty pen and a small notebook and flipped to an empty page.

Monroe stepped forward. "I was showing our client how to use the cameras when we saw their car slam into the gate on the monitors. I ushered her upstairs and into her closet so she could hide while I secured the house. I left my phone on the counter in the kitchen, so I couldn't call the police. Our client told me about a small keypad behind some clothes and thought it was a panic room. We punched in the code left by the previous owners on a small piece of paper stuck in the corner of the panel, and sure enough, it was a secure room. I put her in it and left her with my gun. On the way out of her room, I grabbed her pistol from the nightstand and made it to the bottom of the stairs when I heard the back door forced open."

Ayers furiously wrote while Monroe took a moment for him to acknowledge that he had it down and he flipped to another page. He nodded for Monroe to continue.

"I barely turned around the corner when I was hit by the one wearing the blue sweatshirt with a college logo on it. I threw a punch of my own and hit the second one, the one in the tan hat. He went down and I scrambled up the stairs to the second bedroom. They entered our client's room first, ransacking it, so I made a noise to get their attention. They fell for it and came looking for me. I hit one over the head with the gun when he entered, and he fired shots in a haphazard fashion. The second one fired at me, and I ducked for cover, darting through the bathroom to the third bedroom attached to it, and came up behind him. He heard me and turned, landing a glancing blow to my head with the butt of his gun. I fought, tackling him into the second bedroom, and he lost his gun. It's still under the bed. I subdued him with my arm looped around his neck. As soon as he passed out, I tied them up with rope I found in the garage, and before I could call for assistance, my employer and co-workers showed up."

The ambulance had arrived and two paramedics had Monroe sitting in a chair while they cleaned up the gash on his head. Riley almost laughed when Monroe flinched. He was great at taking care of people but made a horrible patient himself.

"Officer Ayers, did you need anything else from us?" The paramedic waited for an answer after handing Monroe his copy of the form he signed, declining transport.

"No. Thanks, guys." Ayers scribbled more on his notepad.

Riley gave him his account of what happened after he and his men arrived. Annie sat quietly in the background while they talked with the officer. He knew her apprehension along with her history dealing with corrupt cops where she used to live but hoped meeting Ayers earlier would help alleviate some of that.

Officer Ayers peered around Riley. "Ma'am, can I ask you a few questions?"

Annie started to stand and winced.

Ayers held his hand up, stopping her. "You can stay seated."

"What did you want to know?" Annie glanced at Riley.

"I think you need to tell him everything from the beginning and leading up to the two men who just broke in here, including when they ran you down in front of my office." Riley nodded his head to Ayers.

"If it helps me understand the situation that happened today, please tell me everything. It will benefit me to know what I'm dealing with. We have outstanding warrants for the two who were transported to the police department for an armed assault on you with their vehicle and against this man and his employees when they shot at them outside their business. I take this very seriously and will do everything I can to get them charged for those crimes and the ones that happened here today." Officer Ayers smiled at her.

"Riley, do you still have the report you ran on me?" Annie didn't take her eyes off the officer when she asked.

"Yes, it's in my car."

"Can you get it? I think it will explain it faster than me going over every detail that happened before they ran me down." Annie squared her shoulders as Riley left the room.

He saw her strength right then and knew she was ready to fight with him to take Alan down for good, once and for all. He trotted to his car and snagged the folder from his soft-sided briefcase and jogged back to the house.

Officer Ayers thumbed through it, taking his time, and couldn't tear his eyes from the pictures of her wounds. He silently closed it and handed it back to Riley. "Guess he doesn't have a wife who's missing, since you're not married."

"No, I got lucky and found a judge willing to hear my case outside normal jurisdictions due to the blatant discrimination that was against me in Alan's safety net where he lives. I changed my name and moved here. No matter how many times I ended up in the hospital, and they are mandatory reporters of abuse, the cases never went anywhere. I thought I would never get away from him. So, when I found a judge to agree to my divorce proceedings, I couldn't believe it. I tried to stay hidden, but I love to jog. I now see how stupid I was to go out in the open like that. The divorce was final nine months ago. With my name change and the distance I moved, I felt safe. I dared to believe the nightmare that was my life was finally over, that I had something to look forward to...freedom and safety to live again. I should have had a home gym put in here. Anyway, Sam and Mark have worked for Alan since before I was married to him. He told me they were his best friends from college. I didn't think anything about it until I saw what they did for him. They have contacts everywhere because they use Alan's money to influence whoever they need to. I went on my normal early morning jog and was in front of Mr. Strong's building when I heard the engine of the car that is sitting rammed into my gate at this moment. I tried to jump out of the way, but I wasn't fast enough. I rolled across the grass as far as I could when they got out of the vehicle." Annie cleared her throat.

"Do you need some water?" Riley interrupted her statement, his need to take her in his arms almost overwhelming. He wanted to stay and listen but felt he was invading on a moment he wasn't sure she was ready to share with anyone if it wasn't important for the officers to know a little background to what led up to today.

"Yes, please." She smiled at him.

"Go on." Officer Ayers flipped the page on his notebook again.

Annie went over in detail what transpired between his first contact with her and today.

Riley could tell she was nervous because of bad previous interactions with the police. Officer Ayers continued to furiously write. His partner came back in the house after knocking on the door frame of the open front door. Ayers nodded at him.

"They are put on twenty-four-hour holds, and a detective was informed of the charges. I'm going to grab the camera and get some photos before the tow truck loads it up. Ma'am, what door did they force entry to on your home?" The officer rested his hands on his belt.

"The back door." Annie pointed past them toward the back of the house.

"I'll show you. We didn't touch it, so you may be able to get some good prints if they did. I didn't see them wearing gloves when you guys took them out to be transported to detention." Riley nodded to the young officer.

The young officer disappeared through the front door. They all watched him grab a camera out of the trunk of the police cruiser and head to the gate where the tow truck driver was patiently waiting to pick up the car. The numerous bullet holes in the sides told Riley they weren't smart enough to get a different vehicle than the one they used in the first assault on Annie.

"Okay, will you be staying here?" Officer Ayers was done with his note-taking.

"I think so." Annie glanced up at Riley.

Riley closed his eyes briefly and gave a nod, his heart hammering in his chest. "If not here, she'll be at one of the apartments. It will be harder for him to gain access than at this house."

"Miss Divers, are you in fear for your life?" Officer Ayers's bluntness took her off guard.

"Yes," Annie admitted.

"Then I'd like to suggest a protection order. We can have the courts put the Brady indicator on it so if they are caught carrying weapons, it will be a felony charge. Which will be a lot harder to sweep under the rug."

Riley nodded to Annie. "It couldn't hurt. Officer Ayers, I also have more evidence to show that her ex-husband is definitely stalking her. I hope we can get one on him also. I have video of him calling her his property and pulling a gun on me a second time."

Annie jerked her head up at him and gasped.

"I'll definitely put in the request in my report for a detective to apply for one when they take you to court for the other two." Ayers nodded and keyed up his police radio to ask for a report number. He pulled his card out of his pocket and scrawled the number on the back before handing it to Annie.

"Thanks." Annie's hand shook when she took it.

"I suggest you listen to Riley. He's the best officer I ever worked with, and I trust him with my life. If I was to bet on anyone getting you through this, it would be him. He knows domestic violence laws better than anyone I know, even the court system. Your ex-husband will be hard-pressed to find anyone who will listen to him over the reports I'm about to file on your behalf." Officer Ayers nodded to Annie and excused himself before he joined his partner at the back door.

"Can you really keep me safe and all that the officer said you could do?" Annie stared at her feet and didn't look at Riley when she asked.

"I will do everything I can to keep you protected and put Alan where he deserves." Riley didn't wait for a response but joined Bear at the front door when he motioned him over.

"We don't know where Alan is. His car is showing at the hotel, but staff said he also had a rental so he could be anywhere." Bear peeked at Annie, who watched them.

"Annie, we can't track Alan. He changed cars. I suggest you come with us back to the apartment so we can keep you safer there than here." Riley wasn't sure how she would like that suggestion.

"Okay." Annie didn't hesitate in her answer.

"Did you need help grabbing a few things of clothing?" Riley strolled up to her.

"Just help with carrying the bag down after I pack it, please." Annie took Riley's offered hand to help her off the couch.

He stood outside her room while she packed a few essentials in a bag. He nodded at her when she held up her gun. He previously checked and she had a concealed carry permit, so he knew she would be fine if she brought it with her. She nestled it between her clothes before zipping the bag. He held out his hand to take it from her and caught her wince when she twisted to hand it to him.

Riley slung the bag over his shoulder and placed his hand on her lower back to steady her on the way down the stairs. He glanced out of the large front windows and saw the car had been removed from her front gate. He would call a company he used for subcontracted work when he got back to the office to make sure it was repaired as soon as possible. He would also have one of his men walk the perimeter and see if there were any other weak points. They still didn't know how the neighbor accessed her yard without going through the front gate, which he definitely didn't do or he would have shown up on the video footage.

Thirteen

Riley rose early to check on Annie. She stayed in the spare apartment last night, and he had to say he unquestionably slept better with her secured in the building. It was easier for his employees to keep an eye on the outside cameras than on the large grounds around her house. Duffy was scheduled to walk the perimeter to see where the weaknesses were in defending the property.

He punched the elevator call button with his thumb and waited to ride it to the main floor. He would grab coffee and breakfast downstairs. He told Annie to text him when she woke so he wouldn't interrupt the sleep she so desperately needed. He still desired to sit down with her and tell her about her parents. Last night wasn't the night to do it. She was still reeling from what happened at her house. Bear nodded at him as he walked to the coffee pot.

With a cup filled to the brim, he took a sip, and the bitterness of the black coffee hit him hard this morning. He went to his office, past the manned stations of his employees. Everyone was working today to try and help get the evidence they needed to put Alan away for good. No one wanted Annie to go through what she was going through any longer than necessary.

Monroe knocked on his door frame; butterfly bandages held closed the wound he suffered yesterday. He had no doubt cleaned and bandaged the wound himself.

Riley motioned him in. "Whatcha got?"

"No one has seen Alan since before his buddies visited last night. He's up to something. Just don't know what it is yet." Monroe sank into the soft leather chair across the desk from Riley.

"Can we track his phone in any way?" Riley leaned back and steepled his fingers.

"No, we tried several various ways. He must have turned his phone off."

Riley shook his head. "Wonder what he's up to. I know he'll more than likely involve one of his fraternity brothers since the goons are still in jail this morning. Hopefully, the district attorney will seek charges with yesterday's fiasco."

"It's not an election year so he may." Monroe scoffed.

Riley smiled. "Yeah, lucky us."

"Riley, he's back," Bear grunted from the door.

"Oh, fun." Riley rose from his desk.

Duffy unlocked the front door with a head nod from Riley.

"How can I help you? We aren't open for business yet if you are looking for security services." Riley felt like poking the bear this morning.

"Since Megan isn't at her house, where you lied about my friends and had them arrested, I'm guessing she's here." Alan was pompous as ever.

"Sorry, I don't know anyone named Megan." Riley crossed his arms and wondered who the two men with Alan were this time. They weren't state agents; they were in a black utility vehicle.

Alan smirked. "Oh, you must call her Annie then."

"What do you want?" Riley, tired of this man, was not going to play his games.

"We have a court-ordered mental health hold warrant for Annie with concerns for her wellbeing from her suicidal and homicidal text messages." Alan nodded to the man on his left, who pulled a folded court order from his inside jacket pocket and handed it to Riley.

Riley unfolded the paper. This wasn't good. He couldn't go against a court order even though he knew she never sent those texts, and if Annie went with him, she wouldn't survive. It had a judge's stamp on it, and it was the judge that was on the other side of the state. He wasn't sure this could hold up in a court here. He turned to Bear and gave him a short curt nod. "So, do you have a search warrant to search this building?"

Alan smirked and nodded to the other man, who pulled another piece of paper out of his jacket pocket. This one was a state-ordered search warrant. Riley turned to Gavin Bruce's desk, his legal guru and nighttime employee, and handed both to him. Gavin, who wouldn't be in today if it wasn't for the mandatory monthly staff meeting, flipped through the pages and read them through again before he stood. He whispered in Riley's ear. Riley smiled and turned back toward Alan.

"Sorry, this isn't a valid search warrant, the address isn't for this building. By state statute code four nine eight seven point four, it has to be for the exact address you want to search. Nice try. Now, I'd like you to leave." Riley handed the warrants back to the two men as if Alan wasn't there.

The one spoke in hushed tones to Alan, whose face turned several shades of red. "Are you kidding me?"

"Bye." Riley's employees rose and all placed their hands on their guns.

Alan stormed out of the building, slamming the door open against the frame.

"Gavin, I owe you lunch! Now how do we fight the mental evaluation hold? We all know as soon as she gets in the car with him, she won't live through what he has planned for her." Riley locked the front door.

"We get her before a judge for a competency hearing in her request for a restraining order. Call Ayers and see where the paperwork is that we need to get to court this morning. We can go for an emergency protection order with Alan listed as a hostile party putting her life in jeopardy. We can even go as far as getting one for you since we have video of him pulling a gun on you more than once. Then when he gets here, this jurisdiction's judge's order will supersede that of the judge that's in his pocket, making his mental health request null and void. We can also serve him the subpoenas to appear in court for the full order. One second in front of this judge will get her full order granted and she won't have to worry about any phony orders from his judge. We can even go as far as having his friend investigated for going outside his jurisdiction and removed from the bench. That will put a pretty dent in his plans." Gavin threw his feet up on his desk.

"Do it before they come back. Are you sure you don't want to move to day shift and join the land of the living instead of only rising after the sun sets?" Riley headed in the direction of his office. He knew Gavin had clout in several judge's courtrooms because of his knowledge of the law and his previous stint as the youngest prosecutor before his military career. He never lost a case and didn't make his father very happy when he ditched it all for the army.

Riley's phone buzzed, vibrating across the desk. He saw a text from Annie; she was awake and asked if Alan was just in the building. Riley stood and stalked to the elevators as he punched in his reply that he was on his way up.

The elevator doors closed after he selected her floor. He would give her the news in person and have her ready to go to court for her hearing to get Alan and his two minions served with papers to stay away from her. He knew a piece of paper wouldn't do anything, but to have that would only help his case to keep her safe and Alan away from her.

The elevator dinged and the doors opened to her floor. She stood in the doorway waiting for him. She looked so small this morning. He tried to smile, hoping to ease her tension and held up the bag of bagels and cream cheese together with coffee and juice.

"Okay, what's going on?" Annie peered up at him. He noticed she didn't step to the side to let him in.

"We need to talk and it's going to be a long conversation so I think you may need to sit down for this one and eat while we discuss what's going on." Riley motioned to her apartment.

She didn't move. Her eyes widened and he wondered what ran through her mind about what could be wrong. He hoped he could convince her that they had a plan and that it would help keep Alan from trying to get to her in this building. If she went back to her house, it would be harder to keep her safe. After several agonizing minutes where he thought she wouldn't let him in, she stepped to the side and swept her arm in the direction of the living room.

"Tell me everything and don't keep anything from me." Annie perched on the edge of one of the chairs that faced the sofa, picking a bagel apart, nibbling on the small bites.

"Alan showed up this morning with a court-ordered mental health evaluation hold for you." Riley stopped when she gasped. He continued, "He also had a search warrant to look for you, but it had the wrong address on it. It was for your house. It won't take him long to have his friend change it to this address. I won't be able to keep him out with a court-ordered search warrant."

She started to get up. "I told you I have to leave again."

"Wait." He held up his hand. "It wasn't a valid search warrant. We sent him away. Gavin thinks he has a way to keep Alan from taking you and to get the judge in his pocket removed from the bench. We're still gathering evidence to show his friends have been covering up his crimes. In the meantime, Gavin said if we can get you in front of a judge here and present your case, he may issue an emergency protection order to keep Alan from you so he can't serve you with the mental health hold warrant."

"He'll also have the judge look into his order and see if he can nullify it since it wasn't issued in this jurisdiction. Gavin is also looking at presenting this order from his buddy to the state level so all future attempts to get at you won't be valid since there is an old, antiquated law most people don't know about that one jurisdiction can't supersede another one without the local court's knowledge." She raised her eyebrows. "Don't ask. He studied old outdated, quirky laws everyone has forgotten about as a hobby. He's making calls now." Riley rushed through the explanation to keep her from rushing from the room and leaving.

She lowered back into the chair, "Do you think that'll work?"

"We are going to try and we'll also get Officer Ayers to testify on your behalf. Get ready. We'll try to get you in front of a judge hopefully in the next hour before Alan comes back with an adjusted search warrant. We're also going to submit for a protection order for me since he has pulled a gun on me twice, and we have video evidence of that to show the judge. And we're also trying to have the protection order cover this building, as added protection." Riley rose from the sofa.

"I'll be ready to go in ten minutes. Do you want me to wait up here or come down to the lobby?" She started for the bedroom and then waited for Riley to answer.

"Stay in here. I don't want him to see you if he comes back before we can get a judge to see our case. I'll let you know what I find out. We may go ahead and leave and drive around so we aren't here when they get back, making it harder to serve you with the hold order." Riley rose from the couch and nodded at her before he closed her door behind him.

He rode the elevator to the top floor to grab a shirt and tie before he checked in with Gavin. He hoped Gavin had some good information for him when he got there. He fished a light blue button-down shirt and a maroon tie out of his closet, changing as fast as he could before rushing from his apartment. Time was short on what they needed to accomplish this morning. If Alan got hold of Annie, he knew he would never see her again, and his heart hammered in his chest as he thought of what she would go through. He didn't want to admit to himself, but he was ready to break the law to keep her safe. In a quick silent prayer, he asked for God to watch over them as this maniac tried to take Annie to torture and kill her, and to thwart his actions and for them to be victorious today. He muttered "Amen" out loud as the elevator doors opened at the lobby.

He straightened his tie as he approached Gavin at his desk, who was grinning from ear to ear. "I guess you got something good for me?"

"Judge will see you and Annie as first docket today since his other case asked for a continuance not even ten minutes ago." He smirked after giving a chin lift. "He said to bring all the evidence and he will be more than willing to fit you into the docket." Gavin handed Riley the tablet with the videos loaded with Alan pulling a gun on him and his goons shooting at the building after running Annie down with the car.

"You are good!" Riley quietly thanked God for this run of good luck. He wasn't sure how Gavin was able to get the person representing the other case to ask for continuance, but he definitely owed them one. He yanked his phone out of his pocket and sent Annie a text to join him as soon as she could and to let her know that the judge would see them.

Not even two minutes later, the elevator doors opened to Annie dressed in a simple solid blue dress.

"Riley, Officer Ayers said he'd meet you at the courthouse to testify on Annie's behalf," Gavin called out as they headed to the back entrance of the building.

Riley raised his hand but didn't turn around, so he knew he heard him, but didn't want to delay getting Annie in front of a good judge. Not one who was corrupted by money and toxic friendships.

He held the open door for Annie and helped her sit in the car. It was low enough to the ground that she grunted, no doubt at the pain in her side, as she angled into the seat. It had been five days since she'd been run off the road. Any normal person would still be taking it easy, but Annie, she didn't have the luxury to take care of herself because of her ex-husband, who was bent on making her suffer. Riley would get her to the courthouse so she'd have a chance at living her life without the fear of being hunted.

Riley slid behind the wheel and cranked over the engine. It purred quietly as he shifted into drive and sped out of the parking lot. He knew the courthouse was several miles away, but they had plenty of time to make it. He didn't initially tell Annie when he spotted Alan's vehicle turn around at a red light, almost running two other vehicles off the road, and following them.

"Annie, I need you to hold on. Alan is behind us." He glanced over at her.

"He's going to win again, isn't he?" She closed her eyes. Defeat was written on her face.

"Not yet he hasn't." Riley tapped his screen for his car to dial a contact on his phone and waited for Bear to answer.

"I see him, sir. Hold on." Bear's voice filled the car.

The next light turned yellow as Riley hit the intersection and turned red before Alan could catch up when the car separating them braked, causing Alan to stop for the light. Riley punched the accelerator as the next couple of lights stayed green for them. Annie glanced at Riley, who only smiled at her and then winked.

"Next two are keyed up ready to go. He's stuck four lights behind you now." Bear's confidence flooded the speakers in the car.

"Thanks." Annie peered over her left shoulder.

"Ma'am." Bear disconnected when Riley made the light by the courthouse and pulled into the parking lot.

"We have to hurry. Once we're inside, officers that run court security will be there to help us if we need them." Riley jumped out and hustled around to the passenger side.

"Let's do this." Annie grabbed his hand and let him help her out of the car.

They fast-walked without injuring her and made it to the building before Alan could find a parking space. Riley rushed them through security screening since everyone knew him there. The bailiff ushered them before the judge, who banged his gavel to silence the courtroom.

"Please present your case," the judge ordered.

Officer Ayers slipped in and walked up to the front. "Your Honor, I have statements of a home invasion given by Miss Divers yesterday when two colleagues of her ex-husband showed up and rammed her gate with their vehicle, disabling it, and broke into her house with the intent to take her against her will to their employer, her ex-husband."

The judge took the papers from Ayers and then turned to Annie. "Please tell me why you feel you need an emergency protection order."

Annie started with the first time Alan hurt her. The judge patiently listened up to the point where she was run off the road by Alan's goons. There was a commotion outside the courtroom, and the judge looked up from reading the statement that Ayers handed him, by peering over the top of his reading glasses perched on the bridge of his nose.

Ayers whispered to Riley, "I had security detain him and put the metal detector to extra sensitive."

Riley hid the smile and pressed his lips together as Alan stormed into the courtroom, trying to straighten his tie while he held his shoes, a sock, and belt. The judge banged the gavel and ordered silence in the courtroom. He glared at Alan as he dropped a shoe, trying to feed his belt back through the loops on his pants. "Sir, I object to these proceedings!"

"Duly noted. Go ahead with your evidence." The judge nodded to Riley.

"Your Honor, I have video evidence of the ex-husband pulling a gun on me twice when he thought I had Miss Divers in my building." Riley motioned to his tablet.

The judge motioned him forward and had him queue up the videos one after the other and sat there watching them.

"Those are fake videos!" Alan burst out as he took a couple of clomping, uneven steps with only one shoe on.

"Excuse me. You don't yell out in my court. If I have any questions for you, I'll call on you. But until then, you will sit there quietly and not say a word. And you will address me as Your Honor!" The judge glared at Alan.

"Your Honor, I just wanted to show you I have a warrant to have Megan put on mental health evaluation for a ninety-six-hour hold due to suicidal and homicidal statements she sent in a text message to me two days ago!" Alan stormed up to the judge's bench.

The gavel sounded throughout the courtroom. "Bailiff, please escort this man back to the seats. You are not to approach unless I give you permission. One more outburst and I'll find you in contempt!"

Riley showed the last video when the judge prompted him, of Alan's goons running down Annie and then shooting at her. The judge hid the shock on his face when the car impacted into Annie's side, but his lips pursed into a thin line.

"Miss Divers, did you send any text messages from your phone to your ex-husband, threatening suicide or with homicidal tendencies?"

"No, Your Honor," Annie meekly answered.

"Here, look at this!" Alan again approached the bench.

"Sir, you are in contempt of this court! I told you not to approach *my* bench without my permission!" The judge banged the gavel again.

"But look!" Alan practically tossed his phone to the judge.

"I find you in contempt again!" The judge was now beyond mad.

The bailiff radioed for another officer to join him in the courtroom and removed Alan back to the first row of seats.

Another officer joined the bailiff so that one stood on each side of Alan, who was now waving his court order mental health hold on Annie.

"Officer Ayers, can you please bring me that paper this man is ignorantly waving around?" The judge's frustration had reached a boiling point.

"Yes, Your Honor." Ayers took the paper to the judge and smirked at Riley on his way back to the chairs.

"Sir, this court order isn't valid. Why would you go to a jurisdiction that is halfway across the state to get a judge to grant you this when there are judges here who handle this county? Do you have the evidence you showed this judge to get this order instated? And according to this so-called blatant disregard to follow the laws you don't even have her name on this. You have Megan Montgomery and I am clearly talking to Annie Divers."

Riley said a silent prayer when Alan spoke up. "Of course not. The judge has it! And she has fake documents with different names on them. Her real name is Megan Montgomery."

"Well, in this county, I am the only one that can issue this type of hold. Are the texts still on this phone you threw at me?" When Alan confirmed they were, the judge scrolled through the text labeled Megan. "So, if I click on her name and hit dial, her phone will ring. Miss Divers, do you have your phone with you?"

"Yes, Your Honor, but it is turned off out of respect for the court," Annie quietly confirmed.

"At least someone respects my authority here. Please turn it on and let me know when you are ready." The judge pressed dial after Annie had motioned that her phone was ready for his call. Nothing happened. The judge raised his hands.

"She must have more than one phone!" Alan burst out.

"Miss Divers, do you have more than one phone?" The judge sighed his question.

"No, Your Honor."

"This is null and void per this court due to the name not being correct on the order. The messages didn't come from her phone, which was proven since this didn't ring to her. I am granting full emergency orders to both parties on behalf of what I have seen in this courtroom. Bailiff, make sure this man is served for both of the orders. Sir, it is by order of this court that you are not to have any contact with either party that stand to my left. You are also here by order to relinquish your firearms. I'm attaching a Brady indicator to both of these orders. If you are found in possession of a firearm while these are valid, you will be charged with a felony. I am also ordering these to be active for at least a year. We will revisit these cases a year from tomorrow. If you try to contact her by any means, through third parties or any other attempt, you will be charged with these violations." The judge banged the gavel.

Alan lunged toward the judge. "You don't have the authority over me to do that!"

The judge banged the gavel again. "I now hold you in contempt of court for a third count. Bailiff, take Mr. Montgomery to detention, where he will spend three days. One day for each count of contempt. Now, do you think I don't have the authority to do that? Because if there are any more outbursts from you in my courtroom, I'll tack on a day for each occurrence."

Alan snapped his mouth shut and glared at Annie and Riley as the bailiff slipped a handcuff around one of his wrists.

Riley put his arm around Annie and steered her toward the doors with Ayers in tow. "We need to wait for the paperwork and the service sheets so we have proof he was served with the full orders," he whispered to her.

"You are mine! Do you hear me? I will get you back and then I'll show you that you are my property! Sam and Mark will keep you company until I get out of this podunk little town and back where I belong!" Alan hissed under his breath.

The court stenographer's fingers flew over her device in a blur. Her enormous eyes looked even bigger behind her thick glasses as the shocking scene unfolded before her.

"Bailiff!" The judge almost broke his gavel when he hammered it onto his bench.

"Yes, Your Honor?" He turned toward the judge.

"Did he just say what I think he said?"

"That he just threatened this young lady, and that he called her his property, and that the two men I assume were in the vehicle that ran her down the other day will be sent to capture her? Yes, Your Honor, that is what he said." The bailiff gave a single stiff nod to Riley.

Annie held his arm in a vice grip as she glanced back and forth between Alan and the judge.

"Sounds like a threat to me, and the order hasn't even been valid for more than two minutes. Officer Ayers, please issue a threat report and log it, with me and the bailiff as witnesses. The orders are now extended to two years. Bailiff, make sure the court tacks on one for each of his friends, a one Sam Berger and a Mark Murphy, so they are issued orders to stay away from Miss Divers and Mr. Strong."

An additional officer appeared when Alan started yelling at the top of his lungs about the rude, inappropriate mishandling of the law. It took all three of them plus Ayers to finish handcuffing him and haul him down to the holding cells until he could be transported to jail to serve out his days.

Annie blew out a sigh. "That really worked?"

A court clerk came over and took their IDs to finish the paperwork once they were outside of the courtroom. They sat there stunned. They would have a three-day reprieve of Alan in which they could work on gathering evidence to put him away for good. Riley stood when the bailiff approached them. He shook Riley's hand and smiled before he handed him the paperwork and their IDs.

"Haven't seen the judge that mad in a long time. If he hadn't come in and shown what a jerk he was, not sure the judge would have granted these. Guess someone upstairs was looking out for you." The bailiff sauntered off toward the courtroom.

Officer Ayers met them outside to walk them to Riley's car. "Sorry, have some bad news for you."

Riley's car had four flat tires and a broken windshield. His shoulders slumped as he looked at the damage. He grabbed his phone and called Bear. "We'll need a ride, and send us a tow."

"We got him on camera, so I'll add this to the report I already have going against him." The officer pointed to the camera mounted at the top of the light pole. "They're new. No one knows they're there yet."

"Guess that's a good thing." Riley sighed.

"Oh, got more good news for you, though." Ayers smiled.

"What's that? Not sure we can handle this much good news in one morning." Riley leaned against his trashed car.

"Judge is sending the paperwork to state court to have Alan's buddy investigated for issuing illegal mental health holds. Apparently, the paperwork wasn't sent through the right channels. My guess is that he's been twisting the law for so many years, he didn't hesitate this time but didn't take into account another judge seeing it or noticing Annie's name change. Alan threw his own friend under the bus flaunting his order in front of this judge as if it superseded everything in this county. He may even give us evidence on Alan to help us drop this case on him." Ayers smiled.

"Yeah, too bad we couldn't get evidence on the four people he killed," Riley muttered.

"Four?" Annie frowned as she stared at him.

"Wait, you mean to tell me he's murdered people?" Ayers narrowed his eyes.

"We don't have evidence yet. And it didn't happen here." Riley tried to not look at Annie.

"I thought it was only his two ex-wives. Who else did he kill?" She stepped in front of him.

"Later. I don't think this is the place to have this conversation." Riley wouldn't meet her eyes.

"Oh no! No! He didn't!" Annie spun on her heels and faced away from him, taking in deep breaths.

"Annie, I didn't know how to tell you." Riley put his hand on her shoulder. She batted it away as a sob tore through her throat.

"Okay, you have to tell me. Who else?" Ayers wouldn't let it drop. Riley said too much in front of him. He had to report what Riley told him.

"Her parents." Riley watched her shoulders slump.

Ayers twisted his body around so he faced her. "Miss Divers?"

"Can you please take me home, Officer Ayers?" Her words hitched and caught in the back of her throat.

"Annie, please don't do this. I just didn't know how to tell you. Then this happened this morning, so I wanted to get this in order first before I told you," Riley tried to explain as she started to walk away, his heart stuck in his throat. Ayers held up his hand to Riley to indicate that he would handle getting her safely home. What he didn't know was that they had her at his office building to keep her away from Alan. If she went back to her home, she could become an easy target.

"I'll take her home. With him in jail for three days, maybe she'll be able to figure some things out. After I drop her off, you and I need to talk." Ayers walked to where Annie stood and nodded and motioned toward his patrol car to signal that he would take her home.

Riley's heart ached at the pain Annie was going through. He knew he should have told her sooner. Why didn't he? Because he didn't want to hurt her. She would feel betrayed by the information he'd withheld, and it would only hurt the trust that he had built so far. He slid the phone from his pocket but didn't dial as Bear pulled into the parking lot followed by a tow truck. They watched them load up the coupé and told them where to take it. Then he jumped in the vehicle Bear arrived in.

"Where's Annie?" Bear put the car in gear and pulled out of the parking lot.

"She figured out about her parents. She had Officer Ayers take her home." Riley watched the pavement fly by out of the passenger window.

"What about the orders? Did the judge grant them?" Bear concentrated on the road.

"Yes, thank goodness. Alan showed up and only cemented the case for us. Judge put him in jail for three days for contempt. He didn't like being told to be quiet and someone listening to Annie instead of him."

Bear smiled. "You know, that's good news!"

"Yeah, but I lost all trust I had built so far. I should have told her as soon as I found out about her parents yesterday." Riley sighed.

"You only just found out. She can't blame you for not running to her the split second you knew. The goons made bail this morning. Charges are being filed but they are out and about. We still need to keep an eye on Annie." Bear's news was like a punch to his gut.

Riley grabbed his phone. "I hoped they would be held longer. We finally get Alan out of the way for a couple of days only to have the goon squad back on the loose."

Bear waited for Riley to finish his conversation with Officer Ayers and then looked at him as they pulled into the back parking lot of the office. "Is there anything Ayers can do to convince Annie she still needs our help?"

"I don't know. I hope so, but I'm not holding my breath." Riley shook his head as he wrenched open the back door harder than necessary.

He marched into his office and booted up his computer for the account on Annie. He blew out his breath when he saw that she had disabled all the cameras inside the house. He printed off the invoice for the installation of everything and gave her a discount. She had been adamant about paying for the service and equipment he installed on her home. It was a hefty figure but he had no doubt she wouldn't hesitate to pay for the safety of being able to view the outside of her home while locked inside, from the comforts of her office. The outside cameras were still up and operational; for that, he breathed a sigh of relief. At least she hadn't turned everything off. He put her invoices in a folder and headed for the elevators.

He felt he invaded her space as he entered the apartment they had for her. The bag she brought still sat on the bathroom floor. The only things that looked unpacked were her toothbrush and toothpaste. Everything else was thrown into the top of the bag. He zipped it closed after he added what was on the sink and was carrying it to the elevator when his phone buzzed in his pocket.

Ayers's name lit up his screen. "Riley," he answered.

"She is safe in her house. We need to talk. This house has good security but with Alan in jail for three days, his friends will be on a rampage and she needs someone to have her back." Ayers's voice echoed; Riley could tell he stood somewhere in the lower level of Annie's house.

"I'm on my way. Tell Annie we still need to talk. Maybe if I tell you everything in front of her, it will restore the trust I lost this morning." Riley slipped his folded phone into his pocket and waited for the elevator doors to open. His phone also carried his account's monitoring system in an app he had created for the purpose to keep track of the high-end accounts he worked hard at securing. His phone opened into a tablet to access the camera's not only on his building but also on the delicate elite accounts he followed.

The elevator dinged as the doors opened. He set the bag on the floor as he rode down to the lower level. When he arrived at the main floor, he slid her bag out to the hall with the toe of his left foot before marching over to Bear's desk. "Do you have the extra set of keys for fleet vehicles?"

There was a set already on the corner for him. He snatched them and nodded before he started for the back door. He snagged Annie's bag from the hall as he made his way to the back parking lot. He used the remote to find which vehicle Bear had chosen for him and trudged to it when the horn honked and the lights flashed.

He sat behind the wheel for a couple of seconds, trying to calm himself with a few deep breaths, before he put the car in reverse to back out of the parking space. He didn't know how to fix what he lost. She was so fragile in the trust department already. The fact that she had faith in him as much as she had after what she endured with the monster she married, shocked him.

The drive was short and he still didn't have any answers on how to repair the distance with Annie. It would undoubtedly be hard for him. He could only explain his struggle by telling her why he had kept her parent's truth from her as long as he had. Hopefully, Ayers would help with that since he knew the judge as well as Riley did. A blow such as the knowledge of the murder of her parents could only jeopardize their case in front of this specific judge. A frantic emotional woman in his court rarely got any special treatment. She needed to present herself as the calm, daring woman he knew her to be. He remoted himself through the gate and parked in front of the house. It didn't matter now if someone knew she was here since her ex had her tracked here weeks ago.

He approached the front door, and Ayers stood on the other side when it opened. He was on his cell phone and hurriedly mumbled and then ended the call. "Strong."

"Everything okay?" Riley studied Ayers.

"Oh yeah, just checking in with my sergeant." Ayers averted his eyes and pretended to take in the space around them as if searching for something.

Riley stepped into the foyer with Annie's bag and set it next to the stairs. "Where is she?"

Ayers motioned toward the living room at the back of the house. Riley nodded and strolled through the kitchen toward Annie. She had her feet curled under her with a plush burgundy blanket thrown over her. A wine glass was half empty in her left hand. He cringed. Alcohol would only make her grief that much worse, and she could spiral out of control if she let it consume her.

"Annie?" Riley waited for her to acknowledge him and prayed God would open her heart to him and listen to what he had to say.

Fourteen

Several agonizing moments went by before she peered up at him, eyes glazed over; her heart dropped at the disappointment and sadness in his eyes. She motioned to the chair opposite hers as she went back to staring out of the floor-to-ceiling windows that offered a serene look to her backyard that spanned several acres. She loved the space; it was so open and tranquil. She never felt closed in like she used to when she lived with Alan. He had a few acres but it was so full with a pool for entertaining, the gazebos—yes, he had three—and the outdoor cooking area. There was hardly a blade of grass for someone to enjoy. No expanse of a yard to let nature be.

"Annie, I'd like to start by apologizing." Riley sank into the overstuffed cushion of the high-backed wing chair that matched hers. He waited for her to look at him again before he continued.

There was a tear balancing precariously above her lower lashes when their eyes met. She blinked it away. She took another sip of the wine that already affected her. She just wanted the pain to go away. To forget that if she had never let Alan into her life, her parents would still be alive. How scared were they when they knew they were going to die? Did they suffer?

"First, I didn't know how to tell you about your parents. Everything happened so fast with Alan's friends trying to get to you in your house. Then the luck we had getting you before a judge today. The judge who saw our case is not the easiest judge to convince that you needed his help to keep Alan away from you. I've seen it too many times in the past when I took other victims to him. If they were emotional in the least little bit, he would deny their case. He has never been one to believe a woman just because she was crying. So, for that I'm sorry, I was trying to get your case accepted and didn't know how the murder of your parents would affect you before appearing in front of that specific judge." Riley took his time and calmly spoke every sentence.

"Miss Divers, he's right. I've seen that judge refuse a plea for help on numerous occasions just because the woman cried in his courtroom. He sees that as a sign of attempted manipulation, trying too hard to seem scared. He's a hard one to get any protection order approved. Today, we got lucky that Alan spun himself to be out of control, and the fact that he acted like he owned the courtroom couldn't have been better for us. It was exactly what the judge needed to see," Ayers backed up Riley's claims.

Annie finished her glass and reached for the cabernet. She tipped it to the right and then the left, but no liquid swished around in the green blown-glass bottle.

"Annie, that wine won't help the hurt. It'll only make it worse." Riley leaned forward and put his hand on hers.

She glanced down, staring at his blurry hand before she finally nodded. "Where do we go from here?"

"I want to do everything by the book, so, first of all, I brought your invoices for the services you requested to pay for. This will help prove you fear for your safety." Riley held up the folder for her.

"Thanks." She thumbed through the pages and glanced at the summary page with the amount due and didn't blink an eye. She shoved the blanket off her legs and stood. Faltering, she clutched the side of the chair for support. She closed her eyes as the room spun.

Riley and Ayers both started to reach for her but stopped when she opened her eyes. She lugged herself to the office as if her legs were tied down with weights. She opened a side cabinet, blocking part of their view as they lingered in the doorway. She spun the dial on her safe. It took three tries before she was able to get the combination correct. She grabbed the second envelope to the left and turned to her desk. Pulling bills out, she counted the exact amount the invoice was for.

"You don't have to pay me in cash." Riley's eyebrows rose as she took the envelope back to the safe and locked it away.

"I pay for almost everything in cash. No paper trail for Alan to find me. Although now that he knows my name and address, I guess there's no reason for that." She put the money in a new envelope she pulled from the second desk drawer on her right and printed her name on the outside in beautiful script handwriting before she rose to hand it to Riley.

"Miss Divers?" Ayers stood to the side as she sauntered past him to the kitchen.

She pulled another bottle of cabernet from the built-in cooler and then reached for the corkscrew. Riley closed his eyes and hung his head. She ignored his disapproving movements. She was hurting too much to care about how her actions affected him.

"Annie?" Riley took the corkscrew from her as she fumbled while trying to get the cork out of the new bottle.

"I'm fine. Thanks for the security system. You can let yourself out." Annie took the unopened bottle of wine to the chair and set it on the table, nudging the already empty green-tinted glass bottle so that it sat perilously on the edge of the table, wobbling just enough that it almost tumbled over.

"Miss Divers? I wanted to go over with Riley what information he had on the murders of Alan's wives and your parents. Do you mind if we discuss that here? I think you're in danger. Sam and Mark made bail. They're out." Ayers sat on the arm of the chair across from her, feet planted squarely on the floor. His hands were clasped together, his fingers intertwined as his muscled forearms rested on his legs.

She didn't answer right away; she schooled her emotions as she stared out the window. The pain of her parents' deaths kept her on the brink of an emotional collapse. She knew one small word or show of compassion would send her over, and she wasn't sure she would survive a hit like that.

"I don't care." Annie's eyes never left the window.

Ayers nodded to Riley; he must be thinking the same thing: that she was on the edge. If they discussed this in front of her, would it be her undoing or would it give her a reason to fight harder?

"These are two autopsy files on both of his wives. We called in a few favors to get these before anyone found out they still existed and destroyed them to cover up for his crimes. These shouldn't exist but apparently, God was looking out for Annie on a level no one realized, with the initial reports still obtainable and not wiped out. I wonder if someone was just covering themselves and kept them hidden from those who helped an animal cover up his crimes." Riley pulled several folders from his soft-sided briefcase.

"Wait. There are two reports for each wife?" Ayers peered up at Riley.

"The official reports are doctored to hide the true cause of death, stating all the injuries were from the crashes because both women weren't wearing seatbelts." Riley's eyes never left her.

She tried not to react, but it was hard to stop the shiver that traveled down her spine. She struggled to tell everyone how connected Alan was and how many people helped him cover up his crimes. Granted, at the time she thought it was only his abuse of her. Numerous murders were now accumulating with Alan as the culprit. How did you fight someone like that?

Ayers flipped through the pages, reading each line for line. He whistled when he saw what looked like photos of women and glanced up at her. Riley never stopped monitoring her while she kept her gaze low, observing them through her lashes. She ignored him when he would glance at her and just looked at her empty wine glass.

As he finished reading the last report, Annie excused herself, went around to the front foyer, and closed herself in the bathroom. Several steady breaths helped her control her emotions. Her hands gripped the edge of the sink to keep them from shaking. How did she not know what he was capable of? Physical abuse absolutely, but the anger seeping off the two alpha males in her house was staggering and she was choking on the visceral rage that hung in the air. Ayers's next words had her stopping dead, hiding that she was back in the room as she listened in.

"This is pure anger and rage taken out on these women. Did she have anything this serious?" Ayers shook his head at Riley as he handed back the folders. "And where are the original reports? These look like copies."

"No. The worst ones, it appears, were when he was planning their deaths and he knew he wouldn't need to explain away any of their injuries. She has been cut, beaten, bruised, and branded. The original reports are in a safe place." Riley's baritone tense voice lowered.

"I'll need those originals for my report as evidence." Ayers shuffled the pages back into the folder.

Riley sat back and crossed his ankle over his knee. "They will be kept hidden until then, if and when we get before a judge. The copies are good enough for now to start the process of opening these cases back up."

"I'm sorry, Riley, but you aren't a cop anymore. I'll need those originals." Ayers closed the files.

Narrowing his eyes, Riley glared at Ayers. "I'll see what I can do. I don't have them myself."

"What else do you have?" Ayers peeked up as Annie sauntered back into the living room but not before snagging the corkscrew from the counter, giving Riley a look daring him to try to take it from her.

"These are on the crash involving Annie's parents. Check out the pictures of the back bumper after reading the report." Riley's attention was back on her, and it felt as if her skin was branded with his gaze.

Annie's hands shook when he said the folder was on her parents. She clenched her fists and took a couple of deep breaths before attempting to remove the cork from the bottle again. The cork's pop sound, as it sprang from the glass, echoed through the house. She left it attached to the corkscrew and filled her stemless wine glass to the rim. She went back to staring out the window before she finally took a sip from the newly filled glass, her fingertips turning white as Ayers reached for the file on her parents.

Riley glanced at Ayers, who only grimaced as she took a larger gulp when he opened the file. He took his time and reviewed every page. He stacked them neatly upside down on the other side of the open file as he went through every sheet.

• • • •

HIS PHONE BUZZED IN his pocket, and they both looked at him as he excused himself and stalked to the foyer to answer the call. "Yeah."

"They tried to get Alan out of jail. That didn't go so well for them since they were served with the full orders the judge issued. Just wanted you to know," Bear informed him.

"Thanks. Do we know where they are now?" Riley peered through the sidelights by the front door.

"Nope, they had an animated conversation with a very ticked-off Alan. Apparently, voices were raised and they were escorted from detention before being served with the papers stating they can't have a gun or go near you or Annie. No one has seen them since, and that was approximately an hour ago."

"Okay, thanks. We'll keep an eye out here. She's still on for surveillance of the outside of the house so make sure it's monitored twenty-four-seven." Riley waited for Bear to say he copied before disconnecting and slid his phone back into his pocket.

He ventured toward the living room as Annie emptied the bottle into her glass. Ayers stared at her, shaking his head. Riley closed his eyes; she would be in danger if she was so inebriated that she couldn't even stand.

"Annie?" Riley called to her as he leaned against the pillar that held the support for the beam dividing the living room from the kitchen.

She didn't respond and only drained her glass. That was two bottles of wine she consumed in a short period of time. She was very petite and the wine would be more than she could handle.

"Is this right, Strong?" Ayers held up the photos of the damage to the bumper.

"Yes. Our question is, how's there damage to a brand-new vehicle's rear bumper if a front-end crash is what killed them?" Riley noticed Annie flinch.

She reached for her glass, but it was empty, so she tucked her hand back into her lap under the blanket that covered her legs. A single tear trekked down her cheek.

"I'm sorry, Annie. Did you want us to discuss this case back at my office?" Riley squatted next to her chair.

"I'm fine. Can I see the file?" She finally looked at him after she finished her slurred question. The effects of the alcohol in the wine dotted her cheeks, flushing them red. Her eyes didn't completely focus on Riley.

"Yes, of course you can. I suggest you look at it when you're sober." He placed his hand on her arm. "I won't hide anything from you. You can have access to every file we have on this case."

She nodded as another tear slid down her cheek. Ayers closed the file and stood. "Miss Divers, I think you should lay down and rest. I know you're still hurting from your injuries from a week ago. Can we help you upstairs?"

The blanket dropped to the floor where she shoved it from her legs before she tried to stand. She swayed. Riley and Ayers rushed forward, each grabbing an arm to steady her. Clasping her hand in theirs, they gripped her elbows with their free hand on either side.

"I'm fine," Annie slurred.

"Yes, I can see that, come on." Riley guided her to the stairs at the front of the house.

She glared at him as her knees buckled. They waited patiently as she gained her footing again and started up the stairs one stumble at a time. She mumbled something that neither one could understand and shrugged it off when they didn't respond.

The stairs took several minutes to maneuver. Riley resisted the urge to sweep her up into his arms to save time and put her in bed himself. Her legs gave out at the second to last step as her head lolled forward. He shook his head and picked her up, cradling her in his arms. He didn't have a choice now. He nodded to the door for Ayers, who had it open before he got there. Ayers pulled down the blankets for Riley and helped cover her back up.

Ayers shifted the trash can from the bathroom and put it next to the bed. "Just in case." He started for the stairs.

Riley didn't join him but leaned against her door frame, shaking his head.

Ayers clasped him on the shoulder. "This isn't your fault."

"I should have told her sooner," Riley admitted.

"And it would have ruined the case for her." Ayers started down the stairs.

Riley followed. "Yeah, and for that, I hurt the trust that I built up so far."

"Okay, maybe, maybe not. Let's look at the cases we have so far. How many people does this guy have in his back pocket?" Ayers snagged the folder on Annie's parents from the side table where he placed it.

"Check this out." Riley pulled another folder from his bag, showing Ayers the array of frat brothers in the pictures. They had been able to identify every one of them.

"Whew, that's a lot of clout to have on your side. A judge, sheriff, coroner, enforcers, and attorney. This is worse than I thought. At least the judge will be busy covering himself from what Alan exposed of his illegal activities today. But these others could cause problems." He studied the picture that had everyone labeled with their name and their job title.

Riley knew it was a lot to take on, but maybe they could get ahead of this and shatter the bond of this fraternity that stared at them from the matte finish photo that lay on the slick surface of the table. "Coroner evidently kept both files on each wife. That tells me he's a possibility of being turned against the others. If he kept his original findings with his signature this long, then who's to say we can't use that against him, showing his name on two different versions. Same with the local police department that did the initial investigation into her parent's crash. Look at the report. It shows County coming in and taking over, pushing out the local department, and filing a different report. I think someone hid this report in case it hit the fan."

Ayers placed the pages back into the folders. "Yeah, agreed. Let me make some phone calls. Can I get copies of these?"

"Those are yours. I have the originals somewhere safe." Riley glanced up the stairs.

"Okay, let me see what I can figure out. I have a couple of friends of my own that Alan can't buy off." Ayers smiled and shook Riley's hand. "Hey, you haven't completely lost her trust. It's just hidden for now, but I think it's still there or she would have turned the entire security system off."

Riley blocked the sun with his left hand to deflect the glare off Ayers's windshield as he turned his police cruiser around to head toward the gate. He hoped he was right and that it wouldn't take long for him to build that trust again.

Since it had been a busy morning, he sent a text to Bear that he would be walking the perimeter to reinforce the security of the property. He flipped his phone open to the full seven-inch tablet mode and created a folder to save the images to, so he could access them when he got back to the office. The morning was heating up to be a scorcher. The six-foot wrought-iron fence started at the front gate, and he began there, following it down the east side of the property.

A pine tree had sprouted and grew through the fence line part of the way down the east side, pushing the wrought iron over and weakening the joints on the next section. He took a picture and edited the photo, labeling it as tree removal.

Halfway down the east side, he found another tree encroaching on the fence line, making it easy for someone to climb in and access the yard. Shaking his head, he also labeled it for removal. Now at the back corner, he started across following the back of the fence. About forty feet from the corner, he found two sections laying on the ground. He took a picture of them and noted they were freshly cut. The ends hadn't started to rust yet even though the elements would have started deteriorating the metal immediately. He spun on his heels and took in the back of the house. It really was a beautiful home with floor-to-ceiling windows overlooking the vast backyard with no other houses in the line of sight from the windows.

He turned back to the fence when rustling to his right caused him to pull his firearm from his side holster. Silent lateral steps moved him closer; he never took his eyes from the spot where the rustling came from. Footsteps behind him, crunching through the fallen pine needles, alerted him that there were two people. He spun around but it was too late. Something thudded against the back of his skull. He sank to his knees as the world disappeared to blackness.

Fifteen

Riley heard scuffling close to him while someone pressed something against his head. He swung and lunged up. His fist connected with something solid, sending a jolt through his wrist. They yelled as his vision started to clear. Monroe came into focus; he held his jaw. "Monroe?"

"Gee thanks." Monroe shook his head and moved his jaw from side to side as his hand absently rubbed down over a reddened area.

"Annie?" Riley tried to get off the ground but Monroe held him down.

"Boss, you definitely have a concussion. You need to get checked out. We have an ambulance coming." Monroe waved the paramedics over as they appeared around the east edge of the house.

"Annie?" Riley didn't get a glimpse of who hit him but could guess, and they would have been here for Annie.

"She's still asleep. Bear's with her." Monroe moved out of the way for the paramedics to check on Riley.

He closed his eyes while the paramedics took his pulse and checked his breathing, including blinding him with their stupid little penlights. "Am I good to get up? I need to get inside."

"Sir, we'd like to get you checked out at the hospital. We're told you were unconscious for several minutes. You have a concussion but need a scan to make sure there isn't anything else going on internally." The paramedics started packing up their bags.

"I'll go later." Riley took Monroe's extended hand to help him off the ground. He handed him back his semi-automatic he had out earlier before he was embarrassingly knocked out cold. He blew out his breath as his vision swam from suddenly standing. Why hadn't they used his gun on him? Or had they not considered that since they were known to carry their own weapons? Why only knock him out?

"Please sign this refusal form, and we'll be out of your hair," the paramedic ordered in a short, clipped tone. They dealt with Riley before, and ever since going to work in the private sector, he only let them transport him twice to the hospital in the last two years.

Riley scribbled his name on the signature line and started for the back door. "Fill me in."

Monroe caught up to him. "We saw them on the cameras and immediately sent everyone we could as soon as they took you out. It looked like they were trying to figure out what to do with you, so we got here before they made entry to the house."

"They cut two fence panels. We need that repaired asap. I didn't get to finish walking the perimeter when they ambushed me. They shouldn't have been able to get to me." Riley cringed when he felt the blood in his hair on the back of his head.

"They hit you pretty hard. You really need to get looked at." Monroe opened the back door for him.

"Later." Riley marched up the steps and shook his head when the room spun.

Monroe grabbed his elbow. "Boss."

"I know. Just let me check on her." Riley took the stairs two at a time.

Bear filled the doorway to her room but moved to the side when Riley joined him. "She's still asleep or passed out. I can't tell."

"Passed out. She isn't taking the news of her parents very well." Riley noticed she hadn't moved so much as a muscle.

"I'll stay with her until you get back from the hospital," Bear suggested.

"Thanks," Riley nodded to Monroe; he knew he shouldn't try to drive. He was more worried about hurting someone if he passed out than hurting himself.

"Let's go. Tracker is trying to follow their trail in the woods with Duffy. Bear is with Annie, and we have Erickson watching the monitors at the office. Gavin called in a few favors from the state-level courts. With what the judge requested this morning and Gavin's calls, they got the ball rolling on the investigation on Alan's little friend in the courts on the other side of the state." Monroe unlocked the car with his remote.

"Thanks, sounds like you guys are on top of things." Riley leaned his head back and closed his eyes. The throbbing behind his skull made it hurt to keep his eyes open, but he couldn't take the time to deal with it and keep Annie safe.

"Sir," Monroe waited for Riley to look at him. He only raised an eyebrow when he continued, "Did we lose her?"

"No, I did. I should have told her about her parents as soon as I found out. She blames me for that, not anyone else."

"She can't shut us out. It will get her killed. Alan is furious and in no uncertain terms told his men to get her so he can finish what he started when he gets out. He's gonna come for her with only one thing on his mind. He will take her back to where he can get away with her murder, and she won't stand a chance."

Riley blew out a breath. "Yeah, I know." He rubbed his closed eyes with the palms of his hands.

Monroe pulled in front of the emergency room entrance and waited for Riley to get out and then pulled to the side parking lot, searching for a space. He jogged through the doors, joining Riley before he could get the nurse's attention.

"What's your complaint?" The nurse's monotone voice grated in his ears.

"I have a concussion. Just not sure how serious it is," Riley informed her.

"Oh, you diagnosed that yourself?" She pursed her lips and raised a single eyebrow, twirling a pen through her fingers. It showed off her overly long acrylic nails, done in an obtrusive pea green that was not a flattering color.

"No, the paramedics did after they responded to the assault scene where I was knocked unconscious for..." Riley looked at Monroe.

"At least seven to ten minutes," Monroe answered.

Officer Ayers sauntered through the emergency room doors. "Strong, heard you were jumped."

The nurse's attitude changed as soon as the officer joined them. "I'll get a doctor right away for you, sir. Please fill this out."

He took the clipboard from her and swiped a pen from the cupholder outside the window that surrounded her station. He ripped the stupid pink daisy flower that was secured to the end with gauze tape and threw it down on the counter. Why did people have to add such annoying things to something as simple as a pen?

"Who did you tangle with now?" Ayers placed his hands on either side of his duty belt and watched Riley fill out the admittance form.

"I don't know. You'd have to ask Monroe. He caught it on the cameras outside of Annie's house." Riley scrawled his name at the bottom of the form and rose to hand it back to the nurse.

"It was Alan's friends," Monroe offered.

"Well, that's a violation of their court order to stay away from you and Annie." Ayers grabbed his notebook out and furiously wrote. "What time did this happen?"

Monroe pulled up his phone and tapped a few times on the screen. "Fourteen-thirty-four."

"I heard they caused a ruckus at the jail downtown, trying to get Alan out of lockup early." Ayers almost smiled.

"That is where they were served with the full orders, so they know they aren't supposed to be at Annie's," Riley offered for Ayers to include in his report.

He nodded and jotted it down in his notebook before sliding it back into his front shirt pocket.

The doctor stepped out and called Riley's name. Monroe and Ayers sauntered out of the building as the nurse pulled the curtain around the non-private emergency room bed.

"So, I heard you were knocked in the head and lost consciousness."

"Yes ma'am." Riley hated hospitals. It reminded him of his wife. He missed her still, even though it had been eight years. She was his rock in life, and when she was gone, he felt lost until he found her Bible in the bottom drawer of her nightstand one night as he looked for anything of hers to hold onto.

It was worn and the pages were marked up with colored pens. He started reading where her bookmark was; it talked about God's love and plan for His children. He remembered the bitter feeling that if God loved His children, why would He let them suffer like his wife did? He kept reading and it talked about the gifts in heaven. He crumpled next to the bed and cried himself to sleep. When he woke the next day, he continued reading. He couldn't stop, he was hooked. The next Sunday he didn't work, he visited the church she'd attended, and felt odd. She'd talked about how great the pastor was and that he preached directly from the Bible.

He sat in the far back pew and didn't talk to anyone and avoided eye contact. He didn't know the words to any of the songs they sang. Something stirred inside him. He left there confused about his feelings and went back home to read more from the Bible. Several weeks later, he went forward during a benediction and accepted Jesus as his personal savior. The emotions that overwhelmed him almost scared him away from going back, but he did, and that was over seven years ago.

As the doctor was going through his exam, he wondered what Annie believed. He thought about her smile as the doctor asked him a question. He didn't hear it. "I'm sorry, what did you ask?"

The doctor frowned. "We need to get you in for a scan if possible. You do have a concussion, but I'm not overly concerned about it. Your vitals are good and according to your chart, you aren't unfamiliar with concussions and are not always the most cooperative patient when it comes to staying at hospitals for any length of time."

"So, can I go? I know to come back if I have a persistent headache, vomiting, or slurred speech."

"Have someone stay with you to monitor you over the next day or so." He scribbled on his chart and left the room.

Riley sighed. Another thing he would need to worry about while Alan's men were after Annie. He was ready to get out of the hospital and see what they could dig up on Alan. They were already down an afternoon and needed to take advantage of every second he was locked up to dig up dirt on him.

Monroe and Ayers lingered outside the doors when he exited the emergency room. "Let's go."

"What did the doc say?" Monroe unlocked the car.

"Someone needs to keep an eye on me." With Monroe's chuckle, Riley turned toward Ayers. "We need to get Alan charged before he leaves detention. How fast can we get reports pulled from the other county?"

"I already have some calls in to friends at the state level. I pulled in some favors on this one. I should hear back from them shortly. I'll keep you up to date on what I find." Ayers jumped behind the wheel of his cruiser and pulled out of the lot a few seconds later.

"Take me to Annie's." Riley leaned back and closed his eyes as Monroe angled the car out of the parking space. He had a headache, if you could categorize the pounding and pain as a simple headache, but tried to ignore it.

"Bear said she's still out. How much did she drink?" Monroe's eyes never left the road.

"Two bottles."

"That's a lot for someone her size. Unless she drinks like that all the time."

"No, I don't think she does. She was shocked by the revelation about her parents. I'm sure the abuse she took didn't bother her as much as finding out about their death by her abuser's hand. She will blame herself." Riley opened his eyes.

"That wasn't her fault," Monroe countered.

"She won't see it that way. She'll blame herself for not leaving him sooner. I know how victims blame themselves for everything. Even if I told her he probably would have killed them whether she left him or not, it wouldn't matter. She'll still question everything around that time and wonder whether she could have stopped it." Riley sat forward as they pulled into Annie's driveway.

He felt his pocket for his cell phone. It wasn't there. He let them in through the front door. Bear peered around the wall, gun in hand. He shook his head when he saw Riley and motioned with his head toward the kitchen as he holstered his weapon. Annie stood behind the counter with bread, meat, cheeses, and condiments all laid out.

"Bear, what do you like on your sandwich?" she asked.

Riley smirked and raised his eyebrows at him.

"I tried to tell her I don't need her making me no sandwich, but she insisted," Bear stammered.

She spread her hands over the items on the counter and motioned to all three of them.

"I'd love a sandwich, but I can make it." Riley joined Annie at her right side.

She flinched when he reached for the bread. She set the knife on the counter for him while she stood on her tiptoes to get another plate. He reached past her to help and watched her knuckles turn white as she gripped the counter and closed her eyes. He smiled at her and handed her the plate.

"Thanks." She slid it over to where he stood at the countertop slathering mayonnaise on the bread. "I heard you were hurt today."

"I was walking your perimeter as part of your contract. I found two sections of fence that had been cut away. As I was inspecting the cuts, someone hit me in the head. I think it was Alan's two friends." Riley piled on the deli meat and cheese and handed it to Bear.

"Sam and Mark?" Annie offered.

"Yes," Bear said around the huge bite he took of his sandwich.

Annie smirked then frowned. "I thought they were still in jail from the attack in my house yesterday."

"They made bail. Alan is still in for the rest of today and two more days after that. So, we at least have him out of the way." Riley finished constructing his sandwich and placed all the items on the counter back in the refrigerator before taking a bite. Monroe declined one for himself.

Annie silently walked out of the kitchen and came back and placed four over-the-counter pain pills in front of him, before she grabbed two bottles of water from the door in the refrigerator.

"I only need two." Riley grabbed two pills from the brown swirled marble surface and took the bottle she offered him.

"Yeah, the other two are for me." She blushed as she popped the other two in her mouth.

"Are you okay?" Riley gazed down at her waiting for a response.

Annie pursed her lips together before meeting his eyes. "Yeah, I will be. Although food will help absorb the rest of the alcohol in my system."

"I'm sorry for not telling you immediately when we found out."

"No, you were right. I would have been too emotional to be any good in that courtroom today." Annie ventured to the chairs by the back windows.

"Alan's two friends were also served with the court orders today when they tried to get him out of jail. They will be charged with being on your property and in violation of that order and the assault on me for mine." Riley stood next to her.

"But what good does that do if they can't catch them?" Annie appeared so much shorter than he was when she didn't wear shoes. She didn't even come up to his shoulders.

"We will. I promise you that." Riley noticed Tracker working his way to the house from the perimeter fence.

Annie grabbed his arm, her hand like a vice grip. "I just want this to be over."

Riley placed his hand over hers. "That's what I'm trying to do." She didn't flinch but managed a smile. His heart raced and he nodded to her.

Tracker let himself in through the back door. "Sir?"

"Go ahead, she needs to know everything on her case." Riley wouldn't keep anything from her. She needed to know what she was up against. Maybe it would help her to find the strength to fight against him one more time.

"They came in on foot from approximately a mile away. They had a car waiting. When we gave chase, they were able to get away. They had Alan's Porsche this time. We were able to get a video of them leaving the area. You can see who's driving and who's in the passenger seat. It will be hard to explain what they were doing here against court orders." Tracker nodded to Annie.

"Thanks. Can you get that information and video to Officer Ayers? He's taking lead on this and has involved some friends on the state level." Riley stepped to the side for Tracker to leave by way of the front door. Bear joined him and handed him several file folders. He nodded and left.

"What's that?" Annie eyed the folders, her pulse in her neck quickened as she swallowed hard.

He knew she saw the same files that Ayers had perused earlier and wasn't sure if she had been too inebriated to remember the one on her parents was in there also. "Everything we have on your case. I promised to share everything with you."

She squared her shoulders and motioned to the dining room table. "I'm sorry about earlier."

"It's okay. I have no clue what you're going through, but we're here for you and will get you through this." Riley spread the folders out in front of her in the same order he showed them to Ayers, leaving her parents' murder for last. "Start with these two. There are some graphic photos in there that may be hard to look at. Just let me know if it's too much, and I'll redact what you don't want to see."

Annie inhaled deeply and held her breath for a split second before she released it, straightened her spine, and opened the file for Alan's first wife. She quietly read each sheet of information Riley had. After reading a page she would turn it over and continue with the next one. When she got to the pictures of the injuries, she silently cried. He got the sense that she knew the pain and fear these women went through at the hand of this monster. She closed the first folder and pulled the next one toward her and opened it to the first page.

She read the second one in the same fashion. The second set of pictures didn't make her cry this time. She was angry. He stiffened as she reached for her parents' folder. He didn't remember breathing while she read it. The pictures of the damaged vehicle didn't seem to be new to her.

"Okay, explain these to me, please." She spread every picture out on the table in the order they were in the folder.

Riley pulled a chair next to hers and pointed to the first picture. "Okay, see the damage to this side of the bumper?"

She nodded.

"This is paint transfer from another vehicle hitting this section. The report showed they had a new vehicle. There wouldn't be damage on this area of the vehicle if the brakes failed causing them to careen down a hill and die from a front-end impact crash like they put in the report. There would only be damage to the front because that impacted the tree."

"Okay, what about this one? The same thing?" She slid the next photo over onto the first one.

"Sort of. This dent shows something impacted the rear bumper, but this is not from the same hit as the first one. There were two impact points causing your parents to lose control. But again, there wouldn't be any damage to these two sections of their car if they had indeed had a front-end impact. Notice the airbags deployed from the rear, showing that the hit on the rear was enough to deploy the rear and side bags. If it was a front collision, only the front airbags would deploy." Riley glanced at her to see if it was registering what he was telling her.

"Okay." She slid the next two pictures over, her fingers trembling. "These are showing that they hit the tree, right?"

"Yes, self-explanatory. The car should look like that from this angle with brakes failing and them hitting at a high speed."

Annie pushed the explained pictures out of the way and put the last picture in front of her. "This is cut. This isn't a failed brake line, is it?"

"You're right. It's cut. I think the police department that tried to work this crash before county deputies appeared on the scene kept this evidence for a reason. To cover them if something was ruled differently than County decided on this crash. There are times when County supersedes city ordinances, especially if it's a rural road where this occurred. Cities have no problem stepping aside on a crash where people died and letting County or even a crash on a highway be taken over by that agency, such as highway patrol." Riley waited for another question but none came.

"My parent's death isn't my fault. I wanted to blame myself today for the fact that if I had left him after the first time he hit me, they would still be alive. Now, I don't think that's true. He would have killed them for sport just to hurt me, whether I stayed with him or left." She clenched her fist in her lap.

"I think you're right. He planned on killing them no matter whether you were with him or not. He's had his friends cover up his crimes for so long that he feels he's above the law now. I think this started before his first wife. I need to call my office and get them to look at Alan's past before his first marriage and see what they can dig up. It may not be enough to help with these cases, but I also don't believe his first wife was his first victim." Riley gathered the folders together and stood and then moved the chair back around to the side of the table.

Annie's hand covered his in an instant. "Thanks for showing me these."

"I'm sorry about your parents." Riley's eyebrows pinched together as his headache grew worse.

"Are you okay?" Annie stood.

"Yeah, head just hurts a little." He shoved the files into his briefcase.

"Did you get checked out for that?"

"Yes, concussion, but I'm just supposed to have someone stay with me to make sure I'm doing okay." Riley didn't tell her that the doctor wanted to do a scan.

"Well, I can make up the couch for you, then we can keep an eye on each other." Annie blushed and hurried to the hall closet, snagging sheets and blankets from the shelf. She busied herself making up the couch for him to sleep on.

Riley pulled his phone from his pocket and called Bear. "Hey, see what you can dig up on Alan before his first wife. I'm thinking there's no way she's his first victim. There had to be cases leading up to her. Maybe we can get some dirt on him he won't expect us to be able to find."

"Yup." Bear disconnected.

"I have to ask..." Annie interrupted his thoughts.

"Sure, anything." Riley spun on his heels toward her.

"So, Bear, huh?" She smiled.

Riley laughed. "His last name starts with Bear and because of his size, people started calling him that, even back in school. It stuck and as long as I've known him, since we were kids, we've called him that. If anyone called him by his given name, he probably wouldn't answer."

"What's his given name?"

"Shamus Bearden." Riley chuckled when Annie full-on belly laughed. It was an amazing sound that touched him deep in his heart. He hadn't felt that since his wife.

Annie smiled again as she held a blanket in her arms. His heart raced. The sun was starting to set. His men knew he was staying at her house tonight to keep an eye on things. Tracker was in the wooded area behind her estate while

Erickson watched the front gate. Bear was on duty at the office, monitoring all exterior cameras.

"I'm going to make sure everything is locked up." Riley strolled to the front door and let himself out. The sky was bathed in purple hues as the sun hit the horizon. He was curious what tonight would hold with Alan's goons still on the loose. At least with Alan in jail, he would be the one they wouldn't need to worry about as they tried to catch some sleep.

The walk-through gate was unlocked. He frowned. This shouldn't be unsecured. He knelt to inspect the locking mechanism and found someone had wedged rocks into where the latch would catch, securing the gate. He pulled a knife from his pocket and dug the pebbles out then closed the gate. It was now secured. He sent a text to Bear to keep an eye on it overnight. Bear acknowledged his text and Riley started back for the house when Alan's Porsche roared by as they gunned the engine, flying past the house as soon as they saw him. He shook his head. They just didn't give up. He sent a text to Ayers, who let him know they would put extra patrol in the area for the night.

He was sure they wouldn't hesitate to let Alan know he was staying in the house with her. Alan would be furious. Riley almost smiled as he thought about him sitting in a jail cell for the next two days, stewing over the fact that he was with her.

As he closed and locked the front door, Annie approached the railing at the top of the stairs. She wore a pale pink tank top and dark heather gray shorts. He couldn't tear his eyes from her.

"Is everything okay?" She took a step back, clutching a hand to her throat.

"Looks like they messed with the lock on the walk-through gate. I fixed it and it's now secure. They drove by while I was out there. Alan will find out soon enough I'm staying here tonight. Even though it's for security, he will put his own evil spin on it to justify what he wants to do to you." Riley had promised her he wouldn't keep anything from her. He waited to see how she took the news.

"Won't his head explode when he finds out," she stated with a smile, and then she disappeared through her bedroom door. The soft snick of the latch echoed down into the foyer.

Riley laughed and strolled to the back door. It was already locked. The office was his next stop. He keyed up all the exterior cameras. He didn't need to dedicate any of the monitors to the interior, since he was here with her, so he could view every angle the cameras picked up outside. His head was pounding and his vision doubled. He fished pain pills out of his briefcase and snagged his bottle of water from the dining room table. He doubled the suggested dose and hoped his headache didn't get in the way of monitoring the house to keep Annie safe.

Footsteps behind him caused him to jump out of the chair and spin around on his heels, gun in hand.

Annie's hand flew to her mouth as her eyes widened.

"I'm sorry, I should have realized it was you." Riley held up his left hand while he holstered his gun with his right.

"No, I shouldn't have walked up behind you like that. I wanted to make sure you had everything you needed. If you're hungry or thirsty, just help yourself to whatever you find." Annie backed up to the stairs, her eyes still on Riley before she scurried up the steps as fast as her ribs let her.

Riley shook his head. He probably scared her as much as she startled him. He closed his eyes as he sat back in the chair to watch the monitors.

Riley sat up, eyes wide, and stared at the cameras. He'd fallen asleep and checked his watch. It was after midnight.

Not sure what woke him, he panned the cameras around. His phone buzzed in his pocket, and he struggled to fish it out. "Yup."

"Did you see something? I saw you panning the cameras." It was Bear.

"No, fell asleep and wasn't sure what woke me." Riley rose out of the chair and peered around the doorway.

"Nothing has moved all night. Tracker is still secure in the back wooded area while Erickson is back at his vehicle after walking the perimeter. Oh, by the way, there *is* a gap in the hedgerow to the neighbors to the west. Probably how that cranky old codger got into her yard. I have it flagged to install a fence along that section also." Bear yawned through the phone.

"Thanks. I'm going to lay down and try to get some decent sleep instead of sitting up in this chair all night." Riley disconnected and tucked his phone back into his pocket.

Someone moved around upstairs. He pulled his weapon and edged around the corner to stand at the bottom of the stairs. It was quiet as he stood motionless. Maybe it was Annie? He didn't want to scare her again but knew if he didn't check on her, he wouldn't get any sleep. Gun in hand, he took the steps one at a time and checked the upper level, sweeping his eyes back and forth. Two steps from the top, he heard another noise. It came from the bedroom on the right across from Annie's.

He backed up to Annie's room and glanced in at her bed. She was asleep, curled up on her side to keep her injured ribs up like they did for her when they first helped her.

"Annie?" Riley whispered. His back was to her while he aimed his gun across the vacant hallway from her room.

She rolled to her other side and grunted. Then she rolled back to her non-injured side.

He stepped back to the end of the bed and whispered again. "Annie?"

She bolted into a sitting position. "What's wrong?"

"Get to your panic room. I'm hearing noises in the room across the landing." Riley glanced over his shoulder to make sure she headed to the reinforced room.

"Come with me!" Annie reached for him.

"I can't. Now go!" He stalked to her open door and waited until he heard the door secure in the back of her closet.

He decided to wait and see what made the sound first before calling in the calvary. The house was secure. The perimeter checked. There was no way someone could have made it past everyone to get inside, much less past the locks. One foot in front of the other, he edged to the door next to Annie's. Peering around the corner, he flipped the switch, illuminating the room. No one hid in the spare room. Being thorough, he checked the closet, and then he turned off the light and worked his way around the upper landing to the room directly across from Annie's and grasped the lever door handle. With a deep breath held in, he pushed down on the lever, easing the door open. A muzzle flash flared in front of him, sending orbs of light dancing in his field of vision as something hit his shoulder. He dropped to one knee and fired back, emptying his clip. He aimed for center mass where the flash emanated from.

Sixteen

The front door flew open at the same time the back door slammed into the back wall. "Riley!" Tracker and Erickson's voices intermingled.

Riley turned on the light to someone slumped onto the floor. Blood pooled under the body. "Up here."

Their thunderous footsteps echoed up the stairs and off the walls in the room he stood in.

"You okay?" They both asked in unison

"Yeah, get the police out here." Riley turned and passed them on the way to Annie's room. He quietly knocked on the panic room door and waited for the pressure seal to release, telling him she was opening the door. With the woosh of the seal, he holstered his gun. Her wide eyes let him know how scared she was as she stood there trembling.

"It's okay." He winced when he moved his arm.

"Oh, my gosh! You're shot!" Annie flew out of the closet and dug around in her bathroom vanity, pulling gauze and bandages out by fistfuls.

"I think it's just a graze." He winced when he pulled his shirt sleeve away from his arm.

"Let me see that." She grabbed a pair of scissors and proceeded to cut the sleeve of his shirt from him.

"Police!" someone bellowed from downstairs.

"Up here, Officer. I have my firearm on my hip and both my employees are armed. We have one suspect down for good. I haven't finished clearing the rest of the house," Riley announced as he sauntered toward the railing. Blood ran down his arm.

"Leave your hands where I can see them!" the officers announced as they started up the stairs.

He held his hands in surrender as they walked up the set of steps, guns drawn. Riley's employees did the same, keeping their empty hands in plain sight. The first officer took Riley's firearm and tucked it into the back of his pants before holstering his weapon. He took cuffs out and clipped them around one of Riley's wrists. He grunted as the pressure of his arm wrenched behind his back pulled at his wound.

His partner did the same with Erickson and Tracker, who complied with his orders. They marched Riley's employees downstairs as Annie came out of her bedroom with bandages in her hand. "What are you doing? Can't you see he's been shot!"

The officer pointed his gun at her and ordered her down to the ground. She dropped the bandages as Officer Ayers came through the front door. One glance up the stairs and he holstered his weapon and his partner followed suit. "Officer, she's the homeowner and she's okay. Annie, come on down to me." Ayers motioned for her to join him.

Tracker and Erickson sat on the couch side by side. Annie trembled as she grabbed the bandages off the floor and walked around the officer, giving him a wide berth. Ayers put his hand on her shoulder. "Are you alright?"

She furiously nodded and he motioned her to where the others sat.

"Officer, you can uncuff him. He's part of her security detail, and they were issued full protection orders today, which I was a witness for." Ayers nodded to Riley.

"Thanks." Riley held his arm as the officer finished taking off his cuffs. "Ayers, the body is in the room across from Annie's. Looks like one of Alan's men didn't follow the orders. He fired first and I returned fire. My aim was better." He locked eyes with Ayers as he passed him in the foyer.

Ayers took the stairs two at a time while his partner radioed in for the coroner to respond together with an ambulance. After only a couple of minutes, he reappeared at the top of the stairs. "Riley, there's no gun up there."

"That's not possible. There was a muzzle flash, and I returned fire!" He started to rise, causing the officers to place their hands on their holsters. He turned to Erickson and Tracker, who nodded that they had seen the gun.

Eyeing the other two officers that had been in the room before Ayers got there, Riley had a bad feeling.

Monroe appeared at the front door with his medical bag slung over his shoulder. Ayers pointed to Riley's location, where Annie held bandages against his shoulder. "Okay, let me see what you have here." Monroe slipped gloves on his hands and lifted the bandages that Annie held over the wound.

"Well, can you clean it up and take care of it?" Riley grunted when Monroe inspected it.

"You need stitches. It looks like it just tore through the outer muscle and didn't hit anything important." Monroe covered the wound back up and wrapped gauze around it to secure it in place.

An ambulance pulled up out front, the lights reflecting off the police car windows flooding the interior of the house with the famous red-and-blue lights penetrating through the night.

Riley glared at Ayers, who was typing something into his phone. "Hey, don't look at me like that. You know the procedure. You were shot; we order an ambulance. And this doesn't look good with there not being a weapon."

"Yeah, because I shot myself." Riley glared at Ayers before meeting Monroe's stare. "Why don't you follow the trajectory and go find that bullet and show it doesn't match my gun."

Monroe raised an eyebrow at him. He knew it wasn't right to take his frustration out on Ayers, who was only doing his job. The first two officers were in a huddle by the front door and kept squinting at him as if he was the criminal. One disappeared out the door for several minutes as they waited patiently for a supervisor and paramedics and then approached.

"You said you have filed several reports regarding that man upstairs?" He folded his arms over his scrawny chest, trying to make himself larger than he was.

"Yes." Riley wasn't sure what he was getting at.

He took a second to peer over his shoulder and then back at Riley. "Our system doesn't show any reports filed with you as a victim or otherwise."

They were interrupted when the paramedics came through the door and headed straight for him; he knew the drill. It was standard procedure for any officer on the scene of a shooting. They plodded over to Riley. With a check of his bandage, they nodded to indicate that they would prefer to transport him. He signed the decline of services page and said he would drive himself. The paramedics packed up their bags and left.

Riley took in Monroe's and Tracker's frowns as Ayers finished putting police tape up on the doorway to the spare room as more officers arrived together with a couple of detectives. Riley nodded to the new additions in Annie's house. He had worked with most of them during his years as sergeant at the local department.

It was troubling knowing that there were no reports in the system showing the danger they dealt with over the last couple of weeks. He knew they wouldn't have a problem with this case being self-defense if they could find the pistol, but the missing police reports seemed to be a bigger problem. Hopefully, they were smart enough to know he had been shot and was the victim, even if they couldn't find the weapon itself. The bullet that grazed him just had to be found. Pain radiated down his arm through his elbow when he moved. At least having the full orders would go a long way toward proving self-defense since the man upstairs went against a court order and broke in. He knew they still had to go through the proper procedures to process the scene.

Riley pulled out statement forms for his men to fill out. They were already printed in the format the police department demanded. He winced when he moved his right shoulder to grab a pen to start his statement. He blew out his breath, black dots clouding his vision, sat down heavily on the edge of the couch, and documented every detail of the events that led up to him taking a life.

Ayers joined him but didn't say a word as Riley finished his form. He motioned for him to join him outside. Once out of earshot of Annie, he said, "Okay, do you want to tell me what happened? I already know you were in the right with the full orders and the fact they were in violation of that being in her house. Yet the fact he wasn't armed doesn't explain the bullet graze in your bicep. But walk me through it."

Should he bring up the police reports Ayers said he submitted on his behalf or keep that tidbit to himself? "Everything is exactly as I explained in my statement that's ready to go." Riley waited for Ayers to acknowledge everything he told him.

"Well, he was in her house without permission and direct violation of the judge's full orders. I'll write it up as self-defense, but we still need to figure out about the weapon. It will still have to go to the prosecutor per procedure, but I think you're good here. I'll see how fast I can push it through to have them look at it and decide from there without having the bullet since there is no sign that it hit a wall or anything behind where you were standing. Since this occurred over the stairwell, we may never find that evidence. Sorry, but it will be a while before you get your firearm back." Ayers peered around Riley. "How's Annie holding up?"

"I haven't had a chance to talk to her about any of this. She used my injury to keep herself busy when I first got her out of the secure room in her closet. I'm going to see if I can get her to come back to the office with me and stay in the extra apartment there where it's more secure than her house.

They cut sections of fence from the back. That is why Tracker and Erickson were on-scene so fast. They were already on the property patrolling the breaches in the fence line." Riley blew out a breath.

The pain in his shoulder had gotten worse. He hated to admit it, but he would need to head to the hospital soon. However, he didn't want to leave Annie here without knowing how she was doing.

The question of where the second goon had gone wasn't lost on his men. They knew those two always went everywhere together. But with only one being in the house, he didn't want her to be alone until they could figure out where the other one was.

Tracker approached him when he strolled in from talking to Ayers. "I didn't see anything outside and no tracks from behind the property that weren't there from the other day. He didn't come in through that direction."

"Okay, we need to find the second one. We need someone to stay with Annie until I get back from the hospital." Riley winced when he moved his shoulder.

"Erickson and I won't let her out of our sight," Tracker assured him.

"I'm going to see if she'll go with you guys back to the office and stay there until we get this taken care of." Riley dreaded the conversation that he was about to have with her.

Annie eagerly stood as he approached. "Can you tell me what's going on?"

"They have to process the scene. The coroner will take a little time to get here and take custody of the body for the autopsy. They will ask you for your statement, which you already filled out, but they will also take you to the police department for a video statement. Just tell them exactly what you know and be truthful. If you didn't see anything, just tell them that." Riley wiped sweat from his brow with the back of his hand.

"Shouldn't you go to the hospital?" Annie started to reach for him but pulled her hand back at the last moment.

"I'm getting ready to go, but I wanted to ask that you go with Tracker and Erickson to the office and stay there. They won't be able to get into the building like they got into the house." He hoped she wouldn't want to argue about it and prayed she would see that the best option for them to keep her safe would be to go with them.

"Is that my only option?" Annie glanced upstairs at the yellow tape that stretched across the opening.

"Annie." Riley stepped in front of her view of the upstairs. "We can keep you safer there."

She locked eyes with him. "And how long am I supposed to stay there? For the rest of my life? When does this finally end?"

"I don't know but until we can sit down and come up with a plan of action, it's your safest alternative. If you can just give me two days, then we can sit down after I get back and see what our options are."

Annie only shook her head as Ayers approached them.

"Miss Divers, can I have one of my officers take you to the department for an official interview since you are the owner of the house and the victim of the violation of the full order?" Ayers eyed Riley who wiped his hand across his brow again. Riley ignored him.

"Sure, let me change. Am I allowed to go back to my room?" Annie was halfway to the staircase when she turned around.

Ayers nodded. "Yes, you're okay to go to your room. We already finished in there."

Annie disappeared up the stairs and into her room, closing the door behind her. Riley turned to Ayers. "Don't let her out of your sight. I need to go to the hospital. I'll send Tracker with your officer so when she's done, he can take her to the apartment at the office."

"You don't look so good. I don't think you should be driving." Ayers frowned.

"Erickson, I need you to take me to the hospital." Riley swiped at his forehead again.

"Yes, sir." He jogged through the front door to pull the car around.

Riley didn't want to leave before Annie got back downstairs to him and he made sure she was on her way to the police station with an officer.

"Hey, I'll watch her until we get her in the car and en route to the station."

He turned to Ayers and nodded, heading out to the Audi in which Erickson pulled up in front of the house. Riley turned back to Ayers, who motioned for him to go to the hospital and then pulled his phone from his pocket, typing as Riley headed out the door. He dropped into the passenger seat, leaned his head back, and closed his eyes as they pulled onto the street.

Seventeen

The hospital was packed. They were moved to the front of the line due to his being a gunshot wound. Riley provided the police report number to the emergency room staff along with Ayers's name and badge number. They politely called dispatch, who confirmed his story, and after the confirmation, they whisked him off to be seen by the doctor.

The doctor verified he would need stitches to close up the wound but didn't feel it was necessary that he would need anything more than that. Over an hour later, Riley was on his way out the door to Erickson, who waited in the Audi, after antibiotics and pain meds were prescribed.

Riley's phone buzzed in his pocket, and he wrestled it out with his left hand. "Yeah, Ayers."

"They got her! Mark Murphy was out there waiting. He ran my officer off the road and took Miss Divers!" Ayers's frustration and anger seeped through the phone.

"What?" Riley shot up in his seat.

"We're investigating the crash now. Officer Manning is on the way to the hospital. Riley, there is blood in the car on the passenger side where Annie was sitting. Manning called out an assist. When dispatch broadcast it, every available unit responded. They were already gone before we got there. Tracker is also trying to see what he can find and is on-scene with the officers."

"Where?" Riley's shout caused Erickson to raise an eyebrow. How could he let this happen? Why didn't Tracker stop him? He knew he should have waited for Annie to make it to the police department before he went to the hospital. He flexed his fingers before curling them into fists hitting his thighs; his lungs expanded with each exaggerated inhale. His muscles quivered and heat flushed through his body.

Erickson watched him out of the corner of his eye. Riley just shook his head. With the location from Ayers, he had Erickson reroute to the scene. Maybe Tracker could get what vehicle they left in or any sort of trail if they were on foot; it would be the best place to start. Alan was still in jail for the next two days, and he had no doubt that he would want to deal with her himself and his goon wouldn't have permission to do anything to her. At least that's what he prayed for.

He jumped out of the vehicle and shifted his arm in the sling before joining Ayers and Tracker. "Tell me you have something."

"Looks like they got into another vehicle at this point. Burned rubber from the tires as they left the scene shows they headed east. The treads are from high-end sports tires. Paint transfer shows a silver sedan is the one that hit them. I think he used Alan's Porsche. He won't be happy about that." Tracker motioned to the impact site where Riley could see the silver flecks of paint embedded in the side of the black and white patrol vehicle.

"Ayers. How's the officer? And what happened? I thought you were following her to the station and then would take her back to the apartments." Riley turned on his heels and faced Tracker.

"That was my fault," Ayers answered. "I misplaced Tracker's statement and couldn't let him leave the scene until he wrote out another one. I didn't think it was that big of a deal and that Mark would be out there watching for her. The officer was unconscious when they transported him. Other than that, we aren't sure. I had an officer follow the ambulance, and he will give us updates as soon as he knows anything."

"Okay, I'll say prayers for him. In the meantime, how do we figure out where they could have gone? Have you sent anyone to check on Alan's hotel room?"

"Yes, no one is there, and they don't have any record of his car coming back. Looks like his friend took it out approximately twenty-one hundred hours last night. Coincidentally, the time corresponds with the suspect being at her home. The one who is no longer in play, Sam Berger." Ayers signed the tow sheet and backed up for them to load the vehicle onto the flatbed.

Riley yanked his phone out of his pocket. "Bear."

"Sir."

"See where the tracker is on the Porsche." Riley noted the look on Ayers's face when he mentioned the tracker and then slipped his phone into his pocket. "Don't ask."

"I don't want to know." Ayers keyed up his mic. "Dispatch, please enter Miss Divers as missing, endangered involuntary." Dispatch didn't answer back, but maybe the radio volume was down enough that Riley couldn't hear it.

After the tow truck loaded up the cruiser, the two of them were the last on-scene with Erickson and Tracker headed back to the office. A lot of blood evidence was on the passenger side of the vehicle. His heart thundered in his chest. They had to find her before Alan got out of jail or he would take her back where he could dispose of her and have his friends sweep it under the rug.

His phone rang. "Go."

"Car is down a ravine, just off Highway 24 after mile marker 47." Bear's voice strained through the phone.

"Ayers!" Riley slid his phone into his pocket and jogged to the police cruiser.

"Where at?" Ayers already had his door open, joining Riley.

"Highway 24, just past the Main Street exit." Riley grabbed the seatbelt with his left hand, keeping his right arm in the sling pinned to his body, and pulled it across his chest to buckle in before Ayers put the cruiser in gear.

Their lights and sirens pierced the night as they tore down the road to the location Riley had given his friend. He prayed she wasn't in the car. He was all too familiar with how they worked crashes into their ways of disposing of bodies. He swallowed past the lump as he started to say something and then changed his mind. As they rounded the curve in the highway, lights already sliced through the night, bouncing off the leaves on trees and road signs. The fire truck's water hoses and ropes disappeared over the edge of the embankment. Billows of smoke drifted toward them, shifting and changing shapes as the wind caught and carried it away.

Riley jumped out of the vehicle and bolted to the edge of the road. Ayers caught up with him and held him back with the help of two firefighters when he tried to go over the edge to the car.

"You can't go down there, sir!" One of the firefighters practically shoved him back to keep him from going over the edge. The behemoth of a firefighter towered over Riley with his gear on. He wasn't so sure he wouldn't put Bear's size to shame with his.

"Annie!" He murmured through gritted teeth.

"We don't know if she's even down there yet." Ayers steered him back to his cruiser.

"This is how they dispose of the wives he's killed. He stages crashes over embankments, with ejections. He's throwing it in our face that he can get away with murder! He thinks he's above the law. That he's untouchable. This is the games he plays that Annie warned me about. He sees how far he can push things and what he can get away with. He has the perfect alibi, he's in jail," Riley ranted before stepping forward when he saw a firefighter coming up the rope draped over the edge.

The wire basket with a body strapped down, partially covered with plastic, cleared the top, and wind caught the tarp and blew it back from a small-framed person that was so badly burned they were unrecognizable. He turned away from the scene and blew out the deep breath he sucked in when he saw the corpse and tried not to concentrate on the rolling in his stomach, breathing through his mouth, his free hand landing on his knee as he bent over.

"Stay here. I'm going to see what I can find out." Ayers squeezed his shoulder and jogged to the officers at the scene.

Riley sat on the hood of Ayers's cruiser and dropped his head into his hand. He failed her; he couldn't believe this was how it ended. Alan would get away with this; he sat in jail. There was no better alibi than that. He slid his phone out of his pocket and dialed Bear.

"Did you find her?" Bear's eager voice drifted through the phone.

"I failed her. They pulled a body from the wreckage. They'll need dental records to identify her. Alan knew what to do this time. We may have tipped our hand letting him know we knew he killed his first two wives. She's burned beyond recognition." Riley clenched the fist that didn't hold the phone.

Ayers joined Riley as he hung up. "We'll have to use dental for this. I've already got detectives putting in the request for the coroner's office. Riley, I'm sorry."

"Yeah, me too. We need to find Mark. He's the only other person who had access to Alan's car since I shot Sam at Annie's." As he mentioned her name, his heart stuttered.

"Hey. We're going to get him on this." Ayers walked away to answer his radio and rejoined his fellow officers but glanced back at him several times.

Riley turned when the coroner's van pulled up. The man behind the wheel was hunched over as he hopped out of the driver's side and bumbled around in the back to release the catch on the gurney. The wheels hit the ground hard as he yanked it from the van. The man almost tripped as he pushed it over to the rescue basket. As he spoke with the paramedics, Riley frowned. Something felt off.

The paramedics lifted the body bag onto the gurney and signed the form the man gave them. He quickly shuffled to the back of the van almost, stumbling over his feet. Riley hopped off the front of the cruiser as he closed the doors at the back of the van. The man nodded to him and jumped behind the wheel. Cranking the engine over, he put the van in reverse and turned it around, heading away from the crash.

Riley frowned. "Hey, Ayers."

"Yeah." He joined him as the van's taillights disappeared in the dark.

"Did you know him?"

"The coroner?" Ayers stared after the van.

Riley glanced behind him as the fire department started pulling their hoses coiling them back up to be ready for the next emergency. "Yeah, I haven't seen him before."

"I didn't notice. I was getting details of how the call for service came in from Simons."

"What can you tell me?" Riley crossed his arms, winced, and uncrossed them.

"Witness said they saw the car go over. Female in the driver's seat. No one else was in the car. It was a silver Porsche, plates respond to Alan Montgomery, who, as we know, is in jail. Description matches Annie's. Also, the pieces of clothing still on the body match what I saw her wearing when the officer transported her to the station." Ayers flipped closed the notebook in which he had written down everything.

Riley nodded, opened his mouth to say something, and then closed it again. His head pounded as his heart raced, hammering in his chest. He needed to regroup, think things through and figure out his next move. Right now he wasn't thinking right. Tracker pulled up on-scene but didn't get out of the vehicle. "Ayers, if you need me, I'll be back at the office," Riley mumbled as he rubbed his hand across his chest.

He didn't look back as he lumbered to the Audi and got into the passenger side. This happened way too fast. They had to have been watching the house. He would need to pull up the footage to see if they could spot the Porsche following the officer out of the neighborhood. There was a knot in his stomach. There was so much more he should have done to keep her safe. He even knew what he was up against. He had her file for days!

He sighed and Tracker didn't say a word or even look at him. They were all thinking it. They lost this one big time, and they wouldn't recover anytime soon. Riley bolted out of the car before Tracker finished putting it in park and let himself in through the back entrance. He stormed into his office and dropped into his chair and put his head in his hand with one elbow perched on the edge of his solid oak desk.

The desk was the last thing his wife ordered for him before she died. She wanted him to know how much she believed in him and his dream of starting a security company. He ran his hands over the oak, feeling the grain of the wood under the finish. It was a beautiful desk. Simple, like him, yet solid, it was perfect and exactly what he would have ordered.

Annie's face flashed through his mind. He opened his eyes and slid his laptop over and furiously typed, his fingers hitting the keys with ferocious authority. He pulled every search engine he could think of, going back to when Alan was a kid. Juvie records were sealed but not college records.

He sat back and stared at the screen as his computer worked overtime trying to get the searches finished. The tickers at the bottom of the screen told him how much data they were searching through to find what he wanted.

The screen flashed as his phone rang. He lifted it off his belt. "Strong here."

"Are you okay?" it was Ayers.

"No, but I will be when we put Alan in jail for good together with his little lackey." Riley pushed back from his desk. Between the concussion and being shot, he hurt and strolled to the kitchen to grab water and pain pills.

"Have you found out anything else?" Ayers's police engine surged in the background.

"No, the searches haven't come back yet." Riley shook out four pills from the bottle and tossed them in his mouth, chasing them down with the water he guzzled.

"Let me know when you have something. I got a call back from my friend at the state courts. They are indicting Alan's judge friend for misuse of power and have already removed him from the bench this afternoon. The paperwork Alan waved around court today was illegally filed with no documents to back it up for the hold on Annie. The techs in the detective unit also cracked his phone's password with the search warrant also issued by my new favorite judge. The texts didn't come from Annie's phone but Sam's, explaining why her phone didn't ring in court. He's the one you shot and killed tonight. They changed his name to Annie in the text messages for quick evidence to get her admitted." Even with the good news, Ayers sounded sullen with the loss of Annie's life today.

"Do you think it will be enough to get the judge to turn on Alan and have him charged for the murders?" Riley dropped the water bottle in the trash and then grabbed another one as he headed back to his office.

"Not sure, but state investigators are waiting for a warrant to pick him up and already have the SWAT team on standby, waiting for that order." Ayers's car door dinged in the background, telling Riley he was at the station to type up his reports. It would be a couple of hours before he would have a chance to go home. He had reports on two dead bodies on his hands as well as a violation of a full order, that he had to submit for approval before he could even think about the end of his shift.

"Thanks, I'll call you if I find anything on my search. I'm starting with his college days to see if there are any cover-ups back before his first wife's murder." Riley sighed when he hung up and dropped into his chair behind his desk.

He pulled up the tracking software. Alan's car showed to be moving, no doubt to the police bay for processing. Annie's showed in the same location. Her license must still be in the car. He typed in a few command codes and the blips disappeared from the screen. His shoulders slumped as his computer alerted him that the searches were done. The printer whirred in the corner, made a clunking noise, and then continued to warm up before printing the files he selected. He forgot to call the repairman for his printer. He set an alert on his phone to call the next day.

The printer spit out page after page. Riley sat back and closed his eyes as he listened to the rhythmic sounds as the machine pulled the sheets of paper through the rollers, printing out his search. Sleep found its way in. He didn't hear anything else after a few minutes; all sounds were lost as he started to quietly snore in his chair. Exhaustion finally pulled him under.

Eighteen

A commotion outside his office startled Riley from his sleep, and he bolted out of his chair. Ayers marched over to the doorway. Bear trailed behind him, quietly clutching a folder in his hands.

"What's going on?" Riley wiped his hands down over his face.

"Blood type matches Annie's, but we won't have a full workup completed for two weeks," Ayers informed him.

"We both figured that it would be a match for her. The body was the same height and weight as her, plus with the clothing description that you confirmed yourself—" Riley grunted.

Ayers bit the inside of his cheek and sighed. "I'm sorry, Strong. I know you were trying to keep her safe. I should have kept her with me and transported her myself. If only I had known the other one was still in the area."

"No, you can't blame yourself any more than I can for going to the hospital instead of staying with her. What do we have to keep Alan in jail?" Riley turned to Bear.

"We need to get this to State. Alan wasn't at the conference like he said he was during his first wife's murder. We downloaded every ounce of footage taken. They announced him for the award for his work on the board where he donated hours and hours of medical services, and he never went up for the award. Someone else accepted it on his behalf." Bear handed both Riley and Ayers copies of the photos.

"I have someone already looking into the two separate autopsy reports, so now with this, I'll see if they can push this through. Hold on." Ayers snatched his cell phone off his belt and stalked down the hall toward the elevators, turning his back on Riley. He raised the hand that held the files Bear had given him as he murmured in hushed tones, pacing back and forth from one wall to the other in the narrow hall.

Riley thumbed through the photos. There were a lot of doctors at the convention. It would be harder to prove Alan wasn't there than for him to say he was but just wasn't in any of the photos. What caught his attention was the last couple showing someone else on stage accepting the award for him. All they needed would be for him to say he was there to accept his award and they would be able to prove he lied. But would they be able to prove without a shadow of a doubt to a jury that he was in town the day his wife was murdered? The autopsy reports should be enough to get the case reopened since they had the proof there were two on file with the coroner's office.

"Strong, we need to get these scanned in and sent over to my contact." Ayers clipped his phone back onto his belt.

"Duffy?" Riley pointed to his employee, who raised his hand.

Ayers marched over to his desk and wrote down where they would need the files sent. Duffy grabbed the file and placed the photos into the feeder on his scanner and sent them to the email Ayers gave him.

"What can we do to find the man who killed Annie and put the officer in the hospital?" Riley popped two headache tablets into his palm and washed them down with the cold coffee from the mug he nabbed from his desk. He twisted his mouth and made his way to the coffee pot.

"We don't have anything new. Is there anything you can do on your end?" Ayers dropped onto the corner of an empty desk, resting his hands in the armholes of his vest.

Riley hung his head. "No. The only trackers we had were on the car and her license."

"We didn't recover her license in the vehicle. It may have burned in the crash." Ayers jumped to his feet. "The fire would have scorched the tracking chip, making it untraceable."

"Yes, it would have." Riley strolled up to Bear, who pulled up the tracking software and then slid over out of his way. He snagged the chair next to Bear's station and typed in several commands for trackers that were turned off. A blip popped up on the screen showing Annie's tracker was moving.

"How is that possible?" Ayers peered over his shoulder.

"It's not, unless someone still has it." Riley's eyes bore into the screen.

"Wait. That's the area of the tow lot we use for our patrol vehicles. It's probably just in the cruiser. We haven't logged everything into evidence yet. I'll head over there now and see if it's in there and do a more thorough inventory of the vehicle. It could have been lost down between the seats or something." Ayers sauntered to the front door.

Riley moseyed to his office and grabbed the stack of paper on the printer he started the previous night and slunk down into his chair. He took a gulp of the scalding hot coffee before he read a word on the printouts. His phone buzzed and he lifted it from the desk. It was only his alarm telling him to have the repairman come out for the printer in his office. He scrolled through his contacts with his thumb until he came to the one for his equipment. The phone rang several times before an out-of-breath female answered with their company's name and asked how she could help him. He scheduled a technician to come out at their earliest possible appointment they had available. With that set, he perused the first couple of pages of Alan's college days.

Several hours later, he had a new meaning for the term creep, and it was Alan's fraternity. He lost count of how many complaints were filed against his fraternity that were either squashed or the victim dropped the charges. The college seemed to not only back the group but also praise them that they did nothing wrong and pay off victims to choose another college to go to. Several were never heard from again. Very few chose to pursue the cases; he could count on one hand how many took that route. Monetary donations, larger than any other that year, were given to the college by the fraternity's families.

Three victims of the fraternity's crimes were dead and one was in jail on possession charges, charged under federal jurisdiction since it involved drugs at a school and the amount they found in a dorm room justified the charge. Their defense was that they never used before and they had been planted. The kid was a good kid; she had a clean past and no skirmishes outside the law that he could find when he ran her through his software's search engines. She had now been in federal prison with no possibility of parole for over seventeen years.

Her prison record was of someone hardened by the time and the situations she dealt with daily behind the bars. Bars that were more than likely put around her illegally by the fraternity planting drugs in her room.

The last victim ended up being his first wife, who was later murdered at his hands. It looked like the marriage was a quiet ceremony done before a judge. Magically, that judge happened to be his best friend's father. The paperwork was rushed through and filed with the judge signing off on the marriage minus any witnesses for her side. The two goons that he employed to help keep his crimes hidden were the ones who signed the wedding license. The marriage lasted a short time; they were both still in college when her car went off into the ravine.

Riley stood and stretched his neck from side to side when Bear appeared in his doorway. "I had a cousin look at the autopsies that we have on the first two wives. There's a problem with the paperwork."

"Problem for us or Alan?"

"Alan." Bear raised an eyebrow.

"Tell me." Riley sank into his chair. It was about time they got some good news.

"They died before Alan supposedly got to the conventions. The first wife was dead at least seventy-four hours before he showed up at the first convention as a guest of his father's friend before he became a doctor. Look here." Bear laid the pages on his desk. He pointed to the time of death on the unaltered autopsy and when it shows she died. Then the second form of the official one was filed with the state. The dates had been changed to reflect she died after he arrived to meet his father's friend.

"Then look." Bear handed him the autopsies of the second wife. "Her time of death is off but only by two days. This time it looks like they made an effort to seem more realistic and imply she died close to when her body was found."

"This won't help much unless we can get the coroner to turn on him and testify in court." Riley drained the rest of his coffee with the intent to get more.

"No, check this out. You don't need to. The coroner was too good at his job. My cousin said the insect documentation is all we need to show that the time of death doesn't correspond with what was filed officially. They put her time of death, days after her actual death to coincide with the conventions, and he will testify to that in court with the insect evidence that was originally submitted. I think the coroner had a change of heart when he was asked to modify the files, and kept these without anyone's knowledge." Bear smiled.

They finally had him. Riley slowly stood from behind his desk. They would have to be careful who they let in on this until they could get the charges filed at the state level. Phone in hand he dialed Ayers's number.

A quick conversation gave Ayers the information Bear had. Riley dropped his phone on the desk, then grabbed his coffee cup, ready for a refill.

"What does he think about it?" Bear sounded eager, which wasn't something Riley had ever heard in his voice before.

"Said his guy noticed the same thing and is having a state expert look at the evidence but has already started the paperwork to get warrants issued for Alan before he gets released tomorrow." Riley drained the almost empty pot of coffee into his cup. The bitterness made his jaw clench as the first sip hit the back of his throat.

"Good." Bear sauntered out.

"Annie, I'm so sorry." Riley closed his eyes and leaned back. How could he have failed her so miserably. He knew something felt off; he just couldn't put a finger on it. He would go to her place and make sure everything was secure. It was still part of his job to take care of her house and monitor it, even though she was dead. It was the least he could do for her. He dialed Ayers.

"Hey, Ayers," Riley spoke into his phone as he crossed the office, snatching his keys off his desk.

"Yeah."

"Is Annie's house available for me to enter and make sure it's secured?" Riley frowned when he said her name.

"Yes, the scene has been released."

"Okay, thanks. I'm heading over there now to secure the house and...I don't know, just look around. Maybe we missed something." Riley beeped the key fob and unlocked his car.

"Let me know if you find anything." Ayers disconnected.

Although Annie only lived a couple of miles from the office, it felt like the longest drive he had ever taken. He keyed himself through the gate and pulled in front of the house. As he stood in the entryway, the eerie quiet felt off. He hung his head and lumbered to the office. The monitors were still streaming the video footage of the exterior of the house. He ran his finger over the power buttons for every monitor, turning them off one by one.

A sigh filled the ominous quiet that suffocated him as he sank into the chair behind her spacious desk. An envelope with his name on it caught his eye. The trembling of his hand scared him as he ripped it off the desk. He groaned out loud. "Oh Annie, I'm so sorry." His voice hiccupped in his throat. Tears threatened to spill over his cheeks. He hadn't cried since his wife's funeral. He slid his finger under the flap to release the self-sealing strip and reveal the letter inside.

Dear Riley,

I wanted to take a moment to thank you for everything you have done to keep me safe during all of this. You are the first person I have trusted in a long time. You gave me hope that there were still good people in this world. I have endured more than most people could imagine, and their minds couldn't fathom the evils of some people and what they are truly capable of. If something happens to me, I don't want you to take it personally. I always knew deep down there was a possibility of Alan ending my life. This town, city, you, gave me hope for the first time in a long time that I might have a chance at life after Alan. He is relentless and ruthless. He always has to win, no matter who he has to take out and hurt, or worse, to get what he wants. I've seen the devil in person. I was married to him. I just hope and pray he doesn't take you out along the way. You are a good, sweet person who has a huge heart. Please keep doing what you're doing. You are helping people who need it and can't necessarily ask for it. Don't stop because this one case was unsuccessful. Don't lose who you are because of this one evil man. Just promise me you will put him away and stop him once and for all, the legal way. Show him he can't win everything. I've had papers drawn up to leave you the house and all my royalty payments from my books if something happens to me, and if you are reading this, then it has. Use it to help those who can't get away like I couldn't. Help those who have nowhere else to turn. Be their hope, their light in the darkness, help them find the way to survive. You were my light, when I thought there was only darkness left.

Regards, Annie

Riley crunched the page in his fist and raised his hand to his face. The crinkled page rustled when it made contact with his forehead. He smoothed the page out, refolded it, and then slid it back into the envelope. His heart sank. She knew there was the possibility she was going to die, and she never expressed that to him. He should have let her run.

Riley stood and strolled to the bottom of the stairs. His legs were heavy as he lumbered up the steps one at a time. The police tape still secured the third room at the top of the stairs. The coppery smell of blood mixed with the gunpowder that still hung in the air. He would get biohazard out here and clean the room before it started to smell. Blood could be nasty to clean if left alone for too long.

He skipped the room next to Annie's and went straight for her bedroom. The handgun lay on the nightstand where she left it. He tucked it into the back of his waistband. The Bible was open and, if he wasn't mistaken, to a different page than it was before. He could tell the pages were thicker on one side than the other when he could have sworn it was the other way before. He picked it up and closed it, holding it to his chest as he heaved out a stuttered breath. The closet door stood in front of him with the panic room door open. The space was small but cozy. A couch, small bathroom, and refrigerator occupied one corner. A fold-down bed adorned the opposite wall from the couch with several shelves for things such as clothes, towels, or food.

Riley choked down the sob that rose in his chest. He couldn't let this get to him. His priority was to secure this house and get back to the office. With the door secured to the panic room, he stormed down the stairs to the back door. Everything was secure at the back of the house. Hurried steps took him to the front where he surveyed the rooms. Windows were closed and locked. At the front door, he turned, taking in the house one more time before he pulled the door closed behind him, locking it with the key fob and setting it to lockdown mode. He would have one of his men come out when biohazard arrived to clean the room upstairs. He wasn't sure when he would be able to bring himself to come back. The letter weighed heavily on his mind as he pulled his Audi around, circling the wide driveway so he faced the gate.

Something nagged at him. He stepped from his car and stared at the house that loomed in the background. What was he missing? There was something he needed to do, but he couldn't think what it was. He couldn't bring himself to go back inside and look. He wasn't ready for the emotions that tore at him with Annie's death. He ground his teeth and hopped into his car and took off, remoting the gate open so he barely skated through, his car clearing the still opening entrance by mere inches. The gate closed behind him as he steered toward his office.

What was he missing? He ran through the files in his head. Was it something in there? The wives, the murders, the insect evidence showing they died days before they were reported to have. Her parents' murder. There was evidence in those files; he just needed to connect the dots. Alan was good at covering things up, but everyone missed something. Too many people had their hands in his cover-ups. That was it. He needed to connect Alan to them. How do you get so many people to help you cover up crimes like murder? There had to be a massive event that he held over their head. He would need to look again at the college days. That would be where he would find what he was missing.

Pulling Alan's bank records for payments to shush them up should have been a priority when he was doing his background checks. He snatched his phone from the cupholder when he parked in the back lot and jogged to the building. The coffee pot was full, and he snagged a cup from the cabinet, filling it before he strolled to his office.

"Bear."

"Yeah?" Bear joined him. His hulking form blocked the doorway.

"Bank statements. How can we legally get ahold of those? I want to know if Alan is paying them to cover up his murders or if it's something more. Something he has over them so they are forced to help him conceal his crimes. I think something happened in college they were all involved in that Alan is holding over their heads. Why else would people in such pivotal positions be helping this madman cover up his heinous deeds?" Riley dropped into his chair.

"I'll check with Gavin. His contact at the state level would know how far we can push the envelope on this." Bear turned then stopped. "Hey. Are you okay?"

"Not by a long shot." Riley motioned for him to come in and close the door.

He waited for Riley, who finally pulled the letter from his pocket and handed it to Bear. He was quiet as he opened the envelope, pulled the crumpled sheet out, and read it. His sigh filled the room. "She knew she wouldn't survive this."

"Yeah." Riley tilted his head back and blew out his breath. Tears built in the corners of his eyes.

"This isn't your fault. You can't be everywhere at once."

"I know that, but if I only waited for the transport to the police department, he wouldn't have been able to get to her."

Bear huffed. "You were shot."

"Only a graze."

Bear raised his left eyebrow. "Really?"

"What?" Riley leaned forward and rested his arm across the top of his desk, the sling holding his other arm in place.

"No one could have predicted he was out there waiting to grab her. She was in a police car. Who in their right mind would go for her under police protection?" Bear placed the envelope on Riley's desk after delicately folding the letter and sliding it in place.

Riley wanted to laugh at the hulking man being so gentle with the slip of paper. "Because the only time she would have been vulnerable was on the way to the police department. After that, she would have been secure in our building, which they knew they couldn't breach." Riley slid the envelope across the desk, the paper scraping across the grain surface. He held the letter in his hands before dropping it in the top left drawer.

"He was watching us the whole time."

"Yup."

"When he shot at you, how did he know you were the one opening the door and not Annie? I don't think they had permission to kill her right away. Would they shoot immediately when you opened the door if they thought it was her?" Bear stood.

Riley's head snapped up. "They were watching us."

"I think so. How else do you explain that they shot the second that door opened."

"Take Monroe, clear that house, and check for cameras and listening devices. We should've checked for those as soon as we realized they knew where she was a week before they ran her down." Riley tossed the remote for Annie's house to Bear. Or his house, since she left it to him.

Riley sauntered to his doorway. Alan had been a step ahead of them. How could he have let that happen? Something felt out of place, and the thought that someone watched them would explain why he'd felt so uneasy when he was in the house with her. He leaned against the door frame while Bear grabbed his bug sweeper from his desk and called to Monroe, who grabbed his jacket and jogged after him as they headed to the back door.

Gavin motioned Riley over. "Yeah, what did you find?"

"There are no large withdrawals from Alan's accounts over the past twenty years. There are smaller deductions that match deposits to his buddies Sam and Mark. Those go back years, even during times that he wasn't committing murder, so my guess is they have worked for him since college. Not sure how he codes it for employment purposes, but they make a good living being his little lackeys."

"So, something could have happened so that Alan has blackmail on the others from college. See what you can dig up on that angle. There has to be evidence showing they are tied together. To my knowledge, frat brothers don't help cover up murders just for frat loyalty."

"You got it." Gavin leaned back in his chair. "Riley, this wasn't your fault."

"Yeah, my brain knows that, but my heart doesn't. It still feels like I should have done something more." Riley turned toward his office.

"We all feel there was more we could have done. Let's just catch this jerk and put him away for good, for Annie." Gavin's chair squeaked as he spun around to his desk.

"Oil that chair. It's killing me," Riley called from his desk.

"Yup."

"Oh, and check with records. According to the two officers on the scene of the shooting, there are no reports in the police database for their attacks on us and Annie." Riley pulled out the business cards Ayers had written the report numbers on and tossed them onto the corner of Gavin's desk.

Gavin raised his eyes. "I'll see what I can find."

He knew if they got hold of goon number two, they would never get him to flip on the good doctor. Covering up his crimes for so long, he was just as guilty as Alan was.

He nabbed the property listings that Bear put on his desk. Maybe he could get a location on him and at least get him off the streets. They had enough to charge him for being on Annie's property after the protection order was served to him plus the assault on Riley behind her house.

He grabbed his phone as it rang. "Strong."

"Hey, just wanted you to know that the officer is going to be okay. The brunt of the impact hit on the passenger side. The officer identified Mark Murphy as the driver of the Porsche. He doesn't remember much after the impact except Annie fighting to get away from Mark as he yanked her through the broken window and dumped her in the trunk of the car." Ayers informed him.

"Glad he's going to be okay. Now you can put an APB out for Mark and get his picture all over the news stations. It will only be a matter of time before someone turns him in. He can't run from this one. He'll go down for murder." Riley closed his eyes. That still didn't feel like it was enough for what Annie went through.

"Already done. Phones are ringing in Dispatch. I don't envy them tonight. We have a desk set up for officers to take those calls, but there have already been over two hundred that came in. Unfortunately, it's people calling in asking if there is a reward and that they saw them last week. Nothing concrete yet but I'll keep you in the loop."

"Thanks, Ayers." Riley disconnected.

"Boss, you got to see this," Gavin's voice boomed.

Riley jumped from his chair. The printer was working overtime in the office, between the background searches he ran and the ones his men were working on, trying to put

Alan where he belonged. He wouldn't be surprised if they wore it out by week's end. "What did you find?" He sauntered up behind Gavin, who spun around smiling. His chair squeaked again and Riley cringed.

He pointed to his screen and Riley squinted to read the article that he uncovered. While Alan was in college, there was a frat party where twelve girls claimed rape against everyone in the frat house. He dropped into the chair next to Gavin's desk and continued to read. The college called in the local police department. He remembered the incident. He had just finished the academy and had started his field training when it occurred. His training officer told him that they should be happy that hadn't happened in their city because he would have had to work the report for training.

Twelve girls all gave varying accounts of the evening. There were gaps in their memory of the hours during the party but knew that something happened to them while at the mixer. The local police department said since they couldn't give them all the details, they wouldn't be able to file charges since they couldn't identify their attackers. The girls were distraught and filed complaints against the department, asking County to come in and investigate. Two of the girls overdosed within the first week after the initial report. Girls who had never tangled with the deadly drugs they had supposedly abused ended their lives.

Two others left the school and never returned and said they didn't want to pursue it. They just wanted to be left alone and move on. Three more died in a single-car crash as their car went off the bridge crossing the river that separated the college from the downtown clubs. They ruled it an accident due to drinking and driving. One ended up in prison for drugs on campus while another married the guy. The last three each disappeared, never to be heard from again at varying times during the final week of school. Since they had no victims left, the county dropped the complaint as no victim no crime.

Wait, these were the girls he read about earlier! He sprinted to his office and yanked the pages off his desk before rejoining Gavin. Scanning through the reports, he saw that the names were a match.

This was a blatant disregard for justice. Twelve girls all at Alan's frat party. Was this the key he was looking for that tied them together to cover Alan's crimes for the rest of his life? Gavin pulled up another screen showing Alan out of town with his parents on a ski trip in Colorado when it happened. He wasn't there during the incident but returned the next school day to the accusations against his frat brothers.

One of the girls was the senator's daughter. He swore he would make the fraternity pay and get it removed from campus and shut down. Every single chapter that existed would be demolished. The week after his daughter overdosed—she was one of the first two girls to die after the incident—they had a tragic car crash when his vehicle hit black ice and careened over an embankment. It exploded on impact at the bottom. They had to identify the bodies from dental records. This was sounding too familiar. How were all these crashes covered up like this with no one putting together the connection? Maybe these were the first two crashes they ever did, and since they worked so well, they continued with what they got away with.

"Okay, how do we tie this to them?" Riley leaned back in the chair. "There are four girls missing. Six dead, two parents dead, and two who dropped out and declined to continue with charges. How did no one make the connection that these men were the cause of it all?"

"Who said no one made the connection? What if they did but couldn't prove it?" Gavin shook his head.

This was more bodies than he thought they would find. Maybe Alan disposed of all of these victims and then held it over their heads. But wait. How did he hold it over their heads unless there was hard physical proof that it happened? There had to be evidence somewhere for them in order to be willing to go along with Alan's proclivities for torturing and murdering his wives. He enjoyed exacting that torture way too much. Annie said he loved to play with people and mess with them just for the sick entertainment of it. Would he let his friend get rid of her? Robbing him of the satisfaction of doing the deed himself? Riley stretched his neck and blew out his breath.

"What are you thinking?" Gavin studied Riley.

"There's proof somewhere. Otherwise, Alan had nothing over them. He was out of town with his parents when this happened. Evidence is locked away somewhere that hides this dark dirty little secret. He found it and probably told them he could make their problems disappear, but they would owe him. Pull records on the two that survived but moved back home. I want to see bank statements. Did they take a payoff?" Riley grabbed his coffee cup and stalked to the kitchen.

He rinsed his cup and dropped it into the dish strainer for it to dry on its own and looted a bottle of water from the fridge. What kind of evidence would there be that would be enough to hold this level of blackmail over their heads for twenty years? Video? Audio? His bet was video. Nothing like the prospect of the crime being shown live on TV would make anyone that loyal all these years later to continue to do his bidding. But it's twenty years ago. How degraded would the picture be and could everyone be identified on it? People change a lot over that length of time. Wait, he had the group photo of good ole Alan and his cohorts. They could compare the video to the photo taken at the same time and make identifications that way.

He dialed Ayers's number. "I have something but I'm not sure how it will help."

Nineteen

Riley stared at the ceiling in his apartment. It was no use, he couldn't sleep. Alan had gotten out of jail and hadn't been seen since. With Annie gone, he didn't have a reason to stay around. He was probably back in his hospital looking for the next victim.

Bear and Monroe had found numerous cameras and listening devices in Annie's house a couple of weeks ago after her death. They were short-range, so they had to be close to access the video feed. The cameras didn't have a large memory, so they recorded over every twelve hours. The connection was also spotty, so they probably sat in her neighborhood for days on end just monitoring and keeping an eye on her. He wasn't sure they sat close by or her nosey, cranky neighbor would have called on them. He already had Ayers check the call log to see if anyone called on a suspicious car in her neighborhood. No one had.

He also said he would check to see if they had any friends in Alan's side of the state to walk through a search warrant to look for a video of the incident the night twelve girls were raped. He would see this through to the end for Annie. Every time he closed his eyes, he saw her smiling face and how beautiful she was when her smile lit up her eyes. He knew he wasn't cheating on his wife, but he still felt guilty at the feelings he had developed for Annie in the short time he had known her. He prayed she didn't suffer when she burned to death in the car.

He sat up and looked at the clock across the room. The red glowing light read zero four thirty. He kept the ancient clock just so he wouldn't have to fumble with his phone when he was married and wake his wife when he was working long hours. Then after she was gone, he couldn't bring himself to get rid of the ridiculously large annoying thing. He smiled as he thought of her. The thought that he knew she was the one, the first night they met in the emergency room. Something as simple as her hand on his shoulder and he knew. He refused to admit it, but when he scooped Annie off the ground, he could see himself married to her. He had no clue why that came to mind, but looking back on that day, he knew she was different.

Special.

She felt so small and helpless in his arms. His protective instincts reared their heads. The second her eyes met his, there was a strength in her that shone through. If only he'd had more time to get to know her, the undamaged Annie.

He sighed and rolled out of bed to jump in the shower. There would be no going back to sleep; his mind was running wild with what-ifs. The water fell from his rain shower head as he stood under the spray. His wife had wanted one, but he never got around to putting one in. And then she was gone so fast, he never got around to it before she was ripped from his life. He'd wanted to be there every second she had left.

"Helen, I miss you," he said out loud to himself.

Sighing, he turned the shower off and snagged the towel off the outside of the shower door. The hot water did nothing to ease the tension in his neck and shoulders. He knew if he didn't take something, he would be sore in a couple of hours with a tension headache he wouldn't be able to get rid of. He popped several ibuprofen tablets and then threw clothes on. He flipped the news on while he dropped bread into the slots in the toaster.

Annie's deadly crash was airing on the television again. A picture of Mark Murphy flashed in the lower corner as a person of interest, requesting anyone with information about his whereabouts to call the local police department. Ayers was good on his word about getting his picture out to the news stations. He wouldn't be able to hide very long with his mug plastered everywhere.

The toast popped up and he removed it from the appliance. He slathered butter and jam on both slices. He gulped orange juice between large bites, washing down the breakfast he hardly tasted. His mind wandered to being able to get their hands on that video from college and getting Alan's little cohorts to turn on him and testify about what he did to his wives. They hadn't come up with anything new since Alan's release. With a toothbrush hanging out of his mouth, he flipped through texts on his phone. No news on any of the searches Bear or Gavin ran. This was getting frustrating. They just had to find the right thread to pull to unravel the entire life that Alan wanted to protect.

It was only five o'clock when Riley left his apartment and sauntered down to his office. He stopped at the coffee pot first and poured some into the cup he'd left in the dish drain the day before. It was extra strong and his jaw tightened as the first swig hit the back of his throat. Bear was already at his station when Riley meandered past. "What are you doing here so early?"

Bear turned in his chair. "Looking for anything we can use to lock Alan up. He's been out there living his life as if he didn't have another person killed. And it doesn't help no one has seen him since."

"Yeah, I couldn't sleep either."

"What are you going to do since she left you everything?" Bear furrowed his brow.

"I've been thinking about that. I want to start a side business of helping victims of domestic violence to leave their abuser and disappear like Annie tried to. She was alone and didn't have any help. What if we had helped her disappear? Would Alan have found her if I hadn't convinced her to stay?" Riley gazed through the front windows. The sun wouldn't rise for another hour or so, so all he saw was his and Bear's reflections. He needed a haircut. He never let his hair get this long. He ran his hand through it, proving it was longer than it needed to be.

"That's a good idea. I can put some things together to get out to victims that we are a safe haven they can come to. I have a cousin." Bear smiled.

Riley chuckled and strolled to his office. He jotted down a note to get his hair cut. He pulled his keyboard closer and opened his email account. There were thirteen messages. He never had that many this early in the morning. Clicking on his inbox, he saw they were from his friend at the state office where he got his business license. The first one acknowledged that the agents who showed up with Alan were fired and their credentials revoked after an internal investigation. The second was an automated system email from the state saying something happened to his license files. It said the state couldn't continue to let him operate his business until he paid fines for illegally operating within the state and filed the correct forms again. That would take up to ninety days to push through. The third was from his friend again to say his new contact for a business license was Nick Sanders and that he would no longer be able to be his contact and all future questions were to go through the above-named agent.

Riley's stomach lurched as he opened the fourth email from Hargis's personal email that stated he had no clue who he made mad, but it was rolling downhill fast, and he hoped he had kept copies of the paperwork so he could resubmit them quickly. He added that someone was gunning for him and trying to discredit him so they could shut him down. The next email was also from Hargis, sent a couple of hours after the last one, and simply stated...*I was just fired.*

Riley shoved back from his desk. "Bear!"

"Yeah?" Bear marched into his office.

"We're in trouble. Hargis was fired. They assigned us a new agent and said all of our proper paperwork wasn't filed correctly and as of immediately, we have been shut down until the time they get the correct paperwork files, which could take up to ninety days."

Bear whistled. "Well, that's wrong. You have all the copies of the paperwork you filed when Hargis helped you set this up with the state's seal and notarized."

"I know. Grab the copies of those papers from your stash. During your search of Alan, did you run across anyone with enough clout that could do this? State-level?" Riley clicked on the sixth email. It was from Ayers, stating the files he sent to his state contact were missing and therefore, they were unable to reopen the case on Alan's first two wives.

Bear reappeared with the papers in hand. "I'll check my files but nothing that jumped out at me."

"They also lost the copies of the paperwork showing the two autopsy reports for his wives. Tell me you have the originals hidden and not onsite here." Riley narrowed his eyes at his computer as he clicked on the seventh email.

Bear shifted out of his chair. "I can make them safe in about five seconds."

"Do it. I want several copies made first and the originals hidden offsite."

"Sir." Bear practically ran to his desk. It was the most cardio the man ever accomplished. He tended to focus on building his mass instead of cardio. The copier in the corner of the office started up seconds later.

The seventh email was from the courts, stating that since Annie was no longer alive, they didn't see a reason to keep the protection orders active and dismissed all active orders pertaining to him and her. What was happening? There was no way Alan had this much pull and power to get the state to jump like this and tear away everything he worked to get put in place to protect Annie and himself. Annie's death hadn't even been confirmed yet for them to start filing for a death certificate, at least not until DNA and dental records could be confirmed as a match.

He didn't want to continue reading his emails, but he couldn't stop himself. The eighth email was from Hargis again. *Riley, the two agents that were dismissed before have been reinstated, and they are coming to shut you down. I suggest you make sure you're not there if you can help it. Put a sign on your door saying you are closed and regroup at an unknown location. I don't know what you stumbled into, but it's bad. I get to keep my pension because they legally can't take that from me, but you need to get everything in order.*

Riley hit print and sent out a mass text to all his employees to meet at his house. He glanced at the clock; it was only five-fifteen. Bear hurried in and handed him the copies of the autopsy reports. "They are coming to shut us down and take all of our files. Load all of Alan's and Annie's files in your car and hide them with the autopsy reports. Meet me at my house when you are done. I need to grab a few things here before I join you."

"How bad is this?" Bear grunted.

"Pretty bad. We need to figure out who he knows and how they are tied to the crimes he has committed." Riley opened the next email while Bear grabbed the folders he asked him to as well as all the laptops on the other workstations belonging to his other employees. Then he grabbed all the keys to the cars except the one Riley was using at this time.

The email was from an anonymous source. *There is a warrant being issued for your arrest on capital murder charges in the shooting. The chief of police has put several people on administrative leave. They are stating you staged the place after you killed Sam and that you sent a text to him asking him to come to Annie's house. I know that didn't happen, but you need to disappear until we can get this figured out.*

Riley knew they would come to the office first, so he grabbed his laptop and transferred the files and accounts. Then he set a destruct program to wipe all the hard drives on his computer and those of his employees. He never thought he would use it but had been told by a close friend to have it installed just in case. The program would reset the computers to factory settings continuously until told to stop, erasing everything on their hard drives numerous times.

He jogged to the control room and set the monitors to shut down with a passkey that would only unlock with his fingerprint. With the lower building taken care of, he ran up the four flights of steps to his apartment. He didn't have time to wait for the elevator. He pulled his go bag out and tossed his extra weapons in together with the ammo he kept in his apartment. He took the stairs down, skipping more than he was probably physically capable of on a normal day, but he loved the adrenaline dumps on days like today. He sprinted to his car, got behind the wheel, and peeled out of the parking lot. Headlights on the next hill warned him to pull over and hide. Darting into the next parking lot, he pulled around the back of the building while several county deputy vehicles flew past his location together with state-issued puke-gray sedans. Once the caravan of vehicles passed, he sent out a mass text, telling his team his house may be next and to meet at the safe house.

He set it up years ago under his grandmother's maiden name. He never knew what prompted him to do that but knew God gave him a shove just for this moment. His phone alerted him that everyone received the information and was headed there. He pulled onto the street and punched the accelerator. His heart hammered in his chest.

Alan was more connected than any of them had been able to uncover. He needed to get to the safe house and finish reading the emails. He didn't dare to try while he was driving; he was likely to turn around and march right through the front doors of his office and have a go with the men who were trying to take him down. He blew out a breath and concentrated on the road and where he needed to go so that he would be there for his men, who trusted him enough to sign onto this crazy debacle that was getting out of hand. With his right hand, he flipped through apps on his phone, activating the one to hide his phone. He sent a group text telling his men to do the same.

After tossing the phone into the passenger seat, he white-knuckled the steering wheel. He told himself to relax since he still had a two-hour drive to finish before he could start coming up with a plan to take his life back and put Alan away for good and everyone connected to him.

Twenty

Everyone was already at his cabin when he pulled in. He told them to pull their cars around the back and hide them behind the crumbling barn that needed to be torn down about a century ago. He was finally able to breathe when he saw Bear walk in seconds after him. Everyone made it.

"Okay, sorry to say, everything just hit the fan. Give me a minute to finish getting some details, and then I'll let everyone in on what's going on." Riley yanked his laptop from the bag and pulled up his email after activating privacy on his computer. That way, if someone was trying to find him, it would bounce them around servers and make it hard to determine where his building was located. Bear handed out everyone's laptops, which he had lifted from their workstations.

The next email was from Hargis telling him he hoped he got out of the building safely and that someone at the top was to blame for all of this. He still had friends who were trying to figure out what happened. He would keep in touch if he could, but it may come from an email he wouldn't be able to get responses from. He also stated not to send replies to his email as they were more than likely tracking any correspondence that came in.

An anonymous email broke through his spam filter, unclear who sent it. He could only assume it was Ayers. *Hope you got out. They are watching your house and office like hawks.*

Don't contact anyone other than your employees. I'll continue to send you updates as they come in. Stay safe.

Hargis sent the next email to alert him that they were going to execute a warrant sweep on his building by zero six hundred and had pulled in the local counties to do the sweep. Riley checked the timestamp on the email, and he sent it several hours before the sweep happened. He saw the warrant go out before he was walked out the door. He said he would work on things from his end and asked Riley to pray they didn't find out or he would be in jail also.

The last email was from Anonymous again. *Riley, hope you have read all of this, and it didn't make it to your junk folders. Source at the state level said several people have been walked out and fired on the spot for helping you. Don't trust anyone, not even people you have known for years. Some people can be bought.*

Riley closed his eyes as his men watched him. "Guys, we need to be careful with who we talk to and who we contact while we try to figure this out. Alan is connected well above the level of the county where he lives. This is coming down from state-level."

He filled his men in on the emails and what he did to wipe his computer and about the team of deputies that showed up at the building after he got away.

Bear was the first to speak. "I have all the original files hidden in a safe location. I brought duplicates so we can figure out what the heck is going on." He passed out files to everyone in the room.

"I have contacts no one knows about. I'll make some calls." Duffy plucked his phone from his pocket.

"Scramble your phone," Riley warned.

Everyone grabbed their phones and set them to scramble. Thanks to Erickson, they had software installed that was better than any app you could download. It not only scrambled the signal so they couldn't trace it, but it also scrambled their voices, except for the person they were talking to.

Gavin Bruce piped up, "I think I know where this is coming from. I took some of the files home and perused them since I couldn't sleep. Look at this." He slid a page down the dining room table they all sat around, to Riley.

Snatching the page off the table, Riley's eyes grew wide. "Are you serious?" This was worse than he thought. He closed his eyes and shook his head.

The others murmured among themselves when they saw the page Riley passed around. The connection was through the judge in Alan's back pocket. His cousin was a congressman the same age as they were. He didn't see this coming.

"Wait, he was at the fraternity with his cousin. They both pledged the same one." Gavin narrowed his eyes as he continued reading the file.

"He wasn't in the group photo. We already identified everyone in it." Riley strolled to the kitchen and started coffee. They would need a lot to get them through this.

"The photo was taken after the incident where twelve girls were raped. Maybe he didn't want to be connected to them?" Gavin offered.

"Maybe, but how did we not know this?" Riley held his cup as if the coffee pot would work faster if he stood staring at it.

"The congressman was not only in the fraternity, but he was also the chapter president. Being the president, they don't always have their pictures taken with the rest of the boys. He was also at the party. His name is on the reports filed against them. He was listed as the instigator and aggressor of the roofies that were dumped in the punch bowl. He and his buddies drank from a keg out on the lawn so they wouldn't get drugged with the girls." Duffy joined them at the table.

"So, do we have proof of this that we can use against him, or is this going to be another issue with he-said-she-said?" Riley was done being patient. He shifted the pot from the machine and filled his cup. Then he replaced the pot to collect the rest of the rich dark roast he used at the cabin.

"If everyone is getting booted from their jobs, it's going to be hard to convince anyone to take a chance and issue a search warrant to look for evidence." Bear was next in line for coffee.

"Well, you guys are already in enough trouble being with someone who has a warrant out for murder. If they find you here, you could serve time also. Anyone who wants out, no hard feelings. This is more than any of you signed on for." Riley perched in the chair at the head of the table.

"I ain't going anywhere," Bear grumbled.

"Yeah, where are we supposed to go anyway? I kinda got used to seeing Bear's ugly mug every day at the office."

Duffy's phone rang and he answered it while stalking away from the table as everyone chuckled around them.

"Thanks, guys." Riley rubbed his hands across his face. "This could get rough before we clear it up."

"Well, like Alan is so fond of saying, he has no clue who he is messing with." Gavin continued to flip through the pages without looking up after his comment.

"We have to do this for Annie." It was the first thing Monroe had said since Riley arrived.

"For Annie," Riley muttered to himself.

They all stared at him for a second before putting their heads back down and studying the files in front of them.

Duffy rejoined them. "Okay, my guys are working on a few things. They have clout and a few contacts themselves that Alan will never be able to match."

Riley raised an eyebrow at him.

"You don't want to know, and trust me, I don't want to jinx us, so mum's the word for now." He smiled his lopsided grin that usually made everyone else smile. Today wasn't a day for those smiles, though.

"Duffy, your contacts come through on this, and I'll owe you big time." Riley grabbed the file on Alan and started at the beginning. Maybe he missed something that would jump out at him now.

Monroe stood and excused himself, his phone in his hand. Riley knew he had contacts but never talked about them. He wasn't sure if they were of questionable character or if they were so far up the chain, he didn't want anyone to know. His computer alerted him that he had a new email sent to his laptop, remotely jumping through a proxy server to mask where he was. He had no clue what all Erickson did in the technical capacity to hide them, but he was good and well worth his pay. Everyone stopped what they were doing while he read it. Ayers informed him he was put on desk duty and not allowed near the Alan Montgomery case and that he would be lucky if he still had a job by the end of the day. He told Riley to stay safe and work his magic. Ayers was often surprised at what he could accomplish with the contacts his employees had. He hoped they lived up to those levels of praise this go-around.

Riley was done rereading Alan's file, and Monroe still hadn't rejoined them. He snagged the next file off the table, on the judge in his little game of power. He started at the beginning. Coffee didn't last long with all of them needing the caffeine. A couple of his employees worked the overnight shift and had opted to grab a couple of hours of sleep. They stretched out on the couches in the back of the cabin that had been added on after he bought it. He put several sofas in there for group gatherings. This was as good a time as any to test out their sleep-worthiness.

"I need to call a cousin." Bear jumped out of his seat. They all smirked and then went back to reading. Riley stretched across the table to snag the file he had been reading. There were two, both the original autopsy reports on Alan's wives. He furrowed his brow and wondered what Bear was antsy about.

His phone rang and he didn't recognize the number. He answered anyway. "Hello."

"What are you doing answering your phone? I was going to leave you a message." It was Hargis.

"I have my phone scrambled. No one can hear us or trace the call from my end. What about your end?"

"Prepaid. Just bought it with cash," Hargis threw back.

"Good enough. What do you have?" Riley rubbed his temples with his thumb and the middle fingers of his left hand while he stood to grab something for his throbbing headache.

"So apparently, you pissed off a congressman."

"Tell me something I don't know."

"Wait, you know? How could you keep me in the dark that a congressman may be involved?" Hargis's voice rose an octave.

"We figured it out after you sent us into hiding. We didn't know either. Alan bragged about knowing people higher than we did. Just didn't know it went this high." Riley popped a couple of over-the-counter pain meds into his mouth and chewed them. They were bitter but he knew they would work faster crunched up than waiting for the outside coating to dissolve in his stomach.

"Oh, sorry. Well, I have a few friends also, and he really made me mad, so I made some calls. The help won't be immediate, but I have some people working on a solution. Hang in there. I just wanted to talk to you to make sure you were okay."

"Yeah, we're good for now. Thanks for helping. This went wrong so fast we didn't see it coming." Riley plopped back into his chair.

"Anytime. The deputies didn't find anything in your office, but you'll need a new locking front door. Nice job on the computers. They were livid when they couldn't even boot them up without going through the set-up screens." Hargis laughed.

"Figured as much with the doors. I'll send someone to secure the building who doesn't know anything."

"Okay, stay safe and I'll keep in touch." Hargis disconnected.

"Anything new?" Monroe had rejoined them at the table.

"Hargis said our building was an annoyance of non-information for the deputies. Bear, can you send a cousin over to secure the building? Our front doors are malfunctioning." Riley couldn't help but laugh if just for the relief of the pent-up stress he felt. He prayed this was in God's hands and that the outcome would be what God had planned for it.

"On it." Bear paced from the table to the front of the cabin.

Who knew a few weeks ago that saving Annie's life would put him on the front lines like this with his own freedom hanging in the balance? He pictured her face and knew he would do it again in a heartbeat to keep her safe. She was truly the innocent victim in all of this. He wondered if anyone checked her house to make sure they didn't go there. That would be an option if they needed another place to stay. Would they even put two and two together that he had access to it?

His phone rang again with an unavailable number. "Yes?"

"Hey, are you safe?" It was Ayers.

"For now. Tell me you have something to stop this downslide we are going through."

"Not yet. My ex-partner is keeping me in the loop without the brass knowing about it. I told him not to cross a line and get himself in trouble. Deputies made access to your building this morning. Luckily, you weren't there. They were incensed not being able to access your computer system. They also issued warrants for your men for being accessories or directly involved. Tell them to stay out of sight. Shockingly, the bodycam footage disappeared after I logged it in, but I had a copy on my computer. Someone is making my reports disappear."

"Thanks. Would you get in trouble if you forwarded me the video?" Riley didn't want to jeopardize his job.

"Already done. Should be coming over any minute."

"Okay. We didn't make the connection to the congressman until after all of this went down. Apparently, the judge in his back pocket is cousins with the congressman who also happened to be the chapter president that year of their fraternity."

Ayers whistled. "Riley, it's rumored that he has dirt on every elected official above him in the state and he is eyeing the governor's spot next year."

"Not after we get done with him. Keep yourself out of the spotlight. Just hang back and let us figure some things out. We are working contacts we have and hope to start shedding some light on the event in college that started all these cover-ups. Don't worry about getting your buddy to do a search warrant for evidence. We'll think of another way to bring it to light." Riley didn't want to risk his job and his pension over something he started.

"Gotcha. Let me know if you need anything. Keep the number I called you from. It's my friend's prepaid, so they won't be able to trace it back to me." Ayers said bye and disconnected.

"Well, everyone here is now an accessory, and there are warrants out for you also. Hope you don't mind close quarters for a while." Riley rose from the table, pushing back his chair. The legs scraped and bounced along the warped floor he hadn't gotten around to repairing yet.

He started another pot of coffee brewing and sauntered toward his bedroom, grabbing his bag on the way. What were they going to do? He knew it would be a waiting game for their contacts to start their own investigation into this. Not sure how much time they would have before they found this cabin and tied it back to him.

"We may need to move," Riley told them as he leaned in the doorway to the dining room.

"I have a place we can locate to," Bear offered. "My cousin owns it."

They all laughed at that. "No, I was thinking Annie's. Tracker has a way to sneak us in the back. We only take a couple of cars and leave the rest here."

"The police will be watching that house," Bear grumbled.

"Yeah, but if we can sneak in and keep the lights off, they will have no clue we are hiding right under their noses." Riley smirked. Alan wasn't the only one who could manipulate a situation to work in his favor.

"Let's go." They didn't hesitate to grab their bags and wake their sleeping colleagues.

They decided to take the largest cars so they would need fewer on the road. Tracker pulled up a map of the streets behind Annie's. They could easily slip in the back way without going through town and past their building, which was no doubt under surveillance.

"We need to cover the windows and keep the lights out at night. She has an old codger nosey neighbor who won't hesitate to call the police if he sees someone moving around his dead neighbor's house." Riley cringed and headed for the door.

Twenty-One

They crowded around Annie's back door while Riley let them in. Most of them being ex-military, they were all experts at moving silently through the yard, keeping to the shadows, and staying out of sight. Riley secured the door behind them and led them to the office, which had blackout blinds on the windows. With the door closed behind them, they turned on the monitors and accessed their cameras back at the office building. If you didn't know what to look for, someone would miss the well-hidden six deputies camped out, watching the building.

Riley quickly logged out of the system. "Okay, if you need to move about the house do so in the dark. There's a bathroom on the lower level off the kitchen and two upstairs. Stay out of the taped-off bedroom unless you enjoy the smell of blood. If for some reason they send someone to search this house, everyone head to the panic room. They won't have the code to get in. Erickson, get the interior cameras up and running and linked to our tablets so we will know when they clear the house if it comes to that."

Several of his men donned night vision goggles. He couldn't help but laugh and shake his head. He knew Annie's house, so he had no trouble maneuvering over to the couch he slept in before. If he could manage a couple of hours of sleep, it would help him stay alert. He was wearing himself down, and that was never a good idea when so much was in jeopardy. Glad Helen wasn't here to see this. She would be beside herself worried about him.

The images of Annie's burned corpse being pulled up the hill in the basket flashed behind his closed eyelids. The movement of his men around the house over the next hour lulled him to sleep, exhaustion taking over. If something happened, they would let him know.

His phone vibrated in his pocket and woke him. Again, it was a blocked number, so he answered. "Well well, Mr. Strong. How are you holding up? I hear you have a bit of a mess you are dealing with. Please let me know if I can be of service in taking care of anything for you. I told you, you had no clue who you were messing with." Alan disconnected.

Riley was now wide awake. The sun peeked on the horizon.

"Was that who I think it was?" Bear broke the silence.

"Yup, he said he warned me and asked if there was anything he could do to help."

"That son of—" Riley's phone interrupted Bear.

"Unavailable" showed on the display. "Yes?"

"Riley, are you sitting down?" Hargis was on the line.

"Yes, as a matter of fact, I am."

"The DNA doesn't match! I called a trusted family friend. They ran it through behind the scenes, putting a rush on it. I can't tell you how we got it, but it doesn't match!"

Riley bolted off the couch. "Wait? What?"

"It doesn't match. I had a friend grab samples and run them outside of normal channels. It wasn't Annie in the car. They have her!" Hargis disconnected.

Twenty-Two

Riley stared at his phone. His men gathered around him. "That wasn't Annie's body in the crash, and Alan has had her for two weeks!"

Several tried to speak at once, and Riley held up his hand. "We need to find her and now. Who knows what he's been putting her through." He ran his hands through his hair and blew out his breath. They had her for weeks. He couldn't breathe.

"I have his property records. Hold on." Gavin used his night vision to find the right file and hand it to Riley, who marched to the office.

Everyone crowded into the cramped space and shut the door so they could turn on the light. Riley flipped page after page. Most of the properties were in the county where he lived. But he just called him. "Bear, trace this number and check where it just called from." He handed him his phone.

Bear withdrew his phone from his pocket and dialed, no doubt, one of his cousins. "Hey babe, I need you." Bear blushed when the guys smirked. "Thanks. He's right here in town," Bear informed them when he hung up.

"Babe?" Monroe grinned. "Do you have nicknames for all your cousins?"

"You're sick. It wasn't a cousin. Leave it alone." Bear turned to Riley.

"What properties are here in town?" Riley spread the pages across the small desk that the monitors had taken over when he installed her security system.

"There's nothing in town that I know of." Gavin scrunched his forehead as he thought about the files.

"Okay. Did we run properties on his goons?" Riley turned to the others.

"I did but not sure if the file is here or not. Hold on." Duffy scurried from the room, closing the door behind him. A few seconds ticked by when he rejoined them with several folders in his hands. "Here's all of their properties."

Riley handed out files to everyone to check. Frantic page-turning filled the silence as they all held their breaths waiting for the aha moment to hit. Several tossed their folders on the desk, muttering there was nothing in their file.

"Here!" Riley pulled the deceased one's records from the stack.

Bear peered over his shoulder. "That's not that far. But do we chance going after her when all of us are wanted?"

"No, we can't." Riley snagged his phone from his pocket and sent a quick text to Ayers giving him the location.

"Will handle," came the reply.

Riley dropped his phone on his desk and clasped his hands together. She was alive this whole time. They should have been looking for her. "I need to be there for her."

"You go out there, and they will arrest you for murder." Bear put a hand on his shoulder.

"Yeah, I know but she's been alone with Mark and Alan for two weeks. I can only imagine what they are doing to her!" Riley rocked back on his heels.

"If you want to go get her, we're with you," Monroe piped up.

Riley's phone vibrated across the desk. He read the text message. "They need more evidence," Ayers responded.

"We aren't waiting!" Riley tapped back, tossed his phone on the desk, and stormed out of the office.

No one needed to ask what to do. Everyone suited up to go in. Riley couldn't ask for a better bunch of employees or friends than the men who stood in the room with him. He tugged his vest on and put on the duty belt he bought when he left the precinct. They would need to cross the backyard, and the sun was already announcing its arrival. There would be no stealth mode leaving the house, and they would be giving up their safe place if someone caught them. He didn't care if he had to spend the rest of his life in jail for a murder he didn't commit if he saved Annie. He glanced back at his men and knew they felt the same way. He gave a quick curt nod and stormed through the back door.

The drive felt as if it took forever. Thirty-four minutes later and traveling above the posted speed limit—a chance they had to take to get to Annie as quick as possible—they pulled down the hill to the small house nestled in the trees off the main road. Riley jumped from the car and strolled to the last car in line and pulled his weapon. "Okay, guys. This could get nasty real fast. Anyone wanting out, no ill will whatsoever. I just can't leave her in there with him after all he's put her through already."

"Let's go," Bear answered for everyone.

They stalked to the edge of the trees and peered around the row. Alan's large black SUV sat in the driveway next to a small beat-up four-door sedan with no insignia on it. A scream pierced the air. It was Annie. They all started forward before the scream finished. Riley and Bear, together with Monroe and Duffy, took the front while the rest jogged around the rear of the house. A tap on his shoulder told Riley it was time to go get him. He kicked in the door and checked from left to right. No one was in the front of the house. Stretched between the table and counter was a small tripwire.

Riley held up his hand to the men that came in the back and pointed to the wire. He had no doubt they would double-check every place they stepped from what they had seen in the military during deployments. He wouldn't worry about his men; he needed to get to Annie. They were quite capable of diffusing anything they came across, rendering the devices inert. Another scream escaped through the floorboards. Riley scanned the room for a basement door.

Bear pointed to the corner of the rug partially folded over. Riley nodded and silently moved to grab the opposite side of where Bear stood. They watched Bear's fingers count to three and yanked the rug back, exposing a trap door. Riley took a deep breath and waited for Bear to open the hatch.

Alan's raspy voice filtered through the floorboards. "So, you thought you could get away from me, huh?"

Riley frantically signaled Tracker, who started recording the event.

"Do you know what happened to the first two wives who thought they could leave me? Me! Do you know how many women throw themselves at me and want me?" Alan screamed.

Riley cringed and motioned for Tracker to continue to record everything then motioned for Bear to open the hatch.

He lifted the handle and eased the door up and away from the stairs that were below it.

"Let me go!" Annie screamed.

The unmistakable sound of a slap reached him at the top of the stairs, and Riley had no doubt it was Annie. She cried out, confirming his suspicions a second later. He started down the first step and then knelt to get a better angle on what he would face when he came to the bottom of the stairs. Off to the right, boxes were stored for what looked like years. The basement flooded on more than one occasion from the telltale water lines on the walls and disintegrating boxes piled in the corner.

A muffled scream reached him as he took another step down. The stairs creaked and he grimaced as the board under his foot wobbled rubbing against the nails. He pointed to the step and then returned his hand to his gun. Bear nodded in acknowledgment. Another step down, he peered into the basement.

"I told you, you are my property. You belong to me and now that you are a cash cow with your lovely book that you wrote, we'll get remarried happier than we were the first time and you will admit the mistake you made in ever leaving me. Then once you get a couple more books published, there will be such a horrible accident that you won't survive. I, of course, will be heartbroken. You were the love of my life, but I can live with the heartache since you are still alive in your books and, of course, the royalties that will add quite nicely to my income. I'll be set for life." Alan's pompous monotonous voice drifted up the stairs. He talked down to her as if she were nothing, to be thrown away when she was no longer convenient for him. A phone rang. "What is it? I told you not to interrupt me!"

Riley crept down two more steps.

"What? Now? Thanks for the heads up. I'll move locations. They won't be able to get here before I get her moved." Alan's voice stressed on the last sentence. "Okay, looks like we have to move, so hold on. Let me get you something to help you relax."

Riley still couldn't see them, but the sound of his voice bounced off the cold sweating concrete walls, where black mold crept up through the mortar grooves, inching along in spiderweb-like trails. They were around a corner that a wall blocked. He inched down the rest of the stairs and blew out a sigh when they didn't hit any more creaking stairs. The question was, where was Mark? He only heard Alan's voice and Annie's. No doubt his men were keeping an eye out while they were disabling the tripwires in case they needed to make a quick escape.

Annie's muffled screams pierced the basement, and Bear grabbed his shoulder to stop him from lunging around the corner.

"There, now. You have my mark even deeper than last time. Ooh, that has to hurt. Now come on, I have to get you ready to travel." Alan chuckled. "Come on, play nice and stop trying to kick me. Be a good wife, and in a minute, we can kiss and make up and be like it was when we were first married. I know you miss that, but your punishment needed to be doled out to show you who owns you. We need to move first—no more honeymoon cabin for now—but I'll make it up to you."

The hairs stood at attention on the back of his neck. He nodded to Bear and Tracker before inching around the corner. Gunfire interrupted him as he put Alan in his sight, who removed a hypodermic needle from Annie's back. Annie's eyes widened and locked onto Riley's as she lifted her head. Relief flooded her face and tears trickled down her cheeks.

"Well well, if it isn't Mr. Strong." Alan stepped behind Annie who was tied to a table face down. Her shirt was torn open and almost shredded across her back.

Riley clenched his jaw as Bear moved around to his left. The room was small, so with four of them it was crowded, and then Tracker joined the group, filming everything from behind Riley. He held the phone with his left hand while his right held his sidearm.

"Alan, give up. You're caught," Riley calmly relayed to him.

"I hear you have a felony warrant issued for your arrest for murder. I think I'll land on my feet like I always do, unlike you. The way you lured Sam to the house and killed him and had your friend shoot you so it looked like self-defense. That wasn't nice, Mr. Strong." Alan's monotone voice held no emotions. The man was a sociopath.

"Oh, that will be cleared up quickly once we show the video to a judge and show him I never sent those texts."

Alan inched closer to Annie. "You have to admit, you didn't plan on being on the run, did you? Hiding from the law you used to uphold and took your oath so seriously. Self-righteously thinking you were above everyone else."

"Yes, I didn't see that one coming, although I never thought I was above anyone else. That is where your faults lie. Nice move with the congressman. Too bad he will be removed from office by the time you are convicted of murdering your two wives and Annie's parents."

"Why, Mr. Strong. I have no earthly idea what you could be talking about. I'm a grieving widower who lost two women I loved dearly. Life hasn't been kind to me, but Annie and I rekindling our love and remarrying, I think will help relieve some of that ache." Alan lifted a knife running the dull end over her back.

Annie flinched and almost cried out but clamped her mouth shut, scrunching her eyes. She trembled. The welts on her back that showed through her torn shirt told him Alan had been busy the weeks he had access to her. The branded mark on her shoulder was ugly and swollen. He had branded her again on the opposite shoulder of the previous one. Her skin was scorched and burned. He couldn't imagine the pain she went through while he held that to her. The cufflink lay on the table next to her together with the torch he used to heat it.

"Like my handy work? I learned about the fun of burning with Sheila. She was the first that I took time with. Annie here will get more of this when I get her back home where she belongs. Then we can go over the lessons again about what being a good wife entails." Alan's eyes shifted to the corner. Riley and Bear spun on their heels as a shot rang out.

Mark Murphy collapsed in front of them as Monroe hung through the opening, gun trained on him. Blood ran from Mark's shoulder. Riley spun back to Alan, who had a gun to Annie's head.

"That is two of my friends you have murdered now. I'll make you pay for that." Alan's finger twitched as it curled around the trigger. "Although they were getting sloppy. Maybe some of my new friends will help fill the void."

"Not sure how you think that will happen. You pull that trigger and you will be dead before you hit the floor." Riley aimed center mass while Monroe joined the group.

Alan flinched. "You still have no clue who you are dealing with. You won't win this, Mr. Strong. Do you really think she's worth the hassle she's already caused you? You lost your business, your freedom, with the warrant hanging over your head. Come on tell me. Is she worth all of that?"

"Yes." Riley didn't hesitate as he spit out the answer.

Annie raised her head, her eyes drooping. He gave her a quick single nod then raised his eyes to Alan. "Wow, she got to you, didn't she? Do you know she was worthless and poor when I met her? She didn't amount to anything until I shaped her into the woman she is today."

"She's a stronger, better person than you could ever hope or dream to be. Being penniless doesn't make someone worthless. Step away from her and put your hands up." Riley inched forward.

Annie pulled on the ropes that held her. Her arms strained against the tension as she tried to pull free. Alan glanced at her and then at Riley. "She is strong, I'll give you that, but it also made her the most fun so far."

"Did you really have to kill her parents?" Alan flinched at Riley's question.

"They died in a horrible car crash. I was there for Annie when she grieved for them, like the good husband I am." Alan's clipped response was as cold as the man himself.

"So, the damage to the back bumper pushing them over the embankment had nothing to do with their deaths or the cut brake lines? We have the original local police report. They kept it in case it ever came back to visit them. They ruled it a homicide, but the county shut them down from being able to pursue the case and find a suspect." Riley took another step forward. A couple more and he would be at Annie's side.

"Try and prove that in court. I was in my office with a very prestigious patient who will vouch for me at the time of their deaths." Alan jumped when Mark Murphy moaned behind Riley.

Monroe spun around and double-checked the cuffs he used to restrain Mark's arms behind his back. He turned back to Riley and nodded that everything was still secure.

Riley snorted. "Do you really think Mark Murphy will back you up in court? His freedom will be on the line if he survives the surgery he'll need to remove that bullet. We already have witness testimony that he assaulted an officer and kidnaped Annie. Although I'm confused why, if they knew where she was for weeks before making contact, they didn't grab her sooner."

"They didn't have permission. Their job was to monitor and report back to me what was going on. I had to rearrange my schedule and have another doctor cover my scheduled surgeries, and her name is Megan Montgomery! She is *my* wife!" Alan spit out, his voice changing from his monotone dull brusque tone as it rose two octaves.

Annie flinched and tried to shrink away from the anger Alan spewed behind her. Alan took a breath and lowered the gun to the table as Duffy and Gavin joined them in the room, edging around so no one was in friendly line of fire. Alan straightened his tie and unrolled his shirt sleeves on the no doubt high-priced dress shirt he wore.

He stepped out from behind the table she was still tied to and peered down at Mark Murphy. "You all will pay for this."

Gavin and Duffy put cuffs on Alan and had to use two pairs. They marched him upstairs while Riley snagged a knife off the table and cut the bindings that held Annie down. Bear tore through the corner pile of clothes and pulled out a large shirt, handing it to Riley. He draped it over her shoulders, wrapping it around the front of her as she sat up. She trembled as she tried to button it. Riley helped her as she cried.

"Are you okay?" He let Monroe squeeze in by the table and take her pulse.

"You came for me." She clutched his hand before her eyes closed.

Riley lowered his head. "I'm sorry. It would have been sooner, but we thought you were dead."

She slurred, "You came for me."

Monroe nodded to Riley and helped her to stand. Her legs wobbled and Riley scooped her up. She threw her arms around him and buried her head into the side of his neck as his heart raced. "You came for me."

"I'm so sorry. I failed you, Annie. They should have never been able to get to you." He trudged up the stairs as Monroe and Bear lifted Mark from the floor and dragged him up the dilapidated warped steps.

Red and blue lights danced and reflected off surfaces as they crested the top of the stairs. Ayers frowned at Riley when he saw Annie in his arms. Alan was sitting in the back of a patrol car while his friend's handcuffs were switched out to the officer placing him under arrest, in front of the cabin. "Riley, you shouldn't be here."

"I couldn't wait for the police to do something. She was in danger." He marched past Ayers to the waiting ambulance. Annie tightened her arms around him and started trembling worse than she already was. Her breath came out in quick pants.

"Yeah, but now, I have to arrest you. There's still the warrant for the charge of murder." He unclipped the handcuffs from the back of his duty belt and waited for Riley to lay Annie on the gurney.

She clutched his hand her fingers turning white. "Don't leave me!"

"Annie, I have to go with the officers until we get this cleared up. Alan is in custody and Mark is out of the equation with his injuries." Riley pried her fingers from the hand she clung to.

"I'll make sure she's taken care of. Annie, I'll meet you at the hospital, but right now we need to get this scene secure and figure out what happened." Ayers placed Riley's hands behind his back and clicked the cuffs around his wrist. He used his key to lock them so they wouldn't tighten while he rode to the police department.

Riley nodded to Annie, her eyes wide with fear as she shook her head before it fell to the side and her body went limp. They loaded the gurney into the back of the ambulance.

After the ambulance pulled away seconds later Riley spun to Ayers. "There are explosives in the house that I'm not sure my men were able to defuse. Tell the deputies to be careful."

Ayers sprinted to the door and ordered everyone to get out of the cabin. Men rushed from the doors. The deputies nodded as he explained what Riley told him and immediately shut off their radios while one jogged to the edge of the driveway, calling in for their EOD unit and bomb-sniffing dogs. The doors stood open to the detention van. His men were being loaded into the back as a deputy approached Riley.

"Deputy, I'll take him in." Ayers stepped forward.

"Sorry, it's a county warrant. We get to take him in." He pushed on Riley's upper back toward the van.

"Ayers, don't let Alan out. He kidnapped her and tortured her. Get to the hospital. Keep her safe. He'll come for her." Riley stepped into the back of the van.

Ayers nodded. The van bounced along the gravel driveway, and Riley had to plant his feet against the side to keep from being tossed around. He looked at his men. "Sorry guys, it could take some time to get us out of this one."

Riley looked around. Monroe was missing from the equation. His eyes met Bear's, who only winked and then smiled. "I have a cousin." Oh, boy.

Twenty-Three

Her head throbbed and she had a searing pain in her shoulder. Voices mumbled around her as someone rolled her to her side. An icy cold penetrated the skin around the burn Alan gave her. She sucked in a breath.

"Annie?" She knew that voice, but her head seemed as if it was filled with cotton.

She tried to move her hand, but her foggy brain wasn't able to send the right signals to the rest of her. What had Alan injected her with? It wasn't the first time he drugged her to manipulate or torture her. She cracked her eyes open before shutting them against the painful light in the room. She let the darkness take her under again.

"Annie, I need you to open your eyes." There was that gentle voice again.

She partially opened her eyes to take in her surroundings. She was in the apartment. Her hand obeyed her this time when she raised it to her head.

"No, don't touch your head. Glue is holding that cut closed. I finally got it to stop bleeding." Monroe came into her field of vision.

She wanted to sob with relief it wasn't Alan.

"Shh, you're okay. I took you from the back of the ambulance with the paramedics' help and brought you here. You have several cuts on your back and, of course, the new burn from his cufflink, but you'll be okay. There is no internal damage as far as I can tell. Is there any pain besides what I listed? Anything that tells me we need to get you into a scan to make sure there aren't any internal injuries?" Monroe still held her hand.

"No, he didn't hit me like he normally did. He was ranting about being in jail for as long as he was and taking it out on Mark, asking where Sam was. He turned back to me when I said Sam was dead. I should have kept my mouth shut. That is when he started striking me across the back and continued several times a day. I don't know what he used this time. I don't know how long that went on. I kept blacking out." Her raspy hoarse voice didn't last long before she closed her eyes again.

"Hey, stay with me, okay?" Monroe tightened his grip on her hand.

"Is everyone good? What happened while he had me?" Annie opened her eyes fully, clearing her vision.

Monroe's tight-lipped smile gave away how bad it was. "That is not something you need to worry about right now. Just concentrate on you."

She noticed his flinch when he stood, and his hand flew to his side, where blood stained his shirt. "You're hurt!" She tried to sit up and cried out when the shirt she was wearing scraped down her back.

"Whoa, stay down. I'm fine." He barely managed a smile, and that's when she noticed how pale he was.

"You are not fine!"

• • • •

RILEY WAS SHUFFLED through the system, his fingerprints and mug shots taken. Deputies tried to get him to talk to them, to which he only replied with, "Not without my lawyer." His men replied the same and were put in separate cells since it involved murder charges. They didn't want them talking to each other to get their stories straight. Of course, there was only one story, the truth, and Riley trusted that God would make sure that was the only story the judge believed.

Ayers nodded at Riley as he strolled toward his cell. "Riley."

"Ayers." Riley wasn't sure who to trust. But he hoped the friend who he worked side by side with for years was the man who stood in front of him now.

"Don't say anything. Annie never made it to the hospital. I know you had something to do with that, and you need to tell me where she is. The paramedics said she asked them to pull over and that she had a friend picking her up. I had a safe house to hide her away with a friend set up to watch over her, but I can't help her if I don't know where to find her. Where did you stash her? You're not a cop anymore; you can't run off acting like you're a superhero doing what you want. There are laws for a reason and a way we do things." Ayers tilted his head to the side. Frustration swept over his features before he schooled his reaction. He was ticked and Riley wasn't sure what bothered Ayers more: Annie not letting him help her or the fact someone picked her up without his approval.

"Friend?" Riley narrowed his eyes.

Ayers held up his hand. "I tried to follow the ambulance when a car cut me off, and I hit every red light in the city trying to catch up. I tried to pull over a silver Audi that left the parking lot where the ambulance was parked, and they broke several traffic laws. I put a bolo out on the sedan, which disappeared down an alley. All she told the paramedics to pass along was that he was almost as good as a doctor but less classy."

Riley smiled and pressed his lips together. Now he knew where Monroe went. "I actually had nothing to do with that." He nodded for him to continue. He would be able to relax a little, knowing she was with one of his men. Monroe would put his life on the line to keep her safe.

"You will be taken in front of a judge tomorrow. Get yourself a good lawyer. Someone who can stall until we can figure this out and get evidence in front of the judge of Montgomery's crimes. Until then, it is his word against yours, and we already know who is on his side. You will more than likely be held without bond until your case goes to trial. I know that Audi was one of your fleet vehicles. If you can get hold of him, have him turn himself in. It's for his own good. I will not give up my retirement and be terminated for aiding and abetting a fugitive. We have been friends for a long time, Riley. I don't want this to come between us." Ayers did an about-face and marched from Riley's cell.

He breathed a sigh of relief. Annie was safe and with Monroe. He couldn't ask for a better outcome than where she was right now. With his feet kicked up, he stared at the ceiling. There had to be a way to connect the congressman to Alan's crimes. What happened to Tracker's phone and the video? Did the police confiscate it? If they did, would the video be erased by someone on Alan's payroll? He closed his eyes as tension pulled at the base of his neck. A headache was something he couldn't afford to deal with right now.

Someone screamed at the top of their lungs about injustice. Riley closed his eyes as the pounding in the back of his head started. Great, this was going to be a long day.

"Riley Strong, your lawyer is here to see you." A guard announced as he stepped in front of Riley's cell.

He squinted at the guard; he hadn't called a lawyer.

"Come on, let's go." Impatience radiated in the guard's words.

He stood and put his hands through the opening for the guard to handcuff him. Being on the right side of the law for so many years as an officer, this was an experience, he had to admit, that bothered him more than he thought it would. Stepping back, he waited for the guard to signal for the door to be unlocked. The loud buzzing as the lock disengaged, bouncing off his porous cinderblock cell walls, echoed through the jail.

The guard pointed down the hall. "This way."

Riley entered the interrogation room, sat in the chair, and waited for the guard to attach his handcuffs to the table. As the guard exited, a tall blonde entered, sharply dressed in a navy-blue suit with the skirt modestly hitting just above her knees. Riley had never met this woman before and wasn't sure what to expect.

"Mr. Strong. I have been retained to be your counsel. This will be a quick meeting to just get acquainted and introduce myself. I'm Isabelle. The charges are ridiculous and outlandish. I have been apprised of the situation to which these charges were linked. I met with a judge about the men who work for you. They have all been released and the charges were dropped since they weren't in Annie Divers's residence at the time of the shooting. There was no evidence that tied them to the incident in question. Now, with that said, you were there and that is where it gets sticky. The judge refused to have the charges dropped. Well, you did shoot and kill him. What I hope to present to the judge will be irrefutable evidence that you in no way lured Mr. Berger to the residence with the explicit intent of killing him, due to the lack of bullets found at the scene. The gunpowder residue was explained with a story about how they were at the shooting range a couple of hours before he received this so-called text from you and not from firing at you. That, in fact, Mr. Berger went there with the intention of killing you and taking Miss Divers against her will." She took a breath and met his eyes.

Riley raised an eyebrow at her. He didn't know what to say. Who hired her and threw enough money at her to push up their court times to get his men released? She was good, whoever this woman was that stood in front of him, and she at least got a reasonable judge to hear her arguments in regard to his men.

"Mr. Strong. Trust me, we have a mutual friend, who is tired of letting the *devil* win." She smiled.

He sat forward in his chair. "Is she okay?"

"Yes, I believe you know who is protecting her at this time. She feels it's best to stay hidden until the court date with the devil so she can stand up to him once and for all."

"Thank you, God." Riley breathed out closing his eyes and lowering his head.

"Yes, we need to thank Him. You care for her, don't you?" Isabelle narrowed her eyes, studying him.

"She's suffered because of Alan. I've never seen such a blatant case of domestic violence covered up as the one he's committed. I want to see all of them brought to justice." Riley started to pull his hands to his lap but forgot he was handcuffed to the table.

"That wasn't a no." Isabelle smiled. "There are several things in the works. Be patient. I'm trying to get you out of here as fast as possible. She said to trust her on that."

"Thank you, Mrs...?" Riley stopped.

"Miss Mathis. I'll leave you my card. If you need anything, don't hesitate to have someone get hold of me. I'll be working on getting you out in the meantime." Her staccato-clipped steps from her tasteful pumps filled the room as she stalked around the table and knocked on the door. The guard came in and unlocked his cuffs, releasing him from the metal ring bolted to the surface.

"Can I get something for a headache?" Riley squinted at the bright lights in the hall.

"I'll see what I can do." The guard smiled.

Riley remembered seeing him when he transported prisoners to the county lockup back in the day. He always showed the guards respect. They did a job he would never want to do. Deal with these knuckleheads on a minute-by-minute basis. No thank you, he thought. He preferred being out on the road in the cruiser than locked in a building with uncountable inmates.

The guard released his hands from the cuffs and strolled down to the other door. Within a few minutes, he came back with a couple of pills and a small glass of water.

"Thanks." Riley tossed the pills in his mouth and followed them with a gulp of the water the cup held.

"Good luck with your case. I hope everything works out and you get out of here. You don't deserve to be in here. You're one of the good guys." The guard nodded to Riley and sauntered down the hall.

He smiled as he lay on the bunk that his feet almost draped over the end of. At least Annie was safe and Alan couldn't get to her. Monroe would keep her safe and be able to look after the injuries she suffered yet again at Alan's hand. He cringed when he pictured the brand on her shoulder and how deep it looked this time. Too bad they couldn't flip Mark to testify against Alan. With their history, Riley knew that would never happen. They had been through too much and both were implicated in crimes a mile long. He was tempted to call Monroe's number and have him accept his call, but he knew that would only tip off the deputies, who no doubt would be listening to any calls he made.

If his attorney was half as good as she seemed to be, he could be out of here as early as tomorrow once she got them in front of a judge. The fact that his men were already out and free to dig up what dirt they could on Alan and the congressman made it much easier for him to get some sleep tonight. They would no doubt rendezvous with Monroe and put that many more bodies between Annie and Alan. His men never broke the law to end up in jail like today. Sure, they skirted it pretty close a couple of times but never to the extent that they were arrested. It would be a personal vendetta for them to put the nails in Alan's coffin and have him put away for good. They also liked Annie, and what they saw in the basement of Mark's cabin would only make them that much more protective of her.

His mind was a blur of ideas and thoughts as he lay in his cell studying the ceiling. He wished he had his files to go over so he could find a link to the congressman being at the frat party where the unthinkable happened to those twelve girls. He closed his eyes and was asleep before he could contemplate the last time he slept and how tired he was.

The hum of the fluorescent lights aroused him before they blinked all the way on. He opened his eyes wide and then rubbed his palms against them. His feet dropped to the floor and his boots hit it with a thud. He strolled to the sink and splashed water on his face to wake himself up. He had slept through the night. He couldn't remember the last time he slept that sound since meeting Annie. She was safe and that was the last thought he remembered he had before he'd drifted off. Knowing she was with his men eased that part of stress in his life.

The day guard stood in front of his cell when he turned around. "The judge wants to see you."

Riley strolled to the bars and put his hands through the opening, waiting to be handcuffed. "What time is it?"

"Zero six thirty," came the reply.

"Little early to see a judge, don't you think?" Riley raised an eyebrow.

The guard smiled a lopsided grin. "You have a pesky, determined lawyer who's got friends."

"Guess so." Riley was impressed.

Their rubber-soled boots were quiet as they made their way to the back hallway that led prisoners to court. Prisoners were never paraded through the main hallways to the courtrooms. It only panicked citizens when they saw them in shackles.

Judge Kinsley tried to hide the yawn behind his hand as Riley entered the courtroom. Staccato footsteps sounded on the marble floor behind him. He turned to see his lawyer in a cream-colored suit today with black stiletto heels that made her taller than he was.

"Mr. Strong, you are back in my court again today, I see. Earlier than I normally would like to see prisoners. Miss Mathis, please go ahead." The judge banged his gavel.

"Your Honor, I would first like to thank you for the amended time for seeing my client. Second, I am petitioning for the charges to be dropped in regard to the blatant attempt to get Mr. Strong out of the way so Alan Montgomery could abduct his ex-wife and continue his abuse of her."

"Hold on. Let me read this for a moment." The judge perched reading glasses on the end of his nose as he perused a file handed to him by the bailiff. He flipped a page and continued to read.

"Isn't this the same Sam Berger that I issued a court order to stay away from Miss Divers and Mr. Strong here?" The judge peered over his glasses.

"Yes sir, he broke into the victim's house and was armed with a gun. But per your order and decision, he was not supposed to be in possession of any firearm due to the Brady indicator on the protection order you filed."

"And was this man issued the service on that protection order?"

"Yes, Your Honor. On the third page down, it shows your deputies serving him with that protection order when he came and tried to bail out Mr. Montgomery, who was being held in contempt of court before his served time."

"Then how is this a possible murder charge when the man blatantly went against court orders and had a gun?" The judge scowled at the prosecutor.

"Your honor, we have evidence that Mr. Strong sent a text to this man, asking him to come to the house. Where we hope to prove he lured him upstairs with the guise of working out the situation and murdered him when in fact he never had a gun on him at that time."

"Well, we already know how Mr. Montgomery likes to send fake texts to suit his situations as he deems fit. Where is Mr. Montgomery in all of this?"

"He is being held for kidnapping his ex-wife and torturing her for days until Mr. Strong was able to locate them and rescue Miss Divers," Isabella answered the judge in short, to-the-point statements. Riley knew that would go a long way with this judge.

"So, he went against my court orders to stay away from his ex-wife the same as Mr. Murphy?" The judge flipped to the third page, nodding as he read the service of the protection orders.

"Sir, we will not be pursuing charges in that matter due to the fact that the orders were rescinded when Miss Divers was presumed deceased and were no longer valid through the eyes of the court," the prosecutor rambled.

"Excuse me, sir. I believe only I can rescind those orders! And I don't believe the identity of the person in the car had been released. Now, had it?" Judge Kinsley raised his voice.

Riley bit his lip. The prosecutor stepped over the line, and it only made him wonder who had contacted him to say the orders were no longer valid if the judge was this mad.

"Well sir, I believe the paperwork had been filed to get those orders rescinded and that they couldn't be valid when the victim is no longer alive." The prosecutor tugged at his tie. He just messed up and he knew he couldn't take it back. Sweat beaded on his top lip.

"She isn't dead, is she? And what about the orders to keep them away from Mr. Strong? His were still valid as you claim because he was never dead, was he?"

"No sir, but since Miss Divers was the victim and he wasn't, it didn't make sense to keep his valid also."

"I am the only one authorized to make them valid or not, Mr. Prosecutor, and he was deemed to be a victim in this court's eyes by me, so they were still valid! Since you don't have that authority, I'm requesting an investigation into these trumped-up charges against Mr. Strong. Bailiff, make sure the protection orders are still valid in the system. The victims are both still alive and in need of protection, apparently, unlike what the prosecutor seems to think. Mr. Strong, you are released on your own recognizance until the incompetent man to my right can come up with evidence that you did the things he wants you charged with. Mr. Prosecutor, I suggest you get some hard evidence besides doctored texts and present it in my court one week from today. Bailiff, Mr. Strong is free to go. Please make sure his belongings are returned to him." The judge slammed his gavel onto his bench and stood, muttering under his breath.

The bailiff removed Riley's handcuffs and shook his hand. "That's twice God was looking out for you that I know of."

"Isabelle Mathis, I can't thank you enough. I need to meet up with my men. Where are they?" Riley shook her hand.

"I'll take you to them." She smiled, her shockingly white, bleached teeth were a drastic contrast to the red lipstick she wore.

He wanted to run from the courthouse but stowed his enthusiasm at seeing Annie to make sure she was okay and safe. "Do you think they can come up with evidence to get the charges pushed forward?"

"No. You should be good. If they had any evidence, they would have thrown it at the judge to keep you locked up longer. Mark Murphy is still in the hospital, tight-lipped and not speaking. Mr. Monroe is a good shot and only wounded him. We hope when this goes to court, he will throw Montgomery under the bus to save himself on capital murder charges. The body from the Porsche never made it to the morgue. We were lucky that samples were taken from the scene, or proving it wasn't Annie wouldn't have happened as fast as it did. We won't know the identity of that victim until we can locate her remains. Annie said when they took her, they had her change into different clothes. She can now only assume it was to put what she was wearing on the dead woman they wanted you to think was her." Isabelle used her key fob to unlock her Jaguar.

"Is she okay?" Riley was itching to see her again. After thinking she died because of him, he just wanted to sit in the same room with her and see how she was doing and handling this new round of abuse she'd had to endure.

"I'll let her tell you the details she wants to tell you. Don't push her. She'll need time to recover from what they did to her again. Let her come to you when she's ready. She will be able to heal from her physical wounds, but he pulled her back down into the dark tunnel she was in before she escaped from him through her divorce. My firm was the one who was able to get a judge to see her outside her husband's little friend's courtroom." Isabelle turned down the street his office was located.

He raised an eyebrow at her when she pulled into the back lot.

"Would you think to look for her here?" She shut the car off and popped the door locks.

"No, can't say that I would." With all the times he tried to get her to stay in the apartment to keep her safe, this was where they ended up. He'd figured she would disappear as she wanted to do before it got to this point.

"I have a meeting, so I'll let you talk to her alone. Mr. Strong, please don't push her. Let her come to you."

"I know. I used to work domestic cases when I was an officer. It would only hurt the trust between us if I pushed it." Riley smiled.

Isabelle turned the key to restart the Jaguar's engine that hummed like a well-oiled machine. "She's an amazing woman. Don't hurt her."

Riley's brows knitted together. He closed the door to her car for her to leave and make her next meeting. He stared at the back of the building for several seconds before he strolled to the doors. Bear met him and had them open, waiting for him.

"How is she?"

"Good, considering that madman had her for two weeks. Amazing lawyer she found for us, huh?" Bear locked the door and scanned the back lot.

"She hired her?" Riley looked at the ceiling as if he could see through the next two floors to her apartment. He'd had his suspicions.

"Yup, said we saved her life, so it was the least she could do." Bear sauntered past Riley, bumping into his shoulder as he passed.

Riley jogged to catch up. "How are we on evidence to keep Alan in jail for good this time? That is, if the prosecutor will put a hold on him and not let him out on a signature bond like he has done for murderers in the past."

"Still working on it. Sasha tried to go in and clean, but Monroe headed her off at the door and let her know she didn't need to clean that unit until she was told otherwise. Some of the guys are still hurting after yesterday's run-in with Mark Murphy before he made it downstairs to take a shot at you. Duffy took one to the shoulder and will be released this afternoon from St. Mary's, while Gavin took a hit to the head from the butt of the gun. Monroe was stabbed but said he stitched himself up, and he refuses to go to the hospital, even though the charges were dropped against him. He won't leave her side until he knows you are with her.

Stubborn jerk." Bear dropped into his chair, and it groaned under his weight.

"I'll send him down. Take him to the hospital. I'll make it an order if he wants another paycheck from me. Good call on Sasha. I don't want her wrapped up in any of this. Maybe we need to give her a couple of weeks off with pay until this is cleared up." Riley jammed in the button on the elevator panel with his thumb, to take him to the apartment Annie was in, harder than he intended. Mad he hadn't known some of his men were hurt, he decided he would check on Duffy after he checked on Annie and made sure Monroe went to the hospital.

The door stood open as he approached the doorway. "Hello?" Monroe's ghastly pale skin shocked him. "Get to the hospital now. Bear will take you."

"Yes, sir." Monroe didn't argue, only ambled to the door and disappeared through it.

Riley knew it was bad if he didn't debate about going to the hospital. Annie appeared in the doorway to the bedroom. She was dressed in a loose-fitting t-shirt and shorts, and he could see the welts and bruises up and down her legs. "Are you okay?"

Annie threw her arms around his neck. "Thank you."

Riley wrapped his arms around her, careful not to hold her too tight. From the time she was run down to getting taken again to Riley finally getting to her had only been about three weeks. He had seen what Alan did to her back, and no doubt she would be in pain. She shook as he held her, and he realized she was crying. "Shh. It's okay. I've got you. He'll never get you again."

They stood for several minutes while he held her and let her cling to him as if he were her lifeline; no matter how long she needed him to anchor her, he would. Fear radiated through her as she continued to sob. His heart hammered in his chest, as her fingers dug into his shoulder muscles, and it took his breath away. He wanted to keep her safe and away from anyone who could ever hurt her again. She was strong enough to leave him if she was strong enough to make it through this. He wasn't going to push her away.

"Oh, my gosh. I'm so sorry. I don't know what came over me." Annie wiped at the tears on her face and then at his shirt. She stopped as if she just realized what she was doing and pulled away.

His heart ached to hold her again. Great, he had it bad. "Come on, sit down so we can talk." He motioned to the couch.

• • • •

THIS TIME, THEY DIDN'T keep a cushion between them but sat next to each other, their knees touching. She clasped his hand, afraid to let go. "Riley, I'm sorry he's putting you through his little games. I should have told you earlier about the congressman being part of their elite group. I didn't think he would involve him. With next year being an election year, he usually shies away from helping Alan during those times. I didn't realize he would go after you like he did and that you wouldn't be safe from his games."

"This isn't your fault. No more secrets, though. I need full disclosure so we can fight this together." He covered her hand with his other one. "Tell me what you can about their relationship. Something happened in the early years of college with a party while Alan was out of town. We think he has evidence of a serious crime that occurred and Alan helped them clean it up. Hence, they pretty much do his bidding now when he needs something cleaned up."

Annie furrowed her brow, thinking back to one night in particular. "You know, I think something did happen. Alan used to gloat when he was drunk about being able to get away with murder. I never took that comment seriously until I got to know him. He mentioned a party and that he had elected officials in his back pocket because of what happened that night." She narrowed her eyes and bit her lower lip, trying to remember what he said.

"What else can you tell me?" Riley hoped it was what he thought it would be. Finally, an edge they were looking for to break this wide open and take him down once and for all.

"I'm thinking. There was something he said years ago. He had brutally beaten me. I lay there and let him think I was still unconscious so he didn't start up again. He was on a rant. Bragging. I can't...give me a minute." She lurched off the couch and paced from wall to wall.

She appreciated how Riley sat back and let her work through the memory. She muttered to herself as she repeated what he rambled about that night. Several phrases she repeated numerous times, trying to trigger what she couldn't recall as she worked through the onslaught of images from that horrifying night.

"Video!" Her eyes opened wide. "Oh, my gosh. He has a video. I think I took it when I left him."

"What do you mean, you think you took it?" Riley rose and towered over her as she stalked to him and peered into his eyes.

"He used to record his *training* sessions of him beating me and make me watch them later when I was on the verge of needing another lesson. His voice was digitally changed, and his face was never on the screen. It was focused on me and what he put me through. I grabbed the flash drives on my way out of the house the last time. I never wanted anyone to see them. Even though his friends helped him cover up his abuse of me, I kept them for some reason and couldn't bring myself to erase them. It never seemed to matter who I went to; he knew someone to twist what I was saying so it looked like I was either clumsy or that I set it up. A few of his friends had seen them but they didn't care. They refused to help me; it was so frustrating. I felt like I was nothing. When the divorce was final, all I wanted was to leave and never have to see him again. Oh, my gosh. I forgot I had them. I have to get back to my house. I have them hidden." Annie charged toward the door.

Riley put a hand on the handle, stopping her forward motion. She gasped and stumbled away. "Sorry, I didn't mean to startle you, but hold on. He could still have people looking for you. Let me grab a few guys and a new phone so if we need to call for help, we can. Can you give me five minutes and come down to the lobby, and then we'll go as a group?"

"Sure. Could this be what puts him away for good?" Annie had hope in her eyes for the first time since he met her. It was a good look on her.

"Let's pray it is. We just have to get this in front of a good judge in that jurisdiction since it can't be filed in any other city but where it happened. Murder is another thing. That goes to state-level, but domestic violence and rape have to be filed where they happened. I ran into cases like this all the time when I was on the force. We had to refer victims back to the agency where they lived. They never seemed to understand why, but that's the way the law is for these types of reports. The only other option is to have someone higher up who has authority over the smaller agencies to come in and do a sweep of the corrupt individuals hiding the crimes." Riley spun back to her when he opened the door. "To still keep you informed on everything we found out, I must mention they had hidden cameras in your house, watching you for at least the last week. We found them the days after we thought you died in that crash."

Her hand flew to her mouth and small black dots danced in her eyes. Riley rushed to her. She gasped for air as if she couldn't breathe. "Annie, it's okay. We took them all down."

She clung to his arm and closed her eyes. He put his hand on the side of her face. Her heart stuttered as she leaned into him. He held it there while he rubbed his other hand gently across her upper back. His hand didn't brush against any of the marks that Alan put there. "Shh." He kissed the top of her head.

Her wide eyes met his when she glanced up. "I'm sorry, I don't know why I did that." Riley stammered.

"It's okay," she whispered as she touched his cheek with her hand. She backed away from him but didn't say another word.

• • • •

"MEET US DOWNSTAIRS in five minutes, okay." He felt the heat in his cheeks as he closed the door behind him.

He shook his head as he rode the elevator to the first floor. When the doors opened, Bear walked in the back door.

"Monroe?" Riley frowned.

"Doing some scans since he may have internal bleeding. He said he would call when he was ready for pick up." Bear tossed the keys onto his desk.

"Get everyone together. We need to go to Annie's. She may have the evidence we've been hoping to find on the party."

"What? Are you serious? Why didn't she say anything?" Bear threw out the questions as if an auctioneer.

"She didn't know it until now." Riley slid the first drawer open on his desk and grabbed the phone that lay on top of two others. He always had more already loaded, ready to go. He turned the phone on and waited for the screen to boot up and activated it wirelessly. His contacts popped up and he punched in Ayers's name and sent him a text telling him the good news. This would let him know if he was the trusted friend he thought he was. He didn't tell him all his men would be with him but that he was taking Annie home to grab evidence about the party that would expose the congressman for the hoax he was.

Ayers responded, asking to keep him in the loop and telling him that the prosecutor was pulling his hair out, yelling at the sergeant about needing evidence to present to the judge on Riley's murder case. He had also been teamed back up with his partner and was no longer riding a desk.

Riley congratulated him and slipped his phone into his pocket. The elevator dinged, announcing Annie's arrival on the lobby floor. He grabbed another gun from his locked safe and slid it into the holster on his side. He threw on a light jacket to hide the firearm. Since he was facing felony murder charges, he didn't want to press his luck with the local police department and push any unwanted buttons with the brass.

Annie lingered around Bear's desk when Riley left his office. Tracker, Erickson, and Bear all rose from their seats when he motioned for them to leave. "I told Ayers I'm taking Annie to her house to grab evidence that will put the congressman away for a long time."

"Is that wise?" Bear grumbled.

"We have to take the congressman out of the equation before we take down Alan once and for all."

Annie stopped and Tracker almost ran into the back of her.

"It's a hunch. I think we can trust him, but I'm testing that theory with the information I fed him."

Annie took a step back and bumped into Tracker. She sucked in air as she spun around, unaware he was so close to her.

"He doesn't know we have three other people going with us. You will be safe." Riley offered her his hand.

She held out her hand and then retracted it before finally taking his, letting him lead her from the building to the sports utility he unlocked. The three men jumped in the back, hidden by the dark tint on the windows. Riley smirked at Annie's almost-giggle when she glanced at the three who were shoulder to shoulder in the back seat and pulled out of the parking space.

Within a couple of minutes, they were at her house and pulled around the back. "Keep hidden and out of sight in case information was leaked about us being here."

Riley held the door open for her, and she headed straight for her office. She opened the same credenza door she had when she paid him cash for the security system on her house. The dial on the safe clicked with every number she passed. The lock disengaged when she reached the last number. He strolled up behind her as she dug to the back of the easily six-hundred-pound safe nestled into the furniture. A hidden panel pulled free when she tugged on the top right corner. It was similar to the hidden panel he had in his safes at the office. Several flash drives fell onto the shelf. She fisted them, pocketing one and handing the rest to him. He almost asked her about the one she had when they heard the front door crash in.

He wrapped his arm around his back and guided her so she was directly behind him and then pulled his gun. Her hand gripped the back of his shirt.

"Police!" a voice boomed from the front of the house.

Riley placed his gun on the top shelf of the safe and motioned for Annie to secure it. There was a lot of cash inside, and he didn't want someone to easily be tempted by that much money.

"We're in the office at the back of the house," Riley announced.

"Stay where you are. We will come to you. How many are in the house?" the loud, booming voice asked.

"Just me and the homeowner, Miss Divers." Riley blew out a breath and closed his eyes, counting to ten before he opened them again. His heart rate slowed as he controlled his breathing.

Flashlights bounced off the marble counters, reflecting across the kitchen to the office. "Put your hands up, Mr. Strong."

Riley raised his hands and felt Annie's hands tighten their grip, twisting in his shirt. "It's okay."

"Who are you talking to?" The deputy demanded, shining his flashlight in Riley's eyes blinding him to who joined them in the room.

"Just the owner of the house."

"Miss Divers, please step out from behind Mr. Strong."

She threw her hands in front of her eyes when the light passed over her face. She inched around Riley but stayed so that her back was to his chest. Her trembling caused him to tense.

"Please walk out to us, ma'am." He continued to blind them with the light. He knew exactly what he was doing, and it was against procedure to do that, no matter who the subject was you were talking to. It was just as effective to shine it across their chest or waist to still be able to see their face.

She spun to Riley, eyes wide. He smiled down at her. "Just listen to them and trust me."

Her hand rested on his chest for a split second before she turned and faced the deputy, walking forward with her hands up.

The second deputy, who had yet to speak, spun her around. He threw her against the counter and yanked her arms behind her back, cuffing her violently as she cried out.

"Be careful. Her ribs won't be completely healed yet, and she has injuries down her back," Riley spat out.

"Ma'am, you need to come with us. The congressman needs a moment of your time."

She attempted to pull away, but the deputies lifted her off the ground by each grabbing her under the arms and carrying her from the house. She was no match to their size and strength.

With her secured in the backseat, they jumped into the front of the cruiser and turned the key. Nothing happened. The deputy in the passenger seat jumped out and had the driver pop the hood. Riley dumped the flash drives in a fake potted plant in the living room and then sauntered to the front door.

"Come on, try it again," the deputy, with his head under the hood, called out to the driver.

"What's wrong with it?" The driver stuck his head and upper body out of the window.

"Who knows. Call for another car to take her to the congressman." The passenger slammed the hood down.

"Problem, deputies?" Riley leaned his shoulder against the front door frame.

"Did you do something to our car?" The one outside the car unholstered his weapon.

"I was inside the entire time when you drove up and secured Miss Divers in the backseat. Which I might add is against the law since she hasn't done anything wrong."

"Who are you to tell us about laws?" The deputy raised his gun.

"Well, I used to be an officer for over twenty years and ended my career as a sergeant, so I might know just a little about laws." Riley stood to his full six-foot height and flexed his muscles in his shoulders but didn't move toward the deputy.

Flashing lights dotted the skyline, announcing another cruiser was entering the neighborhood. Riley tensed, wondering if it was the deputy's backing unit. Ayers stepped from behind the wheel while his partner stepped from the passenger side.

"Can I be of some help, deputies?" Ayers rested his hands on his duty belt, watching the one with the firearm pointed at Riley.

"This man disabled our vehicle while we were in the house," the driver exclaimed.

"How is that possible when I was in the house with you?" Riley gave a curt nod to Ayers, who eyed Annie in the back of the county cruiser. Ayers was the only one besides his men who knew they would be at the house and what time.

"That's okay. We have another unit coming to transport our prisoner." The driver sidled up to Ayers, who took two steps to his left from the deputy.

"Prisoner?" Ayers released his weapon from his holster but didn't pull it just yet.

"She is wanted in questioning for a few state charges." The deputy nodded his head.

"I'm sorry, I'm not sure you have the right person. She was run through the system this morning, and no wants or warrants were found for her." Ayers raised an eyebrow at Riley.

"Well, there was one entered this afternoon."

"Why would you be taking her to the congressman for warrants? And I don't believe you read her her rights," Riley interjected.

"Oh, he just wants to clear the air after everything Miss Divers has been through and talk to her in person to maybe take care of the little misunderstanding." The deputies were horrible liars and Ayers flinched when one deputy approached him again.

Ayers's partner pulled his weapon and pointed it at Ayers as the deputy who kept edging forward pulled his own weapon and pointed it at Ayers's partner. "What do you think you're doing?" Ayers demanded.

"Sorry, I like you and all, but I answer to a higher power, I don't want to spend another twenty years working before I can retire. You can take our car to transport her if you need to," the officer offered.

"Thanks, buddy." The deputies yanked Annie from the backseat and tossed her in the back of the police cruiser. Ayers's partner backed up to the vehicle and tried to open the back door when the deputy in the passenger seat shot him point-blank under the vest.

Riley's men stood three wide across the gate opening. Ayers ran to his partner, disarming him and then yanking off his vest. The bullet had entered just under the bottom edge of the front plate. The passenger had the perfect angle to pull off such a shot. Ayers's partner gasped for air as blood spurted from the hole in his stomach.

Ayers grabbed his hand. "What on earth were you thinking?"

"It was a lot of money. You know my mom's been sick and I couldn't pay all the bills. I figured so what if I helped them here and there. The money was more than I make in a month. Just a few more favors for them, and then I could be caught up on bills and go back to the job with no one aware of anything. You're the one who suggested...I...I..." He closed his eyes. Ayers searched for a pulse and hung his head.

Riley grabbed his backup weapon from his waistband and ran to the car with Ayers on his heels. The deputy in the passenger seat pointed his weapon at Annie through the grate that separated the prisoners in the back from the front. "Do it and she dies." He smirked.

He wouldn't be able to get her out of the car without being shot and wondered if their orders were to bring her in alive or in any condition they could. He wasn't willing to take that chance with her and nodded to the men covering the gate to let them pass. Bear grunted and turned the gate back on so they could leave.

Ayers grabbed his radio and called for an assist on an officer down. "Riley, we need to talk. What the...my partner is dead! Dead!"

Twenty-Four

Every police car in the city sat on Annie's street. An officer was shot and killed. The officers were furious. Ayers got in Riley's face. "Now tell me how I lost my partner tonight. Never mind that he took a payoff to tell congressman's flunkies where to find you. But every report I filed about Alan has disappeared from the system. I can only assume he had something to do with that."

"Annie may have video evidence linking the congressman to twelve rapes at a party at the frat house while he was the chapter president. We came here to see if she had it." Riley's heart broke at the thought of the sergeant tasked with telling that officer's sick mother that he was killed tonight.

"How on earth would she have a copy of that?" Ayers put his hands on his hips.

"Alan recorded every time he abused her and made her watch, threatening to do it again. She took the drives when she left him so no one would know what she endured. Apparently, she didn't look at what she was taking and that one was mixed in."

Ayers marched to the back door, started to turn around, and then slumped his shoulders. "Did you get the drives?"

"Some of them. She slipped one into her pocket after she handed me the rest. I don't think she knew I saw her palm the drive. Ayers, I'm sorry about your partner." Riley's voice softened.

"Yeah, me too." Ayers's radio squawked; dispatch informed him that his cruiser was found off the highway in a grove of trees. "Take me to my car."

Riley had sent Bear and the others back to the office on foot. He issued Bear with the task of running through the drives privately in his office and let him know if he came across anything on the congressman. If Annie palmed one and it looked to be the one with the oldest technology, did she take the one they needed?

"We need to get Annie back. He won't hesitate to have her killed. The twelve girls that were raped at that party are all dead except two." Riley slid behind the wheel of his Audi.

"All of them?" Ayers buckled his seatbelt.

"But two." Riley pulled out onto the road and pointed his car in the direction Ayers was informed his cruiser waited for him.

"What kind of storm are you dragging me into? First, I'm put on desk duty. Then you're charged with murder, and now my partner is dead. Riley, this better be the truth or you will have burned every bridge you have." Ayers shifted in his seat.

"A storm I didn't create but am about ready to destroy to get her back."

"I haven't seen you like this in years."

Riley glanced at him. "Like what?"

"Protective. In love." Ayers didn't look his way.

"I'm not in love with her."

"Uh-huh. Sure, you aren't." Ayers had known his wife Helen and said they were the perfect match and complimented each other. He also knew how devastated he was when she died.

"Let's just get her back." Riley pulled his phone from the charger. "Bear, see what you can find for properties they may take Annie to that the congressman owns or leases."

Ayers sat forward in his seat. "There, just over the next rise, I saw something."

Riley slowed as they pulled behind the cruiser. It didn't look any worse for wear. Guns drawn, they stalked to the vehicle and checked the surrounding areas. The car was abandoned.

The keys dangled from the ignition. Ayers popped the locks on the back doors and they both searched the back seat after donning gloves that Ayers pulled from the trunk.

"Is this it?" Ayers held a flash drive that was wedged in the seat behind the driver's side of the car.

"Looks like it." Riley jogged to his vehicle and returned with a laptop that was booting up. He took the drive from Ayers and plugged it in. The drive only contained one file. He looked at his friend, who only nodded for Riley to hit play.

The video took several moments to load. Riley's phone vibrated in his pocket while they were waiting. He put it on speaker. "Go."

"There is only one house registered to our esteemed congressman in this jurisdiction, and it isn't far from Annie's house." Bear hesitated.

"What is it?"

"These flash drives are all of Annie's abuse. Nothing we can use against the congressman, although it may help put

Alan away if we can prove he is the person, but his face or head is never shown in the shots. She begs him to stop on every single one." Bear sighed.

"Thanks, we may have found it." Riley turned up the volume while his phone was still connected.

The video was old and by the look of it started as a videotape according to the lines dancing across the screen, showing the poor quality, before it was transferred to a flash drive. Alan probably got pleasure from watching it over and over. It was a party and looking at the clothes and hairstyles, it could have easily been shot twenty years ago. Front and center, the chapter president, none other than their revered congressman.

It showed drugs being introduced into the punch bowl by the judge, the congressman's cousin. Then orders were given that in no way should anyone drink from the bowl but the sorority that was invited. They marched the girls in. You could easily spot the ones who had pledged but hadn't quite made it into the sorority yet. They were ordered to drink the dosed punch and not leave a drop.

Riley closed his eyes as the girls one by one drank and emptied the bowl. The drugs took a while to cause the reaction the boys were waiting for. The chapter president gave the mandates of which girls were to go first and the order of the men. He shut the video off as Ayers stalked away from the car.

"I need to make a call." Ayers was on the phone before Riley could say anything.

Riley regretted thinking Ayers was in on anything. He didn't need to tell Riley about the missing case files, but he did, helping Riley clear up that mystery of where they had gone or whether Ayers had filed the reports in the first place.

Ayers marched over, snagged the flash drive from the laptop, and popped the trunk lid on his patrol car. Riley's heart sped up until he grabbed an evidence bag and sealed the flash drive in it, putting his initials and date on it. He radioed for dispatch to put him on report call and put on the bag the official city number for the case he just opened.

Riley didn't tell him that his computer simultaneously made a copy of the entire drive while they watched the small portion they did. With all the new technology you could make a copy faster than you could watch nowadays. He now had leverage if the drive disappeared. It wasn't Ayers he didn't trust, but the brass who didn't hesitate to issue a warrant for his arrest when the congressman requested that they do so.

Ayers plucked his phone off his belt when it rang. He turned his back on Riley and had a hurried, very ticked-off conversation with someone on the other end. He said thanks and spun around to Riley. "I'm going to go get Annie once and for all." He stormed off toward his patrol car, not waiting for Riley to join him.

"I'll follow you." Riley pulled the keys from his pocket.

"Riley, you are no longer on the job. This needs to be handled by the book. I'll meet you back at the office." Ayers rolled down the window after getting behind the wheel and started the car. He edged back onto the road, motioning for Riley to move out of the way.

"No, I'm following you, and there's nothing you can do to stop me." Riley narrowed his eyes.

"If you get in the way, I'll have to arrest you for interfering in an official police investigation. Riley, just go to the office." Ayers stared at him for several seconds and then shook his head. "I'll take care of this."

Before Riley made it to his car and turned over the ignition, Ayers was almost out of sight. He floored the Audi, pushing the engine but knew it could handle it.

Lights and sirens from Ayers's police cruiser alerted anyone on the road to get out of his way, and he knew Ayers was in the frame of mind where he wouldn't stop for anyone. Riley dialed up Bear on speaker and told him to lock away the drives on Annie and that he was following Ayers to the congressman's house against Ayers's orders. Bear grunted acknowledgment and then informed him that Monroe was back in the office. But the doctors told him to take it easy or he could easily tear the stitches inside and bleed out in a matter of minutes. Part of the blade had broken off and was wedged against the vein, keeping him from bleeding out before. They removed it and he demanded to be released, and Tracker had just arrived back at the office with him.

"Dope him. Put him in one of the apartments. I don't care how you do it, but I won't take the chance that something happens and he tries to jump in and it ends up killing him." Riley's headache was coming back full force.

Bear rumbled it would be done and disconnected.

He hoped the congressman was conceited enough to think they weren't a threat and was only talking to Annie at this time. Ayers braked hard in front of him and took the next corner on two wheels. Riley knew that frustration. He was mad and would need to get there only seconds behind

Ayers to stop the officer from doing something that would cost him his job. Another cruiser joined them, lights and sirens behind Riley. His phone went off with a text from Ayers that said two words: Stay back.

He stuck to the patrol car's bumper probably closer than he should. They pulled in front of a gated residence. He had no doubt this was where Annie was held. The deputy behind Riley jogged to Ayers and handed him a piece of paper, which Ayers tucked into his shirt pocket while two more patrol units joined them.

Ayers pointed to Riley. "He joins us, no questions asked."

"Sir, that isn't standard operational procedure. We can't let a civilian go in with us." The deputy rested his hands on his duty belt.

Ayers stood toe to toe with the deputy. "He is crucial to this case and retired from the force. He knows what he is and isn't allowed to do once we get inside. He stays."

"It's your funeral if this goes sideways." the deputy stomped over and joined his partner.

The officers from the local precinct nodded at Riley before edging around the gate. He stayed behind them as he tugged on his own vest.

Security ran from the residence, guns drawn. Ayers yelled that he had a search warrant and that they were to either comply or be charged with impeding an investigation. Riley made a mental note to never tick off Ayers. They were ushered into the mansion, which sat easily in the middle of five acres if not more.

Outside, security whispered hurriedly to those in the residence, who only pointed to a back room off the grand foyer. They marched to where they indicated while an officer stayed back with the staff and had them all disarm and put their firearms on a table and then sit against the wall. More officers entered the mansion as they rounded the next corner.

Riley heard yelling and then someone being hit. Ayers reached the door first and motioned for him to join him. He held up his fingers, counting to three before they barged through the double doors. The room they entered had shelves with books floor to ceiling and was at least ten feet high. A ladder on wheels was against the shelves so you could access all the books. His eyes scanned the room and saw Annie gagged and bound to a chair. The congressman was screaming for his security until Ayers waved the warrant in front of his face and shoved him down over the desk in the center of the room.

Red, raised marks from someone's open-handed slaps showed on Annie's face, which told of the anger and no doubt frustration the congressman suffered. Riley untied the gag and released her hands from the ropes that held her to the chair. Ayers turned to Riley. "Get her to the hospital. The keys are in my car if you need to move it."

Riley scooped Annie up. Her arms flew around his neck as he rushed from the room. She clung to him. "That's twice you came for me."

"Yeah, a regular knight in shining armor." He laughed. "If I was good at my job, you wouldn't have been taken in the first place."

"I take it you found the drive in the back of the car?"

"Yes, nice job with that. Why didn't you just give it to me in the first place?"

"I don't know. It was a hunch that was the drive, but I wasn't sure." She tightened her hold as they passed the security, who were now sitting in a row, handcuffed.

Riley skidded to a stop. "Deputy."

"Yes, sir." The deputy responsible for detaining the men took a step toward him.

"The two on the far left impersonated deputies, and the second one in is the one that killed an officer today. I was a witness to the shooting. Officer Ayers has my information if you need it."

The deputy grabbed the man up off the bench, and Riley wasn't sure he would make it out of the house alive as he darted through the door while she clung to his neck. He placed her in the passenger seat of his vehicle and jumped in Ayers's car to move it out of the way. He backed away from the gate around the other city vehicles that were parked haphazardly across the road.

He punched in Bear's number and put it on speaker.

"Sir."

"I have her. We're headed to St. Mary's. They have the congressman in custody."

"Is she okay?"

"Yes, Bear. Thank you," Annie answered.

Riley pulled into the hospital emergency room entrance. He jogged around to her side of the car as a nurse met them with a wheelchair. Once Annie was settled, he told her he would be right back after he moved the car. He didn't want to leave her alone again if he could help it. He lost her twice now to these men; enough was enough.

The nurse wheeled her through the automatic doors that opened as she rolled Annie close enough for the sensors to be activated. He hesitated and debated leaving the car where it was, risking it being towed and ticketed. A spot opened up directly across from the ER doors. He gunned it and pulled into the empty space, slammed the gears into park, and then sprinted across the drive.

He strolled up to the desk to ask where she was as the nurse reappeared with the wheelchair. "I'm sorry. You aren't allowed to be with her, but if you have a seat in the waiting area, we will let you know when you can see her."

"Sue me or call the police, but she isn't to be left alone. Her life is in danger, and I'm the security company she hired to keep her safe." Riley pulled the curtain back, exposing an empty bed that the nurse had told him she took her to. "Where is she?"

"I just put her in the bed." The nurse rushed past him; her mouth fell open. "Maybe she went to the bathroom. She asked where one was before I left."

He glanced down the hall, his eyes locking on the women's lit bathroom sign. "Go make sure she is in there."

The nurse rushed back to him. "She isn't there!"

He called Ayers. "She's gone!"

"What do you mean, she's gone? She left with you. I don't know what game you are playing, Riley!"

Twenty-Five

"Miss Annie Divers?" An average-height male in a cheap suit entered her area from the other side of the curtain the nurse just pulled around her bed. The fabric of his clothes couldn't hide the bulk of muscles, telling her he kept a rigorous workout schedule. There was something in his eyes she trusted.

"Can I help you?" Annie shifted her gaze to the side the nurse had disappeared through and wished for Riley to step around the curtain. She didn't know who this man was, and she could only handle so much crazy in one day.

"US Marshal Troy Talavera, and this is my partner Marshal Curtis Callaway." He pointed over her shoulder, and she gasped as another man stood by her head. She never heard him enter.

"What's going on?" Annie's eyes darted to the ugly fabric around her bed. The thin cloth wasn't much to keep anyone from hearing them.

"We received a call about information you have regarding a current case we have going on, and it was suggested you needed to be taken into protective custody. We know the congressman has a long reach and know you would be safer if we made you disappear until the court date." He shifted from one foot to the other. "But we need to leave now and get you hidden."

His partner, who was behind her, flipped his credentials out of the leather flip wallet they apparently issue with their silver badges, showing the star in a circle with "United States Marshal" stamped in the ring around the star.

"How d-do you know about me?" Annie stammered.

"We can answer all of your questions after we get you moved. You aren't safe, Miss Divers. Please let us help you." US Marshal Talavera confidently held out his hand and gave her a quick nod.

She slipped her small hand into his much larger one and was surprised at the warmth that engulfed her. He helped her edge off the bed, keeping her steady with a hand under her elbow as his partner shifted the back of the curtain out of the way, and they entered a back hallway that stated "Employees Only" on the doors. Another two men with hands on their weapons were stationed down the hallway about halfway to another set of doors that warned they would alarm if they were opened. They didn't. They stepped out into a secured parking lot with a large brown van idling at the curb with another marshal in the driver's seat and a woman in the back, holding the door open.

The thunder of her heart in her ribcage threatened to steal her breath. She didn't get a chance to glance behind her as they situated her between the two marshals in a bench seat while the driver pulled out of the lot. The woman handed Talavera and Callaway a vest she had seen officers wear. They situated it on her carefully, as if they knew the extent of her injuries, and secured the Velcro around her sides.

"You're safe with us, I promise you that. His reach can't get to you now, and we'll keep you safe as we wait for trial." He straightened in his seat after securing a seatbelt around her, his eyes scanning every street they passed.

What had she gotten herself into? "Will I see Riley again? What about my house?"

"We will go over everything once we get you to our safe house. I'm sorry, this is very overwhelming and we usually have more time to get our witness ready for the idea of being in witness protection. But this was time-sensitive and we couldn't take the chance that someone got hold of you again." Callaway offered her a semblance of an apologetic smile.

• • • •

RILEY FILLED HIM IN on arriving at the hospital and explained that by the time he got to the bed the nurse put her in, she wasn't there. Ayers groaned and said he would call him back. Monroe's name appeared on his phone. "Yes."

"Sir, we need to talk. How soon can you get to the office?" Monroe's voice was strained. Riley had never heard him like that. He thought they were supposed to dope him.

"Annie is missing. I'm not leaving this hospital until I find her."

"She isn't missing. Just come to the office."

Riley's blood boiled as he stormed out of the emergency room and jogged to his car. All the lights flipped to green as he approached the intersections. He knew it was someone at his office. Four minutes later, he pulled into the back lot and parked his car by the back door. He didn't take the time to park it in a spot.

"Where is she?" He asked through clenched teeth.

A man in a suit stood at the front door. Riley pulled up, short of storming up to him and knocking him out.

"Mr. Strong. May we have a word." Another matching suit stood in the doorway to his office.

Riley slammed the door behind him. "Well. Where is she?" he spouted as he spun, trying to reign in his anger.

"She's safe at the moment and being taken care of for the injuries she sustained."

"No, you don't get to take her. She's safe here in this office." Riley's face reddened as he glared at the arrogant jerk.

"Sir, you lost her twice, if I may point out. Well, technically, three times if we count this time also." He sat on the edge of Riley's desk, condescending and unmoving.

Riley growled, "That won't happen again."

"You're correct. It won't." He strolled up to Riley and raised his eyebrows before handing him a business card.

"Do I get to know where she is?" Riley stepped out of his way as he took the government-issued non-descript US Marshal's business card.

"Not at this time. I'm sorry, sir. It's for the best and for her safety." He strolled to his partner, and they left the office.

Riley grabbed the lamp off his desk and threw it across the room as he shouted.

"Who was that?" Bear stood in the doorway.

"US Marshals. Know anyone else besides feds who wear suits that hideous?" Riley dropped to his chair and flipped the business card on his desk.

"Won't they be able to keep her safe? Isn't this a good thing, that they're involved? That means someone has been paying attention."

"Yeah, but if they put her in witness protection, I may never see her again," Riley blurted.

"Your attorney called and said the charges have been dropped completely." Bear shuffled out of his office.

Ayers slammed past the front door and stormed in. "The feds took over the case. They took the flash drive and all the evidence, as well as the congressman. Took him right out of our patrol car. My chief even confirmed it, and he wasn't too happy he wasn't kept in the loop."

Riley arched an eyebrow. "They took Annie also."

"What?" Ayers's shoulders slumped.

"We were trying to get people to listen to us. Guess they finally did." Riley put his head in his hands.

"Sorry about that." Ayers hung his head.

"They did drop the murder charges against me, so that's a plus."

"Sir, if I may." Gavin stood in the doorway.

"How's the head?" Riley hadn't checked on his men after the debacle with Alan at the cabin.

"Fine, I've had worse. State shows all your accounts are in good standing, and we have valid state licensing and work permits for your company."

"Thanks, Gavin." Riley was exhausted. They had all been going nonstop for a couple of weeks now.

"You don't look so good." Ayers leaned against the door frame.

"Gee, thanks. I'm getting too old for this."

"I thought you retired and started this company to slow down. This has been nothing but a ride on a rocket ship that crashed at one hundred miles an hour into a brick wall."

Riley rose from behind his desk. "Tell me about it. I'm closing my office for the rest of the day and sending my guys home for much-needed rest."

"Good idea. Hey," Ayers put a hand on his shoulder as he passed him, "if you need anything, you know to call, right?"

"Yeah, thanks."

"I mean it. This one was someone special. I can see how attached you were to her already after only knowing her a few weeks." Ayers rolled his shoulders tilting his head from side to side.

"Just an emotional roller coaster few weeks. I'll be fine."

"Okay, call if you want to talk." Ayers ambled to the front door; all the adrenaline expended from today's activities showed as he walked.

"Guys, go home. Long weekend. Get some much-needed rest. You went above and beyond on this one. I can't thank you enough." Riley wanted to crawl into bed and sleep an entire day.

"Gee thanks, boss." Several shut down their computers while others bolted for the elevators to head to their apartments.

Bear locked the front door. "Is it really over?"

"Looks that way. I just want to know that she's okay."

"I know, but at least she's safe. I wonder how long it will take to get this fiasco to trial?" Bear grabbed the trash cans and emptied them into the larger can in the kitchen.

"I'll get that tomorrow. Don't worry about it." Riley waved him off from trash duty.

Bear smiled. "I'm wide awake. You know I got nowhere to go."

"Thanks." Riley waited for the elevator to take him to his room, where he wanted to shut the world out.

Twenty-Six

His phone vibrated somewhere. Where did he leave it? His palms rubbed against his eyes as he told his brain to wake up. Lurching from the bed, he fumbled around in the dark looking for his phone's screen to brighten again so he knew where he left it. He wasn't ready to turn on the overhead light that would blind him. There it was again. Light showed from the bathroom. It was on the sink and had vibrated down into the basin.

"Strong." He finally answered, anxious and hopeful somehow it would be Annie. He couldn't let his phone out of his sight since the marshals had picked her up.

"Sir, we would like to talk to you about our card member services. This is the last time we will call you with this offer. Please act now to save. If you want to speak with a representative, please press one." The automated recording droned on as he hit the disconnect and promptly blocked the number.

He turned on the shower and waited for the steam to roll over the top of the shower doors. It had been six months since the feds had taken Annie to keep her *safe.* They had all returned to their normal dull lives, but he couldn't get her out of his head. Ayers put in his papers to retire a year early after finding out the chief at his department was also listed as one of those indicted in the cover-ups of Alan's crimes. He prayed he would see her again but knew there was a slim to none possibility of that happening. The water had turned cold, so he stepped from the shower.

Monroe was unusually quiet after the feds took her with them. Almost as if remorse silenced him. He took every job that only required one person as if he was punishing himself. Riley couldn't get him to talk. All he would say was that he was working through something. The mood was somber in the office most days. Ayers had tried to find out the status of the case several times but never could get past that they were still working on the investigation and had no further updates for him at this time.

He kept an eye on Annie's house even though she wouldn't be stepping through the door again. The fridge was empty now that he removed all the rotting food and wiped down all the shelves. The feds still didn't know he had a copy of the video. He saved it on a flash drive and hid it in the newly installed six-hundred-pound safe in his office upstairs in his apartment. All his corporate documents and files on Annie's case were locked inside. Only he and Bear had the combination.

He updated all the software on their cameras and computers. His clients were happy with the security that he provided them, and his business had only picked up when word leaked to the press of his involvement in taking down the corrupt politician. He wasn't sure if that was good or bad, but he wouldn't complain. He turned away questionable clientele and kept all his accounts above board so no one could try to close him down again. He and his team were questioned relentlessly over what they witnessed regarding the corrupt fraternity members. After several weeks, those interviews tapered off and left them sitting on the sidelines, in the dark about the progress of the case.

He prayed for Annie every chance he got and for himself to handle and deal with her not being in his life, even though he never stepped outside the boundaries of client professionalism. He still had a hole in his heart for her. His phone vibrated again. It was a high-end account that was beginning to turn into a royal pain. "Strong," he answered.

After getting dressed while the phone was on speaker, he started the coffee pot in his apartment and continued to listen to the drama they created themselves. He would have dropped the account a year ago, but they were good money and referred all their friends to him. So, if he had to listen to drama every so often, he would deal with it. He gave them his normal spiel on safety and eased their concerns. Their daughter had just turned sixteen and was now driving, making it impossible to keep an eye on her all the time. They thanked him for always being there for them and disconnected.

The sigh he let out filled his empty apartment. Maybe it was time to look at getting a house again. He still had the house he bought with Helen, but couldn't bring himself to live there since her death. It was time to either let it go or move back home. He would take a trip by the house today on his lunch and see what it looked like. A friend took care of it while he decided what to do with it and had moved in years ago, saying it would be easier to keep up with repairs if they resided there. They would love it if he sold it to them, and it would help him to let go of the past.

Everything he owned was in storage in the basement of the office building anyway, leaving nothing left in the house to tie him to it. He rode the elevator down to his office and made a mental note to have the paperwork drawn up so it was ready to go if his friends wanted to buy it. Monroe sat at his desk when he opened the door.

"Monroe?"

"I need to talk to you."

Riley closed the door behind him and sat across from him. "Are you okay?"

"I don't know. I guess it will depend on how you react to what I have to tell you."

"We're friends first and foremost. Spill."

"Annie was picked up by the feds because of me." He hung his head.

"How did you make that happen?"

"They were coming after us, shutting down the business. I made a call. To my uncle who is over the criminal investigative division for the feds. That's not a call I've ever made before. When I told him what we were dealing with and who the players were, he wanted to help. He hates crooked politicians and would like to see them all held accountable for their crimes. I sent him everything we had without asking you."

"I told you guys to pull in markers. To see who could help us. We were in over our heads. You didn't do anything I didn't ask you to."

Monroe slumped in the chair as the air whooshed out of his lungs. Riley saw the relief cross his face.

"I thought you were going to tell me you wanted to quit. I can't replace you, Monroe. You are an integral part of this team. No one else can be an on-scene medic like you can. It wouldn't be the same without you here."

"And here I was worried you would fire me when you found out I'm the reason the feds took Annie."

"She is safe. I couldn't keep her safe with who was out to get her. I was as dumbfounded as you were when he brought in the congressman. We had no clue that was his power play. I just didn't have the same cards that he did, and he called my bluff on being able to keep him away from her. And since when has your uncle been that far up in the ranks of the FBI?"

"Since his promotion last fall. That's why it took me so long to call on this case. I didn't want to rush to him so soon after he got the promotion."

"Are you still in good standing with him? This didn't hurt your relationship with your uncle, did it?"

"Oh, no. Not at all. In fact, his superiors want to know who he got the intel from. They offered me a job." Monroe laughed.

"You thinking about working for them?" Riley didn't want to lose Monroe.

"Are you kidding? And leave this fantastic job with no political agenda like government work? They couldn't pay me enough to work for them." Monroe rose from his chair. "Seriously though Riley, are we good?"

"Hey, we're good. I promise." Riley shook his hand and nodded.

Relief flooded him when he dropped to his chair. Now he knew where the feds were brought into it, and Monroe wasn't leaving. Laughter filtered through his closed door, and he smiled. It had been months since the tension was light enough for his men to laugh. Yeah, they were going to be okay.

A commotion outside his office door startled him. He jumped from his chair and yanked open his door. Alan stood in front of him. He wasn't the same man he was six months ago when he threatened to get his so-called *property* back. Thinner by several pounds, there was no intimidating anyone with his stature now.

"You! I lost my license to practice because of you! You will be hearing from my lawyer." Spit collected in the corners of his mouth.

"I believe you murdering your wives is what got your license pulled, *Mr.* Montgomery." Riley smiled. Since he lost his title of doctor, he felt so privileged and conceited with announcing to everyone.

"It's Doctor!"

"Not according to what you just told me. And I do believe you are in violation of my order of protection. You aren't allowed to be on this property. Although, how did you leave your hotel room? Aren't you on an ankle monitor until your court date? Then you're supposed to be shipped back to your side of the state to stand trial for the assaults and murders that occurred in their jurisdiction." Riley nodded toward the front door when the officers he knew his team would have called, entered.

"What? No, those were dropped!" Alan jumped behind a desk in an attempt to keep it between him and the officers.

Riley almost laughed out loud. Two officers each took a side and casually walked around, putting Alan between them.

"Mr. Montgomery, I believe you are in violation of court orders, and your tracking device stipulates you aren't supposed to leave your hotel room. Place your hands behind your back," the officer ordered.

Alan tried to scramble over the desk in the most uncoordinated effort Riley ever saw. His foot hit papers, causing his feet to slip out from under him, which made him fall headfirst over the front of the desk and right into the officers' waiting hands. They cinched the cuffs tighter than they should have. His partner took him out to the patrol car and placed him in the backseat.

"You guys good in here? Did he make any veiled threats I can add to the charges on him today?" The officer pulled a business card from his pocket and wrote down a number on the back that dispatch issued him over the air.

"No. But why is he still out? Did he make that high bail the prosecutor demanded?"

"Didn't you hear? The state seized his assets. His court date is coming up, and with the way the courts are now saying it's not right to keep a person in jail just because he can't afford bail, judge released him on a signature bond with the conditions of an ankle monitor. He can't afford his attorney, so he had to go with a public defender. Unless he can get his little buddy from his frat days to come over and represent him pro bono." The officer rocked back on his heels.

"Well, that just made my day. Thanks for that." Riley leaned against the door frame to his office.

The officers left with a very deflated Alan in the back cage of the patrol vehicle. Ayers waved at them as they pulled from the parking lot, and he strolled through the front door. "So where do I get to sit when I come to work for you in a couple of weeks?" Ayers surveyed the work area.

"I have a desk ordered. We will put you by the coffee pot so you can start right at the bottom like the rest of us did." Bear roared with laughter.

The rest joined in and Ayers shook his head. "I'm going to have to go through a hazing for a while, aren't I?"

"Oh yeah. And by the way, your desk is the empty one that looks new." Riley turned and strolled to his office.

"Hey, got a minute?" Ayers stood in his doorway, hesitant to enter.

"Yeah, what's up?"

"The trial date has been set. I'm being called as a witness to back Annie's statements that Alan was stalking her and that she hired you to set up security at her house. I would start getting any documents together that you can, to show just cause for the protection orders and her security you were in charge of."

"Thanks. When's the trial? I wonder why I haven't been contacted about it." His heart raced. Would he see Annie there? Would he get to talk to her?

"Wait, you haven't been called? They said it's coming up but didn't give me any details." Ayers waited as if expecting something.

A knock on his door made Ayers turn. He stepped to the side. A man in an ill-fitted charcoal gray suit stood in the doorway with a folded piece of paper. "I'm looking for Riley Strong."

"That's me." Riley rose from his desk.

"Sir, you have been served." The man made a quick getaway, darting out the front door.

He unfolded the paper to see that the feds had called him as a witness at the congressman's trial. It gave a date a week from Wednesday. He jotted down the date and circled it on his desk calendar.

"I'll see you there." Ayers laughed and sauntered out of his office.

Mark Murphy would be well enough to attend the trial. It took a couple of surgeries before they repaired everything Monroe damaged when he shot him. He was being held without bail. Maybe Alan had spiraled so out of control because his nice little lifestyle, with everyone cleaning up his crimes, fell apart. His feet landed with a thud on his desk as he kicked them up on the edge, and he folded his hands behind his head for a split second. He would get to see Annie again. Hopefully.

With the subpoena in hand, he ventured out of his office and gave everyone an assignment for certain files to be pulled for his court testimony. They whooped and hollered for a couple of seconds, stating it was about time, and then went to work on what he needed. Monroe was back to his usual self, and Riley was glad he came to him. He couldn't fault him for who he called. Alan set the bar high, so they needed to go higher.

With the files for his house in hand, he called his friend to see if he was there. "Hey, Roger."

"Riley?" It had been a while since they'd spoken.

"Are you and Rebecca home so that I could come and talk to you two in a little bit?" Riley smiled when there was a pause.

"Yeah, sure. Is everything alright?" Roger's voice wobbled.

"Yes, sorry. Just something I want to discuss with you, and I'd rather do it in person than over the phone." Riley headed toward the back door.

The drive took him down memory lane. It has been far too long since he had stepped foot in the house he owned with Helen. His house wasn't far from the office, but he needed to let go of this part of his life. Angling out from behind the wheel, he snagged the folder off the passenger side, and Roger was at the door waiting for him. The house was a different color. He wondered when it had been painted.

"Roger."

"Hey, Riley. Is everything okay?"

"Yeah, nothing's wrong. Is Rebecca home? I need to talk to you two."

"Rebecca," Roger called out as they entered the house.

"Yeah, in the kitchen." She poked her head around the corner, and her smile widened when she saw Riley.

She hugged him and he hugged her back. "We haven't seen you in so long, young man. How have you been?"

They were several years older than him. Well okay, maybe a few decades, but they were dear friends he'd known for most of his life. "I wanted to talk to you and Roger about the house."

She gasped and her hands flew to her mouth. "Do you need us to move out?"

"Oh no. My gosh, nothing like that. I think it's time I let it go. I wanted to know if you are interested in buying it. I wrote up a proposal and took into consideration the years you paid rent and money you put in to keep up the repairs and deducted that from the sale price." He sat at the dining room table as they clutched each other's hands. Excitement filled the room.

"Oh, goodness! Are you sure?" Rebecca's hand shook as she pulled out a chair.

"Yes, I need to say goodbye. She isn't here anymore. You both know that and tried to tell me for the past five years even though she has been gone longer than that." Riley smiled and slid the paperwork over to them.

Roger flipped the pages and Rebecca gasped. "You aren't asking enough!"

"Actually, I am. Taking into account the repairs you did yourself, the rent. It's been paid off for over a year now, so anything I ask is just money in my pocket. Please let me do this for you. All the years you kept this place going so I could hold on to something that wasn't here is more than I can ever repay you." His heart swelled at the happiness he was giving these two.

"I mean, if you're sure." Rebecca grabbed her husband's hand. "Oh Roger, our own place finally."

Roger smiled and shook his head. Rebecca practically squealed and raced around the table and plowed into Riley, wrapping her arms around his neck.

He laughed and returned her hug. "I'll have a notary come out later in the week, and we can all get together and sign the papers."

"We'll have the payment for you ready to go." Roger pumped his hand up and down in a firm grip.

"Just when you can. No rush." Riley rose from the chair while Roger still held his hand.

"It will be there. Just let us know a date and time." Rebecca hugged him again and then hurried to the kitchen. She reappeared with a jar of homemade jam.

"Oh, now. I'll take a payment like this any day." He took the jar she held out to him. "I'll get back to you about the day later in the week."

He let himself out through the front door and looked back to his friends hugging just inside. It felt right. There was no regret in letting the house go. It took him eight years, but he finally said goodbye to the last thing he held onto after her death. Sure, he had boxes in storage of her personal items, but this was just a house. It took meeting Annie for him to finally see that it was okay to say goodbye to someone who meant so much to him and move on. She was strong enough to move on from such a vicious life, and he was ashamed he held onto his wonderful, blessed past for so long.

Twenty-Seven

The trial was today, and he couldn't decide which shirt and tie to wear. He had testified on so many cases over the years, so why was he so indecisive today? Yes, most of the cases had been when he was an officer, so you wore a uniform, but today was not one of those trials. The files were stacked neatly in his soft-sided briefcase. The federal prosecutor had called him and went over what his testimony would entail so he wasn't worried about what he would say or even about the cross-examination. People didn't bother him or even intimidate him.

Alan would be in court, and seeing him the other week with the weight loss and dire circumstances of losing his practice, license, and home told him he had nothing to worry about. He closed his eyes and pulled out the first shirt his hand came across. It was dark blue. That made the tie decision easy enough. He snagged a silver one that went perfect with it and finished dressing.

It was Annie; he was nervous about the possibility of seeing her. He brushed his teeth for a third time before he left his apartment. This wasn't a date, but it sure felt as if it should be. Would she be able to return to her life after this? Would she move back into her house?

He took the stairs practically two at a time. It was still a couple of hours before the hearing, but he wanted to be there early. With Annie in protective custody, he knew she would be one of the last ones allowed into the courtroom and she would be escorted by her handler who kept her safe these last several months. Something he was unable to do.

Bear whistled when Riley stalked to his office. "Shut it."

"I think she'll like it." He smiled as he stood in the doorway.

"I've worn this a dozen times, even to client meetings when setting up new accounts." Riley didn't know why he was trying to explain himself.

"Either way you look good, boss. Go help put the bad guys away." Bear lumbered to his desk.

"I plan on it." Riley fisted the handles to his briefcase, his keys in his left hand and his mug of coffee in his right.

It wouldn't take long to get downtown at this time of day. No one should be out on the roads this early. He stopped dead in his tracks when he got to his car. All four tires were slashed. He walked around every vehicle in their lot. Not a single one was left with inflated tires. This was no coincidence. Someone went to extremes to keep him from attending the hearing.

He called the prosecutor to see if anyone would be headed to the hearing from this side of town. Then he'd call a cab to bring him back. The phone went to voicemail; he hung up before leaving a message.

"Bear. We have a problem." Riley dropped his briefcase in the first empty chair. "Pull up last night's footage. The tires of every one of our vehicles have been slashed."

"All of them?"

"Well, every usually means *all.*" Riley clapped Bear on the shoulder.

Bear rolled his eyes. "I was just asking."

"I'm sorry, just not something I needed to deal with this morning. I called the prosecutor, but they aren't answering either." He propped himself behind Bear's chair and watched him pull up the cameras.

"Call Ayers. Isn't he supposed to be testifying also? They got the flash drive that they are using to discredit the congressman and charge him with all those crimes in college as well as what he's helped Alan cover up over the years." Bear scrolled to the last time the keycard was used to let Monroe into the building.

He hit play and they watched the screen in fast forward. At zero two hundred hours, shadows moved through the back secured lot. "Why didn't we get notifications of these?"

"Don't know. They should have set off the sensors and sent alerts to everyone's phones." Bear squinted at the screen as the suspects ran from vehicle to vehicle jamming something into the sidewalls.

"Look there!" Riley had him back up the video by five minutes. "They aren't wearing gloves, and that one dropped what he was using and put his hand on my car to balance himself while he bent over to grab what he dropped."

"I'll call the PD and have them send someone over to take prints. Maybe if we're lucky, they are in the system and that can be presented today if it pertains to this case." Bear was on the phone, already dialing before Riley left his desk.

He punched in Ayers's number and waited for it to ring. Nothing. Bear shook his handset to the phone on his desk and put it up to his ear again. "The phones are dead."

"Cell phone too. Try yours." Riley dropped to the chair next to Bear's computer and pulled up the exterior cameras.

Panning to the power box, he saw a shadow move quickly away seconds before the power went out.

"They took out the power box. We have generator backup that should kick in. Not to mention the battery backups to each station. We can keep an eye on what's going on outside." He punched a quick text to Ayers to see if it would go through.

"How do we tell the guys we are under attack if we can't reach them?" Bear grabbed his firearm and stalked to the front doors.

Riley grabbed the police scanner they kept on Tracker's desk so they could monitor police chatter while they were in the building. The scanner's transmit button was removed. How did that happen? Alan. He was in here sitting on a desk the other day. Did he sabotage the radio without them noticing?

Riley joined Bear at the front doors. "Who's here at the apartments?"

"Not sure. I stayed at home last night and came in just minutes before the tires were slashed to finish up some paperwork. I didn't see anything outside when I was out there."

"Use the stairs. Wake everyone."

"The stairs?" Bear groaned.

Riley pinched his lips together for a second. "Well, you could always chance the generator not operating at full capacity and getting stuck in the elevator."

"Stairs it is."

Riley grinned; Bear didn't like small, confined spaces. Riley strolled to his office to open the large safe. Rifles lined his desk as the door to the stairs echoed its closing through the empty office. Monroe was the first to join him and snagged the rifle he was used to and a box of ammo to go with it.

"Set up on the fourth floor where the window opens. They shouldn't be able to see it from below at that angle."

"Agreed." Monroe jogged to the stairs.

Tracker lounged in the doorway. "Is this really happening? Haven't they learned by now, don't take on ex-police and ex-military?"

"Apparently not. We have no vehicles. All tires are flat. Can't make a run for it if we need to. When they took out the power box, it put the building into lockdown mode. They must also have a scrambler because I can't get cell service. I want you set up on the backside of the building."

"Yup." Tracker sauntered out. Nothing phased him. The building could be on fire, and he would still stop at the coffee pot to snag the last cup before leaving.

Erickson appeared next.

"We need to get communication out that we are under attack. Get up on the roof and see what you can figure out and why our phones aren't working. I know you have your little projects, so see if one of those will get the calvary headed our way." Riley handed him the next rifle.

"On it. My guess is they have a jammer to block signals getting out around this building." Erickson stopped at his desk and threw several items—Riley had no clue what they could do—into a bag before slinging it over his shoulder and heading for the stairs.

Monroe jogged to Riley's office. "We need to get everyone off the main level they are setting up a 50-cal out there. It will cut through this glass in no time."

Riley tossed walkies to him and told him to distribute them to everyone and gave him everyone's positions. He jammed the earwig into his ear and turned on his radio as Bear rejoined him.

"Duffy and Gavin aren't here." He grabbed a rifle and slung it over his shoulder, still catching his breath after taking the stairs.

"You know you're supposed to include cardio as part of your workout." Riley handed him a radio.

"Really? You're telling me this now with what they have outside?"

"Monroe told you?"

"Let's get upstairs. Or would the basement be safer?" Bear turned on his heel.

"I sent my men upstairs. I refuse to hide in the basement because it's safer." Riley slung his rifle over his shoulder. "Erickson is trying to get a message out to anyone so hopefully he can get hold of Duffy and Gavin and have them steer clear of this building until we tell them to."

"Got it. Should I stay down here?" Bear eyed the stairs.

"No! Now get going!" Riley shook his head.

Riley's phone vibrated across his desk. He didn't know the number so he hit decline and hit his text messages. If they took the jammer down just long enough to try and contact him, he would be able to get messages out before they reactivated it. The red exclamation mark showed him his last message didn't go out. He hit send as his phone vibrated in his hand. He hit reject and sent a message to Duffy and Gavin to stay away and get police out here now.

The phone didn't ring again, so he checked his texts, including the one to Ayers to get SWAT. All texts showed they went through. Whoever decided to call gave him a chance to alert people outside the building. He jogged to the stairs. His foot hit the first step on his way up when the first shot hit the building. He sprinted up the stairs to the fourth floor and met his men in the hallway. "And it begins. I thought we were done with this, but apparently, they don't want me testifying. I just hope they have Annie under lock and key safe somewhere."

"They have something I've never come up against: blocking our signals out of this building. I can't breach it." Erickson dumped his bag on the floor.

"I got messages out. The not too brilliant people outside tried to call me. I rejected their call and sent messages to Ayers, Duffy, and Gavin. It shows that they went through before they shut it down again."

Monroe sighed as the second shot hit the building. "Not many more of those before they make entry."

"We could try to make it downstairs to the basement. None of the windows above the second floor is bullet-resistant to the degree the lower levels are. I didn't plan on having a full-scale assault on this building when I had it retrofitted."

"Is there a way out from the basement?" Bear huffed as he slid down the wall, his rifle used as a crutch.

"What's wrong with you?" Monroe started to get up when Riley stopped him with a hand held out.

"He's regretting his decision to not include cardio as part of his workout regime."

The others laughed as Bear almost growled, narrowing his eyes. "Really?" His men were used to stressful situations and used humor when most everyone else would be panicking.

"I'm just saying. Car...dee...ooo." Riley steadied himself when another shot hit the building.

"Back to the question 'Is there a way out of the building through the basement?'" Tracker scrambled to the window and peered over the edge just down the hall from them.

"Not that I know of. If we go down there, we will survive the initial assault, but then it will be easy to pick us off once they know we're in the sublevel." Riley checked his rifle and peered through the scope. He adjusted it slightly and then peered through it again.

"Then the basement is out." Bear seemed to catch a second wind.

Riley yanked off his tie, tossing it onto the bag Erickson discarded in the hall. He unbuttoned the top two buttons of his shirt with his right hand as another hit on the building sounded. This one felt different. They made entry; the glass must have been breached.

"We make our stand in this hallway. There are only two ways up. Tracker and Bear, take the back stairs. If we can keep them off this floor until the calvary arrives, we may just survive this. Monroe and I'll take the front stairs. Erickson, see if you can work the radio to pick up the police channel. At least give us an idea if they got my message to Ayers and if they are on the way to save our butts. If one of the stairwells is taking heavy fire, you are my go-to. Back the one taking the most hits and then continue to work on the radio." Riley pushed his master key into the elevator and brought it to the fourth floor. He shut it down with the same key and locked the doors in the open position so they couldn't lower the car without their knowing it.

"It will take approximately thirty-five to forty-five minutes to get SWAT called out, to debrief them, and be en route. We have to hold this building for at least that long." Riley nodded to his men. He then closed his eyes and said a prayer that God would get them out of this and he wouldn't lose any of his friends that had been caught up in this with him.

Riley glanced at his watch. He was supposed to be at the courthouse in less than fifteen minutes. Guess he wouldn't be able to help testify today. All the documents he was going to take were already emailed to the attorney, so he could present those if he needed to. All he had to do was say what was in the documents was the truth. His heart ached because he wouldn't see Annie in court and maybe talk to her again. Would she be disappointed he didn't show? Would she question why?

The radio squawked static and then went silent. Erickson waved his hand at him, telling him to give him another minute. Shots at the back stairwell rang down the hall. Tracker and Bear returned fire. Gunpowder drifted down to him and Monroe. Commotion at the bottom of their stairwell drew his attention. Someone argued and yelled toward them, but it was garbled.

"They have Duffy," Monroe hissed.

"Yes, we do. Come on down. We can talk this out, Riley," a male's voice called out to them.

"Don't come down," Duffy yelled up at him.

Before Riley could stand and approach the first stair, they pulled Duffy into his line of sight and shot him in the head. He dropped at their feet, dead before he hit the ground. Riley stumbled back and gritted his teeth, his hands balled into fists. "They killed Duffy," he announced into the radios so Bear and Tracker could hear it.

Taking the life of one of his men just crossed a line. Riley could take them all out and not be prosecuted. All bets were off. Monroe put his hand on his shoulder. "We need to get into a position we can start picking these guys off one by one. They killed one of us, so we are protected by law to defend ourselves. They have already shown us they will not hesitate to kill."

Monroe nodded. Anger burned behind his eyes. He and Duffy served together and had lived through such devastation overseas; to be killed like this at home was beyond reproach.

"Hey, Riley." The voice was talking again. He couldn't quite place where he knew it from.

"What?" he yelled down the stairs.

"We have your other buddy down here also. Come down now and I'll spare him."

"Who do you have down there?" Riley closed his eyes and hoped they didn't say Gavin.

"Someone said his name is Ayers."

Riley lunged to the railing. A gun at Ayers's temple told him all he needed to know. He wouldn't get out of this one alive. He couldn't let them kill an officer, much less another friend. "I'll trade myself for him. If I come down there, you let him go."

"Done. You're who we came for anyway," the droll voice announced

Monroe held him back. "You go down there and you're dead."

"Yeah, I know, but I can't let them kill anyone else." Riley handed Monroe the rifle and glanced down the hall to his best friend and gave him a small salute.

Bear nodded and disappeared around the corner. Riley's legs didn't want to move. At least he would be with his wife again. He peered over his right shoulder back at Monroe. "Tell Annie I'm sorry."

Monroe started to get up, but Riley held up his hand before closing the stairwell door behind him. His legs were heavy as he descended. He counted three on this side and wondered if he could take any out before they killed him.

On the last landing, the men, dressed in all black with their faces covered, grabbed Riley and hauled him out into the main lobby of his building. Only one pane of glass was shattered. They were smart and had concentrated the shots on one section before waltzing in.

"You said you would let Ayers go if I came down." Riley flinched as one of the men tied his hands behind his back.

"Well, you see, Riley. There's a problem with that." Ayers raised off his knees and wiped the blood from the corner of his mouth before he took his weapon from the second man on his left and holstered it back in his duty belt. "They work for me."

"How could you?" Riley spit out.

"Oh, definitely for the money. See, working for you after I retired was a great option, but I was made a better offer, and I don't have to really do anything for my payday."

"And your partner who died." Riley shook his head.

"I brought him in on it. At his age, it was more money than he would ever make, even with thirty years of service. He jumped at the chance a seasoned officer presented him." Sadness clouded Ayers's features for a split second.

"I trusted you. When did you turn to taking bribes?"

"Oh, about a week before they ran Annie down. I was approached when walking from my car to the house. They knew where I lived. They would have killed my wife and kids. They're connected, Riley. They could do it. So, I figured we would move out of state or even out of the country and away from here with the money I'll get for keeping you from that hearing."

"What could I possibly tell them that would have so much bearing on the case that it would tip the scales for you to do this. Kill an innocent person. Duffy didn't deserve to die the way he did!" Riley started to stand when one of the men shoved him back to his knees.

"Yeah, Duffy. See, I feel really bad about that. I liked him, I really did, but he figured out a few things last night and came to my house, threatening to turn me in. So, we had to detain him and hope his sacrifice would help get you out of the way for today's trial. It was either him or me, and well, we all know by now that I'll choose me any day over someone else." Ayers perched on the corner of Bear's desk. "Good ole Riley fell for it like I knew he would. You weren't supposed to know I was here. Duffy would have just been a tragic accident with you none the wiser, but you had to go and barricade yourself upstairs and force us to use him as leverage to bring you down to us. I was only supposed to delay you getting to court, not kill you, if that makes you feel any better."

"What did he figure out?" Why didn't he come to Riley with it instead of trying to handle it himself? "Why wait until today to come after me? Why the ruse of putting in your retirement and coming to work for me?"

"I switched the flash drives. They only got one of the drives with Alan terrorizing Annie. It will put Alan away for years but also keep the spotlight off the congressman. I snagged one of the drives from the plant you dumped them in. As for not coming after you until now...well, see, for some reason, it was kept secret who was subpoenaed for the case. The defense and prosecutor were sworn not to release any names or they would be charged with witness tampering. The public defender is wet behind the ears and refused to even tell his client. Everyone thought it was only Annie testifying against Alan, and if he was found not guilty and able to explain the video of his abuse of her, then it would go that much easier on the congressman. Every other case hinges on Alan's conviction. We happen to think we can get him off his charges with little to no time served. Claim mental health issues, and it looks like it was just his problems, not anyone else."

Riley smiled. "In regard to Alan, he still has to face murder charges for his first two wives."

"Yes, but that didn't happen here, so they can't present evidence from that case before this judge. You know how jurisdictional boundaries work, Riley. That means no video evidence, no autopsy reports, no crash reports, nothing. I made sure all of that evidence disappeared, and while you were able to get your business account back into good standing—I'm still trying to figure that one out—it still makes you look desperate to save your company and an unreliable witness to what happened involving you. Once he's done with this case and sent home, that won't be my problem." Ayers thrust his chest out.

Riley narrowed his eyes. "You know I made a copy of the video as we watched it. They already have it. They are going to request removal of state charges and replace them with federal ones due to the blatant disregard for the law where he lives. This involved a congressman and the crimes they have covered up over the years. That includes bribery and extortion involving elected officials; that makes it federal. You apparently didn't pay attention in your FTO training or you would realize this would all turn into a federal operation well above local laws."

Ayers lurched off the desk and grabbed Riley by the collar of his shirt. "Tell me you didn't do that!"

"Sorry, I can't tell you that. You don't have much time to run before they come after you. As soon as they realize it was switched, they will know who did it. Your initials are all over that evidence bag. Your pension will be taken away, and you will be charged with tampering with evidence in a federal case." Riley snorted.

"Then why didn't Annie turn over the videos earlier? Why not take him down once and for all?" Ayers sneered.

"Because she never knew the laws and what would hold up and what wouldn't. All she had to go on was what the police drilled into her head all the while she was abused by that jerk. She just wanted to make sure her degraded lessons weren't seen by anyone else, to keep what little dignity that man left her with. But I guarantee with the evidence presented today, Alan and the congressman and all of their little frat boys will know what it's like to lose their freedom."

Ayers pushed him back, toppling him over onto his side. Ayers kicked him several times, which stole Riley's breath. He started to storm to the front windows before stomping back and landing a few more kicks. The men with him didn't know what to do. One jogged up to him and tried to calm him down. He decked him. The other two came to his rescue and held Ayers back. Riley pulled the knife from his ankle and cut the rope around his wrists. He darted to the staircase and took the stairs two at a time.

When he was outside the fourth floor, he knocked four times. Monroe peered through the partially open door and motioned Riley through. "What's going on?"

"It's Ayers. They got to him. He's in charge down there. He isn't a hostage." Riley's breath wheezed out. He wrapped his arm around his no-doubt broken ribs as a radio transmission pierced the silence.

"ETA five out."

Riley smiled. "That's SWAT. Gavin must be working from the outside."

"Can we trust them?" Erickson hovered over the radio holding wires together.

"Who, SWAT? Oh yeah, you can trust him. That's my old captain. He'll take out Ayers himself if given the choice. He hates bad cops. I never saw this coming. I need to be able to send out an email. Erickson, can you make it happen?" Riley grunted while trying to take a deep breath.

"Funny you should ask. I've been working on something. I can get a small burst of network, but it only lasts a few seconds. Get what you need and I'll get it ready for another burst." Erickson scrambled over to his bag.

Riley let himself into his apartment and latched onto the laptop from the kitchen counter. He typed a quick email to the attorney he was supposed to testify for today, mentioning the hostage situation and that Ayers switched the flash drives after they grabbed evidence from his patrol vehicle. He made it back to the hallway and waited for Erickson. He nodded and plugged a device into his laptop. The computer talked to the new device for several seconds and then connected. He hit send and his email popped into his outbox.

The cursor hovered over the screen, spinning incessantly before failing to send the message, saving it to his drafts folder.

"Hold on, try again." Erickson tapped a few buttons and nodded.

Riley hit send. An explosion rocked the back stairwell. Bear and Tracker ran and slammed the door closed. Then they locked it with their key. Something slammed into the door. Smoke rolled under the gap at the bottom of the metal.

The copy of the email flipped over to the draft folder failing to send.

"Erickson, we have to get this to work. If I don't send this email, we'll all be dead."

"Gee, no pressure." Erickson wiped at the sweat on his forehead with the back of his hand and furiously typed on the device. While muttering to himself, his fingers flew over the keys as he coded several lines into the machine, his fingers a blur of motion. "Okay, now."

Riley hit send. Tracker and Monroe ran to the stairwell with wet towels from Riley's apartment and draped them around the bottom of the steel fire door. The curser continued to spin.

Something crashed into the door as they dropped several more towels, ineffective at stopping the smoke that was now pushing curling tendrils of acrid gray around the sides of the dense metal before creeping along the ceiling with nowhere else to go. The longer the smoke continued to pour around the door, the darker it became.

Coughing, they continued to watch the computer attempt to send the email. Monroe darted into the apartment and came out with wet t-shirts to wrap around their heads. It helped for the moment, but it wouldn't last long with how much was collecting against the ceiling. Crouching to stay under the noxious deadly smoke, he turned his attention back to the computer screen.

He prayed God would let it send when the computer beeped to indicate that the message was sent. "Yes!" He clapped Erickson on the back, moved back to his apartment, slid a ceiling tile out of place, and hid his laptop out of sight.

He snagged his rifle from the floor and he grunted as he twisted the wrong way, causing his ribs to yell at him. Pain coursed around his back. "Now let's take back my building."

"How about I check you out first." Monroe palpitated his ribs, earning him several winces, a couple of grunts, and one slow-released breath of pain. "Sorry, man. My guess is cracked if not broken, but I don't think anything has punctured your lungs or you'd have serious pressure in your chest and you'd be unable to breathe as well as you are right now."

"You think this is breathing easily?" Riley snarled.

"Well, easier than if you had air leaking into your chest cavity, putting pressure on your lungs and collapsing them."

Raising an eyebrow at Monroe, Riley snarked, "You may have a point."

Monroe moved to the end of the hall by the windows. "You guys have to see this."

SWAT trucks from County and City were parked outside. Several people, who had accompanied Ayers, were face down on the ground and in cuffs. Ayers shook hands with several of the men on the team before pointing to the top floor of the building. Riley surged toward the stairs. His men followed, yelling for him to stop, that they didn't know if anyone was still in the building and that he had a rifle slung over his shoulder with two SWAT teams outside who wouldn't hesitate to kill him if he ran out of the building like that.

He rolled up his sleeves, dropped the rifle outside the stairwell door, and approached the front door with his hands up. Men yelled at him to stop and drop to his knees. "I need to talk to Captain Marshall!"

"Yo, Cap! Do you know this guy?" a man in full uniform called out from Riley's side, holding him at gunpoint.

"Riley?" Captain Marshall extended his hand and pulled Riley to his feet. "I haven't seen you in ages."

"Sir, I need to talk to you. Ayers is a dirty cop. He took payoffs to keep me from federal court today, and he attacked my building and had one of my men killed." Riley spouted off the facts as quickly as he could.

Riley's men joined him outside, unarmed, of course.

"Are you sure? That's a serious accusation against an officer." Captain Marshall took a step back.

"Sir, have you ever known me to jump to conclusions?"

"No, I haven't, but do you have any proof?"

"Not only do I have it on camera, but I also have boot-sized bruises he left when he more than likely broke my ribs a few moments ago, which will also have been caught on video." Riley glared at Ayers who approached from the side.

"Riley, I'm sorry but I'll have to take you into custody for the part you played in a man's death today in this building." Ayers took a step forward when the captain held up his hand.

"I think I'll watch the video if you don't mind," the captain informed Ayers, who shuffled back. "Officers, please detain Ayers."

"This way, sir." Riley motioned to a desk.

"That is a doctored video. You can't even get cell service in that building. How could he have a camera recording?" Ayers shrugged his arms from the SWAT officer's grasp.

"They run on a separate contained system. They continue to record even if the power is cut." Riley swiveled around in a chair, holding his right side with his arm wrapped around his torso while pulling up the main monitor in the control room, typing with one hand. He split the screen into four separate camera views. One, the front of the building, another with the back stairwell, then the front one, and the final one, the lobby, where he found out Ayers took a payout.

Ayers grabbed at the SWAT team member's gun since they disarmed him, trying to wrestle it away. You can't take on county SWAT. The man took Ayers down without even breaking a sweat.

"My question is, why did you only get upset about a video after Riley said what was on it? Please show me." Captain Marshall pulled up a chair.

Riley pressed the play button after queuing the recording to when the first shot hit the front of the building. He stepped over to a SWAT member and pointed to where Duffy lay. The man nodded and jogged from the building. Seconds later, he came in with a blanket and helped Riley cover Duffy.

Captain Marshall shoved his chair back from the console and spun on his heels. "Men, take him into custody!"

"I'll have a copy made for evidence." Riley shook his hand. He had never seen the captain's face so red.

"No, wait! I can explain!" Ayers struggled against the SWAT officers and was taken to the ground. "Riley, you gotta help me out."

"You killed a soldier who fought for this country! A good man who had family. Who did more tours than anyone in this building! You took a payoff from crooked politicians. You did this to yourself. Man up and live with the consequences." His men joined him in the lobby as the SWAT team hauled Ayers off the floor and dragged him out of the building. His feet never touched the ground.

County deputies stood guard over Duffy after collecting evidence and photographing the scene. They all knew his military ties and his service. Riley glanced at his watch. It was too late to try and get to the courthouse. He jogged up the stairs to his apartment and reclaimed his laptop from the ceiling. He rejoined his men and told Erickson to see what he could do to restore power.

Cell phones blinked and alerted everyone the service had been restored moments after Erickson entered the basement. He reappeared at the top of the stairs with a small black box. He nodded to the deputies, one retrieved an evidence bag and stowed the jammer for safekeeping.

Riley booted up his laptop and was notified of his email being received from the prosecutor on the case and that they were able to introduce the video in court. He would meet him at the office when court was over. That was an hour ago. It took time for SWAT to clear the building. Permits were checked for the rifles in their possession and everything documented. City police were the first ones to leave. Then county SWAT. Riley put in a call to have the window replaced the next day. They surprised him when they said they would be out in an hour. Lights flickered throughout the building as they came on in intervals. The power company sent a truck out immediately. With the power back on, his men were back at work tagging accounts that could possibly turn into client business for them.

They all stood by when the medical examiner showed up to collect Duffy's body. Captain Marshall sent officers to notify his family. Riley lowered his head. There would be a void where Duffy fit into his life. Bear and Monroe didn't say a word as they carried the desk Ayers would have used down to the basement storage. It would be his job to clear out Duffy's desk and send the items home to his family. He snagged an unused folded banker's box and assembled it as he walked over to his desk. Everyone watched him clear out his possessions and empty his desk drawers into the small twelve by ten by fifteen cardboard container.

Monroe wandered over. "Boss, I got this one. I know his wife. I'll take it to her." He held out his hands.

"Thanks." Riley put his hands on the cleaned-off desk, not sure he wanted to ever replace its position. That was something they would worry about in the months to come and see if they could make do without his expertise.

Twenty-Eight

A small man dressed in a simple black suit that screamed lawyer meandered across the parking lot. He hesitated when he saw the window replacement that was in progress and the damage to the front of the building. Riley met him at the door. "It's safe. Everyone's in custody."

"I have to tell you that was probably one of the more exciting trials I've ever been a part of." The lawyer tip-toed over the broken glass, avoiding the broom being pushed across the floor.

"Did the video help?"

"Help? It sealed the case for us. They thought it had been switched out. His true nature came out when some of the best evidence was presented on behalf of your friend. I believe Duffy is his name. I can't even begin to count the number of people who pulled resources and showed up in court, lining the entire back two rows. Where is he? I want to shake his hand." The lawyer looked from left to right, eyeing Riley's men, who had gathered. The excitement from the experience vibrated from him.

"He didn't make it."

The lawyer peered at Riley. "Didn't make it?" The blood in the corner caught his eye and his hand flew to his mouth.

"They sent people to keep me from court today. He was caught in the assault and murdered." Riley refilled his cup from the coffee pot that sat in the kitchen. The lawyer didn't look so hot; he was white as a ghost. Riley wasn't sure he wouldn't pass out.

"Oh. I'm...Oh my. I'm so sorry. I didn't hear." His voice cracked as he stammered and wiped his hand across his brow.

"Thanks. Tell me about the case." Riley dropped to the chair on the side of Bear's desk. He wanted his men to also hear everything. They lost one of their own because of this.

The lawyer started for the nearest chair but noticed the cleared-off desk and glanced to the corner. His face paled further if that was even possible. "Did you want to take this to your office?"

"No. Everyone gets to know what happened. These men are the reason we are still alive, and this building is still open. Along with Duffy, they pulled in markers to help get a corrupt politician out of office. Please go ahead. I'm sorry, your name?"

He marched over, extending his hand. "I'm Simon Robert Sanders the third."

"Okay, Mr. Sanders, please continue." Riley shook his hand and then motioned to the chair next to Monroe's station. Monroe used his foot to slide it away from the desk for him.

"Oh, thanks. Um...well...yes." He put his briefcase in his lap, but it slid from his legs so he set it next to his chair, fumbling, uncomfortable with the surroundings. "So, Miss Divers was a witness to numerous accounts where Dr. Montgomery had meetings with the congressman."

"Mr. Montgomery. He is no longer a doctor." Riley interrupted him.

"Oh yes, I remember hearing that. Well, anywho, she was a fantastic witness even when Mr. Montgomery created such a ruckus that he had to be escorted out of the courtroom as he screamed that she was a liar and not to be trusted. State forensic specialists had the insect evidence that showed that the bodies of his two previous wives had, in fact, been dead days before they were documented in the autopsy reports. The original ones you were able to rescue before being destroyed helped with that." The high pitch of his voice when he was particularly excited about an event would give Riley a headache before he finished, he was sure.

"So, with the switched drive, the court saw the trauma that Miss Divers suffered at her ex-husband's hand." He faced Riley. "She said you had the rest of those secured in this office, I believe."

"Yes, for when she comes back to collect them herself." Riley emptied his coffee cup and looked longingly at the still partially full pot that sat at the entrance of the kitchen.

"Oh, she's not coming back. This has been remanded to the federal level. That is why all of the evidence presented today along with his past crimes was so crucial. We pressed for federal charges, declaring that the state charges would be held pending the federal trial." The lawyer pushed his glasses up his oily nose, only to have them partially slide back down.

Riley's heart raced. "Why not?"

"She is nowhere near safe with all the happenings that have surrounded this trial. The government wants to keep her safe until all the involved parties are brought to justice. That will take...well let's see here. What? Several years? Yes, at least. You see, she was more than just a victim in all of this. She witnessed the majority of the illegal transactions that transpired with the fraternity after she married Mr. Montgomery. I thought you knew that. She wasn't only running to get away from that man but also to hide from everyone who conspired with him to cover up those horrific crimes." He wrung his hands while fidgeting in his chair.

"Years?" Riley lunged off his chair and stomped to the coffee pot pouring another steaming cup. His hands shook. He blew out a breath and steadied his hands before he turned back to his men and reacquired the chair he vacated moments before.

"Well, yes. You see, there are procedures we have to follow and with the powers of the people involved, her life is in mortal danger if she were allowed to just run around willy-nilly. Of all people, being a retired officer, you should know this." His voice returned to his no-nonsense nasal annoyance.

"I'm aware of their pull in their county but surely she could be kept safe in her own home." Riley ignored Bear shifting in his chair beside him.

"Well yes...yes, I suppose, but it was our suggestion that she be kept hidden with federal agents watching her twenty-four-seven. Yes, I think that is the wisest of options. Anywho, several expert witnesses came forward because of Duffy. Autopsies were nullified, crash evidence refuted as haphazardly tampered with. Oh, and her parents' crash was reclassified as murder. Oh, I do say she was so sad but held together so nicely when that decision was made. Alan was charged with, let's see. Oh, where did I put that." He rifled through his briefcase, his glasses sliding down his nose again. "Oh, here it is. One, two, four, then the girls in college, six more. So, ten murders and that is just for starters."

"What about the two who disappeared?" Riley raised his eyebrows.

"Oh, that's the best part! Alan stormed to the bench tossing the bailiff off him, and it took six more officers to subdue him. My gosh, it was such an uproar. But he said he wouldn't be charged for murders he didn't commit and those were all the work of the congressman. Oh yes, it was very exciting, I must say." He shoved his glasses up his nose again.

"Wait. Can that be proved?" Riley dropped his leg, which he had on the corner of the desk.

Simon smiled and edged forward in his chair. "Oh, most assuredly. There are more videos of these events. Since the government has already seized his property, they are searching every room of Alan's house, even knocking down walls. Can you imagine his face if he were to ever walk back into his precious home and have those holes in the walls?" He almost giggled and then calmed himself and slid back in his seat.

Riley bit his lip to keep from laughing. "Please go on."

"Okay. Where was I?" Simon scrunched his nose and narrowed his eyes. "Oh yes, so we have the murder charges for Alan and the congressman. Then the state presented witnesses that the judge was issuing orders above his ability as the judge in his county. He has been removed from the bench permanently, and those charges are pending. Then, oh dear, such a sad thing. While Miss Divers was on the stand, she testified what happened to her when Mr. Murphy kidnapped her and injured that brave officer. He had her for a day and a half until her ex-husband was released from jail for his contempt of court charges. When she mentioned how he tried to violate her, well, Mr. Montgomery came unglued. He jumped on Mark, pulling him up and over the railing, where other criminals sat waiting for their case to be heard, and slammed his head into the floor so many times that they aren't sure Mark will live through those injuries before the deputies and bailiff pulled Alan off him. He then continued to spew all sorts of filth, stating Annie was his property and he never gave him permission to touch her like that. Oh my, it was so scary." The lawyer looked at Riley.

While clenching his jaw, his knuckles turned white that gripped the coffee mug handle. Bear put a hand on his shoulder.

"Oh goodness, I thought you knew." He shoved his glasses up on his nose again.

"No. I did not." Riley set his cup down and put his elbow on his knees and studied the floor. "Please continue."

"Oh no, maybe I shouldn't say anything else."

Riley's head snapped up. "I want you to tell us everything. There were cameras in the court for the news stations, weren't there?"

"Well, of course."

"Then everything that happened in that courtroom is public domain. Please continue." Riley blew out a breath.

"Oh yes, yes. Um, let's see. She told of how she was able to hit Mark and it made him so mad he beat her severely. So sad. Oh, so if Mr. Murphy dies, that will be another murder he will be charged with. The judge sent down indictments on all their frat brothers for the parts they played in covering up all the murders. The sheriff of their county barricaded himself in his lake cabin. When they finally went in, he killed himself." The lawyer shuddered. "The coroner was arrested for falsifying official documents. Tried to say he didn't know anything about it, but the files proved it was his signature so he finally admitted were his. He then offered to be a witness and tell them everything, but the judge didn't blink and advised him he couldn't be counted as a credible witness since he just perjured himself on the stand. This thing will expose so much corruption over the next several years that I'm sure we will be shocked at who is indicted next. With all the evidence that has come to light and still to be presented, we have enough. You won't be called as a witness again. The video really helped to expose the congressman."

"Thank you for coming to give us an update." Riley stood, extending his hand.

Simon vigorously shook it and pushed his glasses up on his nose again. He grabbed his briefcase and meandered to the door. "Mr. Strong."

"Yes." Riley turned toward him as he stood in the doorway to his office.

"Miss Divers said to thank you for everything you did for her. That is one strong woman to get up on the stand like she did. She is the reason we have the case that we do." He disappeared through the door and flinched as one of the workers installing the new glass hammered on the frame.

Bear kicked his feet up. "How many times do you think he got a wedgie in school?"

Monroe spit out his coffee, laughing. Riley's shoulders shook as he held in a laugh on his way to his desk. He needed to see Annie for himself. He didn't know about the extent of the assault. He clenched his fist and wanted to punch something or someone. It would be years before she was finally free from all of this. Why didn't she tell him everything she witnessed? He would have had a different strategy to keep her safe. With his hands on top of his desk, he laid his head on his hands.

"Hey, boss. They're done with the window," Bear alerted him from the doorway.

Riley didn't lift his head. "Just sign the paper for me."

"Will do." Bear's footsteps led away from his office.

A few moments later, the page slid across the top of his desk with a swish sound as Bear brought it to him.

He lifted his head and leaned back in his chair. "I couldn't keep her from more trauma."

"You heard everyone who did everything they could to cover their own butts in this. There are decades of abuse, murder, rape, and probably even more that we don't know about. This is not on you." Bear crossed his arms and leaned his shoulder against the wall.

"I know. How are our cases going? Is everything caught up on our files?" Riley made a mental note he needed to get up the back stairwell and check out the damage.

"Yup, nothing left to do but monitor the accounts and trace the trackers of certain clients." Bear narrowed his eyes. "You know, I think she would see you if she could. We just didn't know how much danger she really was in with all she knew."

"No one knew how much of an integral part of this she was. I'm not even sure she realized it and how it would all lead here. She just wanted to run away from her abuser."

"Yeah, her abuser who is a murderer and psychopath." Bear peered out the door.

"Want to trek up the back stairs and help me assess the damage?" Riley smiled when Bear cringed. "Or you can take the elevator and meet me at the top."

"Come on, I'm just not built for stair climbing. I hit my limit for the next decade today."

Riley snorted and hauled himself out of his chair. "After we check the stairs, everyone goes home for the rest of the week. Paid leave."

No one said anything in response. His guys needed to regroup and figure things out. They would help Duffy's widow plan and pay for the funeral with military honors. When he started this business, he never could have imagined how dangerous it would be. Ayers was a shock. If he could be bought at a high enough price, who else could be?

Twenty-Nine

Riley yanked off his tie and tossed it onto the end of his bed. The funeral today was one of the hardest he ever had to attend besides his wife's. Duffy's widow was beside herself. His men were there every step of the way and never left her side. She clung to Monroe as her lifeline. They were all scheduled to return to work after the weekend. He let them have the days off while he monitored the accounts and covered the business so they could do what they needed to do. A couple spent their entire time with their families. Others went fishing. Bear returned to the office. He didn't have anyone besides cousins, so he helped Riley with the accounts.

Riley had to admit he was glad his best friend showed up. It was hard enough thinking about Annie and not being able to help her, but to walk through the building alone without a soul to talk to made him miss his wife that much more. He tugged a cotton shirt down over his head after he tossed his button-down shirt on the bed next to his tie. Accounts needed to be billed for their monthly services, and he wanted to get that out of the way today; then he wouldn't have to worry about it on Monday.

The elevator took him to the ground floor. He would need to get to the workout room after he sent the billing out. He neglected his workouts the last couple of weeks since he'd found out he was being subpoenaed for court. His printer knocked and chugged to life as he started the printing of the invoice. He jumped to his feet as the last page was spit out from the rollers and opened the front cover. He just had a technician out to fix this stupid thing. Nothing seemed out of place, so he pulled the toner out and peered into the ink-coated interior. It looked dirtier than it should. When he put the cartridge back in, he noticed scotch tape stuck to the top inside lip of the cover. He tugged the tape off and pulled a piece of paper out that was folded over into a small square.

He unfolded the page; it only had three words written on it.

Don't trust Ayers.

It was delicate penmanship. Wait. He yanked the letter Annie wrote him that she left on her desk at her house when he thought she was dead. It was the same. How did she get into his office, much less leave a hidden note? When did she do this? He turned the page over; there was nothing on it except those words.

Bear startled him when he appeared in his doorway. "You never jump. What's got you spooked?"

Riley handed him the note. He read it, turned the page over, and read it again.

"Huh." He handed it back. "Who left you that little gem? Would have been nice to know that a week ago."

"Annie."

"Wait. What? How?"

"It had to have been in there a while. She was in protective custody for over six months. And she hasn't been here since before that. I wonder what she witnessed. I think we need to talk to her. There may be more that Ayers was involved in than we know." Riley rifled through the business cards in the middle drawer of his desk.

"Do you really want to pull her out of hiding for this?"

"What else are we going to do? The least Simon Robert Sanders the third can do is talk to her and ask her about this. That way we won't jeopardize her location." Riley picked up the handset on his desk phone but didn't dial.

Bear stalked to the desk. "What is it?"

"Get Erickson in here." He mouthed "bug," pointed to the phone, and then replaced the receiver.

Bear puffed out his cheeks, extracted his cell phone from his pocket, and lurched for the front doors. Seconds later, he returned and nodded.

Not even ten minutes later, Tracker came in the back door. "I heard we have bugs; I brought my exterminator friend." He pointed to Erickson, who lugged in a large bag with him.

Riley shook his head and smiled. "Start in the office."

Erickson grabbed a toolbelt and snapped it around his waist. Hunkered over his phone, he took the handset apart. He held up a small device he removed and nodded. It disappeared into the pouch he pulled from his belt. "One down."

He worked his way through his office, scanning for anything that wasn't used by them. "Clean except the phone. They can't hijack our software because of the filters I put on them so they had to go old school and plant their own bugs."

"Can we trace them or find out when they were installed so we know when to look at the footage to see who is to blame? And why didn't our sweep find them?" Riley huffed.

"Sort of. They seem inert and impracticable; they scraped the bottom of the barrel for these. I'd say the batteries stopped working so they didn't get picked up when we did our sweep. Is there anyone who was in your office that you would have trusted to be alone?"

"Ayers." Riley yanked the note off the top of his desk that he found in his printer and handed it to Erickson.

He raised an eyebrow. "Who left this little morsel for you?"

"Annie."

"Okay, when was she in your office last? Maybe we can narrow down when Ayers was in here around the same time."

"She's never been in my office." Riley took two steps to the printer and stopped when Bear cleared his throat.

"I'm here to look at a printer?" A young man with a service technician shirt that bore the name of the company his printer was through stood in the doorway. "There wasn't anyone at the front to show me where to go."

"There was a tech out last week." Riley narrowed his eyes.

The young man checked his clipboard. "No, sir. We were going to send someone out, but he got sick and couldn't come in. He quit without notice after that, and we've been juggling accounts to get to everyone as fast as we can."

"There." Riley motioned everyone out of his office as the tech lumbered to the printer.

"Okay, then who was out here last week?" Bear logged into the camera system. He scanned through footage as everyone else stood behind him.

"There." Riley pointed to the tall man on the screen. He wore the same shirt as the man in his office who Erickson was keeping an eye on. They all watched as he retrieved the note from his pocket and reached over the desk to snag a piece of tape from the dispenser.

"Okay, so how do we figure out who he is and how Annie got him to leave me that message?" Riley went to the kitchen and snagged a bottle of water from the refrigerator.

"Look." Bear pointed to the screen.

Riley peered over his shoulder at the frozen frame, showing him steadying the lamp and leaving a perfect thumbprint.

"Have you touched or cleaned that lamp since then?" Monroe jumped up when Sasha strolled in with her cleaning supplies and headed toward Riley's office.

"No!" they all yelled simultaneously.

Sasha yelped and dropped her bucket, her eyes wide and her hands clutched to her chest.

"Sasha, I'm sorry." Riley put an arm around her shoulders while Monroe picked up her bucket. "But can you start upstairs today?"

"Sure, Mr. Strong." Her shoulders trembled under his arm.

"It's okay. We just have a situation going on. When was the last time you cleaned my office?" Riley hit the button on the elevator panel for her.

"I know it's been a while, Mr. Strong. But with everything, I just wasn't wanting to come into the building after it was shot at. When I saw your cars here today, I figured it would be okay with you all here," she rambled.

"No, it's okay. That is exactly what we were hoping to hear. Just clean upstairs and leave the rest for next week. Okay?" Riley held the elevator doors open.

"Yes, sir." Her hands shook as she took the bucket from Monroe.

The elevator doors closed, and Riley marched to his office and snagged the fingerprint kit he'd removed from Duffy's desk off his bookcase. The tech was gone and said the printer should be working like new. He replaced a couple of rollers that the paper was catching on, according to Erickson.

It had been years since Riley attempted to lift a fingerprint. He hoped it was like riding a bike. He twirled the brush through the powder and lightly touched it to the perfectly left thumbprint. The powder clung to the oils left by their fake technician. The tape curved along the lamp, adhering to the side as he smoothed it over the surface. He breathed a sigh of relief when the tape lifted and showed the preserved print. He handed it to Erickson, who grabbed his cell phone before even getting to his desk.

He scanned the print into his computer and booted up his email. As he hit send, he also disconnected his call with his friend Hargis. "They will let us know as soon as they get a hit. If the person is in the system."

"Are they going to put a rush on it so we don't have to wait the three days it normally takes?" Riley scanned the room. They would need to search every inch of this building for other bugs. That was a task he wasn't looking forward to.

"Yeah, now we just have to hope he's in the system." Erickson raised his eyebrows.

Riley gave his employees a chin lift. He didn't need to tell his people when he needed things done. Erickson jumped from his chair and started with the desk closest to his office. He handed out wands to the others to sweep for bugs so they could check the other stations.

Several hours later, they had collected five listening devices, four cameras, a transmitter, and a hard drive that had a layer of dust on it, telling them they hadn't come back to retrieve it yet. They put them all in one of Erickson's special bags to scramble the signals they sent out. "I installed software into our system so they can't transmit the data to the outside. That could be why they had the hard drive installed, to collect what they needed and then they would retrieve it later."

"So, we haven't had a breach in our files or accounts?"

"No. Those are safe and still locked. From the angles of the cameras, it looks like they were watching your apartment, the spare apartment you put Annie in, and your office. Listening devices only on yours, Bear's, and Monroe's phones tell me it was the people who were watching her the closest. Monroe helped her with her injuries, Bear's your right-hand man, and of course you. The bigger question is, who would want that information? Everyone already has indictments on them, so who could possibly need to know what's happening now?"

"Are they even still monitoring or recording at this point?" Riley sat on top of Duffy's desk.

"Yes, until I unplugged the hard drive, where it was storing the audio and visual files. We may need to watch the video and see how far back it goes. That will give us an idea of what day and time on our own footage we need to watch to see who planted everything." Erickson dug in his desk, pulling out cables and wires.

"Can we access it without them knowing or seeing anything?" Riley plopped on the chair and rolled over behind Erickson.

"This is just a storage device. It doesn't send out signals itself. It is just Bluetooth-connected to the bugs in here. With the scrambler we have on the building, they would have to physically be here to view it."

"Pull it up. Let's see what we have." Bear joined Riley as Monroe escorted Sasha from the elevator to the front doors. She was still shaken from being unintentionally yelled at earlier.

"Okay, here we go. I'll open the oldest file. It looks like they are date-stamped, and it starts a new file every day at midnight." Erickson set his computer to play the entire video.

"When is the first video dated?" Riley grabbed a pen and notepad from the desk.

"March fifteenth."

Riley stopped, pen poised over the paper. "Wait, that was a week before Annie was run down. Why would they be spying on us before we even knew who she was?"

"We don't keep video recorded for that long. We won't have the ability to access the system that far back," Monroe huffed.

"Yes, we will. When they hit Annie, I backed up the video for two months before that time and have it saved on my computer. I'll check it when we are done here." Riley scooted his chair forward. He squinted and craned his neck as he looked at the image on the screen. Feeling like an old man, he sighed, knowing he would need to get checked for glasses. His eyes weren't what they used to be.

The video showed them going about their daily activities. They were able to fast forward to when Annie was hit and Riley carried her into the building. His heart roared in his ears when he saw himself holding her back then.

"Okay, you guys keep watching while I go check my records dating back to around the first file on this thing." Riley cracked his neck from one side to the other as he strolled to the kitchen for another cup of coffee.

Once he was behind his desk, he queued up the files on his video system and clicked on the saved files. They weren't there. "Erickson!"

He trudged into his office. "Yeah."

"The saved files aren't on here. Can you work your magic and see if you can retrieve them?" Riley rose from his chair for Erickson to take over and see what he could salvage.

"This could take a minute. Let me see what I can find."

"Okay, I'm heading up to my apartment for a minute." Riley's stomach flip-flopped. What if one of his men was also in on this? How else could someone get to his computer?

No, he couldn't think that way. He knew these men for years, although he knew Ayers for years and never would have guessed he could be bought. He stalked to the elevator. There was still an ace up his sleeve he could play. Would it be enough to catch who was spying on him and his employees?

He let himself into his apartment, and it was spotless. Sasha did a good job for him and had been one of his early hires. She came recommended by...Ayers. No! He jogged to his bedroom and moved his clothes to the side, exposing a safe built into the wall. It stood open. He punched the wall. How could he forget she was a referral from the one man who was now his enemy? His hand felt the back of the safe where he tugged on the corner. It pulled away, exposing a hidden compartment. The flash drives of their camera backups were still in place.

He glanced up at the ceiling and thanked God they were still there. Shaking his head, he trotted from his apartment and took the stairs two at a time. Murmuring came from his office as he walked through the door from the stairwell.

"What's going on?" Riley palmed the flash drive and put his hand behind his back.

"We know who was installing the bugs." Erickson glowered.

"Don't tell me, Sasha," he informed them.

"How do you do that? I would have never guessed her to be our interloper," Monroe growled.

Riley tossed Erickson the flash drive and trusted that he was on his side. "I remembered upstairs that Ayers recommended her. She opened my safe but apparently didn't know I installed a hidden panel, so she didn't find the backups of my backups."

"That's my boy. I taught you well to always have a backup." Erickson grinned ear to ear.

They laughed as he queued up March's videos. The goons' car followed Annie on her morning run. It was an uneventful video. Two days later they watched Officer Ayers following Annie in his personal car while she was on her run. Monroe cussed, apologized, and clamped his mouth shut. That was one of Riley's stipulations to hiring everyone. No profanity in his office space. He knew his wife would get a kick out of that. They all knew and loved his wife so when he told them that was the reason for the rules, they all adhered and never crossed that line, knowing he did it to honor Helen.

"So, he was in on this the entire time." Bear whistled.

All his little comments about keeping her safe, and Riley played into that by acknowledging that he had her and saying she was safe. "This will be a long process. I want all video where Ayers is in and around this building since the files started, saved to five other drives."

"That will take forever." Erickson almost whined.

"We need backups of our backups. A friend told me that once." Riley smiled.

"You got it. I'll need lots and lots of soda." His fingers flew across the keyboard creating files and folders. Dated and timestamped as he found video with Ayers in it.

Riley grabbed his cell. "I'll order in food."

Tracker and Gavin strolled in the back door. "Hear you could use some help."

Riley added to the food order and smiled. "Oh, yeah."

They logged into their workstations and spun around in their chairs to face him, awaiting their orders. Riley gave them assignments and they didn't hesitate to get to work. Joking back and forth, they jumped through hoops to get done what needed to be done. Riley pulled the note from his pocket from Annie that warned him to not trust Ayers. What did she know or see that he didn't? He regretted telling her he could trust him, that there were good officers out there. And for the most part, that's true. Ninety-nine percent of officers were amazing men and women trying to make a change. To be there for the victims when no one else was. They saved lives and put their own on the line to do that job.

"Boss!" Monroe hollered.

"Yeah." He jogged over.

"Prints came back. Guy is in the system. It's her lawyer."

"That man is not who was in here this morning bumbling all over himself?"

"No. Not that lawyer. Her divorce attorney. Works at the same firm where she hired our little blonde bombshell angel." Monroe raised his eyebrows.

She had a way to keep in touch with him. Riley's heart sank that she didn't. "Get me his number. I want to get everything figured out as soon as we can." Riley strolled to the doors as the delivery driver dropped off their food.

Everyone scrambled to either grab pizza or boxes of Chinese, and then hurried back to their desk and continued their assignments. Monroe handed him a piece of paper with a phone number on it. "I'm sure she would contact you if she thought she could."

"Not really sure of that myself. She thought enough to leave a message but not to contact me directly." Riley tapped in the phone number on his cell and then walked to the kitchen.

It rang several times before someone picked up but didn't say anything. "Hello," Riley called out through the phone.

"Mr. Strong, I presume," the breathy voice answered.

"Yes. I hear we have a friend in common."

"That we do. She thinks very highly of you, Mr. Strong, so I am trusting in that value since I have yet to meet you myself."

"But you didn't hesitate to drive how many hours to leave her message for me hidden in the printer." Riley threw out the information he knew.

"I'm impressed. She said you were good."

Riley closed his eyes. "Is she okay?"

A heavy sigh on the other end told Riley the voice was annoyed by the question. "That she is."

"How did she figure out what side Ayers was on?"

"She overheard Mark Murphy talking to someone on the phone when she was in the trunk of the car after the crash with the police officer. Mr. Murphy said Ayers's name. She realized you had no clue how someone you thought was a friend was working against you. At her behest, I placed her handwritten note where you would find it. She has been through a lot, Mr. Strong, and I highly urge against trying to contact her. A new life is what she needs, not to be drawn into another relationship so soon after the dissolution of a marriage that she barely escaped from with her life." He was a mouth breather and every breath he took blew against the receiver when he exhaled.

"We aren't in a relationship." Riley bit the inside of his cheek.

"Sir, I wasn't born yesterday. I can hear it in your voice, especially when you asked how she was doing. By talking to her, I can say the feelings are not one-sided." The attorney sighed, sending another strong breath through the phone.

Riley smiled and closed his eyes. "I just want to make sure she is okay. She needs to stay safe, and if that means staying away from here, then she needs to do that."

"I will relay that message. Furthermore, since we have that business out of the way, I needed to finish telling you the rest of Mr. Ayers's involvement. He also sold Mr. Murphy the cabin in which they held her. He was there on more than one occasion and watched what they did to her, before and after Mr. Montgomery was released from jail. He was the deliverer of the food they ate while in the cabin. At one point, she got out of her restraints and ran, only to be caught by Mr. Ayers, who choked her until she lost consciousness. When she woke, she was back in the basement, this time tied to a table. This young lady has been through enough to defeat anyone and give up on life. She has fought back and stood up for herself. She's an amazing woman, and I want you to realize that before you believe anything Mr. Ayers has to say. I know he's a friend of yours and works at the police department where you did."

"Trust me, I know. He led an attack on my building and killed one of my men. He was taking money from Mr. Montgomery to keep me from testifying in court. That's why I wasn't able to attend. We have him on video and that will be turned over to the police department as soon as they are all copied and put in evidence," Riley calmly informed him.

Heavy breaths filled the air.

When nothing was said, Riley continued. "He is being charged with those felonies and will lose his freedom, his pension, and everything he holds dear when I am done with him. What he did to Annie will only fuel the fire of what I will present to the county deputies I'll call out so they can process this outside of the local police department where Ayers worked."

"Very well, sir. I'll relay that to Miss Divers for you. We both want the same thing for her. To be able to finally live life the way it was meant to be lived. Without fear of abuse or death from the hands of people who vowed to love her. She needs a clean break from everyone and everything she knows. Please let her have that break." He sighed and then disconnected.

Riley pulled the phone from his ear as Tracker joined him in the kitchen.

"Are you okay?" Tracker grabbed a bottle of water.

"I will be. Ayers helped abduct Annie." Riley stormed past Tracker.

He caught up to him as he weaved around the desks. "He hurt Annie?"

Everyone turned from their chairs, and Erickson and Bear lurked in his open office doorway.

Riley relayed what her attorney told him and how Ayers used a hold on her to render her unconscious and take her back to the cabin.

"How could we have been so wrong about him? Who is this guy?" Monroe's face flushed red as he clutched the back of his chair.

"He is a psychopath who is manipulative and a compulsive liar. No wonder Alan was drawn to him. They could probably sniff each other out. How are we on the video copies?" Riley glanced at Erickson.

"Almost done. He really isn't in very many videos here except when we called him to work on cases Alan was involved in. I started a separate file for Sasha. We have her planting bugs in all the places we found them. She was on the phone the entire time. Someone walked her through where to put them and how to go unnoticed."

"Where is Gavin?" Riley turned around in the control room, his eyes scanning the space. Would he ever get the feeling of dread worked out of his thoughts when he didn't see someone and not think they were up to no good?

"Oh, he's on an errand." Bear grinned.

"When you grin like that, it scares me." Riley crossed his arms.

His grin widened. "It was my idea."

Sasha walked through the front doors, escorted by Gavin. "I'm sorry! He made me do it! Hide all those devices!" She threw herself at him. "Mr. Strong, I didn't want to do that to you. You were always so nice to me."

"Sit down and tell me everything." Riley nodded to Tracker, who turned on his phone.

An hour later and part of a roll of paper towels to catch all her tears, they had the full story on Ayers. Most of it they had already figured out. He asked her to plant the bugs. The goon squad approached him the week they found Annie jogging in front of their building. Since it was a daily ritual, Alan naturally assumed Riley was involved with her. Jealous rage kicked in and he started plotting how to take him down and get his ex-wife back.

Ayers told him no initially, but then he threatened to frame him for a crime he didn't commit. He caved and took the money. Once money changed hands, he was stuck. His wife liked the new income and demanded he continue supplying her with new shopping money so she could finally fit in with her rich friends.

Riley motioned Monroe over. "Call County and have them send a deputy to take her statement."

Sasha jumped out of her chair. "Mr. Strong, please, no. I can't go to jail!"

"That isn't for me to decide. If you broke the law, you need to be held accountable for those actions. Time for you to be an adult, Sasha, and face the consequences." Riley strolled to his office as Erickson placed the last flash drive on the top of his desk.

He tucked one into his back pocket and then grabbed another and left his office. Tossing it to Monroe, he said, "Give that to the deputy." He stalked to the kitchen. The cold marble counter he gripped as he blew out a breath felt good on his hands. He was mad and he had to get that anger under control before he did something rash.

The front door opened and he sauntered to the kitchen doorway as two deputies walked in. He knew one of them from when he worked on the force, but the other one was new, young, and he looked nervous. He watched his senior partner and took his queues from him.

"Strong. What do you have for me today?" Deputy Gomez stood, legs shoulder-width apart.

"I have a doozy for you. Hope you aren't at the end of your shift, or you'll be holding over."

"That bad, huh?"

"That messed up. Let me start at the beginning." Riley motioned to his office.

With the door closed behind them, he started when they first saw Annie running in front of their building. While Riley took him through the events that led up to today, the deputy didn't waver once or interrupt him, but let him tell his own version of what he witnessed.

"You weren't kidding. Guess I won't be going to any other calls for the rest of my shift. I'll be typing this report for a week. Let me get criminal investigations out here. Then the detectives can take your statements at the same time, and you won't have to repeat yourself more than necessary." Deputy Gomez keyed up his mic and requested a supervisor and investigation team to his location.

Riley rose from his chair and pushed back from his desk. "Did you want some coffee?"

"Black, please. At least I have a boot who gets to learn what a cluster call is all about."

Investigations arrived and were shown to the conference room where they were offered coffee. Most graciously accepted. His sergeant showed up later and had Gomez walk him through what was happening. His boot looked green under the gills when he heard the type of case it was and that he was taking the lead on the initial report.

Each of Riley's men entered the conference room where they documented their statements. They covered the events of the last six months.

Several hours later, the investigators left the building and took Sasha with them. She was still crying. They said they would request a warrant for Ayers, but since he was still in the local jail, they would have it in the system so he could be picked up on that when he was done with local jurisdiction. This would only tack on charges for Alan on top of the murder indictments that came down through the feds for his involvement from college up to his men being ordered to attack this building.

The sun had set hours earlier. His men looked tired but satisfied with the day's progress in getting their lives back on track. "Guys, again I can't thank you enough for today. It was a rough start with Duffy's funeral and now the sun set how many hours ago. Take the rest of the weekend to relax, and see you on Monday."

Mumbled comments filtered through the kitchen as they made their way to the back entrance and disappeared into the night. Riley double-checked the back door and made sure the auto locks were on. He walked the entire building, making sure every security system and door was on and working properly. Once up in his apartment, he went back to his safe. He opened the hidden compartment and placed the newest flash drive in it before securing the panel back in place. He would change the combination tomorrow; he was too tired for his brain to work on it tonight.

His phone vibrated in his pocket. The name said unavailable but the number looked familiar. "Hello."

"Mr. Strong. Good job today. Looks like Annie was right when she said you could be trusted. I have evidence I forwarded to the sheriff's office to include with the charges they will be bringing today." His heavy breaths came through the phone.

Someone needed to tell him about his breathing issues when he used a phone. "Thank you."

"Annie appreciated you for asking about her earlier, and I wanted to pass along she is fine and safe where they have her."

"Okay." Riley closed his eyes and sank to his couch.

"Mr. Strong, I will not pass along to Annie that we talked again, but I wanted you to know hopefully there is an end in sight with the horrible events that her divorce put into play. She apologizes that you were brought into it and said that she will do everything in her power to make sure that doesn't happen again. Goodbye, Mr. Strong. This will be the last time that we speak. She was released from Wit-Sec last month and has found a place to live peacefully where she can start over and not be reminded of the cruelty of her ex-husband. She's a survivor, don't forget that. She no longer thinks of herself as a victim. She knows the kind of internal force it took to survive. We could only hope to have that same strength in the face of what she went through." The phone disconnected.

Riley stared at the device in his hand and then dropped it to the cushion next to him. He closed his eyes and let his head rest on the back of the sofa. He knew that force was the Holy Spirit in her heart. He was working in her before she ever knew of Him.

Thirty

Riley rolled out of bed as he smelled coffee brewing from his kitchen. He loved his coffee pot, which he set to have that dark rich delicious drink ready for him when he woke. His feet shuffled him down to the kitchen, his eyes barely open. He stood over the pot as it finished running the hot water through the dark roast he preferred to the men's coffee they made downstairs.

It had been a month since Ayers was arrested and charged with his crimes of helping Alan. Mark Murphy had succumbed to the injuries he suffered by Alan in court, so that tacked on another murder charge. The judge and coroner entered plea deals to turn the state's witness against the ex-congressman and Alan. The trials ended in record time, and the court was deciding on the penalty for the guilty verdicts they would return. The jury returned with those guilty results after just a few hours. The cases were about as solid as you could get. The parents of the raped girls cried and held each other as the verdicts were read.

Word through the grapevine was that they thanked Annie for her help in taking these men down and getting justice for their daughters and closure for the families that grieved for them. Her attorney was a man of his word; Riley never heard from him again. After waiting a week, Riley tried to call him and wasn't shocked to hear a recording that the number was no longer in service.

He thought of Annie often, but it was business as usual. His men were back to their normal selves and joked around in the office. He still hadn't filled Duffy's spot but knew the day was coming when he would need to. He was one of his best night workers since he suffered from insomnia; he worked the graveyard shift more than the others. They would need to hire someone who could cover overnights and watch their accounts like Duffy did.

Annie's suggestion to help those who suffered from some of the worst domestic cases came to mind, and he drew up an outline on how to get information out that he could help if someone needed him to. He drove past Annie's house once a week to make sure everything was secure. Her yard was well-maintained and manicured, kept up by a lawn service who received their payments in cash in the mail every month. They said if they continued to receive payments, they would do what they were hired for. No one met Annie; she had filled out an online request and sent payments every month. They tried to email her back to say the payments were higher than what they quoted her, but the email was rejected, advising them it was an invalid address.

He finalized the sale of his house to his friends, who he had never seen happier. There was no regret when he signed the final forms in front of the notary. Helen wasn't there; she was in heaven and waiting for him to meet her there. He prayed for Annie daily and hoped she was safe. He put her in God's hands, and that was all he could do for her at this point. He hoped she was smiling; she was beautiful when she smiled.

His phone vibrated on the counter. He took a huge swig of coffee and grimaced as the bitter flavor hit the back of his throat. Oh yeah, that was the life. The message informed him he was needed downstairs. Oh, what now. Whenever they sent him that message, it was never good news. Too bad they would have to wait. He was going to shower first. He had a meeting with a potential high-end client, so he needed to get ready for that.

Twenty minutes later, he finished tying the silver tie he wore with his dark blue shirt. After sliding his phone into his pocket, he locked the door behind him and strolled to the elevator. He waited patiently; the elevator seemed to take longer than usual to reach the fifth floor. His shoes skidded on the carpet as he didn't pick his feet up all the way when he entered. The silence irritated him as he rode to the first floor. As he straightened his tie, the doors opened. Bear wore a huge grin.

"What?" Riley eyed him and glanced down the hall.

"Took you long enough. But you look good."

"I have a meeting with a potential client at eight, so whatever is going on will have to be handled quickly so I can head out."

Again, Bear grinned ear to ear. "Your meeting came to you. They're in your office."

"We were supposed to meet at a property across town." Riley straightened his tie again.

"You look great. Now, go get 'em, tiger." Bear shoved him toward his office.

Riley stepped through the door. A woman stood with her back to him, staring out the floor-to-ceiling windows next to his desk. She was slender and wore a modest-length dark blue dress. The calf muscles in her runner's legs flexed. His heart slammed into his ribcage. He knew those legs.

But that couldn't be. She was never coming back. She spun around to face him. Annie smiled, a genuine smile that blinded him.

Bear closed the door behind him as he nodded, a smile tugging at the corners of his mouth.

"Annie?" Riley took a step forward; he felt relieved he'd taken the time to shower.

She smiled; his heart raced. "Riley, you look good."

Giant steps took him to her; he couldn't stop himself and wrapped his arms around her, lifting her off her feet. She laughed and wrapped her arms around his neck.

"Oh, I'm sorry. I didn't mean to make you uncomfortable," he stammered after he set her down and stepped back.

"I'm not uncomfortable around you, Riley. You make me feel safe." She put a hand on the side of his face. The heat from her hand traveled down to his heart as he leaned into her.

"What are you doing here? I thought I was meeting a potential client." He couldn't tear his eyes away from her.

"I'm the client. I have a property that I'd like to discuss security measures for." Her smile slammed into him; her eyes sparkled. He never saw her look more beautiful.

"I'm sorry. I don't understand."

"I'm home, Riley. I came home." She pointed to the Bible he noticed on his desk but didn't say anything about. It was different than the one that he urged her to read; that one lay in the bottom drawer of his desk. "I needed to come back to the man who showed me the unconditional love of a Heavenly Father through his actions and words, who told me to do something as simple as read a book. That it would change my world. To let me find Him in my time and not push and demand that I give Him a shot, as that would have driven me away permanently from finding my Savior."

"You...you...He's your savior?" Riley's words caught in his throat, and he found he couldn't swallow past the lump.

"Yes, thank you for giving me a subtle shove in the right direction without being overbearing, which would have turned me off from ever reading the best book ever written."

He cupped her face. Leaning in hesitantly, he kissed her. She kissed him back and the outside world ceased to exist.

Don't miss out!

Visit the website below and you can sign up to receive emails whenever K. A. Moore publishes a new book. There's no charge and no obligation.

https://books2read.com/r/B-A-MAMI-WUMYB

BOOKS 2 READ

Connecting independent readers to independent writers.

About the Author

K.A. Moore, born and raised in Kansas, is a retired 911 police dispatcher with over thirteen years of service and will be the first to tell you dispatchers are a special breed all their own. Her real passion is writing and putting her imagination into works of fiction. Faith-based Christian suspense is her preferred writing theme, with wild, crazy dreams as the backdrop to many scenes that seem to come alive in her writing. As she writes, her Chihuahua scampers for the coveted position of curling up in her lap while creating her stories.

www.ingramcontent.com/pod-product-compliance
Lightning Source LLC
LaVergne TN
LVHW050920080826
845145LV00001B/154

* 9 7 8 1 9 5 7 2 2 3 1 1 7 *